T0059082

TO

THE

SKY

KINGDOM

TO THE SKY KINGDOM

TANG QI

TRANSLATED BY POPPY TOLAND

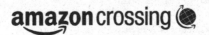

This is a work of fiction. Names, characters, organizations, places, events, and incidents are either products of the author's imagination or are used fictitiously.

Text copyright ©2009 Tang Qi
Translation copyright ©2016 Poppy Toland
All rights reserved.

No part of this book may be reproduced, or stored in a retrieval system, or transmitted in any form or by any means, electronic, mechanical, photocopying, recording, or otherwise, without express written permission of the publisher.

Previously published as 三生三世 十里桃花 in 2009 by Shenyang Publishing House, in 2011 by Baihuazhou Literature & Art Publishing House and in 2012 by Hunan Literature & Art Publishing House in Mainland China. Translated from Chinese by Poppy Toland. First published in English by AmazonCrossing in 2016.

Published by AmazonCrossing, Seattle

www.apub.com

Amazon, the Amazon logo, and AmazonCrossing are trademarks of Amazon.com, Inc., or its affiliates.

ISBN-13: 9781503937420
ISBN-10: 1503937429

Cover design by Shasti O'Leary Soudant

Printed in the United States of America

PRINCIPAL CHARACTERS

Ali, Little Sticky-Rice Dumpling—son of Bai Qian and Ye Hua

Bai Qian—daughter of Bai Zhi, also known as Su Su and Si Yin

Bai Zhi—emperor of the Bai Nine-Tailed White Fox Clan, Bai Qian's father

Bi Fang—Fourth Brother's bird steed

Emperor Dong Hua—head of the immortal audience

Mo Yuan—Bai Qian's old master and teacher of magic from Mount Kunlun

Mystic Gorge—Qingqiu land god transformed from a Mystic Gorge tree

Li Jing—Demon Prince and Bai Qian's first love

Phoenix Nine—Bai Qian's niece

Qing Cang—former Demon Emperor

Sang Ji—the Sky Emperor's second son, former fiancé of Bai Qian, the Northern Sea Water Emperor

Shao Xin—a ba snake spirit, Bai Qian's former serving girl, Sang Ji's wife

Si Ming the Star Prince—the writer of destinies

Su Jin—Ye Hua's head concubine

Xuan Nu—Bai Qian's sister-in-law, married to Li Jing

Ye Hua—the heir to the Sky Emperor

Zhe Yan—a phoenix god who lives in the Ten-Mile Peach Grove

PROLOGUE

She had been feeling completely drained of energy.

"It's because you are carrying the little emperor," Nai Nai said. "Of course you are tired, Empress. You mustn't worry."

Nai Nai was her serving girl, and the only immortal in Xiwu Palace of the Ninth Sky who smiled at her and called her *Empress*. The other immortals all looked down on Su Su because Ye Hua had not formally wed her and because she was not like them: she was just a mortal.

Nai Nai opened the window; a breeze blew through the room, and footsteps could be heard outside. "His Majesty has come to pay you a visit, Empress," Nai Nai said joyfully.

With movements like a wooden puppet's, Su Su pushed herself up from under the embroidered quilt and sat against the bed rail. She had no idea how long she had been asleep, but her head still felt foggy. She had only just woken up, but was still sleepy, extremely sleepy.

She sank farther into the quilt as the black-haired prince Ye Hua, dressed in black, sat on the edge of her bed.

Holding the quilt, she eased herself back. There was silence. She thought he must be angry. When had it started, this fear whenever she saw him? It had become almost a reflex. *You cannot let him know you are still angry with him. You must not offend him,* she thought in confusion.

"Aren't the stars bright this evening?" she said quietly. She had been trying not to tremble, but her voice came out sounding shaky.

"Su Su, it's daytime," he said after a pause.

She moved her hand up to her face instinctively to rub her eyes, but instead her hand brushed against the piece of white silk. She suddenly remembered: she no longer had any eyes. No matter how much she rubbed them, all she would ever see was darkness. As a mortal, she had never fit in at the vast Sky Palace, and this was even more the case now that she was blind.

Ye Hua stroked her face in silence for a long time before saying, "I will wed you up here. From now on, I will be your eyes. Su Su, I will be your eyes."

The hand on her face was icy, and though it was a gentle gesture, it felt like a knife being thrust through her heart. She suddenly had an intense recall of last night's nightmares and became so afraid that she began to tremble and pushed him away. Now she felt even more afraid. "I . . . I didn't push you away on purpose," she hurried to explain. "You mustn't be angry . . ."

Ye Hua took her hand. "Su Su, what's the matter?"

The pain spread through her heart like a drop of ink being sucked into a sheet of thick rice paper. "I've sud-suddenly started feeling very tired," she lied, her teeth chattering. "You get on with your work. I'd like to sleep more. Don't worry about me."

More silence.

She really did not want him to worry about her anymore.

What used to feel like a loving embrace from her beloved had now become unbearable. Sometimes she would wonder why if he liked *that other girl* so much, he had accepted the absurd proposition she had made him back then. Back then . . . back then she was filled with regret about not taking a different course of action. After a while, she heard footsteps. Ye Hua left, and Nai Nai bolted the door.

She sat there for a time, hugging her quilt and feeling desolate. Once her trembling stilled a little, she lay back deep in her bed. Suddenly her head filled with chaotic images: she saw Junji Mountain in the Eastern Desert one moment, Ye Hua's face the next, then the blood-soaked dagger and her freshly cutout eyes.

Once I have borne this child, I will return to Junji Mountain, she decided within this state of confusion. *That's where I belong. This destructive love will end where it started. Soon it will be over.*

She put her hand on the piece of white silk where her eyes should have been, muttering in pain, her voice slightly choked. But she did not cry.

She slept some more, until Nai Nai carefully pushed open the door and came in. "Empress. Empress. Are you awake yet?" she asked gently.

Her throat tightened. "What do you want?" she spluttered.

Nai Nai's footsteps stopped. "Su Jin's serving girl has arrived with a message from Su Jin inviting you to take tea with her."

Vexed, she pulled up the quilt to cover her face. "Tell her I'm asleep."

Su Jin had been fawning on her of late. When she was feeling more positive, she imagined it must be because Su Jin was feeling guilty. Su Jin had been given her eyes; Su Su's blindness was her fault. Su Jin had made Ye Hua cut out her eyes.

These people. She didn't wish to see a single one of them ever again. She didn't even wish to acknowledge one. She was not the same girl who had arrived here three years ago, the naive young thing squirming with unease, nurturing the absurd notion she might gain favor with all of them if she tried hard enough.

• • •

The sun was dropping down behind the Western Mountains when Nai Nai shook Su Su awake. Dusk was approaching, Nai Nai explained. There was a glorious sunset glowing in the courtyard, and a gentle breeze stirred the air. It was a perfect time for her to sit out in the courtyard. She had been asleep all day, and her bones were probably feeling stiff. A little stroll would do her good.

Nai Nai moved a rocking chair out into the courtyard and was about to guide her into it, but Su Su raised a hand to stop her serving girl. She tried to get to it unaided, groping for the table and the wall for support, moving along step by step. Walking was exhausting, and she stumbled a few times, but she could feel a ray of light growing inside herself. She had to learn these skills as soon as possible. It was essential if she was to return to Junji Mountain and live a proper life.

As she sat in the rocking chair, enjoying the breeze, she felt herself becoming dozy again.

She fell into a trance, deep and dreamlike. This dream took her back to Junji Mountain, back to the time three years before, back to when she had first set eyes on Ye Hua.

A dashing young man had collapsed in front of her thatched house. He had black hair and wore black clothing. He held a sword and was covered head to toe in blood. She stood there in shock for a moment before racing over and dragging him inside. She gave him medicine to curb his bleeding and was astonished to see his wound heal up right before her eyes. In less than two days, his life-threatening injuries had completely healed. The young man woke up and quietly looked at her. When he finally spoke, his voice was calm and pleasant. He thanked her for saving his life and told her he was going to repay her. She told him that anyone in her position would have done the same. All she had done was give him a couple of doses of herbal medicine, nothing really. But he was insistent about repaying her. When she told him she wanted heaps of silver and gold, the young man stared at her in puzzlement. "Saving my life is worth more than silver and gold," he said. In all the ages, there had probably never been a savior who felt as helpless as she. Beaten down, she eventually opened her arms and said, "Why don't you repay your debt with your body then?" He looked at her in astonishment.

Her absurd proposition led to the two of them becoming lovers, and she soon fell pregnant.

She had been living alone on Junji Mountain for as long as she could remember. All she knew were the changing seasons and the spirits of the mountain: the birds, beasts, insects, and fish. She had no husband, and therefore no name. The young man called her Su Su and explained that this would be her name from now on. For days she hid the joy she felt from having been given this name.

Later the young man took her back to the Ninth Sky. She learned that he was the grandson of the Sky Emperor. At that point he had not yet been officially named as heir to the Sky Throne.

No one in the Ninth Sky accepted her as his wife. He never told the Sky Emperor he had married a mortal he had met in the Eastern Desert.

One night she went to his bedchamber to take him some broth. No one was standing guard. She heard the head concubine, Su Jin, talking in distress. "Admit it, the only reason you married a mortal was because I betrayed you by marrying the Sky Emperor! But what choice did I have? Is there any woman in the Four Seas and Eight Deserts who could resist the Sky Emperor's affection? Tell me, Ye Hua, I'm still the one you love, aren't I? You only named her Su Su because it reminded you of my name, Su Jin."

She woke up abruptly, filled with terror and drenched in cold sweat. Her dream had depicted the events of the past exactly how they had happened. She lay there motionless for some time before lifting a hand to stroke her protruding belly. It was nearly three years now since she had been with child. The baby had to be due soon.

Darkness had fallen, but Nai Nai had still not arrived to help her get ready for bed. She could not wash on her own yet, and was forced to call out. Nai Nai came over to tuck the embroidered quilt over Su Su's legs. "Wait up a little longer, Empress. His Majesty may still come to visit."

She stifled a laugh. Ye Hua had not slept in her bedchamber once since the incident and would never do so again. However, she did not mind. If he did show up, they would just lie there in silence. She might actually end up angering him.

Being here made her extremely vulnerable. She had not realized it before. She had thought he would always be there to watch over her, but that incident had been a front-on attack, and when the person who harmed you was the only one you actually trusted . . . she clenched her hands, which had begun to shake uncontrollably, making them into fists.

If Ye Hua had told her he was in love with someone else when they were still on Junji Mountain in the Eastern Desert, she would never have made the absurd decision to marry him. She had not even been in love with him at that point. She had just been lonely living by herself between the mountain and the emerald forest year in, year out.

But he had not said anything. He had wed her in accordance with her custom and then taken her back to the Ninth Sky.

That was when things turned murky. It wasn't as simple as it had been when it had just been the two of them on Junji Mountain. She caught constant snatches of gossip about her and the head concubine,

Su Jin. Su Su had an innate ability to remain positive, and had managed to blot out all the rumors.

Anyway, she thought to herself, she was the one he had wed. They had bowed down and praised the great skies and the earth to make their vows. She was carrying his child, and all she could hope for was that one day a love would blossom with Ye Hua.

He seemed to have softened toward her of late. Even if he did not love her, she comforted herself with the fact that he must hold some affection for her.

But then the incident had happened. And she had been woken up from her dream. The price had been losing her eyes, losing her sight.

It had been a bright day with a gentle breeze. When Su Jin invited her along to the Jade Pool to admire the flowers, she assumed it was an excursion for a group of the palace ladies and had foolishly accepted. She arrived at the Jade Pool to discover it was just the two of them.

Su Jin dismissed her palace attendant and led her to the immortal punishment platform, shrouded in mist.

Su Jin stood on the platform and gave a frosty laugh. "Did you know that the Sky Emperor is about to name Ye Hua as official heir to the Sky Throne? At the same time as this, he will offer me to Ye Hua as his wife."

Su Su had never understood their immortal rules and games. She felt the blood surging between her chest and her belly, but felt unsure if it had been roused from anger or confusion.

The concubine stood there in all her finery and laughed again. "Ye Hua and I are in love," she said. "The Ninth Sky isn't a place for a mortal. Once you've had your baby, you should jump down from this punishment platform and go back to wherever you came from."

Su Su didn't know if jumping off the platform really would take her back to Junji Mountain, and she had not considered leaping from the stage.

"Does Ye Hua want me to go back?" she asked in confusion. "I am his wife. I should be where he is."

When she thought back over that conversation later, she realized how much of her own naivety and stupidity she had revealed to Su Jin. Back then her wishful thinking had been that Ye Hua still liked her a little bit, enough at least for a future to be possible. As long as he liked her a little bit, she would stay by his side.

Su Jin gave an amused sigh and grabbed Su Su by the hand. She took her over to the edge of the platform and pushed Su Su's back, pitching her face over the edge of the platform.

Panicked, Su Su's hands wrapped around the wooden mast of the platform, but instead it was Su Jin who tumbled off the high platform. Before Su Su realized what was happening, a black figure flitted past and leaped down off the platform after Su Jin.

Ye Hua stood with his arm around Su Jin, looking coldly across at Su Su, monstrous fury brewing in his dark eyes.

"Don't blame Su Su," Su Jin breathed weakly from his arms. "I'm sure she didn't mean to push me. She just . . . just heard how the Sky Emperor was going to make me your wife and she reacted impulsively."

Su Su opened her eyes wide in disbelief. She had clearly done nothing wrong.

"It wasn't me, it wasn't me! I didn't push her! Believe me, Ye Hua, you have to believe me . . ." Again and again she tried to reason with the young man, sounding panicky and garbled, like a wretched fool.

He waved a hand to silence her. "Enough," he shouted in a deep voice. "I know what I saw."

He was unwilling to listen to her. He did not believe her. With his arm around Su Jin, his brow knitted, and his eyes as hard as ice, he hurried down from the immortal punishment platform, leaving Su Su there on her own.

• • •

She was not sure how she arrived back at her courtyard. All she could think about was the blazing fury she had seen in his eyes. Not long after nightfall, Ye Hua returned and stood before her, looking somber.

"The evil energy beneath the immortal punishment platform has caused serious damage to Su Jin's eyes, Su Su, and by the principle of karmic retribution, you must repay what you owe." He paused. "But don't be frightened, I will wed you here. From now on I will be your eyes." After a pause he repeated, "Don't be frightened. I will marry you here. From now on I will be your eyes."

He had never mentioned marrying her in the Ninth Sky before. She felt a coldness in her heart, anger and fear welling up as one. She could never have imagined herself losing control like that, gripping his hand in near hysterics and saying, "Why do you want my eyes? She jumped of her own accord. It's not my fault. Why won't you believe me?"

His eyes were full of bitterness. "Evil forces linger beneath the immortal punishment platform. Do you really think Su Jin would jump down of her own accord?" he sneered. "Su Su, you are becoming more unreasonable by the day . . ."

She watched in bewilderment as his eyes turned frosty. He was all she had in the Ninth Sky. Since becoming pregnant with his child, she had always imagined that one day, she would stand with Ye Hua, each of them holding one of their child's hands as they looked out over an expansive ocean of billowing clouds pierced through by a thousand rays of sunset light. He did not know how important her sight was to her, the significance it held.

They cut out her eyes. Nai Nai spent three days looking after her, after which Su Jin came in and stood before her. "You'll be pleased to hear that I've put your eyes to good use," she said with a laugh.

It all became clear. This had been Su Jin's intention all along. Su Su had been nothing but a passerby who had somehow been dragged into the confusion. It had been a predestined mortal world calamity.

As time passed, she grew more used to her sightlessness. She no longer confused day with night and learned how to sharpen her ears, to listen out for sounds that helped her distinguish what time of day it was.

She had just finished her lunch when Nai Nai came stumbling into the courtyard. "Empress, Empress," she called breathlessly. "The Sky Emperor has just issued an imperial decree. H-h-he has decided to offer Su Jin t-t-to His Majesty Prince Ye Hua."

Su Su gave a chuckle. Ye Hua had been officially named as the next Sky Emperor some time ago. It was only a matter of time before this news. But Su Jin could not be Ye Hua's primary wife. Su Su had recently heard that the Sky Emperor had an agreement with Emperor Bai Zhi of the Qingqiu Kingdom that whoever succeeded him as Sky Emperor would marry Bai Zhi's daughter, Bai Qian. Ye Hua had never told her any of this. She could have found it out if she had wanted to. She was not as stupid and helpless as they all thought.

She should never have gotten tangled up with these immortals.

She suddenly felt a sharp pain in her belly.

"Empress, what's wrong?" Nai Nai cried out again and again.

Su Su put her hands on her stomach and managed to stutter the words, "I th-th-think I m-m-might be about to give birth."

She fainted during childbirth, but the pain brought her round. When her eyes were taken out to give to Su Jin, she heard that Ye Hua had stayed by her side day and night. While she was giving birth to their child, she only had Nai Nai with her. Intense pain made even the strongest people weak. But she stopped herself from calling out to Ye Hua. She was in enough agony already; she did not wish to add any more.

"Empress, please let go of my hand," Nai Nai begged in tears. "I am going to find His Majesty. I'm going to fetch the prince."

She was in so much pain she could not speak. All she could do was mouth the words, "Stay with me a little longer, Nai Nai, just a short while more."

Nai Nai cried even harder.

It was a boy.

She did not know when Ye Hua arrived, but when she awoke she felt his hand around hers. His hand was ice-cold again, and even though it made her shiver to hold it, she stopped herself from pulling her hand back.

He held the baby and said, "Stroke his little face, Su Su. You'll feel how much he looks like you."

She did not move. She had carried this baby for three years. He had accompanied her for countless days and nights, and of course she loved her child, but she would not be able to take him back to Junji Mountain with her. She had already decided to leave him behind. She did not want to touch or hold him, to develop any form of attachment.

Ye Hua stayed sitting by her side for a long time. He never said a word, not even when the baby fretted and cried.

As soon as Ye Hua left, she called Nai Nai over. She told her servant girl that she had given the baby the name Ali. She made Nai Nai promise to always take very good care of him. Completely unsuspecting, Nai Nai agreed.

Ye Hua came to see Su Su every day. He had never been very talkative. In the past, Su Su had been chatty, but no longer. Most of the time the two of them would just sit there in silence. Luckily her silence did not anger Ye Hua. He obviously understood how frail she was feeling after the birth. During these silences, she would occasionally recall that the last thing she had seen before losing her eyes was Ye Hua's eyes full of coldness. Whenever she recalled that image, she would give an involuntary tremor.

Ye Hua did not say a word to her about his imminent marriage to Su Jin. Neither did Nai Nai.

It took three months before Su Su was fully recovered from the birth. Ye Hua brought her a range of different fabrics and asked her to choose the one she liked the best. He wished to make her a wedding dress.

"I've already explained, Su Su, that I wish to marry you."

She found it strange, his wish to marry her after he had been the one who cut out her eyes.

Later she understood. Ye Hua felt sorry for her. She was a mortal with no eyes, and even though he found her despicable and considered her blindness self-inflicted, he also saw her as in need of compassion. He could have as many concubines as he wished, and giving her the status of his wife cost him nothing.

She knew she had to leave. There was no reason for her to stay in the Ninth Sky.

Nai Nai came out on strolls with her. The two of them repeated the route from the Xiwu Palace to the punishment platform. Nai Nai found it strange, but Su Su explained to her loyal servant girl that she enjoyed the fragrant lotus flowers along the way.

Within a fortnight, she had learned to rely on her senses to navigate her way smoothly between Xiwu Palace and the punishment platform.

Deceiving Nai Nai could not have been easier.

Standing on the immortal punishment platform, she suddenly felt light as the wind. Ali was in Nai Nai's care, so she did not need to worry about him. Standing on this high platform, surrounded by boundless cloud and mist, she suddenly had the urge to explain to Ye Hua one last time that she had not pushed Su Jin, that it was not she who owed Su Jin, but they who owed her. They owed her a pair of eyes and a calm and stable future.

While they had still been on Junji Mountain, Ye Hua had given her a beautiful bronze mirror. He had been about to travel to a faraway place to take care of some important business. Scared that she might get lonely, he pulled this treasure from his sleeve and told her that no matter where he was, all she had to do was call his name into the mirror and he would hear it. As long as he was not busy, he would speak to her.

She did not know why she still carried this mirror around everywhere with her. Perhaps because it was the only present Ye Hua had ever given her.

She pulled out the mirror. It had been a long time since she had called his name, and it felt unnatural. "Ye Hua," she said.

There was a long pause before she heard his voice by her ear. "Su Su?"

She fell silent a moment before saying, "I'm going back to Junji Mountain. Don't come looking for me. I will be fine on my own. Look after Ali for me. I used to dream that one day I could hold his hand and look up at the stars with him, at the moon, the clouds, the sunshine, and tell him the story of how we met on Junji Mountain. That will never happen now." She thought for a moment and added, "Don't tell him his mother is just a mortal, the immortals in the Sky Kingdom all look down on us."

It was a perfectly normal farewell speech, but suddenly she felt herself welling up. She jerked her head upward before realizing she had no eyes: Where would her tears fall from?

"Where are you now?" Ye Hua asked, his voice strained.

"The punishment platform," she said quietly. "Su Jin told me that if I jumped off it, I could return to Junji Mountain. I'm getting used to being blind. Junji Mountain is my home, and I'm familiar with the terrain. I can live there on my own, it won't be hard. You mustn't worry." She paused before saying, "I shouldn't have rescued you back then. If I could go back in time, Ye Hua, I wouldn't have saved you."

"Su Su," he interrupted. "You stay where you are. Don't move. I'm coming straight there."

In the end, she did not go back through her defense, did not explain that she had not pushed Su Jin. They were not going to meet again in this life. Right and wrong, good and bad had ceased to matter.

"Ye Hua, I'm letting you go," she told him quietly. "You must let me go too. We no longer owe each other anything."

The mirror fell from her hand with a clatter, drowning out Ye Hua's fierce roar. "You just stand there. You mustn't jump . . ."

She turned and leaped off the platform. Her long sigh got lost within the fluttering of the wind. *I ask no more of you, Ye Hua. This is the way it should be.*

She did not know that the immortal punishment platform was only meant for immortals, that if a mortal jumped off it, they would simply turn to dust flying and flames dying.

Neither did she know that she was not actually a mortal.

The leap from the punishment platform caused her serious injury. The destructive powers of the punishment platform, stronger than tens of thousands of immortal warriors, split open the seal on her forehead. She did not have any idea of the significance of the red mole on her forehead, which had been there for two hundred years, since the Demon Emperor broke out of the Eastern Desert Bell. In her quest to lock him back up, she had battled with him, and in the course of this battle, he had placed this seal upon her. He took away her appearance, her memories, all her immortal powers and turned her into a mortal.

Everything from the past came back to her, one after another, but within the chaos of her mind, she found a moment of clarity. Enduring the agonizing pain these destructive forces had wrought on her immortal body, she heard a voice inside her quietly speaking. *Bai Qian, you were born from an immortal embryo. You were never required to cultivate any spiritual energy to become an immortal. But nothing in the Four Seas and Eight Deserts comes this easily. How could you possibly become a goddess without experiencing a sky calamity? These last few decades of love and hate, gratitude and grudges have been nothing but your sky calamity.*

She collapsed to the east of the Eastern Sea in Zhe Yan's Ten-Mile Peach Grove. When she finally came to, Zhe Yan gave a huge sigh of relief. "Your mother, father, and brothers have been driving themselves crazy looking for you, and I've been so worried I haven't slept properly in two hundred years. But what's wrong with your eyes? And why are you covered in scars?"

Her memory had been somewhat damaged by the fall from the platform, leaving her in a state of confusion. But she still remembered clearly how she had been hurt. What had it been? Nothing but a pre-destined calamity.

She smiled at Zhe Yan and said, "I seem to remember that you have a medicine to make people forget things they want to forget?"

Zhe Yan raised an eyebrow. "It would appear that you've suffered very badly these past years."

It was true. Thankfully it had only been for a couple of years.

She stood before the hot, bubbling pot of medicine, watching the steam billow off it.

She gulped down the whole thing. Su Su from Junji Mountain ceased to exist, she had merely been someone dreamed up by Goddess Bai Qian, the youngest daughter of Bai Zhi, Emperor of the Qingqiu Kingdom. It was a dream that had involved dreadful suffering, but also some peach blossom romance.

As soon as she awoke from this dream, she forgot it completely.

Three hundred years later.

The Eastern Sea Water Emperor's new son was his pride and joy. To prepare for his son's one-month banquet, the emperor had taken leave from his morning meetings at the Lingxiao Palace for several days. The Sky Emperor turned a blind eye to the Water Emperor's absence, but it piqued the interest of Goddess Duo Bao. Why all the fuss over a simple banquet?

To quell her curiosity, she sought out Prince Nan Douzhen, who had always been on very good terms with the Eastern Sea Emperor.

Life in the Ninth Sky tended to lack intrigue, and these immortals had been charting the Eastern Sea Emperor's absence with interest for some time now. Seeing Goddess Duo Bao take the bull by the horns, they all started to crowd around Prince Nan Douzhen.

Prince Nan Douzhen looked at them in a slightly bemused manner. "Immortal friends, surely you must have heard that Her Highness from Qingqiu has accepted the invitation for the Eastern Sea Emperor's banquet."

Qingqiu was in the center of the Great Desert, not far from the Eastern Sea, and as Prince Nan Douzhen said the name, he cupped his hands together and bowed toward the east and toward Qingqiu. "Her Highness has an eye condition, which means she is unable to look directly at anything bright," he explained. "The Eastern Sea's Water Emperor was worried because the coral walls and glazed tiles in the Eastern Sea Water Crystal Palace are glaringly bright. He has been spending these past few days searching for water-lily grass, which he intends to weave into sheets to cover up anything too bright."

Upon hearing this news, Lingxiao Palace descended into pandemonium.

Her Highness was Emperor Bai Zhi's daughter, Bai Qian. She belonged to the older generation of ancient immortals, and to show their respect, the immortals all referred to her as Her Highness.

When Pangu, creator of the universe, took up his ax and split the sky from the earth, all the great tribes started fighting. This went on without reprieve for many years, and there was a long succession of different rulers in the sky and on earth. Most of the ancient gods had been plundered. Those that were destined to vanish had vanished, and those that were destined to fall into demise had fallen into demise.

Only a very small number of gods remained. They included the Sky Emperor and his family in the Ninth Sky; Zhe Yan, who tended to stay within the parameters of his Ten-Mile Peach Grove east of the

Eastern Sea, keeping to himself; and Emperor Bai Zhi of the Qingqiu Kingdom and his family.

Bai Qian's name could not be brought up without mentioning an incident also involving the Sky Clan, a matter that was meant to be secret but was actually known by everyone.

Fifty thousand years ago, Bai Qian and the Sky Emperor's second son, Sang Ji, became engaged. They should have been the perfect match, but Sang Ji fell in love with Bai Qian's serving girl and broke off the engagement.

Emperor Bai Zhi could not bear the humiliation, and he went to the Ninth Sky with Zhe Yan to meet with the Sky Emperor, seeking justice.

The Sky Emperor was furious with his second son. As punishment, he appointed him as the Northern Sea Water Emperor, thus banishing him to the north. After this he issued a sky decree in which he swore on the honor of the Sky Clan that his successor, the future Sky Emperor, would marry Bai Qian and make her the Sky Empress.

Three hundred years later, the Sky Emperor had gathered together everyone from the Four Seas and the Eight Deserts to announce that his eldest grandson, Prince Ye Hua, was to be the next Sky Emperor. All the immortals in the Ninth Sky felt certain they would soon be drinking the celebratory wine of Ye Hua and Bai Qian's union. But three hundred years on, there was still no news about their nuptials.

Prince Ye Hua already had a son, but no official wife. And Goddess Bai Qian remained in Qingqiu Kingdom, declining all invitations from other immortals.

These two remained unmarried, a fact that oddly enough did not seem to worry either household.

• • •

The audience of immortals gave a restrained sigh and talked admiringly about the Eastern Sea Emperor's good fortune. Her Highness Bai Qian was now respectfully known for not having left Qingqiu for tens of thousands of years. The fact that she had accepted his invitation would raise his prestige no end.

"This really is a matter of great honor for him," Prince Nan Douzhen agreed with a nod. "But the Eastern Sea Emperor has been feeling extremely anxious. He wasn't expecting Her Highness to accept his invitation, and so he invited the Northern Sea Emperor as well. In addition to that, a couple of days ago, he heard that Prince Ye Hua was taking a trip to the Eastern Desert with his son and planned to visit the Eastern Sea on his way back to attend the banquet. These three will certainly run into each other at the banquet, and the Eastern Sea Water Emperor is terrified it could be a recipe for disaster."

This Ninth Sky audience was mainly made up of older, more senior immortals who knew all about the situation between the Northern Sea Emperor, Goddess Bai Qian, and Prince Ye Hua. But there was one who had only recently become an immortal. "Who is Her Highness from Qingqiu?" she asked foolishly. "And why is there animosity between her, Prince Ye Hua, and the Northern Sea Water Emperor?"

This foolish young immortal was baffled by what she was told. With a look of utter fascination on her face, she shook the unpainted white fan in her hand and said, "So the Northern Sea Emperor willingly offended Emperor Bai Zhi in order to marry Her Highness's serving girl? She must be astonishingly beautiful for him to have done that."

Goddess Duo Bao covered her mouth and gave a cough. "I saw the girl once. Sang Ji made her kneel before the Sky Emperor alongside him, imploring his father to accept their love. She is indeed a rare beauty, but she has nothing on her former mistress, Bai Qian. I've never seen Her Highness with my own eyes, but I've heard that she is even more beautiful than her mother."

The immortal prince of the North Pole was the oldest among them. "I saw Her Highness once," he mused, stroking his floor-length white beard. "I was still a boy serving under the Sky Emperor. I accompanied the empress to Zhe Yan's peach grove to admire the peach blossoms. Her Highness was dancing under the branches of the peach trees. I was too far away to see much. I could make out her red dress through the magnificent blossoms. And the way she danced was full of grace, so full of grace."

The assembly of immortals gave a collective sigh and expressed how sad it was for such an alluring beauty to have been jilted like that. Fate always kept you on your toes, they commented, wringing their hands in distress, before parting company feeling very satisfied.

CHAPTER ONE

The oldest daughter from the Ruo River immortal family married into the Eastern Sea family, and within three years she had borne the Eastern Sea Emperor a child, his first son and heir. Both families were extremely happy.

The Eastern Sea Emperor was so proud of this son that he invited everyone between the sky and earth—even me, Bai Qian of Qingqiu—for a banquet to celebrate the boy's first month of life.

Father and Mother had been out of Qingqiu for hundreds of years now, wandering far and wide. And my brothers—Big Brother, Second Brother, and Third Brother—had settled down one after another to start their own families in each of their portioned-off sections of the kingdom. Fourth Brother was off in the Eastern Mountain, looking for his bird steed, Bi Fang, who had flown off. That left me alone in the foxhole, mistress of the house.

I took the invitation over to the curtain of water outside the cave and held it up to the light. I remember hearing that my birth had been difficult for Mother, and the great-grandfather of this Eastern Sea Emperor had sent their family's midwife along to help ease her suffering. I decided it was time to repay this favor. I picked out a night pearl and prepared to travel to the Eastern Sea. The night pearl, with its warm green glow, was the size of a pumpkin. It would be my gift to the Eastern Sea Emperor.

My sense of direction was terrible, so before setting off, I went next door to Mystic Gorge's place to ask for a twig from the Mystic Gorge tree.

The Mystic Gorge tree had black-grained wood and lustrous multicolored flowers that could be used to light the way at night. As long as I had a twig from the Mystic Gorge tree on me, I would not lose my way. In the early days of the huge mists, Old Mystic Gorge actually used to be a Mystic Gorge tree growing on Zhaoyao Mountain in the Southern Desert.

While Mother was pregnant with Fourth Brother, she and Father had an argument. She ran from the house and got lost, ending up on Zhaoyao Mountain. Father eventually found her, but he was so worried about her getting lost again that he dug up the only Mystic Gorge tree on Zhaoyao Mountain and carried it back to Qingqiu, where he planted it on our doorstep.

Qingqiu is an immortal paradise, and after three thousand years of bathing in the sun and the moon and swirling in the energy of the seasons, this Mystic Gorge tree had cultivated enough spiritual energy to transform into human form. Another three thousand years passed, and he became an earth god.

Father gave Mystic Gorge a couple of bundles of bamboo as a celebratory gift, which Mystic Gorge used, along with some thatching, to build himself a three-room hut next door to the foxhole, thus becoming our closest neighbor.

Mystic Gorge handed me my twig with a despondent look on his face, though I couldn't imagine what might be bothering him. I considered asking but knew that if I did, I would probably be trapped there listening to him for a long time and so decided not to meddle. I took the twig and summoned a lucky cloud, which I jumped aboard, and soared in the direction of the Eastern Sea.

Third Brother had heard that I was going to the Eastern Sea to attend the banquet, and he had asked if I would go first to Zhe Yan's peach grove to ask for two bottles of peach blossom wine.

When I was small, Mother told me that Zhe Yan was the first phoenix to be born after the sky was split from the earth, back in the age of primal chaos. He had been raised by Father of the Universe, and he was several ranks higher than the present Sky Emperor.

When I was a child, Father and Mother took me to see Zhe Yan. He raised an eyebrow when he saw me before giving Father a smile and saying, "Is this your new baby daughter? How lovely they are at this age."

Tens of thousands of years before, Zhe Yan asked Mother to marry him, even sending a betrothal gift to her family home. But Mother had her heart set on Father, a man so stubborn and unyielding he found it hard even to nod his head. Zhe Yan and Father had a hearty battle over Mother, after which they became close as brothers. Father and Mother got married on New Year's Day. Father sent a sedan chair with eight carriers to welcome her to Qingqiu, and Zhe Yan was invited to act as master of ceremonies at their wedding.

Zhe Yan was an exceptionally skilled wine maker, even though he himself did not indulge in feasting, gambling, or drinking. "A mysterious god who has shunned the three unwholesome roots and retreated from the mortal world, who has refined interests, and even more refined tastes" was the way he saw himself.

Anytime an immortal invited him to drink and make merry with them, he would simply give a laugh and ignore it.

Knowing this, any immortal who invited him to come and make merry did so merely as a gesture of affection for a god who enjoyed a high ranking within the immortal realm despite serving no great function. He had become far too settled in his own surroundings. Gradually other immortals came to understand this, seeing him as an idle god who was to be respected but not approached, and over the years, they lost enthusiasm for sending him invitations.

Zhe Yan lived a pure and simple life and was wholeheartedly devoted to his peach grove.

I arrived at the edge of the Eastern Sea and counted off the hours using my fingers. I still had a day and a half until the official start of the banquet. I considered Third Brother's request and decided to stop off at Zhe Yan's first. My plan was to ask him for an earthen jug of peach blossom wine, which I could use to fill two bottles to take back to Third Brother, as well as a third bottle to give to the Eastern Sea Water Emperor as a celebration gift along with the night pearl. Even after parceling out these gifts, I would still have some wine remaining in the jug, which I could drink at my leisure back at the foxhole.

It was the height of the peach blossom season, and the Ten-Mile Peach Grove was awash with flowers. The blossoms covered the mountains and plains with their lustrous brilliance.

I made my familiar way into the depths of the peach grove, where I found Zhe Yan sitting cross-legged in a clearing, taking bites out of an enormous peach. In no time at all, he was left with only the stone.

When he saw me, Zhe Yan beckoned me over with a wide smile on his face. "Well, if it isn't the little girl from the Bai family come to pay a visit. You just get more beautiful. Come." He patted the space next to him. "Sit down and let me take a proper look at you."

There were not many gods between the sky and earth who were old enough to call me *little girl*, and hearing the address made me feel as if I were still very young. I felt filled with a mixture of great sadness and great joy.

I sat down as instructed, and Zhe Yan reached out and stroked my hand. I was just considering the best way to ask for that jug of wine when Zhe Yan started to chuckle. "You've shut yourself up in Qingqiu for thousands of years now. What a coincidence that you choose now to come out."

I was slightly baffled by his comment but did not ask him to explain. I just gave a polite smile and said, "The peach blossoms look glorious."

He gave an even deeper laugh. "The Northern Sea Emperor brought his wife here a couple of days ago to admire the peach blossoms. It was the first time I'd seen his wife. She really is rather enchanting." I was unable to even force a smile.

Shao Xin was the Northern Sea Emperor's wife. I was the one who had chosen this name for her many years ago. My four older brothers and I had gone for a day out to Dongting Lake where, there in the reeds, we discovered a little ba snake a couple of feet long who had been tormented to within an inch of her life. I felt so sorry for her that I begged Fourth Brother to let me bring her back to Qingqiu with us.

This little ba snake had already transformed into a snake spirit, but she still moved by slithering on her stomach. Eventually she managed to cultivate enough spiritual energy to turn into human form, and that human form was Shao Xin. Shao Xin spent two years in Qingqiu, recovering from her injuries. Once she was better, she told me she wished to stay with me and repay my kindness.

Father and Mother had already left Qingqiu by then, and Fourth Brother was in charge of the foxhole. He arranged for Shao Xin to become my serving girl. We had never had servants in the foxhole before that, and I had been the one doing the sweeping and all the other housework.

I was so happy with my newfound leisure time that I was rarely inside after that. Instead I spent morning to night out, either at Second Brother's, Third Brother's, or Zhe Yan's. I spent two hundred years of carefree days, until Father and Mother returned with the news that they had found me a husband.

Sang Ji was the Sky Emperor's beloved second son, who lived with him in the Ninth Sky (he had not been banished to the Northern Sea at that point). The Sky Emperor announced my engagement to Sang Ji in front of the entire Four Seas and Eight Deserts. There was not a single immortal who did not hear the news. Following this there was an endless stream of visitors to the foxhole who came around for a chat and to congratulate me.

Fourth Brother and I found this so annoying that we made a bundle of our clothes and went over to Zhe Yan's to hide out in the peach grove. It was while we were hiding out that calamity struck.

After eating our fill of peaches, we returned to Qingqiu to discover that Shao Xin was nowhere to be seen. All I found in the gloomy and dusty foxhole was a letter from Sang Ji, pressed with his seal, breaking off our engagement. He explained that he had developed feelings for Shao Xin and that she was the one he was destined to be with. He apologized for all the upset he had caused.

I did not actually take the matter too much to heart. I had never even met Sang Ji and had no affection toward him. Shao Xin and I had not known each other for all that long, and although we were friends, it was not a friendship that ran especially deep. Even the livestock grazing in the woods are allowed to choose their own mates, and all being equal under the sun, there was no reason why Sang Ji should not be allowed to do the same.

I responded politely, telling them they seemed a well-suited couple. When news of this fiasco finally reached the Sky Emperor's ears, it had not come from me. Apparently it was Sang Ji who dragged Shao Xin into the Sky Emperor's court, and they both knelt down before him, pleading with him to accept their relationship.

This news shook the Four Seas and Eight Deserts. Those with kind hearts said things like, "That poor Bai girl. It was destined to be such a good marriage. Engaged for three years before being abandoned like that. How will she find a husband now?" There were malicious wagging tongues too, saying things like, "Can you imagine having a ba snake as an empress? Or perhaps the ba snake has more allure than the nine-tailed white fox?"

It was at that point Father; Mother; Big, Second, and Third Brothers; and Zhe Yan discovered I had been jilted. Zhe Yan came straight over to find Father and Mother and dragged them all the way to the Ninth Sky to seek justice from the Sky Emperor, although what exactly that entailed I am not too sure.

All I knew was what followed: Sang Ji fell out of favor with the Sky Emperor and was immediately appointed as the Northern Sea Emperor, an even lowlier position than that held by his younger brother Lian Song, the Four Seas Emperor. Any discerning person could see that he had effectively been banished. His marriage to Shao Xin was never recognized.

Father only made one comment on the subject: "That son of a bitch has gotten off far too lightly." Zhe Yan was more philosophical. Both enjoying the drama while also feeling sorry for me, he said, "Ruining his life prospects over a woman—what a fool."

I was young and naive and felt as if Sang Ji and Shao Xin were two protagonists in a drama that had nothing to do with me.

Later the Sky Emperor stood before his court and issued a sky decree that stated that the future Sky Emperor, as yet undecided, would marry me, the youngest daughter of the Qingqiu Kingdom's Bai family, making me the Sky Clan's future empress.

It was a grand gesture, made with kindness. But it was too grand, and to avoid in-family rifts and rivalry, all the Sky Emperor's other sons categorically ignored me. Naturally I was given no input in the matter. To avoid getting on the wrong side of the Sky Clan, no other immortals dared to send betrothal gifts to Father to ask for my hand in marriage either. I was left high and dry, an unmarriageable immortal maid.

Eventually, the Sky Emperor named his oldest grandson, Prince Ye Hua, as his successor. I knew nothing about him. All I heard was that the Sky Emperor had become despondent following Sang Ji's banishment, unsure of which of his remaining unremarkable sons should succeed him. Fortunately, three years later, his oldest son gave him a grandson, an astonishingly bright and talented boy, and the Sky Emperor, an old man now, was freed from his despondency and able to feel joy once again.

Ye Hua was that bright and talented grandson.

According to the Sky Emperor's earlier decree, as heir to the Sky Throne, this young immortal prince Ye Hua was also my future husband. I had heard that Ye Hua already had a concubine named Su Jin, who had been bestowed on him by his grandfather as a display of favor. Ye Hua had a young son too, and I assumed that he was not going to be brimming with enthusiasm at the idea of our marriage. Even though I had no other love interests, I could not get past the fact that he was ninety thousand years my junior. In terms of seniority, he would be referring to me as *Your Highness*, but in terms of age, it would be more like *Ancient Ancestor*. Because of the age difference, I found it impossible to actively pursue the marriage.

The fact that we had been engaged for so long without giving any sign of getting married had become something of a joke within the Four Seas and Eight Deserts.

I blamed Sang Ji more for causing me so much loss of dignity. I kept my animosity hidden, but my hatred became so intense that I often had thoughts of killing him.

When Zhe Yan mentioned the Northern Sea Emperor's visit, I was baffled. It was clearly not his intention to taunt me. There must therefore have been something he wished to tell me, some morsel of gossip he wished to share. I tried to look cheerful and pricked up my ears to listen to what he had to say.

The laughter lines radiating out from the corners of his mouth thickened. "That young girl is suffering from terrible morning sickness. In a few tens of thousands of years, she has given the Northern Sea Prince three children. This will be her fourth. Those ba snakes have remarkable reproductive capabilities. Her morning sickness has left her craving peaches, and she has been begging for them day and night. Peach blossoms are in abundance at this time of year, but finding peaches is a different matter. This is the only place in the sky and earth that has them . . . and that's why the Northern Sea Emperor and his wife made their way shamelessly to my door. They had come such a long way, and I felt it would be cruel to refuse them."

I looked up at him and then lowered my head to smooth out the creases in my dress. I had always seen Zhe Yan as extended family and had imagined that he would see our enemies as his enemies too. His generosity toward the Northern Sea Emperor burned with betrayal.

Zhe Yan looked at me and then burst into laughter. "Look at your face, you've gone green with anger! All I did was give them a couple of contraceptive peaches!"

I lifted my head sharply just as he was lowering his, and we bashed against each other.

He did not seem to notice. "Look at you," he continued mockingly. "As soon as you heard that I gave this groveling young couple a few contraceptive peaches, your heart softened toward them. All those peaches will do is delay the Northern Sea Emperor's fifth child for twenty thousand years or so. It's not going to do them too much harm, and it doesn't make me such a wicked person."

If it was just a matter of delaying the Northern Sea Emperor's fifth child, I was not going to worry about it. A contraceptive peach was not going to kill anyone. And anyway, by jilting me, Sang Ji had brought this misfortune on himself. Zhe Yan had taught them a lesson, and for that I was grateful. Zhe Yan consoled me further with a string of curse words about the bastard Sky Emperor and his lineage of bastard children and grandchildren.

When he finished cursing the Sky Clan, he asked after my family. Zhe Yan always had an endless supply of gossip, and whenever I visited him, I would ask him to indulge me, and receive an eclectic assortment of anecdotes. I had arrived there with my request for that earthen jar of peach blossom wine firmly in mind, but soon I was dizzy with conversation, the talk of families and secrets pulling a veil over the reason why I had come to see Zhe Yan at all.

Night had begun to close in when Zhe Yan reminded me of my purpose. "Your Third Brother asked me for two bottles of wine. I've buried them by the Jade Pool behind the mountain underneath that bare-looking wild ginger tree. Sleep there tonight, and you can dig out the wine and take it back to Third Brother. Those are the only two bottles, so make sure you don't spill any, and don't drink any on the sly."

"How mean you are!" I said with a pout.

He leaned forward and stroked my hair. "You really mustn't drink any on the sly. If you do want some wine, take it from my cellar tomorrow. You're welcome to as much as you can carry." Something occurred to him that made him smile, and he added, "I wouldn't go walking around tonight if I were you either. There's another guest staying here, and it's probably for the best that you two don't run into each other."

I bowed and gave thanks for the wine. Despite his warning, I had already made up my mind to indulge myself with the wine. These trips to the Ten-Mile Peach Grove took a lot more out of me than they used to. Tonight I would drink from the buried bottles; tomorrow I would go to his cellar and take as much wine as I could carry.

His suggestion not to venture out was unnecessary. I was fond of neither drama nor roaming around at night, and I liked social interaction even less. I was not the slightest bit interested in who this other guest might be, and if I could avoid them, I certainly would.

CHAPTER TWO

A little thatched hut that Fourth Brother had helped Zhe Yan build was still standing precariously next to the Jade Pool. Whenever I came to the peach grove, this was where I stayed. It had always seemed run down, even back when I was coming to the grove regularly. Tens of thousands of years of blustering wind, pouring rain, and blazing sun had stripped the hut of any beauty, but still it stood.

I pulled out the night pearl to cast some light inside the dark hut. The glow of the pearl revealed that Zhe Yan was still meticulous about everything and that the bed in the little hut had been made up just how I liked it.

There was a stone plow leaning against the wall next to the door, which I had used to dig holes and plant peach seedlings when I was younger. I laid my fingers on it again now, those two bottles of peach blossom wine not far from my mind.

• • •

The moon in the Ninth Sky was unusually round, and under the light it spilled, it was easy to find the wild ginger tree that Zhe Yan had told me about.

I used the stone plow to dig into the earth beneath the plant and found myself in luck. Straightaway I could see the aventurine wine pot shining through the loose yellow soil, its glittering green reflecting onto some of the wild ginger leaves. I gleefully pulled out the bottles and leaped up onto the roof of the hut with them in my arms. The hut shook a little before steadying again.

The night wind felt cool up there on the roof, and it made me shiver. After a bit of fumbling with the tightly sealed bottle spout, the cork eventually shot out the top, and the aroma of Ten-Mile Peach Grove wine overwhelmed me. I closed my eyes and took in a deep lungful, ever admiring of Zhe Yan's talent.

I had not been given many opportunities for romance in this life, but I did have one great love, and that was wine.

When drinking, it was important to complement the wine with the right blend of natural conditions, scenery, and company. This evening's moon was full, and there were bright clusters of stars overhead. The Eastern Sea peach grove provided the scenery, and there were several crows perched on the roof of the hut beside me, giving certain company. I took a few slurps from the mouth of the bottle, smacking my lips and letting the wine wash over my tongue. I sensed something slightly different about the flavor of this bottle of peach blossom wine.

I took swig after swig, and although I did not have any snacks to accompany it, looking out at the cold moon reflected onto the surface of the Jade Pool provided a nice diversion, and before long I had finished half a bottle.

The wind was picking up, and tipsiness was starting to creep over me, blurring the edges of my mind. There seemed to be a flimsy pink curtain fluttering over the gleaming black night, while a fire began to swell inside my body. I tossed my head from side to side, and with shaking hands I tried to unfasten my lapel. Despite the cold breeze, I grew hotter, eventually my bones seemed to radiate, the marrow inside red with glowing embers. My head was foggy and my thoughts muddled, but I had the vague sense that this was not mere drunkenness. I could no longer deal with the heat, but I did not feel lucid enough to cast a spell to disperse it.

I swayed about before I managed to get to my feet. I wanted to dive into the Jade Pool to cool myself off, but I stumbled and stepped into thin air before plummeting down from the hut roof.

I braced myself for a painful fall, but strangely enough, there was no thud as my body hit the ground. Instead I felt myself being embraced by something very cold, a soothing balm that cooled my body.

After some struggle, I managed to open my eyes, and made out a blurred figure in front of me, wearing a black cloak. Immediately I knew it was not Zhe Yan.

I felt giddy as my head spun. The moon's white light spread out over the entire peach grove, illuminating the flowers and the luxuriant leaves on the branches, making it look enchanted. The layer of mist hovering above the surface of the nearby Jade Pool suddenly transformed into a raging fire.

I clenched my eyes shut, feeling so hot it hurt. I moved toward the source of this coolness, pressing myself urgently against the figure in front of me. I lifted my cheek to feel it against the bare skin of his jaw and neck, cold as a piece of jade. My hands seemed to have taken on lives of their own; trembling, they started to remove the strap from his waist. He reacted by pushing me away. I pressed up against him once more. "Please don't be scared," I said in an attempt to reassure him. "I'm just trying to cool my hands." But he only pushed me away with more force.

I had not used an enchantment spell on anyone in thousands of years, but tonight I did not have a choice. Trying to clear my foggy mind and focus my attention, I opened my eyes to look at him. I was still feeling unsettled: I had no idea how long it had been since I had used such a spell and whether it would still be effective. He seemed confused. His eyes looked dim and unsettled. But then slowly, deliberately, he reached out and clasped me to him.

A pheasant crowed three times, and I gradually started to come to. I had the vague recollection of an interesting dream I had been having. A passionate dream, in which I had behaved with abandon with a young gentleman. My display of lust had been no more than a ploy to cling to him and cool myself against his body. There had definitely been something strange about those bottles of wine Zhe Yan had given me for Third Brother. I stroked my head and tried to remember what the young man had looked like, but all I could remember through the haze was his black cloak and the enchanted peach grove behind him. It felt like both a dream and not.

Zhe Yan's peach grove was not far from the Eastern Sea, and so I was in no great hurry. I went around to his wine cellar in the back mountain and took three earthen jars of wine. I placed these in my sleeve pockets along with the one full and one half-empty bottles from last night and went to bid farewell to Zhe Yan.

He went on about how when I got back to Qingqiu, I was to ask Fourth Brother to come over and help him plow the two thin strips of land in front of the mountain.

"That might not happen. His bird steed, Bi Fang, flew away, and Fourth Brother has been out looking for him," I explained. "It has been a while since he's been in the foxhole."

Zhe Yan looked serious for a moment, rare for him, before giving a long sigh. "I knew I shouldn't have helped him to capture Bi Fang from the Western Mountains. Ah well, you live and learn." I offered a few words of comfort, and he took a few fresh peaches from his sleeves and gave them to me as refreshment for the journey.

Looking up ahead of me, I saw the surging blue waves of the Eastern Sea and puff after puff of lucky clouds in the sky. It was an auspicious day, and you could sense that all the immortals were gathering.

I pulled a piece of white silk scarf four fingers wide from my sleeve and fastened it tightly around my eyes in preparation to enter the water. The Eastern Sea Water Crystal Palace was wonderful but extraordinarily bright, and for the last three hundred years, I had been suffering from an eye condition that made me sensitive to the bright lights.

It was a congenital defect, according to Mother. Her pregnancy with me had coincided with a great flood evoked by the Sky Emperor to punish the inhabitants of the Four Seas and Eight Deserts. Mother had been suffering from morning sickness at the time, and all she could eat was the fruit from Hexu Mountain. The floods, however, rose so high that the waters reached Hexu Mountain, making the whole area barren and denying Mother her fruit. With nothing else she could eat, she became painfully weak, and when she gave birth to me, a scrawny little fox cub, I had this strange eye condition.

The fault in my eyes remained dormant inside me for thousands of years, but three hundred years ago, following a bout of typhoid, it flared up. It was extremely tenacious, and no elixir made any difference. Wise Mother got Father to collect some mysterious light from beneath the Yellow Springs and use it to create a strip of white silk that would provide me with total blackout. Now, whenever I ventured into dazzlingly bright places, I wore it to shield myself from the light.

I dipped my hand into the shallow water. The Eastern Sea water was cold, and a shiver ran up my arm. I summoned some immortal energy to protect myself from the chill. I was in the middle of casting this spell when I heard a girl behind me calling, "Big Sister? Big Sister?"

Father and Mother had given birth to only my four older brothers and me; I was no one's big sister, and certainly had no female siblings. Confused as to who might be calling me, I turned around where I came face-to-face with a line of young girls in silk costumes, presumably family members of one of the banquet's immortal guests.

The girl in purple at the front of the line glared at me. "Why didn't you answer our princess straightaway?"

I looked blankly at the seven girls. The young girl in the middle was dressed in white and had the heaviest golden headpin and the biggest pearls on her embroidered shoes. I stooped and gave her a nod as I asked, "Why were you calling me?" The young girl in white had cheeks like white jade, which suddenly reddened.

"My name is Green Sleeves. I saw that you were shrouded in immortal energy and thought you must be heading to the Eastern Sea banquet. I wanted to trouble you for directions. I didn't notice your eyes . . ."

White silk made from the mysterious light beneath the Yellow Springs was not the same as normal white silk, and covering your eyes with it did not stop you from seeing. As long as I had my Mystic Gorge tree twig, I would have no problem finding the palace. "You're correct. I am heading to the banquet," I told the girl with a nod. "And my eyes are fine. You can follow me."

The girl in purple who had spoken up before now revealed her true spirit. "Our princess speaks to you and you respond with that attitude! Do you not know who our princess . . ." The princess tugged at this girl's sleeve to silence her.

Young immortals these days were most intriguing, so much livelier and more willful than I was at their age. Striding along beneath the water could be quite dull, and soon Princess Green Sleeves's serving girls were chattering to each other. They muttered all along the way, providing me with a source of light entertainment as I walked with them.

"I think that Big Princess shook us off deliberately so that we wouldn't get to the banquet and she could be the cream of the crop," one girl said. "Well, what she doesn't know is that we can find our own way there. We'll have to give her a big dressing down in front of the

Water Emperor when we get there. He'll punish her by sending her off to the Southern Sea for a few hundred years. That will give her a chance to think carefully about what she's done. We'll see if she dares to behave so terribly again after that."

So they are family members of the Southern Sea Water Emperor.

"Big Princess may be beautiful, but she's not a drop in the ocean compared to our princess," another said. "Don't worry, Princess Green Sleeves. As long as you are at the banquet, Big Princess will not get a look in."

I was witnessing squabbling and rivalry between sisters, it would seem.

"The Sky Empress may already have been named, but Prince Ye Hua is unlikely to have eyes for that old Qingqiu woman!" another said. "She's one hundred forty thousand years old, several times older than our family's prince even. I feel so sorry for Ye Hua. Our princess is such a rare beauty, with an appearance unmatched between sky and earth. She's his perfect match. If she manages to get Ye Hua to fall in love with her during this banquet, it will be the first good thing to have happened since Pangu split the sky and earth."

I was stunned to realize that "that old Qingqiu woman" they were speaking of was me. I shook my head, thinking how fickle life was and how fleetingly time passed, not sure whether to laugh or cry.

The more the serving girls talked, the lower the tone of their conversation, until Princess Green Sleeves piped up with an irritated, "Let's please have a break from all your nonsense!"

The more timid among them buttoned up, while the bolder girls stuck out their tongues. The bravest of the girls, the one in the purple dress, was determined to speak at whatever cost. "Rumor has it that Prince Ye Hua has taken his son on a trip to the Eastern Desert. Ye Hua really dotes on his little boy. I've heard that Big Princess has arranged an extremely generous and special gift she plans to give the little boy when they meet. Big Princess has wasted no effort on these measures. You won't let her show you up, Princess Green Sleeves, will you?"

It was obvious from the way she spoke that the girl in the purple dress was well educated and familiar with the sky classics. Princess Green Sleeves went red in the face. "Big Sister and I chose that gift together," she explained. "Who knows if the little prince will like it or not, though . . ."

The princess and her serving girl started to bicker. I walked ahead feeling slightly dismayed. I had not considered that Ye Hua, this bright and talented young man who had made his grandfather, the Sky Emperor, so proud might also be such a heartthrob. Before I had even met him, I had come across two girls nurturing tender peach blossom feelings for him. Adept at both military matters and affairs of the heart, this generation's young gods really were something.

We walked for over an hour before finally arriving at the Water Crystal Palace, located three thousand feet beneath the Eastern Sea.

I was getting nervous that I might have chosen the wrong fork in the road, as the huge palace hall up ahead looked nothing like how I remembered. There was nothing whatsoever connecting it with its name, not a glimmer of sparkling water crystal.

Princess Green Sleeves looked similarly taken aback. "What has this been covered with, water-lily grass?" she asked, pointing at the dark-green palace wall.

"Yes, I suppose it must be," I said, though I was quite unsure myself.

I was wrong to have doubted Old Mystic Gorge's twig, however; it turned out that this dark and gloomy palace was indeed the Eastern Sea Emperor's Water Crystal Palace.

The two court attendants standing at the palace gate were rendered speechless at the sight of Princess Green Sleeves. They hurriedly accepted her invitation and led the eight of us inside, parting the flowers and brushing aside the willows as we went.

As I walked farther inside, I discovered that the formerly dazzling Water Crystal Palace was now even gloomier than Father and Mother's foxhole. Fortunately the path had been hung with night pearls emitting a soft glow, which prevented me from stumbling and falling.

It looked as if the banquet would not start for another few hours, even though there were plenty of immortals already in attendance. They had gathered in the great hall, huddled in groups of two or three. I thought back to Father's birthday banquet some time ago, at which all the guests had shown up, but none of them on time. All the immortals, young and old, had shown equal enthusiasm by showing up early for the Eastern Sea Emperor's son's one-month banquet. The ways of the world had obviously changed, giving today's immortals more time on their hands.

Two palace attendants led Princess Green Sleeves over to the Eastern Sea Emperor, who I saw possessed an elegant charm reminiscent of his ancestors.

I fell to the rear of the group and mixed into the crowd of immortals. I turned to look for a servant to take me to a room where I could have a short rest; it had been a long journey, and I was rather tired. But every being in the hall was staring in awe at Princess Green Sleeves, and there was no one to assist me.

Objectively speaking, Princess Green Sleeves did not compare to the ancient ancestors in terms of appearance; my sisters-in-law were all far more attractive. But it would seem that this current generation of immortals was lacking many great beauties.

The servants were dumbstruck by her loveliness. They wore intoxicated expressions on their faces as they gazed at the gorgeous girl. I felt bad about interrupting them and dragging them away, so instead I wandered up and down the hall for a while and found a quiet way to slip out. I considered if it would be better to take a nap now or to just wait until the banquet, give my gift, have some food, and take my leave early. I remembered that despondent look on Mystic Gorge's face as he had seen me off. I had not asked him about it for fear I would be stuck listening to him go on, but now that I had a moment to reflect on it, I started to feel intrigued and was eager to go back and ask him what was wrong.

I turned this way and that, but even in such a large palace, I was unable to find a suitable place to lie down. I was just about to head back into the great hall, but when I turned, I realized that I didn't know the way. I poked around inside my sleeve, but my Mystic Gorge tree twig had disappeared. With my dismal sense of direction, I was going to have to pray if I wanted any hope of finding my way back to the banquet before it finished.

As I stood there, unsure of which direction to walk, I remembered a philosophy that Fourth Brother had taught me, one that had stuck with me ever since: *There were no paths or roads when the world began; it was only our random walking about that created them.* Losing the Mystic Gorge twig at this moment gave me two options: either I could sit still and wait to be found or I could take my chances by picking a direction and wandering.

The path I chose led me straight to the Eastern Sea Emperor's back garden, which was decorated in luscious green, exactly like the rest of the palace. It had the feel of a maze, and I walked around for more than an hour without coming across a way out.

After a few hours of drifting about in circles, I decided to ask fate for advice. As I approached a fork in the road, I bent down to pick up a branch. I held it in my palm, closed my eyes, and threw. The branch fell pointing toward the path on the left. I brushed the broken bits of leaf off my fingers and started walking toward the path on the right.

Fate has always been a bit of a rascal, and whenever I was required to ask him for advice, I found it sage to act against what he said.

I had been wandering around this back garden for such a long time and had not seen so much as a sea serpent, but only a hundred steps after dropping my branch and going against the advice of fate, I came across a boy who was so plump and pale he looked like a living, breathing sticky-rice dumpling.

This white and tender little rice dumpling child had his hair coiled into two buns, one on each side of his head, and wore a dark-green embroidered gown. He was perched on top of a cluster of green coral, and if I was not looking carefully, I might have mistaken him for part of the coral and missed him completely.

He looked like an immortal's son.

He had his head down, engrossed in pulling the water-lily grass off the coral. I watched him for a while before walking over to say hello. "Little Sticky-Rice Dumpling, what are you up to over there?"

"I'm pulling up these weeds," he said without lifting his head. "Father Prince told me that the coral hidden beneath these weeds is the most beautiful thing in the whole of the Eastern Sea. I've never seen it, so I'm pulling off the weeds to have a look."

Father Prince? So this is a young Sky Clan lord.

I felt sorry for him expending all that energy pulling out those weeds and wanted to lend a hand. I took my fan from my sleeve and placed it before him. "You can use this fan and wave it gently," I explained eagerly. "The grass will disappear without a trace, letting the coral show its face."

He pulled a handful of weeds with his left hand and took the fan from me with his right, and started to give it a little wave. A wild wind suddenly rose up from the ground, and the whole palace shook three times. Waves of dark ocean water crashed down from ten feet above us with a huge roar and the energy of a sword being whipped from its sheath or a wild horse throwing off the reins.

In a matter of minutes, the Eastern Sea Emperor's Water Crystal Palace had undergone a complete transformation and was now glittering brightly.

I was speechless.

The power my cloud fan yielded was completely dependent on the immortal power of the person in whose hands it was held. I had not expected this young sticky-rice dumpling to have such impressive powers.

I wanted to clap my hands and praise him, but I held back.

Sticky-Rice Dumpling tumbled to the floor and landed on his bottom. He looked at me in utter shock. "Oh no, have I caused a catastrophe?" he squealed anxiously.

"Relax," I told him. "You haven't caused a catastrophe. I was the one that gave you the fa . . ."

Before I had finished my sentence, I saw Sticky-Rice Dumpling's eyes open wide. I assumed seeing the strip of white silk covering most of my face must have frightened the young child and was just about to put my hand up to cover it, but he rushed over and grabbed my leg, shouting, "Mother!"

I was stunned and silent.

He continued to hug my leg and give these heartrending cries. "Mother, Mother!" he wailed. "Why did you abandon me? Why did you abandon Ali and Father Prince?" He stopped to give his streaming eyes and runny nose a good wipe on the corner of my skirt.

Cowed by his crying, I racked my brains, trying to recall if I had ever, in all my thousands of years, done anything that could be construed as abandoning a husband and child. As I was considering this, I suddenly heard a deep voice behind me. "Su Su . . . ?"

Little Sticky-Rice Dumpling jerked his head up and called out, "Father Prince," in a quiet voice. He was still clinging to my leg so tightly that it was impossible for me to turn around. Since I was so much older, it felt wrong to bend down and pry his fingers off me by force, so I just stood there with him clinging to me like that.

Father Prince came around and stood in front of me. He was so close that with my head lowered, all I could see was his black-soled cloud boots and the corner of a black cloak embroidered with a faint cloud motif.

"Su Su," he sighed. I realized he had been addressing me before. Fourth Brother often complained about how forgetful I was, but I could still remember all the names people had called me over the last tens of thousands of years—Fifth Cub, Si Yin, Little Seventeenth, and most recently Your Highness—but never had anyone called me Su Su.

Luckily, Sticky-Rice Dumpling let go of my leg at this point to rub his eyes, and I was able to take a hasty step back. "Your eyes seem to be giving you some trouble, immortal friend," I said raising my head to give him a smile. "You must have mistaken me for someone else."

He said nothing, but having a proper view of his face gave me a serious jolt. Little Sticky-Rice Dumpling's father was the spitting image of my revered master, Mo Yuan.

I lost my train of thought. He looked so similar to Mo Yuan, but he was not Mo Yuan. He could not possibly be Mo Yuan. He was much younger, if nothing else.

During the Demon Clan Revolt seventy thousand years ago, the Sky Rivers flowed with turbulent waters while the air danced with scarlet flames. Mo Yuan had locked Qing Cang the Demon Emperor inside the Eastern Desert Bell on the bank of Ruo River, and in so doing he used up all his cultivated spiritual energy, and his soul scattered. I did everything I could to protect his body, stealing it away and taking it back to Qingqiu. I placed him inside Yanhua Cave, where I fed him a cup of my heart blood every month. His body was still lying there inside Yanhua Cave.

Mo Yuan was Father of the Universe's eldest son, and the Four Seas and Eight Deserts' God of War. I had never imagined that one day he might die. Even now I still found myself waking up in the middle of the night from time to time and having to remind myself that he was actually gone. I still fed him this monthly bowl of my heart blood with the conviction that one day he would wake up again, give a faint smile, and call me by my old name, Little Seventeenth. I had spent day after day waiting for him to awaken. It had been seventy thousand years now.

I was so lost in a haze of painful recollection that I didn't notice Sticky-Rice Dumpling's father reaching an arm in my direction until his wide sleeve flapped against my face. I instinctively shut my eyes. He forcefully untied my white silk, stroking my forehead with his cold fingers, and then stopped suddenly.

"Ahhhh! Ahhhh! Deviant! Deviant!" Sticky-Rice Dumpling started to scream in a shaky voice. Deviant was exactly what it was, and the veins in my forehead were pulsing with fury.

"Learn some restraint!" I yelled at him. I had not used such a phrase in years, and it came out sounding strange.

I could not remember the last time anyone had dared to treat me with such flagrant disrespect. I must have scared Sticky-Rice Dumpling, as he yanked the corner of my skirt, bleating, "Mother . . . Mother, why are you angry?"

His father was still for a long time.

Sticky-Rice Dumpling looked first at his father, then at me, before wordlessly adhering himself to my leg, which felt like having a whole fried dumpling stuck to me.

Sticky-Rice Dumpling's father was silent for a few moments before tying my white silk cloth back up for me. He took a couple of steps back. "You're right," he said evenly. "I have mistaken you for someone else. The girl I knew wasn't as imposing or as forceful as you. Nor as alluring. I apologize for any offense I have caused."

Now that we had some space between us, I could see that the lapel and sleeves of the black brocade cloak Dumpling's father was wearing were embroidered with a dark dragon pattern.

Nowhere other than the Sky Emperor's household would immortals have the time or patience to embroider such intricate dragons onto their cloaks. Father Prince was certainly someone extremely influential, his wardrobe alone said as much. I took another look down at Little Dumpling, who Father Prince was attempting to pull off me, and suddenly it all became clear. This black-cloaked man was none other than the Sky Emperor's pride and joy, his grandson Prince Ye Hua.

Half of my anger dissipated immediately.

Prince Ye Hua. Of course. My father's ideal son-in-law. Extremely young. Possibly my husband-to-be.

I felt extremely apologetic toward him, and despite how offensive he had just been toward me, I felt I should be the one saying sorry. He was an exquisite young man of fifty thousand, and he was on the precipice of being tied into a marriage with me, a one hundred forty thousand-year-old woman. It was a lamentable deal for him to have been dealt. I managed to suck the other half of my anger back into my belly. I worried that my stance was not placid enough and my smile not as pleasant as it might be. "Let's not get into a discussion about who has offended whom," I replied. "Things between immortal friends should always remain courteous."

He regarded me with calm and cool eyes.

I moved to the side and let them both pass. Little Sticky-Rice Dumpling was still sniffling and calling out, "Mother."

Realizing that I would actually become his stepmother in the future, I gave him a smile and accepted this address. Little Sticky-Rice Dumpling's eyes shone, and he lifted a foot, getting ready to leap back over, but his father held him.

Prince Ye Hua gave me a strange look, which I responded to with a smile.

Dumpling was still struggling to break free. Ye Hua scooped him up, and the two of them walked around the corner.

In a second they had vanished completely, not even a seam of clothing left in sight.

I suddenly remembered the great banquet. I was still lost, and I had let the two of them go. Who was going to lead me out of the garden now?

I quickly gave chase in the direction they had just headed, but I could see no sign of them.

CHAPTER THREE

I rounded the corner that Ye Hua and his son had disappeared down, and glanced in both directions. From the north I saw a woman striding toward me who, judging by her clothes and her makeup, did not seem to know there was a party at all.

Squinting in her direction, I saw that fate really was up to no good today.

Despite being heavily pregnant, this woman still managed to look light-footed and spritely. I took out my broken-cloud fan and held it in my palm, wondering if a wave from left to right might send her flying back to the Northern Sea. But seeing her pregnant belly, my heart softened and I put it away again.

She walked over and slumped to her knees right in front of me. I moved to the side, not wishing to receive her praise. Looking perplexed, she followed after me on her knees, and I was reluctantly forced to stop. She looked at me and burst into tears. She did not look very different than she had when I last saw her fifty thousand years ago, although her face had become plumper.

I wondered whether the preferred form for female immortals these days was delicate willows or buxom beauties. All the male immortals had seemed extremely taken with lithe-figured Princess Green Sleeves just now, which led me to believe that hers might be the favored figure.

When confronted with people I was not too fond of, I had this quirk of blurting out things I knew they would not wish to hear. I gave myself a little pinch as a reminder to, whatever happened, *not mention her weight*. We had not seen each other for tens of thousands of years, and although I had my issues with her, she was a member of the older generation, and since she had observed etiquette so thoroughly, it would be improper of me to respond with an unkind comment.

She was still looking at me through moist, twinkly eyes, staring so intently that a cold shudder moved up my spine. She lifted her hand to wipe away her tears and choked out, "Your Highness."

In the end I could not stop myself. "Shao Xin, how have you gotten so fat?"

She stared at me in horror. Two red circles sprung to her cheeks, and her right hand moved to her bulging belly, and she gave it a vulnerable stroke.

"I . . . I . . . I . . . ," she stammered before it dawned on her that my words had been a form of greeting rather than a question she needed to answer. She rushed to prostrate herself again, raising her clasped hands in deference. "I was . . . I was in the garden just now when that wild wind blew me to the ground. As soon as I felt that seawater undercurrent, I thought that maybe . . . maybe it was the broken-cloud fan and Your Highness. I hurried over to have a look, and sure, sure, sure enough . . ."

She looked like she was on the verge of tears once more. I was not sure why she was crying, and while seeing her upset like this did not exactly please me, I could not honestly say that it displeased me either.

It would have been perfectly justified for me to storm off under the circumstances, but Shao Xin's pathetic appearance softened my heart. I saw a stone bench to the side and sat down on it with a sigh.

"It has been years since I have left Qingqiu, and I really did not expect to run into an old acquaintance quite so quickly. You must have known I wouldn't wish to meet with you, yet you have gone out of your way to kneel down in my path. You clearly have something you wish to ask for. We used to be mistress and servant, and when you married, I never gave you a dowry, which is something I now have a chance to amend. I will grant you one wish. Tell me then, what is it you want?"

She stared at me in shock. "I knew that you would be angry, Your Highness, bu . . . but why can't you even look at me?"

Before I had a chance to respond, she walked two steps closer on her knees. "You had never met Sang Ji, Your Highness, and you told me you didn't think you'd like him," she jabbered. "You and Sang Ji wouldn't have had a happy marriage. Sang Ji liked me and I liked him. You may have missed on marrying Sang Ji, Your Highness, but you will marry a better man. Prince Ye Hua is a hundred times if not a thousand times the man Sang Ji is. And he is the future Sky Emperor. But if I were to lose Sang Ji . . . I would h-h-have nothing. He's all I've got. I know that you are a wise and magnanimous immortal, Your Highness, and I think the reason you are angry with me is because I left Qingqiu without asking permission or saying good-bye, rather than because I married Sang Ji. Your Highness, Your Highness, have you not always said you wished for me to live a decent and dignified life?"

I turned the broken-cloud fan over in my palm and stroked its surface. "Shao Xin, you feel hatred toward those family members of yours who tormented you in the reeds, don't you?"

She nodded, looking perplexed and suspicious.

"You also know that some of them didn't really want to torment you, but if they'd tried to protect you, they would have been tormented themselves. They had no choice but to align themselves with the strong and bully the weak, didn't they?"

She nodded again.

I lifted my chin and looked at her. "Can you forgive those people who tormented you without a choice?"

She clenched her teeth and shook her head.

I had used such a circuitous route to express the way I felt, but I was pleased to hear my voice coming out sounding friendly and gentle. "That being the case, Shao Xin, you need to put yourself in my shoes and understand that similarly I don't wish to see you, which, under the circumstances, is completely reasonable. I am indeed a goddess, but I have only risen to this rank recently, and I am not as wise and magnanimous as you give me credit for."

She opened her eyes wide.

I had frightened her. She was such a beautiful, timid thing and pregnant, and as a goddess I should not have been so harsh. I felt immediately ashamed.

I lowered my head and looked down at my legs, and my eyes suddenly opened wide too.

Sticky-Rice Dumpling, who I thought had left the garden long ago, suddenly appeared out of nowhere. He started tugging gently at my skirt, a look of annoyance on his pale little face. "Why is Mother denying that she is a wise and magnanimous immortal? Mother is the wisest and most magnanimous immortal between the sky and earth."

I was speechless. "Where on earth did you spring from?" I asked when I had recovered from my shock. He raised his head and pouted his lips in the direction of the coral tree behind me.

Sticky-Rice Dumpling's father, Prince Ye Hua, walked out from the coral's shadow, a faint smile playing on his lips, completely transforming his face. "I wasn't aware that the girl I was talking to was Goddess Bai Qian from Qingqiu," he said slowly.

Hearing this fifty-thousand-year-old youngster calling me a girl made me shudder and gave me goose bumps. "Please don't flatter me," I said after some deliberation. "I am ninety thousand years your senior, and it would be more appropriate for you to refer to me as *Your Highness.*"

He gave a little smile and said, "So Ali gets to call you Mother, while I have to call you Your Highness? Oh, Qian Qian, how do you justify that?"

Hearing him call me Qian Qian made me shudder once more. It was said with a little too much affection.

Shao Xin watched us in complete silence. The scene descended into awkwardness. It had been so long since I had been in a social environment that I was not sure how much of the awkwardness was due to my unfamiliarity with such exchanges and how much was the strangeness of this situation. Under these watchful eyes, I felt compelled to argue back with him.

"You've been hiding behind a coral tree, eavesdropping on us all this time. How do you care to justify that?" I spluttered.

Ye Hua remained calm and unresponsive, but his son slid down from my knees and pointed to the little lane obscured by the coral tree. "Father and I weren't deliberately eavesdropping," he explained. "Father noticed that you were chasing after us, so we turned around. But when we got near, we saw Mother talking with this woman here and thought it would be better if we kept out of sight." He gave me a cautious look. "Mother, were you chasing after us because you couldn't bear to part with Ali? Because you want to come back to the Sky Palace with me and Father Prince?"

What an outlandish conclusion he had jumped to! I was just about to shake my head when I saw Ye Hua giving an emphatic nod and saying, "Yes, Ali, that's correct. Mother couldn't bear to be parted with you."

Little Sticky-Rice Dumpling gave a yelp of joy and looked at me through cheerfully sparkling eyes. "So, Mother, when are we going back to the Sky Palace?"

"We'll all go back there tomorrow," Ye Hua replied for me.

Sticky-Rice Dumpling gave another joyful yelp and continued looking at me through brighter and brighter sparkling eyes. "You've been away so long, Mother. Are you excited to finally be coming home?"

Ye Hua did not respond for me this time. Instead I heard myself give an awkward laugh and say, "Yes, I'm very excited."

They had not given me the chance to explain that the only reason I was hurrying after them was because I needed to be shown the way out of this damned garden! I was in a far more complicated situation now, but at least I had a guide to get me out of this place.

Shao Xin had been quietly lying prostrate on the ground this whole time, turning to Ye Hua every so often, looking aggrieved. If Sang Ji had not called off our engagement, he would be heir to the Sky Throne now, not Ye Hua. Everything that happened between the sky and earth could be explained through cause and effect. Sang Ji had sown the seed of cause, and the effect had naturally been his to reap. I could have caused him a lot of anguish; instead all I had done was add a few drops of water to the seedlings he planted, just a couple of extra drops of anger and hatred that had neither hurt nor stung him. The experience had allowed me to temper myself and become a more magnanimous person.

Ye Hua and his son's sudden reappearance had interrupted my renewal of friendship with Shao Xin, a fact that did not entirely displease me. With lifted spirits, I got ready to leave. Before I left the garden, I went over to Shao Xin and placed the broken-cloud fan in her hands. "Shao Xin, I'll grant you one wish," I said. "Think carefully about what you want, and when you've decided, come to see me in Qingqiu. As long as you are holding this fan, Mystic Gorge won't block your path."

Ye Hua lowered his eyes to Shao Xin and lifted his gaze back up to me. "I thought—" He stopped himself. "You are extremely kind-hearted," he said instead.

I did not feel that this little gesture warranted such praise. It was a matter between former mistress and servant, and while it cost me nothing to be kind to her, for her it was a huge grace. It was not worth trying to explain this to him. Instead I shrugged it off with the words, "You're very perceptive. I've always had a kind heart."

Sticky-Rice Dumpling looked yearningly at the fan in Shao Xin's hand. "I want one too," he said indignantly.

I stroked his head. "You're a child, what do you need a destructive weapon for?" I took a sugar lump from my sleeve and popped it in his mouth.

Ye Hua had a startlingly good sense of direction, and soon he had navigated us out of the garden.

I was not sure that turning up to the Eastern Sea banquet in Ye Hua's company would be such a wise plan. I lifted my sleeve and was about to bid them farewell, but Little Sticky-Rice Dumpling caught wind of what I was doing and gave me an utterly forlorn look. It placed me in an awkward position, and against my better judgment, I appeased him with the words "I have a few small matters to attend to, but we shall meet again tomorrow."

Little Sticky-Rice Dumpling said nothing, and while he did not seem particularly happy about this, he appeared to understand. He flattened his lips and he held out his pinkie finger to hook with mine, as a guarantee of my word.

Ye Hua gave a faint smile. "Qian Qian, it couldn't be that you are scared to arrive at the banquet with us, could it? Are you worried about what people might say?"

Qian Qian. Hearing that name instinctively gave me shivers. I turned to him. "Prince Ye Hua, you seem to be very fond of larking about," I said politely.

He did not reply, but his smile deepened, showing more of that Mo Yuan charm.

Seeing his smile momentarily lifted my spirits, and before I knew what was happening, he had hold of my hand. "So you knew who I was before, did you, Qian Qian?" he asked quietly. "We've been engaged for a while now. There's no reason to be cowed by wagging tongues."

He placed his slender hand casually over mine, a relaxed look on his face and a smile in his eyes. He looked so different from that frosty god who had untied my white silk. It was like looking at a completely different person.

I was not sure how to feel. Nowadays all young men and women who were betrothed seemed to tease each other and lark about like this. Things were much more relaxed and liberal than when I was young. Coming out so rarely meant that I had completely lost touch with the times. But these were rather unusual circumstances. I could have responded to his flirtation, but I found I was unable to get over the fact that I had been alive for ninety thousand years before Ye Hua had even left the womb. Adopting an intimate manner with him felt like it would have been vulgar of me, despicable even. But I was equally worried that pulling my hand back now might make me look like a prude.

After a moment's consideration, I reached out and touched his hair, giving a deep sigh. "When I was engaged to your second uncle, you hadn't even been born yet. Now you're all grown up. Time really is fleeting. It moves in twists and turns, and it can be merciless."

While he was looking at me in surprise, I quickly pulled back my hand. I gave him a nod and then took my leave.

I had not moved more than three steps when the Eastern Sea Emperor, the slender man I had seen dressed in purplish red in the great hall earlier, dropped down from above, landing right in front of me like a wooden stake spearing the ground. "Stop right there! Stop right there! Stop right there!" he shouted.

I took a couple of steps back and gave an admiring sigh. "Water Emperor, you are most agile. Two steps closer and you would have completely flattened me."

His square face was as red and swollen as a piece of coral. He greeted Ye Hua courteously and asked Little Sticky-Rice Dumpling a few deferential questions before turning to glare at me. The tiger eyes in his ragged face looked close to tears. "I'm not sure what I have done to offend you, immortal colleague, for you to come here on our family's day of celebration and take your anger out on my garden."

The mask had come off! He knew what my fan had done. I felt hugely ashamed.

Ye Hua watched calmly from the side, reaching out every so often and running his hand through Sticky-Rice Dumpling's smooth and glossy hair.

I had actually been no more than an accomplice, but since Sticky-Rice Dumpling had taken to calling me Mother, I could not really bring myself to blow the whistle on him. Instead I swallowed the injustice and accepted the blame. I was intrigued by how he had found out it was me who had restyled his garden. I held the question back for a while, but eventually I blurted it out.

The Eastern Sea Emperor glared and grimaced at me. He pointed at me, his whole body trembling. Eventually he calmed down enough to say, "D-d-do you really think you can deny it? The Coral Spirit in my garden witnessed the whole thing. He said that the wild wind was invoked by a little immortal dressed in green. How can you possibly deny that was you?"

I looked down at my green robe, and over at Sticky-Rice Dumpling dressed in dark green, and understood his confusion. There was some ambiguity in the Eastern Sea Emperor's interpretation of the Coral Spirit's term *little immortal*. The Coral Spirit had meant little in terms of stature, while the Eastern Sea Emperor had taken it to mean low ranking. Sticky-Rice Dumpling was Ye Hua's oldest son, and the Sky

Emperor's great-grandson, which meant that his ranking was high, whereas the clothes I was wearing today did not mark me out as a goddess. The mistake was not an unreasonable one.

I was the one in the wrong. The Eastern Sea Emperor had been waiting for a long time for this precious son and had spared no effort for this one-month banquet. I had accepted his invitation with the best of intentions but had somehow ended up causing mayhem. I had not realized I had done anything wrong, but he thought I was denying it. Even though I knew more than he, I decided it would not be wise to get into an argument with him.

The Eastern Sea Emperor looked at me with impatience, his eyes so angry they looked fit to burst. "You, my immortal colleague, have destroyed my garden," he said. "And you don't seem the slightest bit sorry. How can you treat people like th—"

"Water Emperor, you are right to reprimand me like this," I interrupted. I recalled that whenever Phoenix Nine offended me, she would humble herself, fawning and flattering: the exact technique I was going for now. I dropped my head and attempted to look thoughtful. "I was scared and forgot my manners just now," I explained. "I implore you, Water Emperor, please be kind and forgive me. I spend all my time in the Ten-Mile Peach Grove, and the first thing I do when I leave is cause a catastrophe like this. It was completely unintentional, but I can see I have lost the prince's favor, and I have brought shame upon Zhe Yan too. I am extremely embarrassed. Please, Water Emperor, reprimand me, rid yourself of anger by punishing me."

Ye Hua stole a glance at me, his eyes glittering like sunlight.

Destroying a person's garden when you have been invited into their home really was rather shameful behavior. Fortunately for me, Eastern Sea Water Emperor did not seem to recognize who I was, which saved Father and Mother a huge amount of humiliation. Heaping this humiliation on Zhe Yan was a much better option. Back when Fourth Brother and I had been young enough not to know any better, we used to mention Zhe Yan's name any time we got ourselves into mischief. Even when we brought shame upon him, all Zhe Yan would do was give a faint smile. If that shame had befallen Father, he would have skinned the fox fur off our backs.

The Eastern Sea Emperor did a double take. "You mean Zh . . . You mean, you mean the god from the Ten-Mile Peach Grove?" He held his breath, looking solemn and attentive. He had known to honor the custom of not mentioning Zhe Yan by name. This square-faced prince with his wide forehead was actually extremely respectful and observant of hierarchical etiquette, an honorable man.

I pulled the pumpkin-sized night pearl from my sleeve with glee, followed by the wine I had bottled for him. I placed both these items into his hands and gave an earnest sigh. "Does the Water Emperor not believe me? It's no wonder. The god I work for hasn't paid courtesy to another immortal household for tens of thousands of years. Goddess Bai Qian of Qingqiu Kingdom . . ." I gave an unintentional splut-ter here. "She went to visit the peach grove, but sadly she was feeling unwell. She had already accepted your invitation and didn't want to let Your Highness down, so she sent me to offer congratulations in her place." I pointed to the night pearl and said, "This is a pearl plucked from the moon. It is a celebratory gift from Bai Qian. And this is the peach blossom wine prepared by our household prince's own hands." I gave a doleful bow. "Water Emperor, please accept these two gifts as a token of our good wishes. I hope they will brighten your mood. I didn't intend to make any trouble. I am really, really so—"

I was about to shed a tear, but the Eastern Sea Emperor rushed to console me before my eyes had the chance to well up. "Don't talk like that, little immortal. You have come such a long way to be here. It's my fault for not giving you a personal welcome. It is just a garden, and you've made it far brighter anyway." He cupped his hands together in front of his chest and bowed respectfully in the direction of the peach grove. "My son will be eternally grateful to these two gods for showing such concern and giving such generous gifts." He waved his hand. "You must be tired after your long journey, immortal envoy. Please go through to the great hall and revive yourself with a glass of wine."

I offered a hundred excuses, which he countered with a thousand insistences. Ye Hua came over and took my hand as if it were a completely natural thing for him to do. "It's only a glass of wine. There is no need to be so polite, immortal envoy."

My brow was pouring with sweat. "I am actually a boy. I'm simply dressed as a girl today," I explained to the Eastern Sea Emperor, pointing at my right hand, which was firmly encased in Ye Hua's.

The Eastern Sea Emperor recovered from his surprise and mumbled, "Oh, you two must be in a homosexual relationship in that case. And clearly a very serious one."

I had assumed that pretending we were both men would make us less conspicuous, not more so! I had not counted on how enlightened and liberal today's immortals were. All I had done was make matters worse. Alas, I was done for now.

CHAPTER FOUR

The Eastern Sea Emperor walked ahead leading the way, Little Sticky-Rice Dumpling tottered along in the middle, and Ye Hua and I brought up the rear, my hand still tightly encased in his.

I had told only one small lie, which had been to protect his little son, really. He could have just turned a blind eye, but instead he decided to make things difficult for me.

I lost patience, and no longer caring about maintaining my goddess dignity, I cast a magic spell to break away from him. Ye Hua gave a gentle smile and blocked my spell with one of his own.

We battled on like this the whole way, Ye Hua gaining the upper hand because he did not care who saw, while I was trying not to rouse the attention of the Eastern Sea Emperor. Eventually I was forced to admit defeat.

Recently Fourth Brother had dismayed me by telling me how much things had deteriorated since the good old days of the ancient gods. This current generation of immortals was so laid-back and lazy, apparently, and their magic was ailing and their Taoist practice weak. I had believed him. But the spells that Prince Ye Hua was casting in front of me right now were so sophisticated and skillful that it made his grandfather's magic look ailing and his grandmother's Taoist practice look weak.

The Eastern Sea Emperor turned and gave me a weak smile. With his eyes fixed on our joined hands, he said, "Prince. Immortal envoy. We have arrived at the great hall."

Little Sticky-Rice Dumpling gave a yelp of joy and scampered over to grab my free hand. He adopted a solemn and dignified expression, befitting his position as the Sky Clan's great-grandson.

If it had been Ye Hua's head concubine walking in with him, such ostentation would have been all good and proper. But instead, here I was, racking my poor brains to try and make sense of it all. Yes, I was connected to Ye Hua, but not yet in any formal way, and I did not understand what he was thinking dragging me into the banquet with him like this.

The palace door was before us with its gold engravings and jade inlay. I started to feel a dull ache in my head.

All the immortals inside the great hall had been waiting impatiently for the banquet to start, and as soon as Ye Hua appeared, they knelt down in two lines, forming an aisle that led straight to the host's table. As soon as the three of us were seated, they gave praise and sat down in their places. The banquet had begun.

The immortal sitting nearest us came over to give a toast. He raised his glass to Ye Hua before turning to me. "How lucky I am to have the honor of meeting Empress Su Jin," he said with deference. "What good fortune, what good fortune indeed . . ."

Ye Hua stood to the side with his wine cup in his hand, watching impassively as I was forced to deal with this awkward situation.

The Eastern Sea Emperor turned pale and was winking desperately in the direction of the immortal lavishing us with praise. I could no longer bear to watch. I gave a simpering smile and said, "I am actually Ye Hua's long-lost little sister. I am here today as Zhe Yan's envoy."

Ye Hua stopped drinking, and a few drops of wine splashed from his glass. The Eastern Sea Emperor turned and looked at me in bewilderment. The immortal holding out his glass to toast me looked completely mortified. He was not in the position to continue with his toast, nor lower his glass. "I am so sorry," he stuttered, following an awkward silence. "My eyesight is terrible. I will drink this down in penance." I smiled kindly, unoffended, and drank a glass along with him.

After this everyone began toasting each other.

Fox ears are sharp, and between all the clinking of glasses, I could make out the gist of a discussion held between two people at another table.

"It's such a shame Her Highness isn't here today," one said. "Although seeing Zhe Yan's immortal envoy almost makes up for it. Do you think she found out that both Ye Hua and the Northern Sea Emperor would be here for the banquet and that's why she decided not to att—"

"You may well be right, my immortal friend," the other replied. "Her Highness's failure to show up and Zhe Yan sending this envoy to the banquet, it seems as if there is more than meets the eye. Everyone knows that the Eastern Sea Water Emperor didn't send Zhe Yan an invitation on account of his strange temperament."

"That's true," the first one said. "And another strange thing, Zhe Yan's envoy is none other than Ye Hua's little sister."

"I'm not sure about that," the other said. "I've served loyally in the Sky Palace for many years, and I have never heard any mention of Ye Hua having a sister."

"Immortal friend, did you not just see Prince Ye Hua holding that immortal envoy's hand? They looked like siblings to me."

If the Eastern Sea Emperor had announced that the banquet was over at that point, I was certain that these two immortals would have been dancing with glee. There was nothing they wanted more than to find a nice, quiet corner and continue discussing these juicy matters.

Instead they had to put up with the bitter frustration of sitting on the stage and stealing the occasional whisper.

I listened for a long time, but heard nothing else of interest, so I lifted my glass and drank alone. Ye Hua removed the wine bottle from the table with a frown. "You may have a high alcohol tolerance, but don't drink too much. We don't want you getting drunk again."

The Eastern Sea Emperor's wine was seen as the jade nectar of the immortals, but it could have been water compared with Zhe Yan's wine. I was not worried about the quality of what I was drinking, however. I was knocking it back to drown out the sound of people saying humiliating things about me left, right, and center.

The banquet was halfway through now, and I was starting to feel restless. I wanted the meal to be over so that I could return to the fox-hole. But at that moment, the Eastern Sea Emperor clapped his hands together three times.

I sat up straight and watched as a group of delicate, slender, and scantily clad dancing girls spiraled into the hall with silk fans in their hands. I was slightly bemused as to why the Eastern Sea Water Emperor was providing entertainment like this for his son's one-month celebration.

I glanced over at Ye Hua, who wore a bored look on his face. Little Sticky-Rice Dumpling gave a sharp sigh when he saw the dancers. "Oh, it's *her*!" he said. I followed his gaze into the middle of the hall where the dancers in white were arranging themselves into the petals of a lotus flower. The girl he was looking at was in the center dressed in yellow. At first glance I could see nothing special about this girl, although she had a similar physique to the Eastern Sea Emperor.

I turned to have a look at the Eastern Sea Emperor, and he immediately picked up that I was watching him. He coughed, and with an awkward smile, he said, "She's my little sister." He walked over to Sticky-Rice Dumpling and said, "Are you familiar with my sister, Little Sky Prince?"

Sticky-Rice Dumpling looked at me, and after some hemming and hawing he said, "Yes, I do know her," and gave her a vague wave to demonstrate this. "But not very well," he added, stealing a glance at Father Prince.

The Eastern Sea Emperor's sister kept casting anxious looks in Ye Hua's direction, her eyes eager but calm, full of sorrow and joy.

Ye Hua's wine glass froze in his hand, and his expression transformed into that icy one I had seen when we first met.

What were they singing about? Poor flowers falling from trees and cruel water flowing away? A warmhearted girl meets a coldhearted man and wishes to be like a vine wrapped around a tree, but his heart is cold as iron and her dream is not to be.

I gave a satisfied nod at their performance. I poured myself another glass of wine and watched with interest, right up until the crescendo when the music came to a screeching halt. The Eastern Sea Water Emperor's little sister looked at Ye Hua and gave a bow before floating away surrounded by her dancing girls.

Ye Hua turned to look at me with a faint smile. "Why do you look so disappointed, immortal envoy?" he asked.

I rubbed my face and gave an awkward laugh. "Disappointed? Do I?"

I had been forced to put up with so much over the last few hours. Now that the banquet was finally over, I was looking forward to slipping out along with all the other guests. But Ye Hua had other ideas. "Ali wants you to look after him," he said, shoving Sticky-Rice Dumpling into my arms. "I'll be back shortly."

All the immortals came over cupping their hands and bowing farewell. Ye Hua took advantage of the fact that I was distracted and slipped quietly out of the great hall. I had been weighed down by so many trifling matters for so many hours now, and my befuddled brain was only just starting to clear. Realizing the situation I had gotten myself into, my forehead suddenly started dripping with sweat. Ye Hua could not have been serious when he told Little Sticky-Rice Dumpling he was going to drag me back to the Sky Palace with them, could he?

The soft Little Sticky-Rice Dumpling in my hands suddenly felt more like a thorn in my side. I strode out of the great hall, intending to find Sticky-Rice Dumpling's father straightaway and hand his son back over to him.

I asked a couple of young serving boys if they had seen Prince Ye Hua, but none of them had. Taking a different approach, I asked if they knew where the Eastern Sea Emperor's little sister was.

Ye Hua had left in a hurry, but within his aloof manner, I had seen a hint of affection, and within his nonchalance some hidden grace. Based on all the romantic happenings I had witnessed over thousands and thousands of years, it was obvious from this demeanor that he was meeting with some beauty.

The young serving boys pointed to the end of the path, toward the back garden of the Eastern Sea Water Crystal Palace.

I took Sticky-Rice Dumpling to the entrance of the garden and gave a defeated sigh.

I might well stroll into this garden without any trouble, but with my appalling sense of direction, there was no guarantee that I would make it back out again. I deliberated a while, caution advising me to stay waiting by the entrance.

Little Sticky-Rice Dumpling had other ideas. He forged little fists and became quite fierce. "Mother, if you don't go back in and pull the two of them apart, Princess Liao Qing is going to steal Father Prince away." He put one hand on his hip and rubbed his forehead in distress with the other. "Since ancient times, back gardens have been troublesome places. Do you know how many gifted scholars have ended up being bewitched by beautiful women inside them, losing both their souls and their way, eventually leading lives of hardship?"

I was absolutely astonished. "Wh-wh-who tau-tau-taught you that?" I croaked.

Little Sticky-Rice Dumpling looked at me in surprise. "Three hundred or so years ago, a little immortal called Cheng Yu ascended to the white sun in the sky. My great-grandfather the Sky Emperor gave him the title Virtuous Monarch. Virtuous Monarch Cheng Yu. He was the one who taught me that. Am I wrong?" he asked, rubbing his head and looking perplexed.

What he had been told was correct, but the fact that Virtuous Monarch Cheng Yu had dared to teach Sticky-Rice Dumpling such things right under Ye Hua's nose and that his words had left such an indelible mark on Dumpling showed that Cheng Yu was an immortal with a certain flair and capability. He was clearly a bright fellow, and if I ever ran into him, I would be certain to make his acquaintance.

Little Sticky-Rice Dumpling pulled at my sleeve, insistent we should venture into the garden. He was such a tiny thing, and I was scared of putting up any physical resistance. All I could do was try to dissuade him with words. "Father Prince is young and healthy," I explained, "and Liao Qing, if that's her name, is young and of marriageable age. Young men and women yearning for each other is completely natural behavior. If they have already become a couple, we won't be able to spoil their marriage plans. All we'll be doing is interfering. Surely you don't hate Princess Liao Qing enough to wish to ruin her marriage plans? You must learn to be more tolerant."

Little Sticky-Rice Dumpling's mouth flattened, and I realized I might have been too stern. I quickly went to console him, kissing him and stroking him until he calmed down. "She saved my life once," he said quietly. "And I've thanked her profusely. But since then Father Prince has started acting differently. Each time he takes me to Mother's old home in Junji Mountain, *she* comes along too. *She's* infatuated with him."

I felt obliged to have a word. "Gratitude to someone who has saved your life should be deeper than the ocean. It isn't a matter of just saying thank you."

If it were that simple, how much freer and unfettered I would be right now. If it was only the harmonious affection that Mo Yuan and I had shared as master and apprentice that I remembered, I would certainly not have so much guilt and regret trapped inside me.

Little Sticky-Rice Dumpling reflected on my words for a while before stamping his foot. "She doesn't understand that she's crossed the line. She knows full well that Father Prince has a wife, but she wants to ensnare him anyway. She stays in Mother's room, uses Mother's cooking utensils, and wants to steal Mother's husband."

I looked up at the sky, and an image of Ye Hua's face flashed into my mind, looking just like Mo Yuan. Their similarity was astounding.

I could not blame Liao Qing. I had seen that face for thousands and thousands of years, and even as a goddess I had only just managed to keep my desire in check. Being an ordinary woman before such a face must make it so much more difficult not to cross the line. The bit of the story that puzzled me was the connection to the Eastern Desert's Junji Mountain. When had Su Jin had a place there?

I asked Little Sticky-Rice Dumpling about this, and he gave me a rather garbled explanation. Even though I was completely focusing on his words, I could only make out the gist of what he was saying.

Apparently Sticky-Rice Dumpling's mother was not Ye Hua's concubine Su Jin after all, but a mortal. Sticky-Rice Dumpling still kept a painting of his mortal mother on his bedchamber wall. In the picture she was wearing green clothes and had a piece of white silk covering her eyes, just like me. Three hundred years ago, just after giving birth to Sticky-Rice Dumpling, something had made her jump off the immortal punishment platform. I had heard of this immortal punishment platform. If an immortal jumped from it, they lost all their cultivated spiritual energy, but if a mortal jumped, their spirit and soul would fly away and they would disappear altogether. Little Sticky-Rice Dumpling obviously did not understand this part.

Before she was taken to the Sky Palace, this mortal had been living at Junji Mountain. Prince Ye Hua cherished her memory so much that he had placed a seal on her old hut to protect it. Each year he would take his son on a pilgrimage to the little hut, where they would spend a week or two.

I admired Ye Hua's courage. He had not tried to conceal any of this suffering and sorrow from Dumpling. He was confident that his son could deal with such painful knowledge without it casting a shadow over his young mind.

Dumpling and Ye Hua had been fated to know Liao Qing for only a hundred years or so.

Dumpling was in the mountain forest, playing and hunting rabbits once, when his immortal spirit had attracted the attention of a passing snake demon. This snake demon knew who the little boy was and had been just about to eat him to gain the immortal nourishment from his body. Fortunately Princess Liao Qing from the Eastern Sea had been visiting Junji Mountain and had saved his life. Dumpling led her back with him to the little hut on the mountain. The hut had been sealed so it was invisible to outsiders, but Dumpling had been so grateful to her for rescuing him that he had revealed his true identity and taken her inside for tea. The princess had been just about to leave when Ye Hua returned. Princess Liao Qing had been at the age of romantic awakening, and seeing Ye Hua was like being hit by a bolt of lightning. She fell head over heels in love.

Not wishing to be indebted to the Eastern Sea Princess, Ye Hua had promised to grant her one wish. And for the last hundred years, Liao Qing had stayed on Junji Mountain, and whenever Ye Hua and Dumpling came to visit, she would wash their clothes, cook, and make them steamed cakes. Ye Hua did not think it was appropriate for a princess to take on such a lowly role, but when he expressed this, she quietly bowed her head and with extreme modesty said, "This is my wish, Prince Ye Hua. Please don't stand in my way." Ye Hua had no choice but to submit.

I was hearing all this solely from Sticky-Rice Dumpling's point of view. It was clear that Ye Hua was a passionate man, and he might well have found love for this kind and considerate princess in his heart.

Desolation started creeping in. Ye Hua had been alive for no more than fifty thousand years, during which time he had stirred up so much female interest. It was clearly something he had a talent for.

What had I been up to when I was fifty thousand?

Sticky-Rice Dumpling had a strange look on his face. He was regarding me hesitantly, as if there was something he wanted to say, but he was not sure that he should. "As a boy, the worst thing you can do is to appear faltering," I told him sternly. "You don't want to end up looking pathetic. If you have something to say, just come out and say it."

With tears in his eyes, he pointed at me and said, "Mother, you're acting as if you just don't care. Does your heart belong to somebody else now? Is that why you no longer want Ali and Father Prince?"

I was unable to speak. Ye Hua and I had this engagement agreement, but this was the first time we had ever met. It was hard to talk about, and Little Sticky-Rice Dumpling took a couple of steps back and covered his face. Sounding bitter and aggrieved, he said, "Father Prince will marry my stepmother, and Mother will marry my stepfather, and I will never experience family unity. I will be all on my own. None of you will want me." He howled so loudly that my heart gave a leap of fear.

I gave an attentive smile and put my arms around him. "I'm your mother. How could I possibly not want you?" I said.

"But you don't want Father Prince," he accused. "And because you don't want Father Prince, Father Prince will end up marrying Liao Qing. If Father Prince marries Liao Qing, they'll have another baby, and they won't want Ali anymore." The tears were streaming down his face now.

I felt a big headache coming on. I did not want to disappoint him, so I pretended to look love struck, and through gritted teeth, I said,

"Your father is my heart and my soul. He is my precious, my turtledove. How could I not want him?"

By the time I had finished saying all this, I felt so nauseated I was shaking.

Little Dumpling looked delighted. He put his arms around my leg and dragged me into the garden, giving me no choice but to go along. I prayed that Ye Hua was no longer in the garden so that I could avoid the drama of having to cause a rift between the pair.

We went around the arched gateway, and I saw an exquisite pavilion some way off. Inside, a man in a black cloak was standing with his arms clasped behind his back. Ye Hua. And the young girl sitting next to him dressed in yellow was obviously Princess Liao Qing.

Little Sticky-Rice Dumpling tugged at my sleeve. "Mother, you need to step in now," he said. It felt too quick, and I had not had time to prepare. My scalp tingled as I considered how I should launch in. Big Brother was the person I knew well whose life had been most shrouded in peach blossom. What was it my sister-in-law used to do when confronted with Big Brother's peach blossom nymphs? Oh yes, I remembered. First it was the eyes: they needed to be cold. Give your rival the once-over; look at her as if she were a cabbage. Next it was the voice: she would turn to Big Brother and in an ethereal tone say, "I've had a good look at her, and if you like her, husband dear, please take her as a concubine. It is absolutely fine with me, it will be fun, just like having another little sister." This was known as the withdraw-attack tactic. Despite Big Brother's many admirers, my sister-in-law's apparent willingness to accept his future concubines had given him such a sense of gratitude that he had remained unwaveringly devoted to her all these years.

My present situation was different, though, and this tactic was unlikely to be of use. I was still trying to decide what to do when I saw Sticky-Rice Dumpling scampering over to them and kneeling down in front of his father, saying, "I saw you from over there, Father Prince."

Ye Hua squinted past Sticky-Rice Dumpling to where I was. I plucked up the courage to stride over, and bobbing my head in a vague observation of etiquette, I pulled Sticky-Rice Dumpling up from the ground, patted the dust from his knees, and sat down on the pavilion bench, placing him on my lap.

Even without looking, I could feel Ye Hua's eyes on me, making my every movement feel awkward.

"And you are . . . ?" Princess Liao Qing said in an attempt to initiate conversation.

I gave her what was quite clearly a fake smile, and stroking Little Dumpling's face, I said, "The child calls me Mother." Liao Qing suddenly looked as if she had been struck by lightning. I was starting to feel quite guilty. Princess Liao Qing was a pleasant-looking girl. She was not quite in the same league as Princess Green Sleeves, but she was certainly a beauty. I had no quarrel with her; the way I was behaving was just an act. And besides, I was an elder: if anyone were to find out that I was starting a fight with someone younger, and over some romantic business, I would never be able to show my face in public again.

I was feeling miserable inside, but I continued to play my role, still with that same fake smile on my face. "These black clouds above our heads make for a good atmosphere. Little Princess, for you, it seems fitting for a tryst, but it puts me in the mood to write poetry."

Ye Hua was leaning against the pillar of the pavilion, listening to me spout this nonsense.

Little Sticky-Rice Dumpling had no idea what I was up to. He just sat there with his head lowered. I pointed at his forehead and gave an angry laugh. "A thriving pine tree, a charming nest, a cuckoo invades to lay her eggs." Looking again at Princess Liao Qing, I said, "Does that sound fitting, Little Princess?"

She looked shocked. Two lines of hot tears streamed from her eyes. She slumped to her knees in front of me. "Empress, please don't be angry . . . I didn't know who you were just now, or I would never have deigned to be so familiar. I cherish Prince Ye Hua, but I ask nothing of him. I am being pursued by the second prince of the Western Sea. He wishes to marry me and take me out west to live with him. But he is . . . he is a real peacock, always parading himself about. The marriage is drawing near, and I didn't know what else to do. I found out that Prince Ye Hua would be bringing his son to the Eastern Sea banquet, and I used the dance as an excuse to see him. I am willing to spend life after life following Prince Ye Hua, acting as his servant and waiting on him. I have no ulterior motive, I promise. I beg of you, Empress, don't stand in the way of my wish."

So that was what it was all about. This girl had genuine affection for Ye Hua. I was moved by the way she spoke. The Sky Palace was so vast, and I did not see a problem with her being given a small corner to stay in. But this was Ye Hua's own palace affair. If she had not been as genuine and sincere as she was, I would not have seen the harm in causing a rift between them. But after the way she had reacted, I could not bring myself to do it.

Matters of the heart could not really be spoken of in terms of morals and marked as right and wrong. Sticky-Rice Dumpling was still so young. Later he would need careful guidance. When I realized that I had basically bullied this girl, I gave a sigh. I really could not facilitate such tactics again. I picked up Dumpling and was about to stand and walk off, but he reached out and clung to the pavilion bench, looking very upset.

"Mother, you just told me that Father Prince was your heart and soul, your precious, your turtledove. How can you let her just steal him away? You were lying before, weren't you?"

This ordeal was making my headache even worse.

Ye Hua had been leaning against the pavilion pillar, staring blankly. Suddenly he gave a smile and took a step forward, blocking my path. He took a lock of my hair between his fingers. "Am I your heart and soul?" he asked slowly.

I gave an awkward laugh and took a step back.

He took another step forward. "Your precious?"

My laughter came out sounding even more forced.

He trapped me in the corner of the pavilion. "Your turtledove?"

I was unable to make myself laugh this time. There was a bitter taste in my mouth. What had I done? What had I done? What was this wicked deed that I'd done? I closed my eyes, my heart beating fast, and said, "You terrible creature, you know that's how I feel. Insisting on hearing me say these things in public really is just bad manners."

Little Sticky-Rice Dumpling was quivering in my arms, and Ye Hua was standing in front of me, shaking a little too.

I took advantage of his shocked disbelief, and flinging Sticky-Rice Dumpling down onto the pavilion seat, I ran pell-mell away from them all, feeling completely and utterly bamboozled.

CHAPTER FIVE

I had lost my twig from the Mystic Gorge tree, and the sky was growing darker. I had used up all my good fortune getting myself out of the Eastern Sea before evening fell, and I did not have high hopes for getting back to Qingqiu any time before dawn.

The Eastern Sea consisted of four sea roads, one in each direction. Ever since I was a fox padding along on all fours, I had been a land dweller, and these sea roads all looked identical to me. It was only once I got out of the water that I realized I had taken the North Sea road, thinking it was the east.

The moon was high in the sky by now, and shining brightly. I sat on a reef on the Eastern Sea's northern shore, feeling anxious.

I could have gone back into the water of the Eastern Sea and returned the way I had come, but I didn't want to risk the potential embarrassment of running into Ye Hua again. I went over all my options and decided I would be best off spending the night on the northern shore and deciding what to do in the morning.

Lunar April was the most fragrant and verdant of months. The days were warm, but the nights tended to be cold. I was only wearing light clothing, and the white mist rolling off the ocean made me sneeze three times in quick succession. In the end I decided to jump down from the reef and head into a nearby wood.

This wood was nothing compared with Zhe Yan's, but its trees had tall, gnarled branches and thick foliage that helped to block out the wind and the light. Although there was a clear, round moon hanging from the Ninth Sky, radiating brightness, inside this wood I was unable to even see my own hands. I pulled the white silk from my eyes, folded it, and put it carefully away. From my sleeve I pulled out a night pearl the size of a dove egg and wandered around looking for a tree with cradle-like branches that I could climb up and sleep the night in.

It was a wild wood, and despite the glow of my night pearl to guide me, I had trouble navigating in the dark. I stumbled along for ten feet or so before losing my footing and tumbling into a huge underground cavern.

Strange as it seems, I found that I could see much better inside the cave. A moon and some stars shone down brightly from the magic sky inside the cave, while below I could see a flowing stream and a pond and within it a straw pavilion, slightly larger than Father and Mother's foxhole.

Inside the straw pavilion, I could see an intertwined couple.

I had been prepared for the possibility of stumbling upon almost anything, but I had not considered that I might bump into a couple in the throes of intimacy, and the encounter shocked and embarrassed me.

The boy had his back to me and was half obscuring the girl's face with his shoulder. What I could see of her face was delicate and pretty. I had landed gently, but she obviously noticed, as her almond-shaped eyes were full of surprise.

I gave her a pleasant smile to try and calm her, but she just continued to stare. The two of them were still wrapped in each other's arms, but the man must have sensed something was wrong, as he leaned over, craning his neck to look my way. Even with half a pond between us, seeing his face felt like having sizzling lard poured over me on a hot day. I was overcome with feelings of awkwardness and anxiety. Past happenings, memories I had worked so hard to blot out started flooding back into my mind, one after another.

The man seemed preoccupied. He fixed me with a long stare before saying, "Si Yin."

I lowered my eyes. "So it's Li Jing the Demon Emperor," I said solemnly. "It's been a long time since I cut ties with you, Demon Emperor, and Si Yin is no longer my name. I would be grateful if you were to address me as Goddess."

He said nothing, and the girl in his arms gave a little tremor, which allowed me a clearer look at her. It frustrated me what good terms this generation of little immortals seemed to be on with the Demon Clan. I was feeling apprehensive, and tried not to let the frostiness I was feeling show in my face.

"Si Yin," he sighed. "You've hidden from me for seventy thousand years. Do you plan to keep on hiding?" He sounded incredibly sincere, as if he really did feel regret and sadness about not having seen me all this time.

The way he was speaking intrigued me. Our relationship had broken down completely and was replaced by a life-and-death struggle that left me wishing that the two of us had never met. I could not understand why he was now talking to me with such affection.

His comment about how I had been hiding from him seemed hugely unfair. I had been alive for so long, and it was easy to forget details and events. I rubbed my temples, trying to recall exactly what had happened. I still felt that our lack of contact over the last seventy thousand years had not been due to any deliberate evasion on my part, merely fate keeping us apart.

Seventy thousand years ago, the previous Demon Emperor, Qing Cang, was out on a hunting trip. He took a shine to one of my fellow apprentices, Ninth Apprentice Ling Yu, tied him up, and carried him off to the Purple Light Palace, where he planned to make him his male empress. I was out with Ling Yu at the time and was unfortunate enough to be abducted along with him.

I entered into an apprenticeship with Mo Yuan when I was fifty thousand years old. Mo Yuan did not take on female students, but Mother cast a spell to make me look like a boy and gave me the name Si Yin.

Although Ling Yu and I were abducted together, Qing Cang had no romantic interest in me, and I was given many freedoms, as well as three meals a day. I was allowed to roam the grounds, and as long as it did not involve leaving the confines of the palace, I could do as I wished.

Later my thoughts often returned to what might have been if on my third day at the Purple Light Palace I had not eaten that extra bowl of braised pork. If I had left it, today the Four Seas and Eight Deserts might be a very different place.

I had already finished my lunch that day when the chef came along and presented me with this bowl of fate-changing braised pork, which, he explained, came from a mountain boar Qing Cang had hunted down that morning. The chef had cut off a thigh and steamed a couple of bowls of it, giving one to Ling Yu and, since I was there, one to me too. It looked delicious, all glistening with oil, and I did the polite thing and gobbled it up.

Eating this bowl of braised pork on top of my lunch had made me feel very full. I decided to make my routine post-lunch walk slightly longer than usual. It was those extra steps that led me to encounter Prince Li Jing, thus changing the course of my life.

Just like the saying one anthill can bring down a whole dike, the idea that this bowl of braised pork made my life infinitely more difficult is not as absurd as it sounds. I often looked back and thought about how different things might have been and mourned all that was lost.

I could still remember that day perfectly. The sky was bright, and the sun was shining in the distance, and through the barrier of gray-white fog around the Purple Light Palace, it looked like a salted duck yolk suspended in the sky.

The palace attendant walking alongside me started telling me about an incredibly rare winter lotus that had just flowered in the palace. Since I was still feeling full, she suggested I stroll over and take a look, and pointed me in the right direction.

I ventured along the path, shaking my silk fan. My poor sense of direction meant that I wandered around in circles for a long time without coming across this rare lotus. The palace garden was made up of man-made ponds and rockeries, but its luxuriant trees and flowers sustained various birdlife, and I could hear the occasional chirruping of a swallow and call of an oriole, which made me stop and listen in enchantment.

I was happily absorbed in listening to the sound of birdsong and was shocked when a young man leaped out at me, his gown half open at the front and his hair in disarray. He looked bleary-eyed, as if he had not woken up properly, and he had petals stuck to his shoulders. An almost feminine beauty shone through, despite his disheveled appearance.

I gave a vague nod, assuming he must be one of the Demon Emperor's husbands. He looked at me blankly, not returning the courtesy. With a shake of my fan, I continued on my way. But as I brushed past him, he grabbed my sleeve, an intense look of confusion on his face. "Your gown is a very strange color. Stunning though. Where did you have it made?"

I was taken aback and looked at him anxiously, feeling tongue-tied. I was wearing my silvery-purple gown, which I had been wearing for days on end now.

The young man walked around me in a circle, looking me up and down. "I really have never seen such a color," he said earnestly. "I've been worrying about what to give my father for his birthday. I haven't found anything suitable. But this is most unusual. Be a kind chap and exchange this garment with me for something." As soon as he said this, he grabbed hold of me and whipped the gown off me, his snow-white face flushing red and his face turning sheepish.

I may have had a male body, but I was still an innocent little immortal girl at heart, and I had to put up a fight, even though I knew it was unlikely to do any good.

We were both standing by the lotus pond, and a gentle breeze blew over carrying the beautiful lotus scent. Our struggle did not involve magic, just pure, bare-fisted, shirtless rough and tumble. I turned my head in the middle of this scramble and somehow managed to topple us both into the pond. Members of the Demon Clan are known for their sharp ears, and the splash brought a number of people rushing over to see what had happened. Being caught like this would have been very embarrassing for him, so he gestured for me to stay there and keep quiet. I nodded and squatted back-to-back with him at the bottom of the pond.

We waited anxiously like that until the sky went dark, when we assumed it was safe to get out unseen, and we climbed back up shivering onto the bank.

All that time crouching down there together, we had managed to make amends, exchange names, and even start referring to each other as *brother*. This beautiful youngster was indeed connected to the homosexual Demon Emperor, not his husband, however, but his second son. This was Li Jing.

I remember being very surprised to learn that the homosexual Demon Emperor had a son.

Following this incident, Li Jing regularly invited me to drink tea with him, watch cockfights, and share wine. However, having just heard that Ling Yu was going to be forced to marry Qing Cang on the third of Lunar February, I was in no mood for such jollities. Ling Yu had decided he would sooner die than let this marriage happen, and he had already tried to kill himself by bashing his head against a pillar and was now on a hunger strike. I was the only one who could help him, but I was not in any way strong enough to rescue Ling Yu and get us both out of the Purple Light Palace. I had faith that Mo Yuan would come to our rescue, and was keeping my spirits up. I had been counting on Qing Cang's devotion to Ling Yu to keep my fellow apprentice safe and well cared for. I had not been expecting Ling Yu to get himself worked up into such a state.

I spent my days and nights in constant worry.

Li Jing began to lose patience with me. One day he had a tantrum, smashing his wine cup down on the floor. "But that's so easily resolved!" he said when I explained. "Why would you spend your days with that morbid look on your face, worrying when you could have just asked me for help? You clearly don't think much of our friendship, or take me as a proper brother. I promise that I will help you to sneak Ling Yu out of the palace before the second day of Lunar February. Write down anything you have to say, and I will deliver it to him this evening and give him a little peace of mind. I heard he threw himself into the lake yesterday—I had no idea immortals these days were feeble enough to drown in lakes. My father is the only one taking his suicide attempts seriously."

I was speechless. Because he was Qing Cang's son, I had not wanted to involve him for fear of getting him in trouble. But he was insistent, so I quietly went along with it.

I quite clearly owed Li Jing a favor after this, so I joined him in drinking and making merry, which was all I had to offer. The thing that scared me most about drinking was being forced to play sophisticated word games. I was young and had spent too much of my time fooling around. I was always out and about with my gang of silly apprentices, watching cockfights and dog races and swaggering through the streets. Poetry and verse were therefore beyond me, and when playing games that involved a mastery of them, I was always the one who forfeited. For lowbrow drinking games, it was a different story. Whether it was drawing lots, rolling dice, guessing fingers, or number games, I excelled effortlessly. But I wanted to let Li Jing win in order to keep him happy, so I suggested we play these sophisticated word games. Losing them was easy for me, just a matter of talking nonsense and then lowering my head to drink. Trying to lose at the lowbrow games would have been much harder, and the effort involved would have left me scratching my cheeks and pinching my ears.

Li Jing was delighted and started to formulate a plan. He decided on the night of the second to help me to steal Ling Yu out of the palace.

One night I dreamed that Ling Yu did end up having to marry the Demon Emperor, making him empress, while I was forced to marry Li Jing's sister, Princess Rouge. Li Jing gently took my arm in the dream and pointed at Ling Yu, saying, "Si Yin, you may greet your empress mother." Ling Yu grabbed my hand and placed it on his stomach, a golden light shining above his head. "In a few months, Empress Mother will have a baby. It will be your little brother, Si Yin. Aren't you pleased?" My face stiffened, and I gave an awkward laugh. "Very pleased," I said.

I woke up to find my clothes drenched through with sweat. I was just about to get out of bed for a sip of cold water to calm my nerves when, pulling back the bed curtain, I saw Li Jing standing silently by my bed, dressed in a white robe, watching me through glimmering eyes.

I was shocked to see his face. It was around midnight, and although the moon outside the window was not very bright, it provided enough light to illuminate my small room. I lay on the ground, telling myself, *It's not that strange. It's not that strange.* Perhaps he had been unable to sleep and had come to see me out of boredom. He crouched down and muttered incoherently to himself for a while before saying, "Si Yin, I have a secret to share with you. Do you want to hear it?"

If I did not allow him to unburden himself, I would not be honoring our brotherhood. So I gave an unenthusiastic nod and reluctantly said, "Yes, do."

"I like you, Si Yin, and I want to sleep with you," he said shyly.

I had just climbed up from the floor, but hearing this shocked me so much I fell straight back down.

Li Jing had always seemed disapproving of his father's sexual orientation and, as far as I was aware, had always been one for the ladies. The women he kept in his bedchamber were beauties with big breasts, tiny waists, and long legs. I had a boy's body, and although my face was the same as it always had been, my chest was completely flat.

He assumed that my hearing his confession was the same as giving my consent, and so he came over and tried to rip off my clothes. I desperately guarded my lapel, "You've agreed, Si Yin. Why are you acting all coy?" he said angrily.

I was still too shocked to speak, how could I have agreed? The first time he saw me, he tried to pull my gown off, and less than ten days later, he was at it again.

Deciding enough was enough, I hit him, and he fell over. I was surprised by my own strength. I had hit him on a vulnerable spot at the back of his neck, and as luck would have it, he fainted. He crashed heavily down onto my stomach, and I could smell alcohol wafting off him.

I wondered if all this had just been that, a craze born of drunkenness. Thinking it must be cold on the floor, I picked up the quilt and wrapped it loosely around him, rolling him up and pushing him to the end of the bed, before climbing back onto my mattress and drifting off back to sleep.

Early the next morning I opened my eyes and saw him pitifully bundled up by the side of my bed. "How did I end up sleeping here?" he asked, frowning and rubbing his neck.

My mind raced as I tried to figure out the best way to respond. "You were drunk last night," I began slowly. "You came to my room in the middle of the night, telling me you liked me and that you wanted to sleep with me."

He had been scratching his head, and hearing this, he stopped his hand in midair and stiffened while his face turned first green, then white. "I . . . I, I, I can't . . . ," he stammered. "I can't be homosexual. If, if, if I am, how . . . how can I explain to my sister that you are going to be my wife?"

"You aren't homosexual," I told him, drawing my clothes around me, an action I had not expected to provoke such upset.

He pointed a shaky finger at me. "Look at you . . . you're scared that I'll take advantage, aren't you!"

I was stunned. "Well, you did try to rip my clothes off me last night," I told him acerbically.

I did not see Li Jing for several days following this. Before he had been badgering me on an almost daily basis, but after that incident, not a glimpse.

Although he was brash, Li Jing did bring nice wine, and it was entertaining to watch cockfights and cricket fights. After not seeing him for a couple of days, I started to miss him.

During this time Princess Rouge invited me for a wander around the gardens, and mentioned her brother in passing. I learned that Li Jing had been spending his nights cavorting with beauties, having a debauched and merry old time.

Princess Rouge was sweet natured and attentive. "Have you and my brother fallen out?" she asked with concern. "You used to be as thick as thieves. I never saw you two apart."

I rubbed the back of my head and thought back over my friendship with Li Jing, realizing that aside from the drunken move he made on me that night, the two of us had always gotten along very well. But it made me think of the saying wives are like hands and feet while brothers are like clothing. While he was cavorting with these hands and feet, I was the unnecessary piece of clothing that could be cast off. Having a beautiful woman in your arms was romantic. Having a friend lurking like a tiger by your bedside and staring at the beautiful woman in your arms was not. Even though I was not a man, and had no interest in his wives, Li Jing was not to know that, and it was natural he would keep me at arm's length. Being a man was not easy, and being a man with many wives even less so; I felt for him.

Rouge was looking at me anxiously, waiting for my response. It did not seem a very appropriate explanation to give a girl, and after a few awkward moments, I came up with some random excuse that I reeled off.

Soon it would be February.

The Purple Light Palace had been decorated for the nuptials, and the food had improved tremendously.

Receiving my note had obviously reassured Ling Yu, and he had just about managed to remain calm. However, the plan to get him out of the palace was top secret, and I had not mentioned it in my note. As the wedding drew near, he naturally started to panic. In a single morning he attempted to bite off his tongue, poison himself, and hang himself.

I paced back and forth in my room, wondering whether to go and see Li Jing and discuss it with him, see if we could carry out our plan a day earlier. But when I reached Li Jing's bedchamber, two palace attendants stopped me and told me that the prince was not in. He had gone out hunting with a couple of his wives apparently. I left a message for when he returned, saying that Si Yin had an interesting new game and could not wait to play it with him.

I sat in my room, listlessly cracking sunflower seeds between my teeth. It was not Li Jing who came to my room in the end, but Master Mo Yuan.

Mo Yuan had a figure wrapped up in a quilt tucked under his arm, obviously Ninth Apprentice Ling Yu, who had fortunately not been successful in his suicide attempts.

Mo Yuan released Ling Yu and came over to embrace me, wrapping his arms tightly around my waist. We stayed like that for a long time before he eventually released me. "You haven't done too badly for yourself, Little Seventeenth. Ling Yu has lost a lot of weight, but you actually seem to have put some on. All things considered, it would appear that we haven't suffered too much here."

I gave a sheepish grin and held out a handful of sunflower seeds, saying, "Master, have some seeds."

Our escape that night was anything but smooth.

Taking into account the friendship between the gods and the demons, Mo Yuan had hoped not to resort to fighting. His plan had been to creep into the Purple Light Palace and steal Ling Yu and me back out without attracting any attention. This way he would allow the Demon Emperor a chance to maintain some dignity. But the Demon Prince was too foolish to appreciate this, and he moved his soldiers to the front of the palace gate to block our exit. Mo Yuan had no choice but to fight, and the whole thing escalated into a bloodbath.

Ling Yu was unconscious the whole time and did not witness the bloodshed. But I saw it all—the blood and the cracked skulls and ripped flesh. It was horrifying.

Mo Yuan had never lost a battle in his life, and this was no exception. He leaped over the palace gate with Ling Yu and me in his arms. I turned around, and all I could see was Qing Cang with his eight-pronged halberd, standing in the dark red sea of blood, his eyes so full of fury they looked as if they might explode from their sockets.

I did not see Li Jing this whole time.

Mo Yuan carried Ling Yu and me away from the Purple Light Palace. We fled through the night, finally arriving back at Mount Kunlun. Ling Yu was still unconscious, and Mo Yuan and I said nothing to each other the whole way.

I will remember that night for all eternity, although I never wish to recall it.

After racing us back to Mount Kunlun, Mo Yuan handed Ling Yu over to Fourth Apprentice and rushed with me to his alchemy room. He knocked me out with an arm and locked me inside his alchemy furnace.

I started to come to, wondering if Mo Yuan was punishing me, issuing me with a warning for my failure to look after Ling Yu properly. I wondered if he blamed me for his poor apprentice's emotional trauma and his physical demise.

But hearing a loud boom of thunder, I realized that my predestined calamity had arrived. Mo Yuan must have placed me in the furnace so that I could hide and escape it. I had been born an immortal, but rising up through the ranks required hard work and the development of skills. Elevating yourself from a normal immortal to a higher immortal, and then from a higher immortal to a god or goddess took between seventy thousand and one hundred forty thousand years, and it required you to experience two calamities. If you were successful, you would live as long as the sky is wide, but if you were unsuccessful, your life would come to an abrupt end.

I had been Mo Yuan's apprentice for twenty thousand years at that point and was expecting my predestined calamity to befall me at any time or place and in any shape or form. If I had been practicing magic, passing through these calamities would not have posed a problem. But I always hated the magic of deduction and found the scriptures deadly boring. Each time Mo Yuan taught this class, I would use it as an excuse for a nap. Despite all my years of study, all I had learned to do was to tell a mortal their rough fortune, and even this I would get wrong half the time.

I knew for certain that I had not cultivated enough spiritual energy. Facing a sky calamity without these things was like trying to cut a duck's egg from a chicken's stomach: absolutely impossible.

Fortunately I had spent the last seventy thousand years feeling free and unfettered, and if my soul were to fly and my spirit to flutter, I would feel no great regrets. I had expected my sky calamity to take place at some point in the next year, but I had not taken the reality of it very seriously.

I spent some time locked inside the alchemy furnace before it suddenly dawned on me: If I were hiding in here, who would my calamity find to replace me? Sky calamities were completely different from mortal calamities in that once they descended, someone had to undertake them, even if it was not the person for whom it had been intended.

The booming sound of the thunder helped to clear my head, and I tried every way I could to get out of the furnace, all to no avail. For the first time in my life, I was forced to acknowledge that these last twenty thousand years of study had been a complete waste of time.

The next day Master came and opened the lid to the furnace. "Little Seventeenth, I stood by the furnace last night and was struck by your three bolts of sky thunder. You must study better from now on and work on your skills. If you wish to become a god, you can't expect Master to keep experiencing your calamities for you. That's not how it works."

Mo Yuan had suffered my sky calamity for me, and before I climbed out of the furnace, he had gone into confined recuperation. I knelt down in front of his cave for three days, sniveling and weeping, full of sadness and regret. "Master, are you hurt very badly? Are your injuries getting any better?" I asked. "Your lowlife apprentice has worn you out. Don't fall ill, please. If you do, I'll stew my body into medicinal soup and feed it to you to nourish you."

Never in my life had I cried with such abandon and distress.

CHAPTER SIX

I worked really hard after that, spending all my days in my room, studying and thinking deeply about immortal magic and Taoist practice and reading the immortal classics left by the older generation of immortals in my spare time. My fellow apprentices were comforted by the transformation in my attitude.

Every time I learned a new skill, I stood outside Mo Yuan's cave and practiced it. Even though he did not know I was doing this, it brought me peace of mind.

I was sitting in meditation in the peach grove on the back peak of the mountain one day when First Apprentice sent a messenger crane telling me to hurry to the front hall, where a guest was waiting for me.

I snapped off a branch of peach blossoms, as the one in Mo Yuan's room had started to wilt.

He was still in confinement and had not been back to his room, but I wanted to keep it tidy and pleasant so that he had a comfortable place waiting for him when he came out of his confinement.

I walked to the front hall, twisting the branch of peach blossoms in my hand.

I went past the central courtyard, where Thirteenth and Fourteenth Apprentices were sitting under the date tree, taking bets about whether the guest in the front hall was male or female. I assumed that it must be Fourth Brother come to visit me, so I took out my night pearl and hesitantly laid my bet. The person sitting in the front hall looked nothing like First Apprentice had described. It was that member of the Demon Clan: Second Prince Li Jing.

He was sitting in a graceful upright posture in the pear-wood imperial tutor's chair, his eyes half closed as he sipped his tea. He gave a start when he saw me come in.

Mo Yuan had carried out a massacre in the Purple Light Palace, and I assumed that Li Jing was here to take revenge.

Instead he rushed over and grasped my hands with affection. "Si Yin, I've thought it all through. I want to spend my life with you."

My peach blossom branch clattered to the floor. "Give me money, give me money, it *is* a girl!" Thirteenth Apprentice yelled loudly from outside the door.

I was extremely confused. I thought about it a moment before opening the front of my gown and giving him a flash of my chest. "But I'm a boy," I said. "You have such a good relationship with all the wives in your bedchamber. You aren't this way inclined."

I was not really a boy. The fist-sized fox heart under my skin and flesh was not as broad as boy's; it was a girl's: slender, gentle, and delicate. But Mother had tricked Mo Yuan into taking me on, which meant that I was stuck in my male form until I had finished my studies.

Li Jing stared at my flat chest in surprise. "I've been thinking a lot since I left your room that morning. I was scared by my desire for you, and I spent my days surrounded by beautiful women, trying in vain . . . trying in vain to numb myself. It worked at first, but I didn't expect to miss you so much, to think about you day and night. Si Yin . . ." Overcome by emotion he walked over to embrace me. ". . . I will be homosexual if it's for you."

I looked up at the peach blossom wood rafters, not knowing what to do.

Fourteenth Apprentice's laughter drifted over from the distance. "Give you money? Who exactly is meant to be giving who money?"

Li Jing had walked for miles and miles to the remote Mount Kunlun to confess his feelings to me, but in a boy's form, I did not feel that I could return his love. I tried to let him down gently.

It was getting dark and already too late for him to take the mountain path, so I allowed him to spend a night on the mountain. When First Apprentice heard that there was a homosexual Demon Clan member who had come up the mountain to kidnap me, he beat him up and drove him away.

I admired Li Jing's courage. He refused to be cowered by the severe beating First Apprentice had served him. Every few days he would send over his stead, a fire qilin, with a poem describing his heartbreak. At the beginning they read, "We are a pair of lovebirds in the sky, intertwining roots beneath the ground." A few days later, he was writing, "I yearn to see you, which day will it be, this anguish is slowly killing me." A few days after that it was: "My belt is loose around my waist, but no regrets have I, for him I will gladly wither away, become sallow and finally die."

The paper he wrote these on was useful for making fires, and Thirteenth Apprentice, who was in charge of stoking the stove, collected them all up for this purpose. I desperately tried to save them, but Thirteenth Apprentice protested. "You spend all day on the mountain doing nothing but waiting for others to feed you. Waste paper like this is rare. How can you be so selfish?" I felt unable to argue with that.

I was still young, and despite spending all my days with men, I still possessed some girlish sentiment. Li Jing persisted in writing to me despite my lack of response to his poems, and every day his fire qilin would arrive with a new poem.

Slowly but surely he was starting to win me over.

One day the fire qilin brought over a short poem that read, "Life is long, but it has an end, but this sorrow of mine will even death transcend." I was filled with terror, thinking it must be a suicide note. In panic I jumped astride the fire qilin, planning to make myself invisible so that I could enter the Purple Light Palace and convince him not to do it. But the fire qilin carried me to a cave dwelling at the foot of our mountain instead.

It was a natural cave, which had been kept very neatly. Li Jing was sprawled out on a marble couch, and I could not see if he was dead or alive. I felt as if half the sky had just caved in. I jumped down off the fire qilin and went to shake him. I shook and shook and shook and shook, but I couldn't wake him. Feeling completely helpless, I resorted to my weapon. I sent thunder and lightning storms at him along with vicious winds, one after another, but still he did not wake. The fire qilin could no longer bear to watch. "All your weapon is doing is hurting his flesh. Perhaps you should try to rouse the prince's fragile heart instead? Say something that will give him hope."

And that is when I said it. That sentence.

"Wake up and I will accept your love."

Sure enough he opened his eyes, and although he had been brutally ravaged by my silk fan, he beamed. "Si Yin, if you tell me you accept my love, you can't go back on your word. Help me up. You've given me such a battering with your fan that all my bones have loosened."

Later Big Brother told me that romantic ploys were unlike other ploys, more like appeals. And romantic appeals were unlike other appeals, more like ploys. After suffering a period of heartbreak myself, I believe that to be true. However, I did not understand that truth back then.

Li Jing sent away all his bedchamber wives, and I stayed with him. It was Lunar April, and the peach blossoms along the mountainside had just burst into flower. Once Li Jing had been successful in his love crusade, the poetry stopped. There were no more visits from the fire qilin, which delighted First Apprentice, who assumed that Li Jing had finally lost patience and given up.

Li Jing still felt scared when he thought about the terrible beating First Apprentice had given him, and although he lived at the foot of the mountain, he never ventured up it. So it was I who would descend the mountain each day, after I had finished class and gone to Mo Yuan's cave to report what I had learned, where Li Jing and I would have our tryst.

I still remember all the exquisite little things he gave me: crickets woven from coco grass, a piccolo made from bamboo husk, all crafted by his own fair hands, very lovely.

Once he gave me a bunch of bright yellow flowers from a cucumber vine. Back in the Purple Light Palace, Princess Rouge had once told me that her brother had suffered from an eye disorder that made it hard for him to distinguish between yellow and purple. He saw both these colors as a strange shade ordinary people could not even imagine. He gave me these cucumber flowers, thinking he was presenting me with some special rare species. I did not have the heart to tell him what they really were, and besides, a flower was a flower—even if it did come from a cucumber. I dried these flowers and pressed them between the pages of my Taoist practice book for safekeeping.

After my heart had been broken, I could no longer think about that period in my life, about falling in love with Li Jing. Many years had passed since then, and so much had happened, and many of the details had blurred in my mind.

But I remembered the next big thing that happened: Xuan Nu turned up.

Xuan Nu was the youngest sister of Big Brother's wife. When Big Brother married my sister-in-law, she already had an infant in arms. An accident at her maiden home had meant that there was no one else to take care of Xuan Nu. Big Brother and his wife had looked after her for some time, and she and I would play together.

Xuan Nu was a beautiful girl, but for some reason she became infatuated by my looks. She was still just a child, but she would spend all day talking about how she wanted a face just like mine. Listening to her go on like this for a few hundred years was very annoying. She knew that Zhe Yan had excellent face-changing skills, and on her birthday one year, she made a special trip over to the Ten-Mile Peach Grove to ask him to transform her face to look like mine. Xuan Nu got her wish, which made her very happy. I got some peace and quiet, which made me happy too.

Not long after, I started noticing some imperfections. It was not Zhe Yan's magic that was flawed—I just found it disconcerting and dizzying to look at a version of my own face every day. Gradually I started drawing away from Xuan Nu and spending time with Fourth Brother instead.

Xuan Nu grew up and returned to her family home, and the two of us rarely saw each other.

While Li Jing and I were in our honeymoon period, my sister-in-law sent me a letter explaining how her mother was forcing Xuan Nu to marry a blind bear spirit. Xuan Nu had run away from home and was living in their cave dwelling, but my sister-in-law worried that their mother would soon track her down. She and Big Brother had discussed it and wondered if Xuan Nu could take refuge with me for a while.

As soon as I received this letter, I went to arrange a room for her to stay. I went to First Apprentice with a letter explaining that an immortal friend was planning to visit me at Mount Kunlun and asking if they would mind accommodating her for a short time. First Apprentice had been in high spirits lately, and after discovering that my visitor was a female immortal, his spirits soared even higher, and he agreed readily.

Three days later Xuan Nu made her low-key entrance into Mount Kunlun, soaring in on a gray cloud. She gave a start when she saw me. In her letter, my sister-in-law had explained that Xuan Nu did not know she was to be staying with her childhood playmate, Bai Qian, just that I was an immortal friend that they were on good terms with.

Xuan Nu settled down on Mount Kunlun. She looked even more like me these days. "I can't believe she's not your sister!" First Apprentice said. "When you are with her, it's only your listless spirit that allows me to tell you apart."

In truth, Xuan Nu was a little despondent herself, and her beautiful face was looking sallow. I saw her as family and naturally wanted to cheer her up, and so the next time I went down the mountain to visit Li Jing, I decided to take her with me.

Li Jing stood there staring at Xuan Nu in stunned silence the first time he saw her. It was a while before he regained his composure. "Where did this female Si Yin come from?" he blurted out, still staring in disbelief.

Xuan Nu started to giggle.

Seeing her finally starting to look happy, I felt as if a weight had been lifted, and from then on I took her with me to Li Jing's whenever I visited.

One day I was up in the date tree in the central courtyard, picking dates, planning to take them to Li Jing's cave and give to him as a treat once the sun set.

First Apprentice walked over looking bitter and stood beneath the tree. "When I beat up the Demon Clan homosexual who came to abduct you, you whined that I was being too violent, and so I was careful not to beat him to death," he said through gritted teeth. "Now I wish I had done so. I managed to stop him from abducting you, but now he's gone and abducted Xuan Nu . . ."

I lost my grip and fell out of the tree. I managed to lift my head and say, "First Apprentice, can you repeat what you just said?"

He came over to help me up. "I was at the foot of the mountain when I saw him and Xuan Nu walking together in the distance, holding hands. They were looking very friendly."

He helped me halfway up and then stopped. "Hang on." He scratched his chin. "Xuan Nu is a female immortal. How on earth have she and this homoscxual gotten entangled?"

I was off like a bolt of lightning, throwing aside his hand and flying out the door.

Li Jing's fire qilin was dozing outside his cave.

I cast a spell to turn myself into a moth and fluttered straight inside.

Sure enough, there on the marble couch, I could make out the outline of an intertwined couple. The girl underneath who had a face just like mine was panting softly, while the man on top had loosened his long black hair and was murmuring, "Xuan Nu, oh, Xuan Nu."

My chest felt as cold as ice. I could no longer sustain my moth form, and as a gust of wind blew through the corridor, I fell to the floor back in human form. Luckily I was able to stand steady: I had not lost all my Mount Kunlun poise. Li Jing and Xuan Nu both turned their heads at once, looking at me with flustered panic.

I remember walking over very calmly, slapping first Li Jing and then going to slap Xuan Nu, but Li Jing grabbed my hand before I could. Xuan Nu covered herself in the quilt and hid in his arms while Li Jing's face turned first green, then white. We stared at each other for the longest time. Finally, he released my hand. "Si Yin, I have let you down," he said in anguish. "I am not homosexual after all."

I felt too angry to do anything but laugh. "That's very convenient for you. Just decide if you want to be homosexual or not as it suits you. That's fantastic. What about me, though?"

He fell silent a while before saying, "It was ridiculous of me to think I could be a homosexual."

Xuan Nu's cheeks were streaked with tears. "Si Yin, please give Li Jing and me your blessing," she sobbed. "We are in love. You and he are both men and, and, well, it's . . . um . . . improper."

I regained enough composure to laugh bitterly. "So what is proper then—abandoning someone? Seducing someone else's lover? Destroying someone else's relationship? Are these all proper ways to behave?" She went pale and said nothing.

Physically and mentally exhausted, I waved my sleeve and let go of them.

My first taste of love had changed me completely. Realizing that I had been the fool who had actually introduced the two of them upset me even more. It was the pain of losing love, mixed with the pain of the injustice.

All the things associated with Li Jing, all those worthless little presents he had given me, now felt like objects of torture. I burned the lot of them, but it brought no relief. Drowning my sorrows was much more effective than burning things, so I spent three days down in the Mount Kunlun wine cellar, drunk out of my mind.

When I came to, I found myself in Master's arms.

Mo Yuan was sitting against a huge wine jar, a wine gourd in his right hand, while he supported me with his left. He frowned when he saw me awake. "You've drunk too much," he said gently. "It would have been much better to just cry it all out. Emotional pain festers inside the heart. And it's a shame to waste all this good wine."

Finally, with my arms wrapped around his leg, I started to cry. When I had finished crying, I looked up at him and said, "Master, you've finally come out of confinement. Does that mean that you're better? You don't have any lasting injuries or complications, do you?"

He looked at me and gave a faint smile. "It's fine. You won't need to stew up your body to make me any medicinal soup."

My fellow apprentices all thought I was in love with Xuan Nu and was feeling anxious and wretched because Li Jing had stolen her away.

This story I concocted was not a very good one, but Mo Yuan was the only one who saw through it. "Li Jing might have bright eyes, but he is seriously lacking vision," he murmured as he stroked my hair.

After coming out of confinement, Mo Yuan received an invitation from Xuan Ming the Winter God.

Xuan Ming lived deep in the Northern Desert, where he single-handedly administered twelve hundred miles of the Northern Sky. A Taoist assembly was to be held there at around this time, and he sent an envoy to Mount Kunlun, inviting Mo Yuan to the high altar to give a lecture.

As Father of the Universe's legitimate son, Mo Yuan was extremely revered, and when the gods from the Four Seas and Eight Deserts held Taoist assemblies, they were always certain to invite him.

Mo Yuan cast a glance at the invitation in his hand and said, "Lecturing about dharma is not very exciting, but we could go and climb the mountains around where Xuan Ming lives. Pack your bags, Little Seventeenth. You're coming with me!"

Surging with happiness, I hurried to my room to pack.

First Apprentice came to see us off. "Master usually doesn't accept boring invitations like this," he said. "He's obviously noticed how miserable you've been and is taking you away to cheer you up. I know you've had a hard time recently, Little Seventeenth, but Master has been very busy with his own matters, and spending all this time with you on top of it, he must be very tired. You're an adult now. You must start to act like one and put Master's mind at rest. You must learn to be a more filial apprentice."

I gave a sheepish nod.

We spent forty-nine days in the Northern Desert, most of them completely free and at ease.

When Mo Yuan was not lecturing, we headed out to explore the vast mountain range. When it was Mo Yuan's turn to take to the lotus stage, I joined the immortals in the audience, cracking sunflower seeds and snoozing.

Mo Yuan always felt that Taoist practice was a dull topic, but he still managed to talk about it for a long time. Many immortals had come to debate with him on matters such as reincarnation, nirvana, and the unpredictability of the human heart. I was overjoyed to see Mo Yuan coming out victorious every time.

I had managed to put the Li Jing affair almost completely in the back of my mind. It was only in the dead of night when all was quiet that I still had the odd nightmare or two.

Xuan Ming's Taoist assembly was a great success. When it was over, Mo Yuan took me to the Northern Desert for a few days before we packed up our stuff and headed back to Mount Kunlun.

Soon after returning we heard the news that the Demon Clan's second prince had gotten married. It had been a lavish wedding, and the Demon Clan celebrated for nine days straight. Mount Kunlun was now enemies with the Purple Light Palace, and naturally we had not been invited.

The only letter I got was from my sister-in-law writing to tell me how happy their mother was about the wedding and how lucky Xuan Nu was to have me looking after her. I was not a small-minded person. Li Jing may have turned his back on me, but it was probably only puppy love. A few years down the line, I might even have felt relieved about this outcome and could have even met with the two of them and drank to their happiness. If the following events had not taken place.

The night that Mo Yuan had come to rescue Ling Yu and me, he had left Qing Cang seriously injured. Three days after Li Jing's wedding, Qing Cang was finally recovered, as he gave orders for his troops to revolt. He said it was in revenge for his wife's abduction. This was not a very honorable excuse: Qing Cang was not married to Ling Yu when Mo Yuan plundered the palace, and it was unwarranted to call Ling Yu his wife. But despite this flimsy excuse, Qing Cang managed to convince hundreds of thousands of Demon Clan soldiers to revolt. To show his resolve against Mount Kunlun, Qing Cang chose a Demon Clan wife for Li Jing and gave the recently married Xuan Nu a severe whipping and sent her back to Mount Kunlun, dripping in blood.

First Apprentice was extremely softhearted. He wrapped Xuan Nu up in an embroidered blanket and carried her inside.

Mo Yuan suspected it was a ploy, but what could he do? None of the apprentices would have believed him. He just had to turn a blind eye and watch as First Apprentice performed his good deed.

The demon troops marched to within thirty miles of the border between the two clans' territories, and the Sky Emperor sent down eighteen immortal children to persuade Mo Yuan to fight against Qing Cang. Eventually Mo Yuan took out the suit of black crystal armor, which had been packed at the bottom of his case for all these years. He brushed off the dust and speaking calmly said, "Since Qing Cang is using me as an excuse to go to war, and I am the God of War, I have no choice but to go to battle. Take this suit of armor, Little Seventeenth, and inspect it thoroughly. It has been so long since I've used it, and it might have been chewed through by insects."

The old Sky Emperor was very pleased. He sent one hundred thousand sky commanders to fight alongside Mo Yuan and sprinkled three cups of wine over the Sky Gate to send him on his way. As Mo Yuan's seventeen apprentices, we stood in a line, ready to follow his command.

It was the first war I had ever experienced. Flames shot up into the sky, and smoke filled the air for eighty-one days straight. Mo Yuan was the undefeated God of War, and this battle should have been easily won. But as the Demon Clan army was being thwarted, Xuan Nu stole the sky soldiers' tactics diagram and sneaked it back across the border to give to Li Jing. If only we had known that Xuan Nu's abandoned wife performance had been part of their strategy, and her injuries just a ploy to gain our trust. Unfortunately, First Apprentice had looked after Xuan Nu, taken her in, and by so doing unleashed white-eyed terror upon Mount Kunlun.

It had taken a lot of Mo Yuan's energy to recuperate from my calamity, and his primordial spirit was still badly injured. Mo Yuan made use of the fact that the Demon Clan did not yet have a full understanding of battle strategy and led the sky commanders in an urgent offensive. Eventually, he surrounded the thirty thousand injured members of the Demon Clan at Ruo River.

During the final battle, two rows of soldiers lined up along the banks of Ruo River, and thousands of turbulent clouds filled the sky. Until that point I was certain that the outcome was set: the Demon Clan would either hand over a letter of surrender or they would be wiped out. I had no idea that Qing Cang might bring out the Eastern Desert Bell, a weapon with enough force to obliterate everything between the sky and earth, the most powerful weapon in the universe, and also the most destructive.

Qing Cang gave a laugh. "We will not surrender! Not as long as I am still the emperor of the Demon Clan. Either the Demon Clan will rise above the Sky Clan or I will die taking everyone in the Eight Deserts with me!"

Even though the Eastern Desert Bell was a weapon with the power to destroy the world, Mo Yuan was its creator and would naturally know how to defuse it.

I had no idea that Mo Yuan was struggling to even keep himself going. The Eastern Desert Bell may have been his creation, but he had no control over it now. The only way to overcome the wrath of the Eastern Desert Bell was to offer it the sacrifice of a strong and healthy primordial spirit before it had the chance to detonate fully.

I still remember Mo Yuan putting down his sword and leaping onto the Eastern Desert Bell, clinging to it with all his strength. Crimson light burst out from all over the bell, and as it passed through his body, it turned an even richer red. He suddenly turned his head, his lips twitching.

Later, Seventh Apprentice, a proficient lip-reader, told us that Master's final words had been, "Wait for me."

Mo Yuan was the master of the Eastern Desert Bell, and he understood its internal universe better than anyone. Before the bell managed to destroy all his cultivated spiritual energy, Mo Yuan concentrated his remaining strength and cast a spell, sacrificing himself in order to lock Qing Cang securely inside the Eastern Desert Bell.

As soon as the Demon Emperor was locked away, his eldest son, the army general, led his thirty thousand injured soldiers over to the one hundred thousand sky commanders, and quivering with fear, they handed over their letter of surrender.

Later, Fourth Apprentice told me I had been holding Mo Yuan's blood-covered body as this was going on, my eyes red, saying that I would die before accepting the Demon Clan's letter of surrender. I clutched tightly onto my fan and spoke fiercely about how if Master could not be saved, all those under the sky should be buried in the sand. My warmongering talk nearly brought me to blows with the Sky Emperor.

My fellow apprentices were worried about what I was capable of and decided the best thing for it was to knock me out and carry our bodies back to Mount Kunlun.

Fourth Apprentice told me I had been acting like a complete thug, but I could not remember a thing. All I recalled was waking up one night and finding myself on a bed with Mo Yuan, my hands wrapped tightly around his fingers, and discovering that he was not breathing.

The Demon Clan Revolt ended there and led to big changes in the Purple Light Palace. First Prince was imprisoned, and Second Prince Li Jing donned the blue robe and became Demon Emperor. The day he succeeded to the throne, he presented the old Sky Emperor with his palace garden's rare winter moon lotus as a tribute.

The old Sky Emperor sent eighteen upper immortals down to earth to help Mo Yuan's seventeen apprentices arrange his funeral. I have no idea where these astonishing magic powers of mine suddenly appeared from, but in my unkempt state, my hair all over the place, I flicked my fan at these eighteen upper immortals and sent the lot of them running out of Mount Kunlun.

"Master may have passed on, but he made us promise to wait for him," Seventh Apprentice said. "Do you think we should preserve his body in case one day he returns?"

It was like offering a clump of rice reeds to a drowning man.

There was something that not many people in the Four Seas and Eight Deserts knew apart from Qingqiu foxes, but the blood from a nine-tailed white fox had magic properties. If it were fed a bowl of heart blood from a nine-tailed white fox, given once a month, Mo Yuan's immortal body would remain well nourished.

Mo Yuan was a male god, and this blood would therefore need to be given by a she-fox so as to maintain the balance of yin and yang.

Luckily, I was a she-fox, and I had a reasonable supply of cultivated spiritual energy. I stuck a dagger into my heart right then and there and fed Mo Yuan's body with the blood. My heart bled for two days and nights, and I nearly died.

The magic worked. Mo Yuan's body accepted my blood, but to keep his body in good condition would require a continued supply of my blood: no other fox's would do.

I was knotted up with worry. It was around this time that I heard about a possession held by the Demon Clan called the Jade Soul. If placed in Mo Yuan's mouth, the Jade Soul would stop his body rotting. It was a sacred artifact and would be difficult to get hold of.

I decided to put aside my issues with Li Jing and go to see him. I hoped that he would remember those early days of friendship we both had shared and agree to lend me the Jade Soul. The Demon Clan was to blame for the critical state Mo Yuan was in, although the injury had happened in battle, making guilt hard to assign.

I humbled myself, fawning and flattering.

Li Jing sat in his throne inside the glorious Purple Light Palace and looked me up and down. He had become a lot more serious since being crowned Demon Emperor.

"Even though the Jade Soul is one of our Demon Clan's sacred artifacts," he began, slowly and deliberately, "because of our friendship, I would lend it to you in a heartbeat. Unfortunately, there has been a lot of disruption at the palace recently, and some days ago the Jade Soul went missing. I am very sorry to let you down."

I felt as if a thunderbolt had just flown in through the sky and split open my forehead. I felt as if my soul had left my body.

I was making my way out of the Purple Light Palace in a daze when I found myself face-to-face with Xuan Nu, dressed in her finery. "Si Yin, you have come so far," she said in an aloof voice. "Why not rest awhile before continuing on your way. It will look as if you haven't been treated very courteously at the Purple Light Palace otherwise."

Although I detested her, I felt too physically and mentally exhausted to deign to respond to her. I walked around her and continued on my way. She did not seem to realize she was being snubbed and put a hand in front of my face. "Didn't you come here to ask for the Jade Soul?" she asked softly. I saw that she was holding a rock of jade encircled by a flowing halo.

I lifted my head sharply and looked at her. "The emperor gave it to me yesterday as a reward," she said with a giggle. "He told me to rub it against my scars. Qing Cang gave me such an extreme whipping, and while my injuries are starting to get better, I've been left with some bad scarring. It's not very pleasant for girls to have scars on their bodies, is it?"

I looked up at the sky, gave three loud cackles, and cast a spell to freeze her. I took my fan out, and carrying her under my arm, I marched all the way to Li Jing's court. I pried the Jade Soul out of her palm and placed it in front of him.

He lifted his head to look at me, his beautiful face blanching. His mouth opened, but no words came out.

I flung Xuan Nu into his arms and took a step toward the door. With a bitter smile I said, "My biggest regret has been coming to the Purple Light Palace to visit you, Demon Prince. You two are a perfect match. One has the cruel heart of a wolf, the other the cowardly lung of a dog. From this day forth, Si Yin and the Purple Light Palace are bitter enemies."

My youth and pride stopped me from just grabbing the Jade Soul and taking it. Instead I left the Purple Light Palace empty-handed, kicking and punching everyone I passed on the way.

Returning to Mount Kunlun, and seeing Mo Yuan's increasingly dismal color, I did not really know what else to do. At dusk I stole into the alchemy room. I took whatever medicine I could lay my hands on and mixed it in with my fellow apprentices' food.

In the middle of the night, while they were all sleeping heavily, I hoisted Mo Yuan's body onto my back and carried him off Mount Kunlun and back to Qingqiu.

Fengyi Mountain was a small mountain to the north of Qingqiu. Halfway up the mountainside was a cavern in which a large amount of spiritual energy had gathered over the years. Father had named it Yanhua Cave. I placed Mo Yuan's body onto an ice chest inside Yanhua Cave. I was worried that the next time I took blood from my heart, I might be too weak to carry it over to him, so I simply lay down by his side.

Mo Yuan's body was wracked with injuries. I needed to feed him some blood every day until these were better, and a cup every month after that.

I really did not know how many nights I could sustain such intense feeding, but what got me through was the thought that if I died, he would not return either. Instead we would be buried together and would travel through to the Netherworld side by side. That was why I had brought him to Yanhua Cave. It was a place I had chosen as my own final resting place sometime before my sky calamity.

I spent seven days like this and was on the verge of death when I opened my eyes and saw Mother, her eyelids red and swollen.

She had come to transfer to me half of her own spiritual energy. That was what brought me back to life and returned me to my female form. Although I still needed to plunge a knife into my chest every night to get heart blood to feed Mo Yuan, being in Mother's care greatly eased my suffering.

I shook my head and saw that Li Jing had crossed the bamboo bridge and was walking toward me. I remembered that I had fallen into this underground cavern where I had happened upon Demon Emperor Li Jing having a secret tryst with this she-goblin.

He took my hand. "Si Yin, I've been looking for you for seventy thousand years," he said in anguish.

I glanced in bewilderment toward the she-goblin in the straw pavilion. I had heard of creditors chasing debtors, but never the other way around. Especially strange was the case of a debtor who came over specifically to remind the creditor what he owed. However you added it up, Li Jing was the one who owed me.

I shook off his grip and took a step back. He took a step forward, staring at me the whole time. "Do you still resent me? Back at the Purple Light Palace all those years ago, you told me that from that day forth, we would be bitter enemies. But you must know how much I . . ."

I gathered up my sleeves and forced a smile. "Demon Emperor, you needn't be concerned—those were words spoken in the heat of the moment. Nowadays the Demon and God Clans have a peaceful coexistence. All these years haven't been for nothing. I have learned to be reasonable. I will not create trouble where there is none, nor will I disturb the peace at the Purple Light Palace. But you and I should continue to keep our distance."

He looked shocked. "Si Yin, I abandoned you back then because you weren't a girl," he explained quickly. "So I . . . these last seven thousand years, I heard that you had . . . had . . . but I didn't believe them. I've thought about you for all these years, Si Yin . . ."

Hearing the name Si Yin floating around and around my head was starting to make me dizzy. "Who says I'm not a girl?" I asked angrily. "Open your eyes and have a proper look. Do men tend to look like this?"

He was about to come over and take my hand, but his hand stopped in midair. "So you are a girl?" he asked in astonishment. "So back then, back then you . . ."

I moved to the side, dodging him. "Master didn't accept female apprentices, so my mother changed my body into a boy's," I told him. "Since you've brought up the past, Demon Emperor, I have a couple of words to say to you. When you abandoned me and got together with Xuan Nu instead, four qilins welcomed her into the Purple Light Palace, and you celebrated for nine days straight, that was your official wed—"

He waved his hand to interrupt me. "Back then when you were so upset, why didn't you tell me you were a girl?"

I completely forgot what I had been about to say. I wondered how best to respond. "I must have been very upset back then, although I can hardly remember it now. And you adored Xuan Nu, loved her interests and her character, not just her face. It was over between us. What difference would it have made if I'd told you?"

He pursed his lips.

I had been unbelievably unlucky this evening, but now I saw that I had managed to fluster him with my words. I took my opportunity, bidding him a hurried but courteous farewell before turning and casting a spell, taking to the wind, and flying off. On my way up, I made myself invisible to avoid any further entanglements.

All I could hear behind me was his panic-stricken yells of "Si Yin!"

But there was no one left in the world named Si Yin.

CHAPTER SEVEN

I didn't go straight home. I decided to pop in on Third Brother on the way and deliver his peach blossom wine. Third Brother and Third Sister-in-Law were not home, however, and after accepting a little bite to eat from their immortal servant, I entrusted the jars of wine to him and summoned a lucky cloud to take me back to Qingqiu.

I passed Xiazhou on the way and decided to go and pay my respects to Tian Wu, who was buried in the cemetery there. Most of the ancient gods had outstanding faces, but Tian Wu had been the exception. However, what he lacked in quality, he made up for in quantity: he had a total of eight heads. We had been good friends while I was studying at Mount Kunlun under Mo Yuan. However, later, when the inexorable doom was meted upon the residence of the ancient gods, he perished in the fire and lightning. I hurried from Qingqiu to Xiazhou as soon as I heard about the inexorable doom, but by the time I arrived, it was too late. All that was left of him was a heap of bones.

• • •

It was noon by the time I arrived back at Qingqiu.

My feet had only just touched the ground when I saw a glossy little green-clad figure crawling out of the foxhole.

Mystic Gorge came over to me, a self-effacing look on his face. "You've taken your time, Your Highness," he said anxiously. I rubbed my eyes.

The little figure gave a squeal and leaped over to me, his eyes brimming with tears. "Mother, your words are meaningless," he blurted out in anguish. "Yesterday you said you would come back to the Sky Palace with us!"

Mystic Gorge had his eyes to the ground, but he glanced in my direction every so often, clearly holding back the questions. I looked at him and waved my sleeve, giving him permission to speak. He cupped his hands together in thanks and bowed down in front of me. "I deserve to die, Your Highness. I have failed you and your instructions to take proper care of Qingqiu. But what else could I have done with this little immortal? It would not have been appropriate to block the heir to the Sky Throne. And he told me he was dropping off Your Highness's child. Someone of his status, what choice did I have but to let him into Qingqiu? I am sorry that I did not manage to get a message to Your Highness to ask for instructions first, so please punish me as you see fit."

I was astonished. Prince Ye Hua had been here? Had he come simply to pay me back for the scene I had caused during his tryst with the princess?

I had retreated from that scene in great haste and had no idea how things had been left between the two of them. Princess Liao Qing was clearly deeply devoted to him, and in my befuddled state, I had allowed his son to convince me to stir up trouble between them. If Ye Hua had wanted to win her back, he would not have found it hard. To come here just to teach me a lesson seemed unnecessarily mean, and I found myself trembling at the prospect.

Little Sticky-Rice Dumpling hugged my arm and lifted his head. "Father Prince told me that you didn't want to come back with us, Mother," he said with a pout. "He said you were worried you wouldn't like living in the Sky Palace. Well, Mother, you don't need to worry about that anymore. Father Prince and Ali have decided to move over here and live with Mother instead. As long as I'm with you, Mother, Ali can live anywhere."

Hearing this made me feel dizzy. "You're telling me that you and Father Prince are planning to move in with me?" I said, my face turning pale.

Sticky-Rice Dumpling gave a rapid, childish nod. My knees went weak, but Mystic Gorge, as considerate and intuitive as ever, came over and took hold of my arm. "Stay calm, Your Highness," he whispered.

We were both aware of an antecedent to this.

While he was still heir to the throne, the current Sky Emperor had been something of a ladies' man. To curb this, his father, who had been Sky Emperor at the time, had arranged for him to marry his cousin. When he had protested, his father had issued a sky decree sending him to his aunt's for a month of confinement. While he was there, he and his cousin grew very close and married as soon as he returned to the Sky Palace. It was a story people loved to share.

Prince Ye Hua's wish to reside with me in Qingqiu was therefore completely justified, and no one could deny him his right to do so. Unfortunately, all this visit would do was cause me trouble, and I was starting to feel worried.

Mystic Gorge explained how Ye Hua had thrust Little Sticky-Rice Dumpling onto him and clearly felt comfortable leaving him here alone, as he himself had returned to the Sky Palace. As the man who would reign over all the immortals of the Four Seas and Eight Deserts one day, Ye Hua spent his time dealing with chores relating to this role. Although he was planning to come and have a short stay in Qingqiu, it seemed he would still need to travel regularly to the Sky Palace for work.

Little Sticky-Rice Dumpling looked up at the sky, and then at me. "Ali is feeling a bit hungry, Mother," he told me anxiously.

It had been a long time since the foxhole fire had been stoked. "Is there anything to eat at your place?" I asked Mystic Gorge.

"No . . . no there isn't," he responded bashfully.

"Have you not been eating with Phoenix Nine recently?" I asked. "Doesn't she come over every day to cook for you? Surely she hasn't gone back to the cave of her parents?"

"Half a year ago she told me she had to visit the mortal world to repay a debt of gratitude," he said, looking despondent. "She packed up her things and left and hasn't been back since. I'm starting to wonder if the person to whom she owed the favor might be holding her back. When she does finally come back, it might be with a little fox cub in tow."

"Ah," I said with a nod. I was worried that once Little Sticky-Rice Dumpling discovered there was nothing to eat, his eyes would start welling up with tears once more. I had only known him for a day or two, but I already had a good sense of his temperament. He would often stare with this pitiful, moist-eyed expression, but he never seemed to cry. Seeing those tears within the rims of his eyes made me feel like there was a cat clawing at my heart. My neglect made me feel utterly inhumane.

Finally Mystic Gorge could bear the pitiful expression on his little face no longer. He grasped hold of Little Sticky-Rice Dumpling's hand and said, "Would you like Big Brother here to take you to find something to eat? Does Your Little Majesty like loquat fruit?"

I felt my mouth start to twitch. Little Sticky-Rice Dumpling was no more than three hundred years old, while Mystic Gorge was about to turn one hundred thirty-seven thousand. By genially referring to himself as Big Brother, he was doing his usual trick of putting himself down.

I followed them to the market in the east of town. As soon as they saw me, the young immortals in the fruit stall stopped what they were doing. "Good day, Your Highness," they greeted reverently, all of them well versed in etiquette.

There were a number of old-looking folk among them, with white hair and wrinkled skin, but most were positively young compared with me. When Sticky-Rice Dumpling heard the way they were addressing me, he was extremely put out. He ran over to the pine tree spirit selling pine nuts and placed his hands on his round little hips to say, "My mother is young and vibrant and beautiful. Why do you call her by an address that makes her sound so grand and old-fashioned?"

The pine tree spirit's jaw dropped. He finally managed to say, "Your Highness? When did you have a child, Your Highness?"

"Yesterday," I said, glancing up at the sky.

It had been a good year for loquat, and there were mounds of them stacked in bamboo baskets, brightening up the marketplace. Sticky-Rice Dumpling was beside himself with joy to see so many of them.

Mystic Gorge spent a long time looking around, tasting the products of one vendor after another. Finally he decided on the contents of one dark-green bamboo basket. "Choose half a basket of these," he instructed us, pointing at the basket.

Phoenix Nine had taught Mystic Gorge how to choose fruit and vegetables, and therefore I trusted his judgment. I nodded and crouched down next to the bamboo basket he'd chosen and carefully started to pick out the loquat I wanted.

Sticky-Rice Dumpling ran over and tried to do the same, but he was too small, and crouching down, he was completely obscured by the basket. He hung around begrudgingly, whining. He stood on tiptoe and leaned over the top of the basket, picked one loquat and made a gesture of looking at it carefully before taking another and doing the same with that one.

I had been so focused on picking out fruit that I did not notice anyone approaching until a very slender hand with angular bones was thrust in front of me. I thought at first that it was Mystic Gorge and shifted to the side to make room for him. I was surprised when the hand started to jostle with me and grab for the fruit I had chosen. I realized there was no way it could be Mystic Gorge. I followed the jet-black cloak sleeve upward and found myself staring at Sticky-Rice Dumpling's father, who I had expected would still be busy with his duties in the Ninth Sky. He bent down and gave me a cheerful smile.

Ye Hua looked extremely dashing when he smiled.

I did not really want him to stay in Qingqiu, but he was here now: an uninvited guest. I was always extremely courteous to guests and naturally was not about to get into an argument. Instead I switched on my hostess charm.

I flashed him a bright and gracious smile. "Ah, so if it isn't Prince Ye Hua," I said. "We are just buying loquat. If you haven't eaten yet, please join us for lunch!"

The smile froze on his face. He regarded the loquats in my hand with disdain. "Ali's a growing boy," he said. "Is that all you're planning to feed him?"

I gave Sticky-Rice Dumpling's face a light pinch, asking, "Don't you want to eat this lovely fruit?"

Sticky-Rice Dumpling gave a bashful nod. "Yes, please," he said quietly.

Ye Hua stared at me in silence, his hand on his forehead, before grabbing my hand and saying, "Where do you find meat and vegetables around here?"

Before I had time to gather my thoughts, I was being dragged off. "Your Highness, do you still want this loquat?" Mystic Gorge shouted after us, Sticky-Rice Dumpling in his arms. Ye Hua was striding along at a fair pace. Gesturing for Mystic Gorge to catch us up.

"Of course!" I shouted back to him. "We've spent all this time choosing them. It would be unfair not to buy them now."

In no time at all, those from the north, south, east, and west marketplaces all knew that a handsome young man with a small child had arrived in Qingqiu and was staying at Emperor Bai Zhi's cave, and that the chubby little boy had been calling me *Mother* and the man *Father Prince.*

Qingqiu had been at peace for a long time, and even the disappearance of Fourth Brother's bird steed, Bi Fang, had been a subject of gossip among the local young immortals. Hearing this news about me caused them such excitement they did not know what to do with themselves. A gray wolf selling fish in the north of town gave me a whole basket for free. "It's just a couple of fi-fi-fish, but if you stew them up, Your Highness, it-it-it'll be very good for your heal-heal-health," he stuttered.

Ye Hua took the basket and gave a chuckle, "Yes, giving birth to a son takes its toll on a woman's body. She'll need plenty of replenishment."

The gray wolf scratched his head and gave a dim-witted laugh.

Hearing them echo back and forth with their crazy talk of postnatal replenishment was starting to addle my poor brain.

We returned to the foxhole, and Little Sticky-Rice Dumpling gorged himself on so many loquats he gave himself hiccups. Virtuous Mystic Gorge picked up the broom and swept all the fruit peels from the floor.

Helping himself to a cup of cold tea, Ye Hua looked at me and said, "Go and cook us something then."

I threw an impassive glance in Mystic Gorge's direction and sat down to pour myself a cup of cold tea. Little Sticky-Rice Dumpling patted his stomach and reached out a hand. "I want some too, Mother," he said petulantly. I walked over and helped him to a few sips of the cold tea.

Mystic Gorge stood with the broom in his hand, looking distressed. "Your Highness, you are well aware . . ."

"There's a first time for everything," I comforted. "You've experienced the doom of thunder. How can you be scared of this? I'll watch your back."

Reluctantly he traipsed to the stove room.

Ye Hua regarded me with his chin in his hand. "I really do not understand you," he said with a quiet laugh. "Qingqiu is clearly within the immortal realm, yet you govern yourselves as if you're all mortals. The men plow and the girls embroider without a hint of magic or Taoist practice."

He did not have the slightest idea of how a guest should behave, so I decided I was not required to uphold my hostess demeanor either. "If you need magic to solve everything, what's the point of being an immortal?" I asked with a listless laugh. "If we were to live like that, our people would have no challenges and would become very easily bored. I would have to start arranging battles just to give them something to do, a little fighting to keep them entertained."

The teacup clattered against the table. "Interesting," he said with a faint smile. "If you do get to that point and need my assistance, let me know. I could send over a couple of sky commanders to assist."

I was about to cheerfully accept when we heard a blast from the stove room. Mystic Gorge stood in the doorway to the cave with his hair in disarray, wielding a ladle and glaring at me. I stared at him dumbly before leaning over to Ye Hua saying, "Sticky-Rice Dumpling has eaten so much he has the hiccups, and three adult immortals skipping a meal is hardly a matter life or death. Shall we just forgo tonight's meal?" I turned to Mystic Gorge. "Quickly, journey to the mortal world and retrieve Phoenix Nine," I said sternly.

Mystic Gorge cupped his hands together and gave me a deferent bow. "What reason should I give her?" he asked, still holding the ladle.

I racked my brains. "Just say there is something unusual going on in Qingqiu," I said after some thought, but before I had managed to finish my sentence, Ye Hua was dragging me into the stove room. "Put some more wood in the stove and get a fire going. You can do that, surely?" Little Sticky-Rice Dumpling was sprawled out on the bamboo chair, watching us and rubbing his tummy. He turned to face the other way, his breathing gradually becoming deeper and more regular.

It was two days since Ye Hua and I had first met, and already he had his sleeves rolled up and was cooking at my stove as if he belonged there. Every so often he would give me an instruction such as, "There's too much wood on the stove. You don't need any more for the moment," or "The fire's dying out. Can you add some more wood now?"

I suddenly remembered Little Sticky-Rice Dumpling telling me about his mother being a mortal from Junji Mountain. It must have been this poor first wife, the woman who had thrown herself off the immortal punishment platform, who had taught Ye Hua to whisk his spatula around the wok with such panache.

He had a soup ladle in one hand and the spatula in the other now, brandishing them with artistic perfection. I was so impressed that I could not hold myself back. "Did your first wife teach you all this? She must have been an excellent cook!" I sighed with heartfelt admiration.

He looked taken aback.

I realized that by mentioning his dead wife, I had reopened old wounds.

The flames sizzled as they licked the bottom of the wok.

I swallowed and moved silently to the stove to add a handful of firewood. Ye Hua gave me a strange look as he ladled out the food. "She was just like you," he said calmly. "Stoked the fire and added the wood while I did all the cooking."

I was embarrassed and not sure how to respond. He turned around and continued to ladle out the soup. "I have no idea how she managed to survive on that godforsaken Junji Mountain before we met," he said with a light sigh.

He had actually mumbled those sentences to himself, but my powerful fox ears picked up every word perfectly. His sigh was quiet but considered. I had caused him unnecessary sadness.

Ye Hua made three dishes and a pot of soup.

Mystic Gorge had tidied up by then, and I called him over to eat with us.

Ye Hua shook Sticky-Rice Dumpling awake and started plying him with food. Sticky-Rice Dumpling patted his little cheeks. "If Father Prince continues to feed Ali at this rate, Ali will turn into a big rubber ball," the child said grumpily.

Ye Hua took leisurely sips from his cup of cold tea. "Feeding you up into the shape of a rubber ball is a fantastic idea! I won't need to carry you on a lucky cloud into your Qingyun Palace once we're back in the Sky Palace then. I could just roll you there instead."

Sticky-Rice Dumpling lay down in my lap and pretended to cry. "Boo-hoo-hoo," he said. "Father Prince is so mean."

Ye Hua put down his teacup and picked up a bowl. He ladled some fish soup from the pot and gave his son a faint smile.

"So you've found someone to take your side, have you?" he said. "Come, Qian Qian, you need to replenish yourself," he said tenderly, pushing a full bowl of fish soup toward me.

Mystic Gorge started to cough and nearly choked on his rice.

I felt my eyes turning red as I lifted Sticky-Rice Dumpling up from my knees. I smiled as I picked up the soup bowl in front of me. "Be a good little boy and have another bowl of soup," I said.

Ye Hua had fantastic culinary skills. The fish soup was not to my liking, but all the other dishes I ate with great relish.

Lunch was a casual affair, and it caused us all to relax no end—so much so that when Ye Hua asked me if there was a room in the foxhole he could use as a study to work on his documents, I agreed willingly and cleared out Third Brother's old lakeside room for this purpose.

My initial thought was that Ye Hua had come here to punish me. But a fortnight passed and he had yet to even mention the Eastern Sea Water Crystal Palace incident.

Early each morning, a little immortal called Jia Yun knocked on the door. He collected the official documents Ye Hua had worked on the day before, while handing him a batch of new ones.

Jia Yun was Ye Hua's desk official and an extremely dutiful fellow. At first I would shuffle over to open the door for Jia Yun every day, my feet only half in my shoes. After a couple of days, I could see this situation making Jia Yun feel awkward, so I stopped shutting the foxhole door and placed a magic barrier on it instead, which I taught Jia Yun to circumvent.

Ye Hua spent most of his time shut up in his new study, working on his documents. He would wake me up each morning and drag me out the house for a walk, and after dinner he would drag me out for another at dusk. Every so often he invited me into his study for an evening game or two of chess. I was so exhausted that I spent my days yawning, and a couple of times, I fell asleep at the table halfway through our chess game. He never woke me when this happened, he just laid his head down on the chess table with me, and we would both sleep there like that.

When Jia Yun came to collect the documents and saw us like that, he started to get absurd ideas about what we were up to, despite the fact we were both fully dressed.

Even dutiful immortals like him were prone to tongue wagging, I discovered.

Too late unfortunately, only after Ye Hua's main Sky Palace concubine, Su Jin, had sent a palace attendant to the mouth of the Qingqiu Valley to urge Ye Hua to come back.

Mystic Gorge had been standing guard, so luckily I did not have to deal with her.

I just heard about what happened from a group of gossiping young immortals who had been at the scene and witnessed the drama. This palace attendant had been wearing a fluttering black robe of fine silk, apparently, but had been rather plain herself. When Mystic Gorge blocked her at the mouth of the Qingqiu Valley, she sneered, "It's not that our empress is in any way intolerant, and she is aware that this involves the future Sky Empress. However, she has sent me here out of the goodness of her heart to remind His Majesty Prince Ye Hua and Her Highness Bai Qian that they are not yet officially wed. Spending their days lying around being intimate together is therefore rather indecent. Even the old Sky Emperor did not behave in such a way during his younger days. And His Majesty Prince Ye Hua must not forget that he invited Princess Liao Qing to the Sky Palace. It is unfair of him to neglect her like this."

Qingqiu had always been a broadminded and accepting place, and no one concerned themselves about matters such as children being born out of wedlock. It was nothing extraordinary, only intimacy. The group of young immortals who had witnessed this scene found the palace attendant's message absurd, and they hounded her out of Qingqiu before Mystic Gorge had been given a chance to respond.

I considered what she had said, and apart from the false claim that we were spending our days lying around being intimate together, everything else she had said seemed justified. I did not really understand why Ye Hua was still living with me, and I was glad to have an excuse to discuss it with him.

He had the window open and was standing in front of the desk, admiring the lotus flowers near the lake outside. He frowned when he heard what I had to say. "If I want to come and live with you, I damn well will. For all intents and purposes, you are my wife. What business is it of anyone else?"

I gave a blank stare, realizing as I heard this that Prince Ye Hua was indeed my husband-to-be, promised personally to me by the old Sky Emperor.

"Oh . . . oh . . . ," I managed at last. "But if I had married at a proper age, my grandchildren would the same age as you are."

The pen in his hand went still. I glanced at the official-looking document on the table. The bold ink soaked right through the paper. It was beautiful, wonderful calligraphy.

He put down his pen and stared silently at me through cold eyes. I gave an awkward laugh. "I heard the palace attendant say you had invited Liao Qing to the Sky Palace?" I said in an attempt to change the subject.

This was obviously not a favorable topic either.

I was under the impression that all men enjoyed discussing women. When I had been Little Seventeenth at Mount Kunlun and I happened to annoy First Apprentice, all I needed to do was start a conversation about the female immortals he found attractive, and his anger would melt away. But I reminded myself, I was no longer Little Seventeenth from Mount Kunlun, neither was I male in form. Male immortals might enjoy discussing female immortals with other men, but probably did not feel as comfortable discussing them with other female immortals. My question had clearly caused him offense.

But I was learning that men's hearts could be as unfathomable as women's. Ye Hua, who had seemed dispirited a moment ago, staring at me blankly when I asked the question, picked up his pen again, and dipped it in the inkwell. The corners of his mouth lifted into a slight smile. "Walk over and stand next to the window," he said. "Yes, next to the bamboo couch. Oh, actually, why not lie down on it? Tidy up your hair. Find a relaxed pose."

I followed his instructions in a trance before it finally dawned on me that he meant to draw my portrait. He had been sketching away looking very refined when out of nowhere he suddenly said, "Liao Qing would rather die than marry the second prince of the Western Sea. She's been very good to Ali and me, so I took her back to the Sky Palace and got her employment there as a servant. When she has had a chance to consider all her options, she can go back."

I stared at him dumbly. I had not been expecting him to bring up Liao Qing.

He lifted his head, and with warmth in his face, he said, "Do you have anything else you wish to ask me? Please feel free if you do so."

I did actually. "My hand is numb. Can I change positions?"

He did a double take and gave a laugh. He sketched out a couple more lines and said, "As you wish."

I ended up falling asleep like that on the bamboo couch.

When I woke up, it was dark. I had been covered with Ye Hua's jet-black cloak, but he was nowhere to be seen.

CHAPTER EIGHT

I climbed out of bed early the next morning and had a quick wash. I drank half a cup of strong tea before dragging myself to the entrance of the cave to wait for Ye Hua to take me off to the forest with him for a stroll. I had no idea where he had picked up this habit of his, but each morning he would take stroll around the foxhole, without fail, an excursion I was forced to take with him, whether I liked it or not.

There was nothing much in the way of scenery surrounding the foxhole, just some bamboo forest and a couple of clear springs. Walking around these places once or twice was fine, but after the third time, I started to find it tedious. A fortnight later, his enthusiasm for these walks did not seem to be waning in the slightest. The whole thing puzzled me.

Today I reached the cave entrance to hear the pitter-patter of rain outside. I tried to quash my feeling of elation as I put my teacup back down on the table next to the entrance and made my joyful way back to bed.

I was just starting to drift off when I heard footsteps. I opened my eyes to see Ye Hua standing beside my bed. "Some Water Emperor or other seems to have arranged rain for today. If we go out in this weather, we'll just end up getting soaked through," I said, trying to sound disappointed. "We'd better be sensible and stay indoors."

There was a smile playing on Ye Hua's lips, but he said nothing.

At this point Little Sticky-Rice Dumpling, usually still fast asleep at this hour, appeared behind Ye Hua. Giving a joyful squeal, he launched himself up onto my bed. He was wearing a colorful tunic of shimmery embroidered cloud cotton, which accentuated his tender little white hands and bright face. He put his arms around my neck, dazzling my eyes with his gaudy garment. "Father Prince told me he's going to take us out to the mortal world today, so why are you still lazing around in bed, Mother?" he asked in a petulant little high-pitched voice. I looked at him in surprise.

Ye Hua handed me my robe, which was hanging on the screen, saying, "As luck would have it, there is no rainfall today in the mortal world." I had no idea what Ye Hua was up to. If he was unfamiliar with the mortal world, he should be asking an earth god to act as his guide. While studying at Mount Kunlun, I traveled to the mortal world every couple of days, but I never managed to orient myself properly and would make a terrible guide. However, seeing Sticky-Rice Dumpling looking at me through those big, glistening, wet eyes, I felt unable to come out with an excuse.

I jumped off my lucky cloud, and transformed my appearance into that of a gentleman. "For the next couple of days, you must refer to Ye Hua as *Father* instead of *Father Prince*. And me you can call, um, *Godfather*," I told Sticky-Rice Dumpling.

Little Sticky-Rice Dumpling did not understand why, but as always he listened with blinking eyes and gave an obedient nod. Ye Hua kept his immortal form, but used magic to change his cloak for contemporary mortal clothes. He threw me a friendly and appreciative smile and said, "You look very confident and at ease like that."

Having spent twenty thousand years of my life as a boy, the pretense did come quite naturally. I cupped my hands together and bowed in his direction. "You're too kind," I said with a smile.

An older immortal gentleman, a younger immortal gentleman, and a young immortal child all dropped into a bustling town center.

We started walking along, Sticky-Rice Dumpling yelping and squealing joyfully at every new sight, his Sky Clan etiquette completely out the window. Ye Hua did not make any attempt to rein him in, and let him scamper ahead while the two of us followed along slowly.

The marketplace in the mortal world was busier and livelier than the one in Qingqiu. I casually waved my fan around and suddenly remembered what I had been meaning to ask Ye Hua. "Why did you decide that we should come to the mortal world today? Jia Yun brought you a huge pile of documents yesterday morning, and from his expression, they looked like they might be quite urgent."

He glanced at me out of the corner of his eye. "Today's Ali's birthday," he said.

"Oh!" I snapped the fan shut. "That's incredibly bad-mannered of you," I said sternly. "Why didn't you give me some warning? I don't have anything nice to give him. Dumpling thinks of me as his mother. He's bound to be upset if I don't give him something nice for his birthday."

Ye Hua looked unfazed. "If you wish to give him a nice present, why not a night pearl?" he asked.

"How do you know about my night pearls?" I marveled.

He raised an eyebrow and smiled. "A couple of old immortals drank too much during some Sky Palace banquet and got to gossiping. They mentioned this as your gift of choice. You've nurtured the habit of only giving night pearls as gifts for a good many years now apparently. Little pearls for the young immortal, and big pearls for the older gods, all very fair. But night pearls are expensive, and Ali's too small to appreciate their value. It would be a waste to give him one. Why not just give him a really good day out instead? That is sure to make him happy."

I rubbed my nose and gave an awkward laugh. "I have one pearl that's half the size of a person. From afar it looks like a little moon. If we took it to Qingyun Hall and set it up for Dumpling in there, it is sure to make the place brighter than the sun prince's residence even. It might be the Four Seas and Eight Deserts' only . . ."

I was speaking with such exuberance that I stopped paying any attention to what was going on around me. I suddenly felt myself being tugged off the road and tumbling into Ye Hua's arms as a horse-drawn carriage galloped past.

Ye Hua's brow creased slightly. The two horses galloping in front of the carriage suddenly stopped and reared up onto their hind legs, whinnying loudly, and the wooden-wheeled cart that had been rolling along at a flying speed spun around in a circle. The coachman slid down from the driving seat and wiped the sweat from his forehead. "Thank goodness my horses have stopped! They went crazy just now."

Dumpling, who had been running ahead of us, crept out from under one horse's belly with a wailing little baby girl in his arms. The baby girl was slightly taller than Dumpling, and he seemed to be clutching her around the waist and dragging her along.

A young woman suddenly rushed over from the crowd and grabbed the baby out of Dumpling's arms, crying, "Oh, goodness, that nearly scared me to death! Oh!"

The scene seemed strangely familiar. My own mother's face suddenly flashed into my mind, crying so much she was barely recognizable. "Where have you been for the last two hundred years?" she wept as she held me. "How could you do this to me?" I shook my head to cast off the daydream that had appeared so real it felt almost like falling under some spell. Even when I had almost died alongside Mo Yuan in the Yanhua Cave, Mother had not been as hysterical as that woman. It had never been my intention to leave Qingqiu for two hundred years. It happened five hundred years ago. Qing Cang broke out of the Eastern Desert Bell, and the two of us battled fiercely, following which I slept for 213 years straight.

Dumpling rushed over to us, huffing and puffing. "Father, why have you been hugging Godfather all this time?" he asked innocently.

The runaway horses had shaken up everyone, and the lively market streets had fallen silent. Dumpling's childish voice came out sounding loud and clear.

In no time at all, the sellers and pedestrians on both sides of the street who had been shaking their heads and sighing over the runaway horses had turned their beady eyes on us. I gave an awkward laugh, removing myself from Ye Hua's embrace and smoothing out my sleeves. "I took a tumble, and he caught me. That's it," I said with an awkward chuckle.

Dumpling let out a long sigh. "Luckily you tumbled into Father's arms, Godfather. If you'd fallen onto the ground and bashed your beautiful face, Father would have been most upset. Ali too."

I raised my head to look at Ye Hua. "Is that so, Father?" I asked.

The bright eyes of the crowd shifted momentarily to Ye Hua, who remained completely unfazed. He gave an almost imperceptible nod and said, "Yes."

A girl selling noodle cakes near where we were standing seemed to have fallen into a trance. "You're the first homosexual couple I've ever seen," she said.

I snapped open my fan to hide my face and sneaked away into the crowd. Dumpling followed behind me, shouting, "Godfather! Godfather!"

Ye Hua smothered a laugh and said, "Don't worry about her, she's just shy."

● ● ●

It was nearly noon, and we decided to have lunch at a restaurant at the end of the street near the lake.

Ye Hua chose a table on the upper floor next to the window. He ordered a jar of wine and a few dishes popular in the mortal world, and mercifully, there was no fish this time.

A refreshing breeze blew over the lake and toward us.

As we were waiting for our food, Dumpling brought out all the little objects he had just bought and placed them onto the table to look at. Two amusing little clay figures caught my eye.

Before we had been served, the waiter brought up two people and asked if they could join us at our table. A slender young Taoist nun walked over followed by a docile-looking servant whom I recognized. After a moment I realized he was the coachman from the market just before.

The young waiter cupped his hands together and bowed to us in apology. It was only a meal, I thought to myself, and the upper and lower floors of the restaurant were completely full. Dumpling shifted onto my seat, which we shared, and we offered them the two spare seats.

The nun sat down and poured herself a cup of tea. She took two sips before looking across at Ye Hua. Her bottom lip trembled, but she said nothing.

It was no wonder: Ye Hua had adopted his frosty god manner again, so different from the image of the kind, sweet-natured man standing at my stove with a spatula in his hand, stir-frying vegetables.

I helped Dumpling put away his new things. The nun took another sip of tea, looking very nervous. She finally plucked up the courage to speak. "I'm so lucky that you were in the marketplace just now, Immortal Prince, and that you were there to save me," she said, a tremble in her voice. "You helped Miao Yun escape a disaster."

I turned to her in astonishment, and even Ye Hua turned to face her. Miao Yun the nun lowered her head, blushing so much that even her ears turned red. To see through Ye Hua's disguise in one glance and tell that he was an immortal and that he had used magic to rescue them meant that she was an extraordinary nun. In less than ten years, she would probably be levitating up to the sun and visiting us in the Sky Palace.

Ye Hua swept his eyes over her. "There's no need to be so polite. It was nothing. Anyone would have done the same," he said in a flat tone of voice.

Miao Yun's ears were now so red they looked as if the blood was about to start seeping out of them. She bit her lip. "Even a finger lifted by the immortal prince should be viewed as a great kindness," she said in a quiet voice. "Immortal Prince, wou-would you be kind enough to tell me your immortal title so that in the future when I learn to levitate I might visit your immortal residence and repay you for saving my life?"

Surely not. It sounded almost as if this nun might be . . . flirting with Ye Hua?

I suddenly remembered the Mount Kunlun rules about taking on apprentices. Neither age nor family background was important, but female immortals were categorically forbidden.

Mo Yuan must have had a similar problem with women falling for him. I had not been aware of this at the time. It was only now after meeting Ye Hua that it became obvious.

The faces they had been born with had earned them a huge amount of female attention.

Ye Hua took a sip of tea. "Good karma only comes around when it is due," he said in that same flat voice. "You have been on the receiving end of good karma today because you have built up good karma in the past. It has nothing to do with me. Don't concern yourself about repaying me."

He spoke with compelling logic, and Miao Yun bit her lip, saying nothing. Dumpling and I had just finished clearing his things off the table. I lifted my head to give her a smile, which she returned. She looked up at Dumpling, who was waiting anxiously for his food. "What a handsome and well-mannered immortal child," she said softly.

"Children are always adorable. It gives no guarantee what he'll look like later," I said in an attempt to deflect the compliment. "There was one young immortal from my hometown who was unbelievably adorable when he was young. Three thousand years later he vaguely resembles his younger self, but there is nothing remotely special about his face."

Dumpling tugged at my sleeve and looked up at me mournfully. Oh dear, I had gone overboard with my modesty.

Ye Hua lifted his cup and looked at me with a faint smile. "There's no point for a boy being too handsome, is there?" he asked. "A charming face won't help you in a fight like strong pair of fists will. And anyway," he continued, taking a sip of tea, "girls tend to resemble their fathers and boys their mothers, so as far as I'm concerned, Ali is going to grow up with excellent good looks."

Dumpling, who had been looking like he was about to cry, was suddenly radiating good spirits once more. He gave his father an affectionate look and started nudging his way toward him.

I gave a cough and looked at him lovingly. "It doesn't matter what Dumpling ends up looking like. He will always have a place in my heart, and I will always be there to look after him."

Dumpling turned back to me, his eyes brimming with tears of joy, and he started nudging back toward me.

Ye Hua gave a quiet laugh but said nothing.

The wine was the first thing to arrive at our table, but it was soon followed by the food. The young waiter was gracious and considerate, and our pot of sweet osmanthus wine had been heated to just the right temperature.

Mao the Sun Prince was doing himself proud, and the sun was strong but not fierce. The sky was adorned with the occasional puff of lucky cloud, which looked lovely against the line of shady trees.

Drinking a few cups of wine in these blissful conditions made me feel inspired to compose a poem. But Miao Yun and her coachman were not drinking, and after two or three cups of wine Ye Hua disappointed me by asking the waiter to take away our cups.

Ye Hua seemed to have fallen under some kind of spell while we were eating and kept making desperate attempts to feed me. With a tender smile, he forced food upon me with words like, "You love this, have a bit more!" or "I know this isn't your favorite, but it's good for you. Your thinness may not worry you, but it worries me." I knew he was just using me as an excuse to avoid Miao Yun, but hearing him talk like this still made my skin crawl.

Miao Yun was obviously not enjoying being made to listen to this either, and her face turned as white as paper. The coachman sensed the strange atmosphere and quickly gobbled down his rice so that he and his mistress could leave.

Ye Hua finally stopped shoving food toward me and let out a long sigh. "You don't seem comfortable with terms of endearment," he said slowly. "What are we going to do about that?"

I lowered my head and dug my chopsticks into my rice, ignoring him.

We were still eating when Ye Hua's desk official, Jia Yun, suddenly appeared out of nowhere. Fortunately he had made himself invisible; who knows how all the mortals would have reacted to suddenly seeing someone floating in midair in the restaurant.

He mentioned a letter that needed urgent attention, although I switched off when he went into details. Ye Hua turned to me and said, "Well, it looks like I am needed back at the Sky Palace. Will you stay here with Ali this afternoon and show him around? I'll come back and join up with you both this evening." My mouth was too full of rice to speak, so I just gave a nod.

I came out of the restaurant and looked around. The sun was directly above us. It was so hot that the market sellers had moved their things under the awning, while those that had not managed to grab a good spot were packing up to go home, looking miserable.

When I was settling up in the restaurant, the waiter graciously pointed out that I had overtipped him and then suggested I go along to the Free Thought Tea House to listen to their storytelling. The tea was a little expensive, but the storytelling was excellent.

I was certain that there was no storytelling in the Sky Palace, and Dumpling had probably never been to a reading. I grabbed his hand and led him there so he could experience it.

The storyteller was an old gentleman whose hair and beard had both turned half white. When we sat down, he was telling the story of a wild crane repaying a debt of gratitude.

It was a completely new experience for Dumpling, whose eyes sparkled as he listened. Sometimes he would give a knowing smile; other times his fists would ball up tightly or he would let out a deep sigh. At Zhe Yan's I had always had countless books at my fingertips and found this story somewhat contrived and uninspired. I asked for a pot of green tea and sat at the table, letting my mind wander.

It was midafternoon in no time, and the storyteller was hitting his wooden block to shake up the audience with the words: "And if you want to know what happens next, you'll have to come to the next session." I could see the lanterns outside the window were starting to be lit.

I opened my eyes in a daze and looked around for Dumpling, but the place where he had been sitting was now empty. I started to shake, immediately wide-awake.

Luckily I had brought along my water mirror. In the immortal realm, a water mirror functions just like a vanity mirror, but in the mortal world, it can be used to find people. I just hoped Dumpling was in an easily distinguishable location. If he were standing in a nondescript room, the water mirror would be completely useless.

I found a secluded spot and wrote Dumpling's name onto the mirror's surface. A white light shone out in immediate response. I followed the white light with my eyes and stumbled, almost dropping the mirror.

My goodness. The room Dumpling had ended up in certainly could not be called nondescript. It contained a carved rosewood bed on which lay a scantily clad couple. The man was half naked, while the woman underneath him had on nothing but a bright red slip. Decent mortal women did not tend to wear such garish colors. I was starting to feel giddy, but I forced myself to stand up straight and grabbed a passerby. "Excuse me. Do you know which direction the town brothel is in?" I asked.

He looked at me carefully, sizing me up before finally pointing to the building diagonally across from the Free Thought Tea House. I thanked him and raced over. I heard him give a faint sigh behind me and say, "And he looked like such a well-brought-up boy. Who would have thought he would be such a degenerate? Such immoral times we live in."

I knew that Dumpling was inside the brothel, but I did not know which room. I made myself invisible so as not to disturb the madam's business and started to go from room to room.

I searched through thirteen rooms before finally finding him floating in midair, also invisible, his chin in his hand, looking pensive. I reached out and dragged him through the wall, away from the passionately kissing couple on the bed.

My face was burning red.

Luckily their bedroom activity had not progressed past kissing. I had first visited the mortal world during my Mount Kunlun apprenticeship. Thirsty for knowledge, I had read as much erotic fiction as I could get my hands on. There were lowbrow books that could be found in any market for three pennies a copy, and ones so rare that the only copy could be found hidden underneath the emperor's pillow. Some of these books described encounters between men and women, and others men and men, all of which I dabbled in. I used to read them, looking as calm as a plank of wood, with neither my face reddening nor my heart jumping about wildly. But not so today. It was a different situation: I was with a child and witnessing live action. If that was not enough to turn my old face red, I really did not deserve to have Dumpling call me Mother.

There were girls outside the brothel room talking to potential customers in sweet, dulcet tones. They were still conducting their dirty business, but at least these ones were fully clothed.

There was not one quiet spot in the entire building.

A maid walked gracefully past us, dressed in red and carrying a tray of mung-bean cakes. Sticky-Rice Dumpling gave a sniff and turned visible to chase after her, asking for one. I followed him and had no choice but to become visible too. As soon as this maid saw Dumpling, she was enchanted. She stroked his little face, turned to smile at me with flushed cheeks, and then handed him the whole tray of cakes.

I pulled Dumpling into a dead-end corridor and thought carefully about the lecture I was about to deliver. I wanted to make him realize what he had done was wrong, but I did not want to upset him. Today was his birthday after all, and Ye Hua had asked me to make sure it was a happy one.

I gave him a smile. "The storytelling at the Free Thought Tea House was rather good, I thought," I began good-naturedly. "You seemed very engrossed at the beginning, so why did you decide to run off? And of all places, why come to this one?"

Dumpling gave a frown. "I saw a fat boy kissing a young girl in the street. The girl didn't seem to want the fat boy to kiss her, but when she tried to stop him, the fat boy got angry and called a group of ugly boys over who surrounded the girl. The girl looked so scared I had to do something. So I went to save her. I ran down the stairs, but couldn't see any sign of them. A man outside told me that the fat boy had carried the girl into the *flower house*. I was worried they were going to hurt her, so I decided to go in and rescue her. The old woman at the door wouldn't let me in, so I made myself invisible and slipped past her. Oh, I really don't know why the man called it a flower house. I went around the entire place and didn't see a single flower."

On hearing his last sentence, my heart started hammering. *Please, Dumpling, don't have seen anything too awful,* I begged silently.

Dumpling was the equivalent age of a mortal child of three. It was an age when his immortal root was extremely unstable, and he needed a lot of care and guidance. His father had looked after him so well for the last three hundred years. If under my watch he saw things he should not have, he might start to spawn untoward ideas, which would bewitch his immortal consciousness, and Ye Hua would want me dead.

I swallowed and listened to the rest of his tale.

"When I found the fat boy, he was lying out flat across the floor, and there was a man in white next to the young girl, hugging her. Seeing that she was safe, I decided to come back and hear the end of the story, but I went through the wrong wall and ended up in that other room."

Tenth Apprentice and I did so badly in our magic of deduction classes that Mo Yuan sent us to the mortal world as a punishment and made us work there as fortune-tellers. We set up a stall in the marketplace to tell fortunes and read bones. Every few days we would see a decent woman being tormented or molested. If she was unmarried, a knight would draw his sword and roar as he rushed over to defend her, and if she was married, her husband would appear and draw out his sword. The knight and the husband would always be dressed in white when they appeared.

Dumpling rubbed his nose and gave another frown. "There were two people rolling around on the bed together in that room. They were tangled up in a ball together. I wanted to know why they were tangled up like that, so I stayed there for a while to watch them."

My heart pounded. "And what did you see?" I asked, my voice trembling.

He appeared to be thinking carefully. "They were kissing each other, yes, kissing . . . and touching each other, yes, touching." He paused. "Mother, what were they doing?" he stuttered.

I looked skyward and thought about how to answer him. I adopted a serious expression and said, "Mortal people who study Taoism have a practice known as harmonizing and studying one another. That's what the couple you saw was doing. Harmonizing and studying one another."

"Mortals are so wholeheartedly devoted to Taoism," Dumpling said in a wise little voice.

I gave a burst of laughter.

I turned around and bumped my head against the firm chest of someone who reeked of alcohol. I rubbed my nose and took a couple of steps back to get a clearer look. In front of me stood a man with a fan in his hand. His slender eyes lit up as he regarded me. He had a pleasant face, but too much fire in his organs had dulled his skin. He had obviously been *harmonizing* a bit too diligently, and the lust was wearing out his kidneys.

Waving his fan in my face, he said, "I am blown away by how attractive you are, Master."

He looked like a scoundrel from a wealthy family. I gave a sigh. The alcohol fumes he was wafting over with his fan overpowered me and started to make me feel dizzy. I cupped my hands together to give a reluctant bow and uttered the words, "You're too kind."

I grabbed Dumpling's hand to lead him out of the building, but the man leaned over, blocking my path. He grabbed one of my hands. "What beautiful, pale, tender hands you have," he said with a snigger. I was stunned into silence.

My early experiences in the mortal world had taught me that women who went out in public often found themselves being lusted after and pestered like this, but these days even men were not safe. Dumpling was gaping at the man with the fan, a piece of mung-bean cake in his mouth.

I was gaping at him too. The man with the fan had been lucky today: he had managed to grope a goddess. It was the first time I had ever been accosted by a mortal. I did not plan to quarrel with him any longer than needed. I graciously took my hand back to give him a clear message. But the foolish man immediately drew even closer. "I've fallen in love at first sight. Would you . . . ?" The cheeky swine reached an arm to put around my waist.

Most of the time I was a merciful goddess, but encounters like this drained my mercy dry. I decided I would cast a spell to freeze him. I could tie him to a tree in a nearby forest for a few days and give him an experience that he would not forget for a while. As I was thinking this over, I sensed a movement from behind. Someone rushed over and swept me up into their arms. I lifted my head and greeted the owner of these familiar arms. "Ye Hua, you've come just at the right moment!"

Ye Hua grasped me with one hand. A few beams of cold light shimmered from the bright lanterns onto his black cloak. He smiled grimly at the perplexed-looking man with the fan and said, "You've been accosting my wife and seem to have been taking a lot of joy in it."

As the future Sky Empress, technically I supposed I was his wife. And the fact that I had been accosted was obviously humiliating for Ye Hua. Still holding me, he grabbed the lecherous coward and reprimanded him, just as a husband should. I allowed myself to be held while he reproached this lascivious wretch, just as a wife should.

Dumpling had gobbled up half the mung-bean cakes by now and was licking the corners of his lips. "You've made Father really, really angry," he told the man with the fan in an earnest voice. "Father hardly ever gets angry, so you must be really talented. It's time for us to say good-bye to you now. So long!"

Dumpling took up position next to me. The man with the fan was outraged. "Do you know who I am, huh?" he sneered. "Huh—"

But he vanished before he had even finished speaking.

"What have you done with him?" I turned to ask Ye Hua.

Ye Hua looked toward the dim patch after the twinkling lights of the town petered out. "A haunted forest nearby," he said calmly. I was stunned. Great minds.

Ye Hue gazed into the distance and then turned to scrutinize me. "Why didn't you hide yourself when he started taking advantage?" he asked.

"It was nothing but a wandering hand," I said meekly.

He lowered his head, his face expressionless, and planted a kiss upon my lips.

I was too stunned to react.

He looked at me, his face still impassive, and said, "And that was nothing but a pair of wandering lips!"

Something about today was making me feel lighter than when I was a ninety-thousand-year-old youngster. Little Dumpling stood to the side and covered his mouth to giggle. He started choking on the mung-bean cake so hard he could not breathe.

That night we took Dumpling to float lanterns on the lake. These lanterns looked like lotus flowers with small candles burning in their centers. Mortals placed them in the water to make wishes or prayers. Dumpling took hold of his lantern and mumbled his prayers. He prayed for a bumper grain harvest, thriving domestic livestock, and peace and harmony to all under the sky. Finally he was satisfied with his prayers and released his lantern into the water.

His little lantern managed to stay afloat despite the weight of all the prayers it was carrying. It spun in a circle, and when the wind blew, it swayed from side to side before floating off. Ye Hua handed me a lantern too. When mortals prayed they asked immortals for protection, but to whom did immortals pray to ask for protection?

Ye Hua gave a faint smile. "Just make any old wish. You don't really think that saying a prayer and placing a lantern in a lake will make everything run smoothly, do you?" he said, sounding very logical.

I awkwardly accepted the little lantern and walked over to Dumpling to release it with him.

It had been a perfect day.

By the time we were finished with our lake lanterns, Dumpling was so tired he could no longer keep his eyes open. He still had enough strength to mutter, "Let's not go back to Qingqiu tonight. I want to spend a night in the mortal world, see what mortal beds and quilts feel like."

The watchman's clapper sounded, signaling nightfall. We wandered around the streets and alleys, but all the doors with two lanterns hanging on them and with the word *inn* written on them were shut.

The town center was small, but it was a popular place with visitors. We knocked on the doors of two inns before finding one that had a vacant room. Dumpling was fast asleep in Ye Hua's arms by then.

The innkeeper was half asleep himself. "You two men won't mind sharing a bed together for one night, will you?" he asked with a yawn. "There are only three inns in this town, and innkeepers Wang and Li are both fully booked. Lucky for you someone just checked out here, so we have one room free."

Ye Hua gave a barely perceptible nod, and the innkeeper shouted inside for someone. The porter ran out, his arms flailing wildly as he tried to thread them into their sleeves. He ran to the front to take us to our room.

He led us up to the second floor and around a corner and pushed open a door. Ye Hua put Dumpling on the bed and asked the porter to bring us some water so we could wash. At that moment, my stomach rumbled. Ye Hu gave me a meaningful glance and said, "And could you make us a little something to eat while you're at it?"

The porter looked exhausted and clearly wanted to finish waiting on us so he could get back to bed. He quickly reappeared with the water and the food. They were very simple dishes: beef cooked in brine, salt and pepper spare ribs, and spring onion with tofu.

I picked up my chopsticks and took a couple of bites, but that was enough. I was not usually a fussy eater, but Ye Hua's cooking had obviously given me a more discerning palate.

Ye Hua sat under the lamp, reading. He lifted his head to look at me, and then down at the three dishes on the table. "Don't eat them if you don't want to. Just have a wash and go to bed."

It was an average double room with one bed. I looked at the bed and hesitated before lying down on it fully clothed.

Ye Hua had not mentioned sleeping arrangements. He was so decent that it probably had not even occurred to him as a problem. If I were to bring it up, I worried I would come across as uptight.

I moved the soundly sleeping Dumpling toward the center of the bed, placed the big quilt to the side, and lay down on the wall side of the bed. Ye Hua was still sitting under the lamp with his documents.

In the middle of the night, foggy from sleep, I felt as if I had a pair of arms wrapped around me. I could feel someone holding me and sighing into my ear. "I've always known about your temper, but I had no idea how obstinate you were. If you've forgotten the past and former happenings, you've forgotten them. I both wish you would remember and hope you never do . . ."

Assuming it was just fragments of dreams, I turned around and scooped Dumpling into my arms, and stroking him, I fell peacefully back to sleep.

It was already fully light outside by the time I crawled out of bed the next morning. Ye Hua was sitting in that same position, reading his documents. The only difference was that the candles were no longer lit.

I was confused. Had he been reading all night? Or had he been asleep, woken up before me, and sat back down to continue reading?

Dumpling beckoned me over to the table. "Mother, Mother, this rice porridge is nice and thick. Ali has ladled some out for you."

I stroked his head and called him a very good boy. I had a wash and then tucked into my porridge. It was identical in taste and consistency to the porridge Ye Hua made at home.

I lifted my head and gazed at him. With his head still lowered, he said, "You didn't seem very enthusiastic about the food here last night, and I was worried Ali wouldn't like it either, so I used their kitchen to stew us up some porridge."

"I didn't like the food the Eastern Sea Princess cooked when we were on Junji Mountain either, but Father Prince never made food just for me then," Dumpling mumbled. Ye Hua gave a cough.

I had been treated so well and did not want to cause any trouble, so I just lowered my head and focused on the delicious porridge.

CHAPTER NINE

Dumpling and I returned to Qingqiu that morning, while Ye Hua's desk official, Jia Yun, came to accompany him back to the Sky Palace. There was an important matter that he needed to discuss with his court, apparently, which would take a couple of days. During this time, Dumpling and I lived off that basket of loquat and felt very sorry for ourselves. Dumpling ate so much of the fruit that his face turned orange. Tugging pitifully at my sleeve, he said, "Mother, when is Father Prince coming back? Ali wants to eat steamed mushrooms and a bowl of his cabbage and carrot soup."

Mystic Gorge could not bear to see such a pitiful little face any longer. If it was only steamed mushrooms and a cabbage and carrot soup Dumpling was craving, it could not be too hard to make, he thought, stoically rolling up his sleeves and marching into the kitchen. Ye Hua's steamed mushrooms and his cabbage and carrot soup were unbelievably rich and flavorsome, but they were so complicated and laborious to prepare that flowers wilted, trees shed their leaves, and the sky changed color during the process. Mystic Gorge turned the foxhole upside down in his attempt to replicate these two dishes, but still he failed to meet Dumpling's approval.

Dumpling continued tugging at my sleeve. "Mother, Mother, when is Father Prince coming back?" he asked in distress.

Phoenix Nine often used to tell me her experiences of love when she was drunk. She had come to the conclusion that you did not really know what love was until you had tried it. Once you had tasted its sweetness, you could not live without it. There was nothing in the universe as beguiling. I agreed that there was nothing more alluring than love but felt that some things were equally enchanting, like Ye Hua's cooking.

While I was not quite to the same extent as Dumpling with his incessant whining, I found I was missing Ye Hua and his cooking a lot too.

I remembered the first time I had ever seen Ye Hua, at the Eastern Sea Water Crystal Palace. I had only noticed how astonishingly familiar his face was. It was only recently that it had begun to dawn on me that he was the future Sky Emperor, with so many matters to deal with, and what it must have taken for him to get away for three months and do all our cooking for us. Ye Hua was so knowledgeable, kind, and considerate.

Dumpling and I would have to wait until he came back down from the sky before we ate another decent meal. Lucky for Mystic Gorge, I had an idea. As he came over to deliver loquat in time for our meal, I called him over to sit down and eat with us. With joy I explained how he would not need to make any more loquat deliveries.

After experiencing Mystic Gorge's cooking, I realized how tough life without Ye Hua was. I bounded out of the foxhole the following day and put up a notice. I was looking to recruit a young Qingqiu immortal to undertake a cooking apprenticeship under Ye Hua.

The local young immortals were all very eager and formed two long lines in front of the foxhole. "I haven't seen such a lively scene in Qingqiu for a long time," Mystic Gorge exclaimed. "With this many people, it would be best to set up a stage and get the candidates to compete. We can choose the one with the best foundation to study His Majesty's noble craft."

I thought it was a wonderful idea and gave my permission. Mystic Gorge was an efficient organizer, so I left him to it while I went back inside for a nap. By the time I woke up again, the stage was set up.

Qingqiu became a mass of spiraling smoke. Dumpling stood salivating in the foxhole doorway. Ye Hua sat at the side all alone, lifting his eyes to glance at me every so often, a strange expression on his face. Seeing an empty bamboo seat next to him, I strolled over and sat down.

Dumpling launched himself straight up onto my lap. "Mystic Gorge tells me you're choosing me an apprentice?" Ye Hua said, giving a light yawn.

I nodded.

He swept his eyes over the crowd of young immortals rushing around on the stage and the smoke and flames leaping into the sky. He leaned over to me and said, "Tell them they can all leave. They are all lacking the right foundation." He looked me up and down and with a smile said, "You look like you'll do. But you don't really need to learn. As long as one of us can cook, we'll be fine."

He casually got to his feet and returned to his study. I was left there staring blankly, not sure what he meant.

"Which one did His Majesty just choose?" Mystic Gorge asked, skipping over.

I shook my head in confusion. "He didn't like the look of any of them. He said to send them all away."

One morning a week or so later, I was nestled up in Ye Hua's study, flicking through a book of folk stories and crunching on sunflower seeds, while Ye Hua sat with a couple of files in front of him, working through a pile of documents. I suspected that the old Sky Emperor had already started to enjoy the comforts of retirement. He no longer seemed to be attending to any of his matters, and the day-to-day grind had fallen entirely onto his grandson's shoulders.

The lotus flowers in the lake outside the window were fully open and looked stunning. A breeze blew across the lake, and the dragonflies inside the flowers swayed along with the petals while a gentle fragrance wafted out. Mystic Gorge took Dumpling out into the middle of the lake in a little boat, and they picked lotus leaves to dry in the sun and make a refreshing tea. Mystic Gorge was not a dab hand at the stove, but he was good at making tea, another highly skilled job.

Ye Hua put down his document and walked over to the window to open the curtain fully. "You never bother to give the lotus flowers in your lake any attention. You leave them to live or die as they will, and yet they are so beautiful, as beautiful as those in the Sky Palace's Jade Pool even," he said with a smile.

I gave a quick laugh and then reached over to offer him a handful of sunflower seeds. He never ate them, but he took them from me anyway and stood in front of the window, shelling them before handing the kernels back to me. "I would give these to Ali if he were here, but his loss is your gain."

I accepted them gratefully when I heard Dumpling give a sudden shriek from the lake outside. I stuck my head out the window to see Mystic Gorge rushing off the boat.

It looked from his reaction as if Qingqiu might be under siege!

"Come and get some sunflower seeds," I called out to Dumpling, sitting alone in the boat.

He sat there in the middle of the lotus lake for a while, coyly wringing his hands, before turning red in the face and saying, "Ali . . . Ali doesn't know how to row."

I went back to my book. I had just come to the most gripping part when Mystic Gorge entered Ye Hua's study and presented me with the broken-cloud fan. "Ah, it looks as if my second uncle's wife has decided to make an appearance," Ye Hua said coolly.

His family had such an extensive and mysterious lineage that it took a moment to work out which uncle he was talking about. It was only when I looked down at the broken-cloud fan that I put two and two together. His second uncle was Sang Ji, the man who had broken our engagement. And his wife was Shao Xin.

While in the Eastern Sea, I had promised to honor our former master-and-servant relationship by granting her a wish. I had told her that when she had decided what she wanted, she should come and see me in Qingqiu, bringing this fan. She obviously knew what she wanted.

Mystic Gorge's face paled and then darkened as he led Shao Xin inside. I gave him a pointed look, reminding him that Dumpling was still in the middle of the lake in his boat. "Ah!" Mystic Gorge exclaimed, leaping out the window.

Ye Hua continued to read his documents in silence. I continued to read my folktale in silence. Shao Xin knelt on the floor in silence.

I finished the story and noticed I had run out of tea. I got up and went out to brew a new pot, picking up Ye Hua's cup from his desk so that I could replenish that too. When I came back with the tea, Shao Xin was still kneeling there in silence. I took a sip of tea and watched her with bemusement. "You've come to see me, so I expect you've decided what to ask for. Why not just come out and say it?"

She lifted her head, glanced at Ye Hua, and bit her lip.

Ye Hua sat there, calmly drinking his tea and reading through his documents. I put down my cup. "Prince Ye Hua is not some stranger,"

I continued calmly. "You'll just have to be brave and say what you have to say in front of him."

Ye Hua lifted his head and glanced at me with a faint smile.

Shao Xin hesitated before finally starting to speak. "Your Highness, Your Highness, can you help my son Yuan Zhen?" she asked in a timid voice.

I had to wait for Shao Xin to stop sniveling and crying before I understood what had happened and why she had been so reluctant to speak in Ye Hua's presence.

Yuan Zhen was Shao Xin and Sang Ji's first son. Although Sang Ji had fallen out of favor with the Sky Emperor, the Sky Emperor still doted on this grandson and invited him along every time he hosted a banquet.

The Sky Emperor had celebrated his birthday recently. Sang Ji took Yuan Zhen along bearing gifts, and they stayed the night in the Sky Palace. Yuan Zhen drank far too much at the banquet, and he stumbled into Xiwu Palace in this inebriated state and tried to have his way with Head Concubine Su Jin.

I threw a glance at Ye Hua, well aware that Su Jin was his concubine. He looked up at me as he was sorting through his papers, a hint of amusement in his eyes. How unique Prince Ye Hua was: he remained lighthearted even when being cuckolded.

Luckily, he had not actually been cuckolded. Yuan Zhen had reined himself in at the last moment and not actually assaulted the concubine. But Su Jin was so resolute and upright that she had taken a length of white silk and tied it to the eaves of the roof. Her suicide attempt had alerted the Sky Emperor as to what happened. I had heard that the Sky Emperor had previously married Su Jin as his concubine, but when his grandson had taken a liking to her, his doting grandfather had transferred his new concubine over to him.

When the Sky Emperor heard that Yuan Zhen had taken advantage of Su Jin, he felt very sorry for his former concubine and was filled with rage at Yuan Zhen. He tied up Yuan Zhen with immortal ropes and issued a sky decree stating that the youngster would be reborn as a mortal. Only after he had lived out a sixty-year mortal lifecycle would he be reinstated as an immortal.

"Yuan Zhen was a kind and well-behaved boy," Shao Xin repeated again and again through her tears. "He was so caring and careful that when he was out walking, he would make sure not to step on a single ant. He would never have committed an offense like this." I was not convinced by her logic; in my experience, there was no relation between kindness and lust.

Yuan Zhen had been sent down into the mortal world. I stroked my teacup. "If he only attempted to have his way with her, this punishment does seem excessively harsh," I said. "However, the fact that it was Ye Hua's head concubine your son tried to take advantage of and Prince Ye Hua has been in the foxhole, looking after me and cooking me meals for many months now, puts me in a difficult position to help . . ."

Ye Hua picked up a new document. "You don't have to worry about my feelings," he said flatly. "I agree that Yuan Zhen's punishment has been excessively harsh."

I was shocked. "But it was your head concubine he was lusting over . . ."

"I have no head concubine," he scoffed. He stood up to pour out some more tea, taking my teacup to refill too.

I was even more shocked. The rumor within the Four Seas and Eight Deserts was that Ye Hua loved and doted upon Head Concubine Su Jin. Could it all have been just hearsay?

It was not a particularly difficult favor Shao Xin was asking of me. She had found out that Yuan Zhen would encounter his big calamity when he was eighteen in his mortal form, and that it would cause him a lifetime of suffering. She begged me to help him through this calamity and help alter his destiny so he could live out his mortal life in peace.

She was wise to come to me, as I was in a strong position to help. All immortals had the ability to change a mortal's fate, but godly etiquette restricted us from doing it, which meant that even when an immortal was capable of helping in this way, they had their hands tied.

But the Sky Emperor owed the Bai family a favor that had not yet been repaid. If I went before him and asked him to grant me a small favor like this, the Sky Emperor was certain to turn a blind eye to the fact that I would be violating godly etiquette, which would be half the problem solved.

Yuan Zhen had been reborn into an imperial Song family as Song Yuan Zhen. When he turned twelve, he was chosen as heir to the throne. He was fortunate and never wanted for anything, but at age eighteen he was fast approaching his calamity.

Yuan Zhen's mortal-world mother was a strange woman. She was the only daughter of the emperor's tutor and had been sent to the palace when she was fifteen to become an honored imperial concubine, a distinguished and prominent position. After giving birth to Yuan Zhen, she decided she wanted to be a nun, and there was nothing that the emperor could do to dissuade her. The emperor had begrudgingly found her a solitary mountain behind the imperial city on which he had built her a Taoist temple, where he had left her to her devoted religious practice.

When she became a nun, her son usually would have been adopted by the empress and continued to be raised in the palace. Yuan Zhen's mother was extremely obstinate, however, and stated that she would die before handing over her son. She took Yuan Zhen to live in the Taoist temple with her until he turned sixteen, after which time he was sent back to the palace, accompanied by a Taoist nun. This nun was Yuan

Zhen's mortal Taoist master, but she was also a serving girl working for the Northern Sea Emperor, Yuan Zhen's real father, Sang Ji, who had sent her down to the mortal world to watch over his son. When I went down to the mortal world to protect Yuan Zhen and help him through his calamity, I would be replacing this Taoist master of his.

I saw Shao Xin out and then started to make a plan. First I needed to go to the South Pole Emperor's to meet with Si Ming the Star Prince and see if I could pull any strings. I needed to find out the exact day and hour that Yuan Zhen's calamity would befall him and how it would happen. Yuan Zhen's calamity was a mortal calamity. Unlike the sky calamity gods had to pass through, which, once in motion, had to be played out, mortal calamities could simply be averted.

I was not on close terms with the South Pole Emperor and had never even set eyes on the six Star Princes who worked for him. I made the rash decision to go there anyway, knowing that there was no guarantee they would grant me the favor.

"Si Ming the Star Prince has a strange temperament, and even the Sky Emperor would find it hard to get his hands on his destiny notebook to have a look," Ye Hua told me as he sorted through his documents. "I don't think you will have much luck going there without giving prior notice."

I looked at him and frowned.

He paused, sipped his tea, and said, "Actually I might have a way, it's just . . ." He gave me a kind and serious look. "If I help you get the destiny notebook, you must promise me one thing," he said with a smile.

I looked up expectantly.

"You must allow me to seal off your magic when you're down in the mortal world," he said calmly. "What did you think I was going to say? Altering the content of the destiny notebook contravenes immortal rules. Even if the Sky Emperor turns a blind eye, any magic you use to change fate you could suffer magic backbite from. Your understanding of this is probably better than mine. Getting magic backbite more than once or twice is very serious, even if you are a goddess. What if the backbite occurs when I'm about to succeed to the Sky Throne and you are about to become Empress?"

On their accession to the Sky Throne, the Sky Emperor and Empress had to endure eighty-one blasts of wildfire and nine blasts of thunder. Only after this were they allowed to preside over the Four Seas and Eight Deserts. This was the way it always had been. The consequences of backbite from your own magic at this moment would be severe. I considered the implications, and realizing that he was making a lot of sense, I gave him my permission.

After agreeing, something else occurred to me. "But we aren't even married yet," I said. "If you succeed to the Sky Throne soon, I won't succeed with you anyway. We have to be married before I can become Sky Empress."

He put down his teacup and stared at me, and gave a sudden laugh. "Are you upset with me for not mentioning marriage earlier?"

Hearing him laugh like that caused a pearl of cold sweat to drop from my forehead and roll down my face. I gave an awkward laugh. "Nothing of the sort. I meant nothing of the sort."

Ye Hua was used to having hundreds of pressing matters requiring his attention, and by the next morning he presented me with Si Ming the Star Prince's destiny notebook. After he had told me how precious and coveted this destiny notebook was, the most I was expecting was some handwritten copies of the relevant content, even though Si Ming did owe Ye Hua a favor. I had not imagined that he might bring me the genuine article.

Ye Hua handed me the notebook with a sigh.

I flicked through to Yuan Zhen's fate and gave a sigh too.

What a convoluted, up and down, mixed bag of a fate it was.

According to the destiny notebook, between his birth and his eighteenth birthday, Yuan Zhen's life was very peaceful. His misfortune began on the first of June of his eighteenth year.

The first of June was the Vedic Dharma Festival, and the Sky Emperor made a trip to the Suyu River to celebrate with his subjects. He led a large procession of nobles and honored concubines, which included Yuan Zhen too. At noon on the dot, a little pleasure boat floated gracefully into the middle of the Suyu River with a beautiful woman inside, her fine and delicate features half obscured by a circular fan. In the midst of this harmonious and happy scene, a giant Peng bird suddenly swooped down through the sky and took the little boat in its talons, tugging and clawing at it. The boat capsized, and the beautiful woman turned pale with fright as she splashed down into the water.

Yuan Zhen had lived in a Taoist temple all his life and was extremely kindhearted. Being a strong swimmer, he jumped straight into the river after this beautiful woman and saved her from drowning.

Their eyes met though the glittering water, and they fell in love. Unfortunately it was not just Yuan Zhen who lost his heart to this woman. Her beauty bewitched everyone at the scene, including Yuan Zhen's father, the emperor, who also fell instantly in love with her. The emperor wrapped this bedraggled beauty up in a blanket and took her back to the palace with him.

Yuan Zhen felt anguished and indignant, but he managed to conceal his melancholy. The tenth of Lunar June was the Ghost Festival, a time when local officials asked to be forgiven for all their sins. That night, Yuan Zhen became so drunk he lost control, and he ended up becoming intimate with the beautiful woman, who was by now his father's concubine.

The misdeed he had not managed to commit in his immortal life was successfully played out in his mortal one.

Despite his misdeed, Yuan Zhen was actually a filial boy, and waking up to the cold light of day the next morning and recalling his night of joyful congress with his own father's concubine, the guilt hit him hard, and he fell seriously ill. It was nine months before he next left his bed. As soon as he got up, he was told that this beautiful woman had borne a son, and realizing that it could be his, his illness returned with twice the force.

The beautiful woman wished to reignite their affair, but Yuan Zhen felt such intense guilt that the fire of love in his chest turned cold. Yuan Zhen woke up to what he had done and ended the relationship.

More than a decade passed. The beautiful woman's son grew up into a man. When the emperor was ill on his deathbed, this son came to see Yuan Zhen and challenged him for the throne. A huge struggle ensued, and Yuan Zhen, who was a very different man from the boy he had once been, killed the beautiful woman's son with his sword. When the beautiful woman heard the news about her son, she hung herself, leaving a note telling Yuan Zhen that the boy he had killed belonged not to the emperor, but to Yuan Zhen himself.

Yuan Zhen thought about slitting his own throat, but he was the last male heir to the dynasty and had no choice but to carry on living. He sat on his throne, his chest filled with an unbearable sadness. He lived with this misery until he was sixty years old and could finally be laid to rest.

The beautiful woman who fell into the lake had clearly been Yuan Zhen's mortal calamity.

I read all the pages of the notebook relating to Yuan Zhen's fate seven or eight times. Everything seemed to have been organized seamlessly, except for the appearance of the giant Peng bird. Did giant Peng birds actually exist in the mortal world?

Ye Hua placed the documents he had already read under a paper-weight and took a leisurely sip of his tea. "The giant Peng bird was borrowed from the Great Buddha of the Western Paradise." He paused, tutted, and sighed. "Si Ming seems to seriously have it in for this boy. My second uncle, Sang Ji, must have built up some bad blood over the years."

I started to tremble. I had not imagined that Si Ming might be one to bear a grudge. Planning a great drama like this had been no mean feat. If I were to crash my way into the middle of it, changing the fate of one of its characters and messing everything up, who was to say he would not start to resent me too?

Ye Hua took the notebook back, glanced over at me, and smiled. "What are you worried about? He still owes me a big favor."

I thought it all through carefully before leaving and reasoned that the simplest way to help Yuan Zhen dodge his calamity would be to persuade him to feign illness on the first day of June and miss the Suyu River trip. No magic would be required then, and if there was any sign of danger, I could just hide.

Even if I did not manage to hide and got a scratch or two, it was not going to be anywhere near as damaging as magic backbite. I took Ye Hua's advice and let him seal off my entire supply of immortal magic.

I dropped down into the mortal world, where I was met by the immortal attendant who Sang Ji had sent down there to watch over Yuan Zhen. If I was to replace her and become Yuan Zhen's second Taoist master, the first thing I needed to do was win over his elderly mother.

The Northern Sea immortal attendant had done a good job of protecting Yuan Zhen and ensuring his safety up to this point. Yuan Zhen's mother really looked up to this first master of his; her words and actions were all incredibly respectful, treating her as if she were indeed some supreme otherworldly being.

This young immortal servant took me over to meet Yuan Zhen's mother. Running her hand up and down a horsetail whisk, she said, "Every banquet must come to an end, and my earthly bond with His Majesty Yuan Zhen has reached the end of the road. I am not one to just leave, however. Luckily a fellow esteemed Taoist master who has been wandering the world recently happened upon our sacred land and has grown to love the place. I have asked her to oversee and protect His Majesty in my place. This master spent hundreds of years of seclusion in her temple. The fact that fate has led her out of her temple and allowed her to meet Yuan Zhen, giving them this opportunity to become mistress and apprentice, is a rare stroke of good luck for His Majesty . . ."

Coming so highly recommended, Yuan Zhen's mother embraced me wholeheartedly and called Yuan Zhen over straightaway and got him to praise me as his new master.

When immortals were reincarnated as mortals, they usually retained an element of their immortal bearing. Yuan Zhen was no exception. Even though he was only eighteen, he already had the elegant and graceful bearing of an immortal.

He bowed down graciously in front of me, and before we had even performed his apprentice ceremony, he was already calling me Master. I looked him up and down and gave a satisfied nod. "You seem to have good immortal foundations. I would be happy to take you on as my apprentice."

Yuan Zhen's mother was overjoyed.

I accompanied Yuan Zhen back to the Eastern Palace, where the eunuchs in charge assigned me to a quiet courtyard. It suddenly dawned on me that I had successfully managed to infiltrate myself into the great drama set up by Si Ming the Star Prince of the Ninth Sky.

I heard a couple of female palace attendants gossiping inside Yuan Zhen's palace the next day. They were talking about how happy the emperor had been yesterday morning when he heard that his son's Taoist nun had finally left. By that afternoon he found out that she had been replaced by another Taoist nun, and he became extremely angry. He spent the whole evening in a foul mood, and this morning he was still seething and had been taking it out on innocent officials.

The emperor's anger was understandable. He had a very weak lineage, and despite working hard to remedy this, Yuan Zhen was still his only son. He wanted his son to help to take an interest in national affairs and contribute to the country, but these Taoist nuns arriving one after another were teaching him how to live like a recluse instead. The emperor was not to know that neither Yuan Zhen's old master nor I was recruiting Yuan Zhen as an apprentice in order to help him cultivate the spiritual energy needed to become an immortal; Yuan Zhen was a fallen immortal after all and had no need for spiritual cultivation practice.

The emperor had no idea about my actual mission and was in no great hurry to meet me. I spent a whole week at the palace without even setting eyes on him.

Yuan Zhen was making very good progress as an apprentice. He seemed to want to make use of me and would turn up every day with a pile of Taoist texts in his arms and pester me with difficult questions. The books on profound theory gave me the biggest headache, and every time we discussed it, it zapped three years off my supply of immortal cultivated energy.

It was still one month until the first of June.

After spending a couple of days with Yuan Zhen, I worked out what I needed to do. Yuan Zhen came across as a modest, cautious, and amiable apprentice, but he had an immature mind and found everything new and exciting. If you told him to head east, he might set off toward the east, but as soon as your back was turned, he would turn around and head west instead. That was how he was about everything.

If I were to deal with his calamity using a direct approach, I would simply urge him not to go on the trip to the Suyu River. He would be certain to ask me why, however, and any reason I used to dissuade him would only end up piquing his curiosity and might well lead him to tag along secretly with them without my knowledge, just to see what would happen. Many of life's joys and sorrows were caused by *seeing what would happen*. The direct approach would not work; I had to rethink things. Yuan Zhen's situation needed to be handled in a more careful and subtle way.

What if when the time came for the beautiful woman fate had chosen to hurt Yuan Zhen to fall into the water, I leaped in to save her first? Oh, but what if there was a shift in fate and she fell in love with me instead? How would that work out? No, it was no good, no good.

What if when the time came, I had gathered together a few other women, and when the beautiful woman showed up, I arranged for them to all to sit with her in the little pleasure boat on the Suyu River? They would be jumping off left, right, and center, and Yuan Zhen would be unable to save the beautiful woman from the pages of the destiny notebook. Oh, but what if Yuan Zhen rescued another woman, but the destiny in the notebook transferred the other woman's fate to this new woman? This too was no good.

I brooded over the matter day and night. I caught my reflection in the mirror and saw that all my fretting had started to make me look old and haggard. I still had no idea what I should do.

Already it was Lunar May.

That evening I was sitting under my lantern, fretting as usual. I pondered this matter until late in the evening, when I decided it was time to get some sleep. I opened my eyes to extinguish the candle, but as I did I saw Ye Hua, who should have been in Qingqiu, strolling over with a cup of tea in his hand and a serious expression on his face.

I hesitated awhile, convinced I must have fallen asleep and started dreaming. He took a sip of tea and gave me a suggestive smile. "I haven't seen you for a long time, Qian Qian, and I've been missing you terribly. Have you been missing me too?"

I gave a jolt and leaped from my chair. He supported his chin in his hand and looked at me with bewilderment. "Have you become crazed with joy? Don't go to bed just yet," he said with a laugh. "I've got something important to tell you. Can you guess which immortal has been reborn as Yuan Zhen's mortal world father?"

I was feeling very tired. "Which immortal has been reborn as his father? Well, it's not your grandfather the old Sky Emperor, that much I know for sure," I said flippantly.

He turned and sat down on the edge of my bed to stop me from lying down. He gave the space next to him a casual pat. I hesitated before sitting down.

He picked up a cup of tea from the table. "Wake yourself up a bit," he said, passing it to me. "No, it's not my grandfather, but you're not far off. It's someone I'm sure you're familiar with."

He had my full attention now.

"It's Emperor Dong Hua," he said slowly.

I snorted the tea out through my nose.

Could Yuan Zhen's mortal life father actually be Emperor Dong Hua? That was a familiar one to me.

My niece Phoenix Nine had held unrequited love for Emperor Dong Hua for over two thousand years. Whenever she was drunk she would whisper on and on to me about Dong Hua this, Dong Hua that. Even now I could bring to mind everything she had told me about him as if it had happened to me personally.

• • •

During the age of primal chaos, Emperor Dong Hua had been over-lord of the sky and earth. Now he was the head of the immortal audience, and although his position in the Sky Clan was beneath that of the Sky Emperor, the Sky Emperor had to consult with him before making his decisions. I had heard that Emperor Dong Hua had gone to the Thirteenth Sky Taichen Palace recently, where he was keeping a low profile, looking after the immortal book of records. All the alluring she-goblins and mortals who had cultivated enough spiritual energy to turn into immortals needed to notify him, and all immortals needed to praise him before they could ascend to the rank of god or goddess.

Emperor Dong Hua was always very calm and detached. He sought and desired nothing and remained blank-faced and indifferent toward others. Father rarely praised anyone, but once I heard him say, "There are so many immortals in the Four Seas and Eight Deserts, but no one has an immortal bearing like Emperor Dong Hua."

When Phoenix Nine was still a little fox cub, she used to be extremely plucky, even before she had fully developed her immortal powers, and she would often run out of Second Brother's cave and scamper around stirring up trouble. Once when she was doing this, a tiger spirit tried to kill her. Just as the spirit was about to pounce, Emperor Dong Hua turned up and he saved her life.

As Phoenix Nine grew older, she developed a deep affection for Dong Hua, which led her to demean herself. For a few hundred years, the poor thing dropped well below her rank and acted as Dong Hua's immortal servant in his Taichen Palace. Dong Hua treated her with indifference, which she found extremely upsetting. It was only a few decades ago that she finally managed to relinquish her affection for him.

I was astonished that Emperor Dong Hua, such a powerful, unyielding, upright man who was unswayed by riches or lust and free from any kind of scandal, had somehow committed such a terrible offense that he had been cast down into the mortal world as a punishment.

Ye Hua leaned back against the bed rail. "Emperor Dong Hua wasn't sent down to the mortal world as a punishment from the Sky Emperor. He went of his own accord!" he said with a laugh. "He wanted to have a proper experience of mortal life. Firsthand understanding of old age, illness, death, sorrow, the bitterness of living with those you hate, the pain of separation from those you love, seeking but not getting, the confusion that comes from greed and desire and all the other ills of humanity. That's why I've come to warn you that while you're changing Yuan Zhen's destiny, you must be careful not to do anything that might change Dong Hua's destiny too."

Ye Hua's words made me feel both elated and afraid. The elation was due to the fact that so much time had passed and so much had been left to chance, and most things in the universe had changed beyond recognition, but Emperor Dong Hua was still as proud, upright, and outstanding an immortal as ever. The fear was whether it would be possible to successfully protect Yuan Zhen through his calamity involving the beautiful woman without affecting the fate of the other party within this destructive love triangle. It was going to be extremely tricky.

There seemed to be a great wind outside, blustering so hard that the window frames creaked. Feeling chilly, I got up to close the window and returned to my bed to find that Ye Hua had taken off his cloak and was shaking out the bed quilt.

I looked at him in shock. He skillfully made the bed before turning to me and asking, "Which side do you normally sleep on, the inside or the outside?"

I looked first at the bed, then at the floor. "I'll just sleep on the floor," I said earnestly.

"If I had bad intentions toward you, it wouldn't matter if you were sleeping on the floor or the bed. I would still get my way," he said airily.

"If you had your magic at your fingertips, we could fight it out together and both end up the worse for wear. But oh, I've sealed off your magic powers, haven't I? From the way you're behaving, Qian Qian, my guess is that you don't trust yourself . . ."

I wiped the sweat from my forehead and generously peeled back the cover. "You've got me all wrong, Prince Ye Hua," I said with a laugh. "I was just worried you'd be uncomfortable sleeping in such a small bed. You choose which side you want. I usually sleep on the outside."

He looked at me and gave a faint smile. "Can I trouble you to blow out the candles in that case?"

With Ye Hua on the inside of the bed and me on the outside, we finally drifted off to sleep.

The courtyard I was staying in was called Purple Bamboo Garden, which contained a thick forest of bamboo, living up to its name. It was cool at this time of year, and this evening particularly so. All we had was one thin quilt between us, which Ye Hua and I were forced to share along with the bed and the pillow. I lay on the edge of the bed with my back to him, my arms and legs outside the cover, getting cold, and without my immortal energy to protect myself, I was soon shivering.

Ye Hua's breathing became long and deep, and it sounded as if he was already asleep. His body smelled faintly of peach blossoms, which was driving me slightly crazy. I wondered when this long night would come to an end.

Ye Hua turned around. I shifted toward the edge of the bed. "Do you want me to sleep with my arms wrapped around you?" Ye Hua asked from behind me. I was too surprised to respond. He turned around without a word, and I reflexively continued to move away from him until I dropped off the edge and landed on the floor with a thump.

He gave a chuckle. "I was just thinking to myself that if I didn't put my arms around you, you might roll off the bed, and sure enough that's exactly what happened!"

"This bed is just too small," I said with frustration.

He reached out to scoop me up off the floor and pushed me to the inside of the bed. "You're right. The bed really is too small," he said sarcastically. "Even though when we're lying flat on our backs, there is enough room between us to sleep three or four people, it really is too small."

I gave a chuckle.

The inside of the bed provided terrain that was easier to attack from than to defend, and I found it even harder to fall asleep. Ye Hua was lying very close to me, and that peach musk of his wafted over, providing worse torment than the Netherworld's eighteenth layer of hell.

Just as I was sighing to myself, Ye Hua leaned over and looked right into my eyes. I looked back at him in astonishment. "I've just remembered something I wanted to ask you," he said calmly. I held my breath. "Qian Qian, do you know the god Si Yin?"

I gave a start and pulled the quilt farther up. "Oh, Mo Yuan from Mount Kunlun's Seventeenth Apprentice. I've heard of him, yes, but I've never met him. After the Demon Clan Revolt seventy thousand years ago, he and Mo Yuan were said to have gone into seclusion together."

Ye Hua gave a sigh. "I'd thought you might know a bit more about him."

"Are you implying I have some hidden secret?" I asked with a yawn.

"The Sky Emperor was still heir to the throne during the time of the Demon Clan Revolt. When I was small he often used to tell me I looked just like Mo Yuan." I nodded to myself in agreement. It wasn't just his face, but his physique too.

"There's nothing about this written in the history books, but according to the Sky Emperor, Mo Yuan was obliterated during the Demon Clan Revolt, turning to dust flying and flames dying," Ye Hua continued. "That means there was absolutely no way he could have gone into seclusion with Si Yin. The old Sky Emperor sent eighteen high-ranking immortals to Mount Kunlun to arrange Mo Yuan's funeral, but Si Yin chased them off with his fan. Soon after, Mount Kunlun's First Apprentice reported the disappearance of both Si Yin's and Mo Yuan's immortal bodies."

I gave a gasp. "Oh, really?" I said feigning surprise. I felt a dull ache in my heart.

He nodded. "There's been no sign of Si Yin for seventy thousand years. But recently I heard that Demon Emperor Li Jing has been searching high and low for this Si Yin. Yesterday one of his servants gave me a portrait of Si Yin, which he said was painted by Li Jing the Demon Emperor."

My heart started hammering.

"Qian Qian, when I saw it, I thought it was you dressed as a boy."

"Well, that's the stupidest thing I've ever heard!" I said in an attempt to sound shocked. "If that's true, that means there are two people walking around the Four Seas and Eight Deserts looking just like me. I'm not familiar with this Si Yin, but Demon Emperor Li Jing's wife is connected with my clan. She's my sister-in-law's youngest sister, and she could almost be my double."

He pondered it for a while. "Is that so?" he said finally. "I'll pay them an official visit if I get the chance in that case."

"Ah, will you now?"

He smiled. "I can almost hear you grinding your teeth! Even if your sister-in-law's little sister does look like you, she almost certainly wouldn't have your charm."

I looked up to the top of the bed curtain and gave some offhand response. His ability to use such obvious flattery without even blushing meant that he must have been very practiced at it. It was admirable, really.

Ye Hua did not say any more about it, and very soon he was asleep. He had a pleasant sleeping manner, not snoring, grinding his teeth, or thrashing his limbs. I stayed awake for a long time, and it was only in the middle of the night that I finally became drowsy enough to nod off. In the hazy space somewhere between sleep and waking, I suddenly recalled an important fact. Just as I was about to consider it further, it drifted out of foggy mind and floated away.

During the night I felt as if a pair of ice-cold hands was gently stroking my eyes.

CHAPTER TEN

Ye Hua was a cruel man.

We were not in Qingqiu, and there was no reason why I should accompany him for his morning walk. I would have been perfectly within my rights to laze around in bed for an extra hour. But no, he insisted on pulling my pitiful form up out of bed.

I was still wearing the same dress as yesterday, which was now completely creased, but I could not be bothered to change. I sat down in the chair, poured myself a cup of cold tea, and covered my mouth to give a yawn.

Ye Hua appeared to be in a very good mood. He slipped his cloak on gracefully and fastened the strap around his waist. He sat down in front of the bronze mirror and said, "Come over and bind my hair."

"Are you talking to me?" I asked in surprise. He picked up a wooden comb. "I heard from Mystic Gorge that you had excellent hair-binding skills."

I was skilled at binding hair, having had much practice over the years. We had rarely had serving girls in the foxhole, and Fourth Brother never learned to bind his own hair, so I always did it for him.

He gave a dazzling smile and handed me the wooden comb. "I have an audience with the Sky Emperor today, and I need to look well-groomed."

Ye Hua had lustrous hair that was soft, black, and glossy, and the wooden comb easily glided through it. Coiling up his hair and piling it onto his head was the trickier part.

There were a jade hairpin and a jade crown on the vanity table. I picked up the pin, and once I had attached it to the hair, I placed the crown on his head. I had not done this for a while, but I had not lost my skill.

I saw Ye Hua smiling at me in the bronze mirror.

I looked him up and down. This hairstyle really did accentuate his immortal good looks. Satisfied, I placed the comb back on the vanity table.

I saw that Ye Hua was still smiling to himself in the mirror. He took hold of my right hand as I was putting down the comb, and in a low voice he said, "In the past you always used to . . ." I could just make out a subtle movement in his eyes, like a ripple in calm water.

Oh dear, I hadn't been bewitched, had I?

I gave a half bow, which, with my left hand still on his shoulder and my right one under his on the vanity table, was not easy to execute. I was not sure what to expect from this sentence of his starting with "In the past . . ."

He slowly released my hand, but did not continue his thought. He just smiled, pulled a slightly decrepit-looking pearl bracelet from his sleeve, and placed it in my hand.

It was obviously a good-luck charm, one that could turn calamities to blessings. He stood up in front of the bronze mirror and gave a reluctant smile. "You should wear this bracelet. You're just like a mortal now, and although you are not going to run into great danger in the mortal world, it's still wise to take precautions."

He was acting a little out of character today, his mood swinging between joyful and anxious. I did not want to aggravate him by saying anything rash, so I agreed.

He nodded and reached out to stroke my face. "I will head to the Sky Palace now in that case." After a moment's silence, he continued, "Last night I was so distracted by the important matter that I completely forgot to tell you something. On the first of Lunar June, at the hour in which fate turns the way it will, if you hold Yuan Zhen back and arrange for someone to push Dong Hua into the water instead, he'll be the one who saves the beautiful girl from drowning. Yuan Zhen will be freed from entanglement without it obstructing Dong Hua's experience of human pain and suffering. Everyone will be happy."

As soon as he had imparted this information, he turned around and was gone.

I thought back over all the things Ye Hua and I had been busy discussing the night before, but not one presented itself as this "important matter" he had just mentioned. I decided to disregard it for the time being and think about what he had said after instead.

He really had come up with an ingenious method. Only someone removed from the situation could view it with such clarity. I had been dithering about for so long now that all I was doing was making myself more confused.

Thinking of a solution to this big concern made me feel as if a huge rock that had been pressing down on my body for weeks had been lifted. I felt weightless and infinitely more relaxed.

I ran my fingers along the leaves of the mimosa plant in the pot on the windowsill, feeling light as a feather. I sat down and drank another cup of tea, still feeling light as a feather. I had only finished half the cup when I suddenly I remembered the thing that had occurred to me as I had been drifting off. It was a really dreadful thought.

According to Mystic Gorge, Phoenix Nine had gone to the mortal world to repay her debt of gratitude. All I knew was that some mortal had done her a favor, which she had gone to the mortal world to repay, an explanation I had accepted without giving it another thought.

Thinking it over more carefully, I realized that in all her thirty thousand years, Phoenix Nine had owed a favor to only one person, and that was Dong Hua. His immortal magic was much more powerful than hers, which made it difficult for her to repay him. Could she have come to the mortal world to find Dong Hua in his reincarnated form and repay the debt that way? It had taken so much for her to make a clean break from her destructive love for Dong Hua. A few days of fussing over him could easily reignite those feelings. For the sake of Second Brother and Second Sister-in-Law I had to act.

I jumped to my feet, changed my clothes, and ran out into the courtyard. I needed to go see Yuan Zhen, the disciple who zapped three years of my spiritual energy each time we met, and ask him whether a young woman had arrived at the palace half a year ago with a phoenix-feather birthmark on her forehead.

Phoenix Nine's mother was from the Red Fox Clan. After she and my brother had married, I was expecting the birth of a mottled little half-red, half-white fox cub.

Instead after three years of pregnancy, she gave birth to an exquisitely adorable little fox cub as red as pigeon blood with one white circle on her ear and four white paws. When she was a year old, she transformed into human form with a phoenix-feather birthmark on her forehead. It was a beautiful birthmark, but it made changing form difficult for her, because whichever human form she took, this birthmark was always visible. Second Brother was rather lazy, and due to this phoenix-feather birthmark and the fact that she was born in August, the ninth month, he gave her the rather unimaginative name Phoenix Nine.

Yuan Zhen had impeccable timing, and before I had even left the courtyard to find him, there he was striding toward me, two scriptures in his hands. His eyes lit up when he saw me. "Master," he greeted with reverence.

Yuan Zhen was an inquisitive boy, and I was not able to just come out and ask about Phoenix Nine. I considered it for a moment before pulling him over to a stone bench and sitting down.

Yuan Zhen gave a cough and said, "What's wrong with your neck, Master? It looks as if . . . as if . . ." My hand flew to my neck, but I felt nothing. He pulled a mirror from his sleeve and handed it to me, and I saw a red mark, as if a mosquito had bitten me. What gall that mosquito had, daring to suck the blood of a goddess!

What luck that mosquito had too. One suck of my blood would provide him with thousands of years of cultivated spiritual energy, enough to transform him into a mosquito spirit probably.

I nodded and sighed in admiration. "You noticed this small, insignificant red mark. And I've heard that you are so kind you won't even tread on an ant. These are extremely good traits."

Yuan Zhen turned red in the face. "What do you mean?" he said, looking at me.

"Well," I said, "in order to stop yourself treading on ants as you walk down the road, you need both a kind heart and a careful mind. A kind heart and a careful mind together make an integral whole."

Yuan Zhen stood up so that he could pay full attention to the information I was relaying. I stroked my chin, and in a wise voice I said, "Taoism gives rise to one being, one being gives rise to two, two beings give rise to three, and three to thousands and thousands of beings. These thousands of beings have originated from nothing, and the process is complicated and delicate. Studying Taoism is a complicated and delicate process too. As your current master, I wish to examine your awareness of the complex and delicate nature of the world."

"Please go ahead, Master," Yuan Zhen said solemnly.

Matching his solemn tone I said, "Before you turned sixteen, you lived in the Taoist temple, and after you turned sixteen, you moved to the imperial palace. It is not my intention to vex you with difficult questions, so I will just ask a couple of things, one about the temple and one about the palace."

Yuan Zhen pricked up his ears.

"In the temple where you lived, there was a nun who always wore white," I said. "This nun had a duster she used a lot. What kind of wood was the duster handle made of?"

He thought about it a long time, but could not recall. It was just a nonsense question I had concocted on the spot, so of course he could not answer it. With feigned composure I continued, "Since you are unable to answer that, I have another question. You must listen carefully and consider what I am asking fully. There's a woman in this imperial palace with a birthmark the shape of a phoenix feather on her forehead. What is her name, her ranking, and in which palace does she live?"

He contemplated it awhile before saying, "Master, your question about the temple has highlighted my ignorance, but your question about the woman with the phoenix-feather birthmark I can answer. It is Honorable Concubine Chen, who lives in Lotus Bud Courtyard. Honorable Concubine Chen never actually used to have this phoenix feather on her forehead, but last December she fell into the lotus pond and was taken seriously ill. Her medicine wasn't working, and for a while it looked like she might not make it. But then suddenly she recovered. Since then she has had this phoenix-feather marking on her forehead. A couple of the other honorable concubines asked a Taoist master to examine the marking, and he claimed that it was a goblin marking. My father, the emperor, didn't believe it, but he's been keeping his distance from her since then anyway."

I was right. Phoenix Nine had come after Dong Hua. I was impressed that this Taoist master could tell it was a goblin marking. Yuan Zhen looked at me anxiously. "It's not easy to cultivate such close attention to detail," I said with a nod. "You have the rare gift of a meticulous and attentive mind, which is the foundation of Taoist practice. But you need to cultivate further attentiveness. You can leave now.

Rest from your scriptures today. Go away and think about your attitude toward Taoist study."

Yuan Zhen wandered off forlornly, his head drooped, a sight that made me feel very bad. Yuan Zhen did not need to be any more attentive than he was already. I watched him stumble off and then called over a serving girl and asked her to lead me to Honorable Concubine Chen's Lotus Bud Courtyard.

As Phoenix Nine's Qingqiu family, we appreciated that she owed Dong Hua this favor, and as her aunts and uncles, we saw it as our debt too. Nevertheless, today I was going to try my best to convince Phoenix Nine to go back to Qingqiu.

The courtyard I was staying in was a prestigious one, as it was not far from the emperor's back palace.

I had rushed straight there without thinking to write a note announcing my visit, but seeing a servant girl on duty in the main courtyard, I reported my visit to her instead. Not long after, a waiting girl led me inside.

There was a pavilion inside where a round-faced girl was feeding fish. Apart from the phoenix-feather shape on her forehead she was unremarkable in her appearance. This was Phoenix Nine in her mortal form. I gave a sigh. Phoenix Nine, the Bai Clan's only granddaughter, had been such a free spirit. It was distressing to see her in such a desolate place, demeaning herself by feeding Dong Hua's fish.

She heard my sigh and looked up from the fish.

"Phoenix Nine, your Aunt Bai has come to see you," I said, my voice filled with disappointment and frustration.

She had been in the mortal world on her own for half a year now and had obviously been feeling very cut off and lonely. Hearing me call her name, she felt overcome with sorrow and rushed toward my arms.

I opened them wide for her.

Squealing, she rushed straight past me and to the serving girl who had led me in, and it was this girl who received her crushing hug. I was not sure whether to continue to hold my arms open or not.

Her whole face was contorted in panic. She was crying and desperately shaking her head, saying, "No, Aunt Bai, don't take me back with you. I love him and I can't be without him. No one can keep us apart, no one!"

I was so shocked by her reaction that I took a step back. This could not be the little red fox from our clan, surely? Phoenix Nine could be a silly girl at times, but she was always composed and had never been known to cry and fuss in this way. Even when she felt upset by her feelings for Dong Hua, she rarely let it show, choosing to drown her sorrows in Zhe Yan's wine instead.

Seeing her in front of me now, clinging to her serving girl and wailing to high heaven, I felt so shocked I could not speak. All I could do was shake my head.

Seeing me shake my head only made her cry harder. "A-aunt Bai . . . please have mercy. Please don't stand in my way! I'll do anything you ask, but please don't stand in the way of what I've come here to do!"

The serving girl in her arms was trembling like a leaf in the wind. I felt the corners of my mouth twitching. Phoenix Nine suddenly squatted down, clutching at the front of her robe. Her serving girl leaped up into the air as if she had been stung and ran off yelling, "My mistress is vomiting up blood again! You, quickly go and tell the emperor! You, hurry and fetch a handkerchief! You, rush and fetch a washbasin . . ."

I covered my mouth to give a cough. "Come on, calm down. If you carry on vomiting blood, you'll choke. I'll leave you now if that will make you feel better. See, I am going now."

I found the serving girl who had led me here standing at the side of the courtyard with her mouth agape, and we both took our hasty leave.

• • •

The whole way back to Purple Bamboo Garden, I thought about how unlike Phoenix Nine Honorable Concubine Chen's emotional behavior had been. But she did have that phoenix-feather marking on her forehead, and she had recognized me as her aunt straightaway. As an immortal, all Phoenix Nine needed was to borrow a mortal body to live in the mortal world; she should not be affected by the emotions of the mortal whose body it had been. *It seemed almost as if . . . No, but it couldn't be . . .* I stroked my forehead as I thought. *She wouldn't have used the two lives incantation on herself, would she? Not when it was forbidden in Qingqiu.*

There was nothing inherently wicked about the two lives incantation, all it did was allow you to change your personality for a certain amount of time. Sometimes young immortals doing business in the marketplace in Qingqiu performed the two lives incantation on themselves.

Under its spell, it would not matter how many difficult customers they had to deal with; all they would have for them was looks of heartfelt sincerity and smiles as splendid as chrysanthemums. There were never any unpleasant exchanges or fights. But it was obviously not an honest magic, and it violated the immortal code of conduct. Later Fourth Brother and I agreed to forbid it.

But why would Phoenix Nine have performed this incantation on herself? I spent a long time trying to work it out, but it failed to make any sense. I took a nap that afternoon, planning to return to Lotus Bud Courtyard in the evening.

Phoenix Nine was considerate enough to save me the journey.

I had a table set up in the back courtyard and was sitting out there eating dinner on my own. There were few stars, and the moon was bright, and with such a thick growth of bamboo, it felt like being in a lush forest. I had been enjoying my meal in these picturesque surroundings when all of a sudden she appeared on the courtyard wall, covered in bramble branches. She jumped over, landing on my dining table, and all the crockery smashed to the floor. I quickly leaped out the way, rescuing my cup.

She climbed up miserably from under the table and straightened the crooked bramble branches on her body. She knelt down in front of me in a great show of etiquette. "Aunt Bai, your unworthy niece has brought you brambles as a sign of penance. I know that I have done wrong, and I am very sorry."

I wiped a couple of drops of oil from my sleeve. She had left Honorable Concubine Chen's body and for the time being was back to her usual appearance, which was much easier on the eyes. "It appears that you've performed the two lives incantation on yourself," I said. Her face went red. She gave an admiring sigh and told me how wise I was.

I wanted to help her up to her feet, but when I saw all the oil on her body glistening in the moonlight, I changed my mind and just lifted a hand, instructing her to rise while I went over to the stone bench to sit down.

I took a sip of tea from the teacup I had rescued. "I can understand why you've come here to repay Dong Hua's debt of kindness, but why did you need to perform the forbidden two lives incantation on yourself?" I asked with a frown.

Phoenix Nine's mouth immediately opened out into a wide circle. "Aunt Bai, how do you know that I've come to repay my debt to Emperor Dong Hua? Si Ming the Star Prince said that Emperor Dong Hua's mortal reincarnation was top secret, and only a few people in the whole of the Four Seas and Eight Deserts knew."

I took a leisurely sip of tea and remained silent, trying to look mysterious. She started to tremble violently. "Aunt Bai, all this concern and interest in Dong Hua, you haven't fallen in love with him, have you?" She wrung her hands in sorrow. "Emperor Dong Hua is more attractive than the Northern Sea Emperor, his magic is more sophisticated, and he is a more suitable age for you, but you must know, Dong Hua's heart is made of stone. If you've fallen in love with him, you have a very bleak future ahead."

I looked up at the moon. "Fourth Brother will be back from the Western Mountains soon," I said casually. "He was the one to forbid the two lives incantation. One unthinking Qingqiu immortal thought the ban was just for show and continued to use the incantation regardless, and Fourth Brother ended up banishing him from our kingdom."

Phoenix Nine jumped straight up from the stone bench, and supporting herself on the bundle of bramble branches, she cupped her hands together and bowed down toward me with reverence.

"When I was a serving girl in Dong Hua's residence, I did a favor for Si Ming the Star Prince. Si Ming was very grateful to me, and when he discovered that Dong Hua wished to be reborn as a mortal, he arranged for an immortal disciple to let me know as a way to repay his favor. I have been feeling so unworthy. Dong Hua saved my life so long ago, and I still haven't repaid him. When I found out he had asked to be reincarnated as a mortal, I knew it was my chance to repay him. I entered his dream when he was fourteen in his mortal form and asked him whether he had any unfulfilled wishes or desires."

"And what did stone-hearted Dong Hua say to that?" I interjected. "It couldn't have been that he wished neither for riches, honor, nor land, just to find someone to love?"

"Aunt Bai, how *are* you so wise?" Phoenix Nine asked in astonishment. I snorted my tea out of my nose. Could Dong Hua have really become so . . . so trite? Phoenix Nine dabbed away the tea I had sprayed onto her face and continued bashfully. "During his mortal life, the emperor has experienced some very fickle women. So in the dream he asked me to pair him up with someone who would love him wholeheartedly and never leave or abandon him."

"So you decided to match him up with yourself?" I mused.

Phoenix Nine gave a nod and then shook her head. "Matching him with me would be meaningless. Si Ming the Star Prince went through

Dong Hua's destiny for this life. He is not fated to meet a woman who will truly love him. Instead, on the first of Lunar June, at age thirty-seven, he will meet the girl of his dreams at the Vedic Dharma Festival. Sadly this girl will fall in love with his son, Prince Yuan Zhen. I may have come to repay my debt to Dong Hua, but I can't rewrite his fate in the process. As it happened, half a year ago, one of his honorable concubines reached the end of her predestined life. After thinking about it long and hard, I decided to borrow her body and offer him true love. Before the emperor's love calamity befell him, I wanted to fulfill his desire by giving him a brief taste of how it feels to be truly loved. By the time the woman he is destined to fall in love with appears, I would have accomplished my mission and would be free to go, not having altered his fate in any way."

I lowered my head and sighed. "Have you not been tormented enough by that man? Have you not suffered enough heartbreak? Now he wishes to find someone to fall in love with! If he'd had this desire when he was an immortal, with your infatuation you'd have fully repaid your debt by now."

"You're right, Aunt Bai," Phoenix Nine said in dismay. "At first I thought that I'd found a way. I was infatuated by the emperor for over two thousand years, and even though I eventually fell out of love with him, I didn't think it would be hard to rekindle some of that former feeling. But how enigmatic true love is. It can't just be brought out on demand. I spent a long time preparing myself, but when I borrowed Honorable Concubine Chen's body and went to see the emperor, I didn't feel even a glimmer of affection for him. I couldn't even find it in myself to say a few kind words. I felt awful to have let him down."

"Dying embers are hard to reignite, and past loves hard to rekindle," I comforted. "You mustn't blame yourself."

"But I have made this journey down to the mortal world now," she said, sounding grave. "I have incurred a large debt to the keeper of the Netherworld for keeping Honorable Concubine Chen's body fresh for me and stop it from rotting. Giving up without having repaid my favor to Dong Hua would be like suffering a double loss. I thought about it long and hard for a couple of days . . ." She paused. "And I decided I had no choice but to perform the two lives incantation on myself. I spend the days bound by this magic, acting in accordance with Honorable Concubine Chen's former personality, which allows me to adore the emperor. It is only after the sun has set that I am released and return to my old self.

"I had no idea what Honorable Concubine Chen had been like when she was alive. Each night when I recall what happened during the day, I feel extremely anguished and ashamed."

"You mustn't brood over this and feel ashamed," I told her against my better judgment. Suddenly I thought of something important. "You haven't taken advantage of Dong Hua since turning into Noblewoman Chen, have you?"

She looked shocked. "Honorable Concubine Chen wasn't very favored at the best of times. After I took over her body, this birthmark appeared on her forehead, and that bastard Taoist master told them all that it was a goblin marking. Although the emperor didn't leave me completely out in the cold, he hasn't come to Lotus Bud Court to visit me since then either."

"Well, what's the point of acting like you're so in love with him then?" I asked in surprise.

"Truly loving someone requires absolute dedication. I can't simply love him when I see him and stop loving him when we're apart."

I yawned. Seeing Phoenix Nine back to her usual calm self made me start to feel a whole lot better. If she could repay her debt smoothly and without a hitch, her uncles and I could stop worrying about her. It was all going to be fine. I thought it through carefully and was just about to tell Phoenix Nine to go back to her palace, clean off all the oil, and get ready for bed when an immortal wind started to bluster and propitious vapors to appear.

Zhe Yan suddenly appeared in midair, looking rather worn-out, which was rare to see. He could not have angered Fourth Brother again, could he? I drained my tea without batting an eyelid. Sure enough the first thing he said was, "Young lady, has your fourth brother come to see you recently?"

I shook my head. "Isn't he still in the Western Mountains, looking for Bi Fang?" I asked.

"He's been back a few days now," Zhe Yan said with an awkward smile. He put a hand to his forehead. "Bi Fang really was feisty and hard to tame."

He was just about to go off when he thought of something else. He turned to me and said, "There's something I forgot to tell you. The day after you went to the Eastern Sea banquet, the Sky Emperor's grandson, Ye Hua, came to the peach grove, looking for you. He was asking about something you'd done three hundred years ago."

"Oh?" I said in astonishment.

"I told him that five hundred years ago you were taken seriously ill and slept for two hundred years straight," he said with a frown. "He left after that without asking anything else. Young lady, you haven't had another marriage engagement fall through, have you?"

That hard-fought battle I had waged against Qing Cang was naturally not something that could be shared with outsiders. Qingqiu had not been enemies with Qing Cang, and as a Qingqiu goddess, I had no justification to attack him. I muttered to myself for a while before saying, "No, I don't think so. I haven't seen any sign that Ye Hua might want to call off our engagement."

"Well, that's good," he said with a nod. Then he leaned toward Phoenix Nine and said, "Fourth Brother really misses your cooking. Please come to the peach grove when you are free."

"I'm too busy," Phoenix Nine said, shaking her head.

Zhe Yan looked at her and said, "Your two lives incantation worked very well," before disappearing.

"Aunt Bai, he's threatening me," Phoenix Nine said, looking very upset.

It would be difficult to find anyone in the mortal world who was both able and willing to push the emperor into the water in front of a crowd. Everything was set to help Yuan Zhen pass his calamity. I was just missing this critical component: someone to push the emperor.

I had thought Phoenix Nine might be the right person to take on this huge burden. She thought it through very carefully before saying, "Being bound by the two lives incantation, I forget who I really am during the day. I think that I have always been Honorable Concubine Chen and have her personality. I spend my days adoring the emperor so much all I can do is cry and vomit up blood.

"Bound by this magic, there is no way I would be able to push the emperor into the water. In fact, the way Honorable Concubine Chen is, you should be praying that she doesn't ruin your plan by stopping whoever you find to push him."

What she was saying made complete sense, and I did not force the issue. If I could not find anyone else, I would have to be the one to push him. But the emperor had never been fond of Taoists, and I was not sure if I would even be allowed onto the same boat with him.

Luckily, Yuan Zhen had a mother who doted on him with heart and soul, and not just his mortal mother in the temple. Although the one in the temple worried about him, most of her heart was devoted to questions of immortality, and mundane earthly matters were often overlooked. The mother who doted on him and also concerned herself with these mundane earthly matters was his immortal mother, Shao Xin.

Shao Xin had come down to the mortal world to see how Yuan Zhen was and how preparations were going to help him through his impending calamity. When I saw her, I asked her to take on the monumental responsibility of pushing the emperor overboard.

My idea was a logical one. When the time came, she could use immortal magic to make herself invisible. When the predestined beautiful woman appeared and everybody was focused on her, Shao Xin could stand behind the emperor and give him a light shove, toppling him over into the water. But there was a hitch to this plan too. She would be using immortal magic to change Yuan Zhen's destiny, and since Shao Xin was pregnant, it would not be right to ask this of her. If she did suffer her own magic backbite, it was likely to impact her unborn baby.

My eyes dropped to Shao Xin's bulging belly, and I muttered, "It would be dangerous for you to take this on. We need someone sturdier."

After thinking it through, Shao Xin suggested getting her husband, Sang Ji, to do the dirty deed.

CHAPTER ELEVEN

A few days later, it was the first of June.

The information in the destiny notebook was correct: the emperor did take all his officials and a crowd of concubines and nobles for a dragon boat trip on the Suyu River. Despite the fact that I was his son's master, the emperor did not hold me in high regard, and I had not been ranked highly within the imperial palace. Some officials from the Department of Rites were more insightful, and realizing that I was a supreme being, they ensured that I was among the officials in the dragon boat. I found myself positioned next to a couple of eighth-level advisers, but from here all I could see of the emperor was the back of his head. Three feet away from the emperor's head, I could see the back of another head, which looked rather like Honorable Concubine Chen's.

Mao the Sun Prince was doing himself proud, and on the day of Yuan Zhen's and Emperor Dong Hua's predestined calamities, the sun was shining and the air was sizzling hot. There were a couple of clouds floating in the sky, but they were wispy and looked as if they might just evaporate away from the heat.

The Suyu River was not very wide, and the emperor's sizable dragon boat took up almost half its width. Both sides of the river were crowded with the emperor's subjects, who must have started arriving at dawn to find good spots to watch from. The dragon boat was not going to be traveling down a very long section of the river, and there were far too many people to fit on the banks, which meant that some had climbed up trees or onto nearby houses instead.

The officials rowing the boat were having a tricky time, as they had to ensure that they steered the boat right down the center of the river. If it deviated an inch in either direction, it would look as if the emperor were favoring the citizens from that side of the bank over those on the other. Rowing with such precision meant that the boat moved along at an almost unperceivable pace.

The people sitting in the boat were so hot under the bright sun that their thighs had started shaking.

It was almost noon. I stuffed two pieces of gold leaf into the hands of a young court eunuch working at the back of the boat and asked him to bring Prince Yuan Zhen over. This eunuch was swift and agile. I closed my eyes for a couple of seconds, and by the time I opened them again, I saw Yuan Zhen bounding over.

He was wearing a sky-blue embroidered robe, and his face had a handsome, youthful glow. When he saw me, he raised an eyebrow and his eyes sparkled. "Master, what is so urgent that you have to call me over at this moment?" he asked and gave me a charming and delicate smile.

I had thought of a way to deal with his inquisitiveness. I was quiet a moment, building up the suspense before gathering up my sleeves. "A flickering Taoist light has just shone through my chest and illuminated many profound things that normally remain in the dark," I explained in a wise voice. "I remembered with fondness how dedicated you are to Taoist practice, and since I have arrived at this truth, I wish to share it with you. Would you like to hear it?"

Yuan Zhen cupped his hands together and bowed. He stood with his head lowered, waiting to hear what I had to say. I cleared my throat to make myself sound more commanding. Despite napping through Mo Yuan's classes for all those thousands of years, much must still have managed to seep through, because providing a mortal with an hour-long lecture on Taoist practice posed me no problem whatsoever.

I lectured Yuan Zhen on Taoism while waiting for the beautiful woman from Si Ming the Star Prince's destiny notebook to appear. It was almost midday, and I was feeling apprehensive.

I was getting toward the end of my lecture when Yuan Zhen, who had been looking as if he wanted to say something for a while now, finally cut in. "Master, you've repeated the part about dual person Taoist practice, cultivation of qi, and harmonization of the soul four times now," he said.

"Of course I've repeated that part four times!" I said in false exasperation. "I've done so for good reason. You need to consider the significance of the number four. You also need to consider the significance of this aspect of Taoist practice and the reason your master went to the trouble of explaining it four times. Considering the significance of various factors is an integral part of studying Taoist practice. If you don't understand your master's efforts, you are going to have a very hard time cultivating spiritual practice."

Yuan Zhen buried his head in his hands.

He had interrupted me mid flow, and I tried to remember which part I had repeated four times. I decided to just continue talking about dual person Taoist practice, cultivation of qi, and harmonization of the soul.

I went on and on, speaking until my mouth and tongue turned dry and I had to gulp down two large pots of tea. Finally the beautiful woman from Si Ming the Star Prince's destiny notebook appeared.

I did not get to see her from my position at the back of the boat. Even craning my neck, all I could see were the backs of a lot of heads.

I knew that she had arrived, however, because hovering above us I could see the giant golden-winged Peng bird, the creature that Si Ming the Star Prince had gone to the trouble of borrowing from the Great Buddha of the Western Paradise.

In all my years, I had never seen an emperor dive into the water to save a beautiful woman. Any moment now I would have the chance to enjoy this rare spectacle, and the prospect gave me a blood rush. To keep Yuan Zhen reined in, I needed to remain calm, however difficult this sounded.

People on both sides of the river suddenly stopped their whooping and cheering, and a wave of silence moved up the boat. I scanned the sky for the giant golden-winged Peng bird, but it was still just a small dot in the sky, and it could not have been the bird that silenced the crowd.

It must have been catching sight of the beautiful woman that had rendered them speechless.

Yuan Zhen was still deeply immersed in the expansive realm of Taoist philosophy and had not even noticed the spectacle unfolding around him. I felt comforted by this and continued to talk on the subject, while taking the odd surreptitious glance up at the giant golden-winged Peng bird, which was now swooping toward us.

The Great Buddha's giant Peng bird was extremely powerful, and each flap of its wings could send it soaring three thousand miles. Today it was disguised as a mortal bird and was unable to fly with as much force and vigor as it was used to. It kept its wings retracted as it flew slowly through the sky. It had probably never felt so pathetic flying before, and hung its head and looked despondent.

I watched the tormented Peng bird floating through the sky until it was right above the Suyu River. It circled gently through the air before extending its wings and diving down, before soaring slowly back up again, all its movements extremely gentle. I could not imagine that it had ever flown with such delicate grace.

But its movements obviously did not look so gentle from the perspective of the mortals watching from below, and they began to shriek with a terror that filled my ears with a constant roar. One old adviser next to me pointed a shaky finger and said, "I didn't know giant Peng birds actually existed, let alone such fierce ones flying as fast as this."

Yuan Zhen was still fully absorbed in the wonders of Taoism and lost to the outside world. The beautiful woman ought to have fallen in the water by now. I sat there calmly, waiting for the splash that would signal Sang Ji to push the emperor into the water from the front of the boat.

Finally I heard it and nodded to myself in satisfaction. Sang Ji had succeeded in pushing Dong Hua into the water. Excellent.

I was still nodding to myself when I heard Honorable Concubine Chen shouting, "The emperor can't swim! Oh, goodness gracious . . . he can't swim!" This was followed closely by another splash and another. Splash after splash after splash.

I stared in dumbstruck horror. Oh my. Despite planning everything so meticulously, we had not given a moment's consideration to whether Dong Hua in his mortal form might actually be able to swim. Who was going to dive into the water and rescue the beautiful woman now? I scrambled toward the front of the boat. Honorable Concubine Chen's roaring had snapped Yuan Zhen from his reverie, and he dashed in front of me in a panic.

There had been so many flaws in the carrying out of our plan already, but it was still vital to stop Yuan Zhen from jumping into the water. Dong Hua's fate may have been altered, but the very least we could do was make sure that Yuan Zhen's was altered along with it. Finding a moment's clarity within all this chaos, I rolled up my sleeves and grabbed Yuan Zhen by the arm.

As he was racing toward the front of the boat, Yuan Zhen turned and gave me a serious look before continuing to sprint on ahead. Everyone cleared the way for the heir to the throne, and we were soon at the front. We squeezed past the thick crowd and found ourselves standing behind the mast column.

I looked down past the column to see a very strange scene. A number of brightly dressed officials of all ranks were bobbing around in the Suyu River. Those that could not swim were choking on water and yelling to be saved while those who could were swimming back and forth, dipping their heads in the water, swimming a bit farther and shouting "Emperor!" When they came across a colleague who had leaped into the water without being able to swim, they would grab them, and together they would swim back and forth in search of the emperor.

The sheer volume of people in the river was making the search for the emperor more difficult. Standing inside the boat gave me a panoramic view out over the river, and I saw that while all his officials were swimming up and down in a desperate search for him, the emperor was actually being held firmly in Honorable Concubine Chen's slender arms as she swam her exhausted way toward the dragon boat.

After Sang Ji had pushed the emperor into the water, Honorable Concubine Chen must have alerted the crowds with her shouts of "His Highness can't swim!" and the emperor's eunuchs had displayed their undivided loyalty by diving into the water to save him.

Some of them could not even swim, but stirred up by the eager crowds, they had pulled up their sleeves, gritting their teeth, and jumped in as well. Those who had not lost their minds to blind panic worried about how it might look if they were the only ones who did not jump in, so in the end they felt compelled to do so too.

The emperor's bodyguards were all able swimmers and could have easily rescued the emperor. But there were now so many people floundering around half drowning and in need of saving, all of them pillars of the country, and their workload was increased to no end.

Honorable Concubine Chen had already dragged the emperor up onto the boat while his bodyguards were still busy swimming around rescuing these floundering officials. There was so much chaos that no one paid any attention to the beautiful woman from the destiny notebook who had also fallen into the water.

Yuan Zhen's only concern was the fate of his father, and he remained completely oblivious to the beautiful woman. He had been about to throw himself off the boat to rescue the emperor, but fortunately a couple of old eunuchs were on hand to hold him back. The emperor was in no state to help and was clearly of no use to the beautiful woman.

I was momentarily distracted, but when I looked back to the woman, I saw her paddling to the bank, tears streaming down her face. The emperor was half drowned and in a very sorry state.

Honorable Concubine Chen had been the only concubine to jump into the water after the emperor and had singlehandedly managed to save his life, which had automatically elevated her status. Aware of what had happened, the empress made all the other wailing concubines stand to the side and allowed only Chen to be near. Chen wailed to high heaven and bashed her head against the boat. "Wake up, Your Highness, wake up!" she cried. "You can't leave your eunuch and concubine servants!"

Soon she was grasping at her throat and vomiting up blood again. She yelled a while and then vomited up some blood, yelled a bit more, vomited a bit more. There were a couple of worldly old imperial doctors among the attendees, who rushed over and dragged Honorable Concubine Chen away from the emperor. They approached their patients, hands trembling as they opened their medicine cases and inspected them before giving their diagnoses.

The outing was abandoned. The dragon boat could finally be rowed like a normal boat, the officials in charge no longer constrained by precision steering. Under the heir to the throne's command, they held their heads up high, shook open the flag, and traveled full speed ahead, all the way back to the imperial palace.

I beckoned to the young eunuch I had bribed earlier and asked him for a jug of water. Yuan Zhen had successfully avoided his predestined calamity, but Dong Hua and the beautiful woman had missed each other completely.

I knew of Dong Hua's position as head of the immortal audience and all the cumbersome matters he had to deal with. It could not have been easy for him to find the time to be reborn as a mortal, and I felt terrible for having destroyed his predestined love calamity so completely and utterly.

I wiped the sweat from my forehead and took a sip of water. I had made a pig's ear of things while dealing with this Yuan Zhen matter, but at least I had achieved what I had set out to do. I counted on my fingers how many days I had spent in the mortal world, thinking to myself that the mortal world was no more interesting than before.

I decided that tomorrow I would go with Yuan Zhen to the temple behind the imperial palace and bid farewell to his mother. And that would be that. I would be free to return to Qingqiu. The only problem was that my magic had been sealed off, and I was not sure how I was actually going to get myself back to Qingqiu.

Phoenix Nine had told me that after today's Vedic Dharma Festival when Dong Hua had met the girl of his dreams, she would be free to leave. Dong Hua's fate had been altered, but it had not been Phoenix Nine's fault. Besides, she had risked her life to save his life, and by so doing had completely repaid her debt to him. As soon as the sun had set over the mountains, I would go and find Phoenix Nine, and tomorrow we could both return to Qingqiu together.

I went back to the Purple Bamboo Garden to take a rest.

By the time my serving girl gently shook me awake, it was already pitch-black outside. I ate a few leisurely bites of food and asked her to bring out a lantern to carry as she accompanied me to the Lotus Bud Courtyard.

It was hard enough for me to find my way around the imperial palace by daylight, but at night when all the palace lamps were shining and the whole place was filled with a hazy yellow glow, someone like me who had been there for less than two months found it impossible to tell one palace hall from another. My serving girl carried the lantern, pushing back flowers and parting willows as we walked along, completely familiar with the route. I followed her in silence, full of admiration for her sense of direction.

As we were passing a garden pavilion, Yuan Zhen suddenly intercepted us. The serving girl gave a curtsy and uttered a respectful, "Your Majesty."

Yuan Zhen drew his hands up into his sleeves and accepted her praise with modesty. He glanced at me. "Master, I have a matter I would like to discuss with you," he said in a stilted voice. "Would you please join me in the pavilion to talk for a moment?"

I went over, noticing that he was looking slightly timid. I gave an involuntary shudder. I had left him looking after his father that afternoon. But his appearance concerned me. Could destiny have found another way of tangling his fate up with that of the beautiful woman? If so, Si Ming the Star Prince and his destiny notebook really were a force to be reckoned with. Yuan Zhen led me to the pavilion and sat down.

A refreshing evening breeze was blowing from across the lake. I looked at the expression of yearning on his face and sat down on the stone bench in silence.

For a while he simply sat there with a silly grin on his face. Then he reached into his sleeve and carefully removed something and held it out to show me. "Look, Master, isn't it adorable?" I glanced at his hand and did a double take. I gave a sorrowful sigh. *Yuan Zhen, oh, Yuan Zhen, you troublesome fellow. Do you have any idea what you have in your hand?*

Obviously not. Beaming with joy he said, "At noon when the boat was nearing the shore, I took up the back of the procession to order the officials. And that's when Little Darling here dropped down from the sky. Oh, it wasn't as small then. When it opens up its wings, it's half the size of a house, and so powerful. It was going to land on me, but it's such a thoughtful little darling that it was afraid of hurting me, so it retracted its wings until it was this size before hurtling into my arms."

The *little darling* nestling in Yuan Zhen's arms was the giant Peng bird from the Great Buddha of the Western Paradise, only now it was no bigger than a magpie. It may have managed to shrink itself, but it had not managed to extinguish the golden light emanating from its body.

Within the midst of this golden light, the bird hung its head, looking despondent. When it heard itself being referred to as *Little Darling*, it closed its eyes and trembled. I took a closer look and saw that both its legs were tied with immortal lock bells. They were used in the Ninth Sky to trap spirit birds and animals. No wonder this golden-winged Peng bird had not been able to return to its original form. At this size it was as vulnerable as a piece of meat on the chopping block and completely at the mercy of others.

I had been concerned when I saw the giant golden-winged Peng bird floating through the sky at noon. It had been flying with such restraint that I worried it might strain a tendon. My fear must have been realized. Why else would it have hurtled into Yuan Zhen's arms like that?

While looking at the bells on the giant Peng bird's legs I must have gone into a trance. "My former master gave these to me," Yuan Zhen explained, snapping my attention back. "When I was twelve or thirteen, there was a she-lion spirit who lived behind our temple, and she used to go on and on about wanting to be our steed. Sometime later, she was abducted by a male lion spirit from the next mountain, and the bells have been sitting here ever since. But now Little Darling can use them."

Little Darling trembled again.

"Ah," I said, nodding. "You've obviously thought a lot about this, but have you considered that the creature you have in your hand . . . has an owner? If you decide to keep it, you might find yourself in trouble when its actual owner comes looking for it."

He frowned. "That's why I wanted to discuss it with you, Master," he said, a hint of reproach in his voice. "I know that you are a supreme being, so I hoped you would be able to help me. Little Darling is a spirit bird, and its owner is clearly not a mortal. I'm just an ordinary mortal with a limited lifespan. When I die and my body returns to the soil, Little Darling can naturally be returned to its real owner."

I looked at Little Darling, which was desperately shaking its head. Because it was in bird form, its neck was not as flexible as a human neck, and when its head moved, its whole body moved too. Yuan Zhen held Little Darling in front of me, saying, "Mistress, see how excited Little Darling became when he heard I wanted to keep him!"

Little Darling collapsed in a heap, playing dead. Yuan Zhen looked at me with a mixture of hope and sorrow. My heart felt hot. I considered what he had just said and realized it had been a reasonable request. I had destroyed Yuan Zhen's predestined love match, which was bound to make the next half of his life fairly dull. To raise a beloved spirit bird and keep it by his side was sure to bring him comfort and help him while away the years. And despite the fact that he called me Master, I had never given him an apprentice ceremony, which was not good form on my part.

I was certain that if I were to go to the Great Buddha of the Western Paradise to explain the situation and ask if he would not mind lending his golden-winged Peng bird out for a little while longer, he was certain to be acquiescent.

I gave a considered nod and said, "I agree." Little Darling let out an unhappy caw. Yuan Zhen tucked Little Darling back into his sleeve and grabbed my hand with joyful excitement. "Are you really saying yes, Master? I'm not dreaming, am I? I thought I was being delusional just asking. I never thought that you would actually agree . . ."

He would have continued talking, but at that moment a familiar voice resounded through the sky. "What are you two doing?" it asked. I looked up in surprise to find Ye Hua, who I had not seen in over a month, standing in midair, backlit by the cold, clear moonlight, his face impassive and his eyes shining as he watched Yuan Zhen and me. Behind him stood another immortal wearing a sapphire-blue tunic, a half smile on his kindly looking face.

For over a month, apart from Phoenix Nine, the only faces I had seen were those of strangers. Seeing a familiar face, and the one of the very person I knew could release my sealed-off magic, I became very excited.

In the play scripts I read in my spare time, old friends who reunited usually took each other by the hand and dragged each other off to a bar to share a drink and lament about how long it had been. That was what reunions between old friends should be like.

Ye Hua and I had not been apart for long, but it had been an absence. Yet here he was, standing in midair, without even a proper greeting to offer me. I was not very impressed.

Yuan Zhen took hold of my hand, trembling slightly. I gave him a reassuring look and turned to the two immortals standing in midair surrounded by steaming propitious vapors. "Come down from the sky, you two," I reprimanded. "The moon shines tonight, and the wind is strong. You are in the presence of a mortal who can't appreciate your immortal airs and grace. It isn't fair to scare him like this."

I spoke with authority, and the immortal in the sapphire-blue tunic cupped his hands together and bowed to me before stepping down from his cloud. Ye Hua looked Yuan Zhen up and down and stepped off his cloud too.

It turned out that Yuan Zhen really was one of those mortals unable to appreciate immortal presence. He had already had one big scare today. I was just about to call the serving girl with the lantern, who was still waiting by the path, and ask her to take him off to lie down, but when I looked up, I saw that she was on the ground, her lantern toppled onto its side. Apparently she was not one who was able to appreciate Ye Hua and his companion's immortal presence either.

Yuan Zhen's hands were shaking more severely now. I gave a sigh. My first ever apprentice and he went weak at the knees at the mere sight of an immortal. I thought that gently stroking his hair might comfort him.

I was about to reach out my hand but gave a jolt when I saw how red and shiny his face had become. His cheeks were as red as the yolk of a salted duck egg. Staring at me through sparkling eyes, he said, "M-M-M-Master, I've seen an im-m-m-mortal. I-I-I've seen my first immortal . . ."

I retracted my hand in silence. He dashed joyfully over to Ye Hua, gave a humble bow, and said, "In ancient times, Xuan Yuan the Yellow Emperor practiced the cultivation of spiritual energy and built up virtuous karma. He reformed the military, researched meteorology, planted corn and grain, appeased the people, and divided the land into square plots, and by so doing, he attracted the attention of the phoenix that flew about the rafters. Has news of my father the emperor's benevolence and impeccable behavior reached the sky and the gods too? Is that why you two immortal princes have arrived here in the middle of the night?"

I gave a quiet sigh, followed by another. Oh, little one, no, it was not news of your father's benevolence and impeccable behavior that reached the sky and the gods. It was news of the love calamities you and your father were destined for.

Ye Hua looked Yuan Zhen up and down, a faint smile on his lips. He glanced at me and said, "I'm sorry to disappoint you, but this trip to the mortal world is a personal one. I'm here to visit my wife."

Yuan Zhen looked at Ye Hua and then followed the line of his eyes to me. He scratched his head in bewilderment. I smiled shyly at Yuan Zhen. "He's come here to see me," I explained.

Yuan Zhen looked at me in astonishment. Ye Hua tilted his head, admiring the dark surface of the lake outside the pavilion. My destiny with Yuan Zhen had come to an end, I realized. Tomorrow I could leave.

Ye Hua had arrived at just the right time. Immortal destiny had allowed them to run into each other today and had also given me an opportunity to excuse myself and say good-bye.

Before I had the chance to think up a good excuse for leaving, the immortal in the sapphire tunic who had been standing quietly to the side used a golden light to strike Yuan Zhen on the forehead, toppling him face-first onto the ground.

The immortal in the sapphire tunic gave me a reserved smile. "You mustn't be concerned, Your Highness. All I've done is erase Yuan Zhen's memory of seeing the prince and me tonight. Thanks to your gentle hands, His Majesty Yuan Zhen has a promising future ahead. My only fear is that seeing two genuine immortals might vex and bewitch him. Yuan Zhen has caused a slight change to the emperor's destiny, which I have come here to remedy. I would be grateful, Your Highness, if you could point me in the direction of where I could find Phoenix Nine. I need to ask for her help."

This immortal in the sapphire-blue tunic was quite a smooth talker. The effect on Dong Hua's destiny could in no way be described as a *slight change*.

I was a magnanimous immortal and understood that he was completely within his right to reprimand us. He was so good with words and had this kind and gentle face, which made it hard to scowl at him and ask for justice for the way he had treated Yuan Zhen and the poor serving girl, both sprawled out on the ground.

I decided to leave the mortals toppled over as they were. "If you rely on her to show you the way, you'll be wandering around until tomorrow morning," Ye Hua told the immortal dressed in sapphire blue. "You'll go around the entire imperial palace before you happen upon the courtyard where Phoenix Nine lives. You'd be better off finding a local earth god to show you the way." The immortal in the sapphire-blue tunic gave me a bemused look and went in search of this earth god. I gave a hollow laugh. Ye Hua was in a strange mood. His quiet words sounded bitter, and I wondered if someone in the Ninth Sky had upset him.

I had already succeeded in my mission to help Yuan Zhen pass through his calamity, and Ye Hua had no reason to keep my magic sealed any longer. The immortal in the sapphire tunic managed to track down an earth god, and I followed the three of them to Lotus Bud Courtyard, saving me the hassle of finding my own way there.

We were about to leave when I saw that Yuan Zhen was still sprawled out on the ground. There was a cold night breeze, and although Yuan Zhen did not have a frail build, he wasn't particularly sturdy either, and it would be unfortunate if he were to fall sick on top of everything else that he had been through. I was a compassionate immortal, and more than anything I hated to see people suffer. So I got the immortal in the sapphire-blue tunic to cast a spell to transport Yuan Zhen to his bedchamber so he could lie down and rest in his bed.

Ye Hua regarded me with cold eyes.

As we were making our way through the palace, I worked out from what the immortal in the sapphire tunic had said that he had to be Si Ming the Star Prince.

Ye Hua had told me that the Star Prince had a strange temperament, but he seemed very good-natured based on what I had seen of him this evening.

Ye Hua must have come with Si Ming to help him remedy Dong Hua's fate, and the comment he made about visiting me must have been just a joke. I could not pretend I hadn't noticed the frosty atmosphere coming from Ye Hua. I turned to him and said, "I just heard you say that you'd come here to visit your wife, yet here you are rushing to Phoenix Nine's living quarters. Could you have been won over by Phoenix Nine's outstanding charm and grace and started to develop feelings for her?" I asked in a teasing tone of voice.

He tilted his head and looked at me. I could not tell what he was thinking. There was a hint of a smile in his eyes, but he said nothing.

Si Ming the Star Prince gave a chuckle from up ahead. "Prince Ye Hua has had a very busy day. He called me down from the Sky Empress's Flat Peach Conference, explaining how some goddess had altered Yuan Zhen's destiny and in the process accidentally altered Dong Hua's too. Dong Hua won't be able experience his predestined calamity now, and Ye Hua was worried that when he eventually returned to his immortal body, he might hold a grudge against the goddess in question. I hadn't had a chance to taste a single one of the Sky Empress's flat peaches before Prince Ye Hua was tugging me down into the mortal world to set things right. I was surprised to find that the goddess in question was Her Highness's niece, Phoenix Nine. When I last saw Phoenix Nine, she was an upper immortal, but I hear she has become a goddess since then? That happened very quickly."

Ye Hua gave a cough, and I gave an awkward laugh. "Yes, it happened very quickly," I said to Si Ming. "Very quickly indeed."

We arrived at the entrance to Lotus Bud Courtyard, and Ye Hua floated gently past me, saying, "Si Ming has come to remedy Dong Hua's destiny, and I came with him so that I could see you." He made himself invisible and dived through the main entrance to Lotus Bud Courtyard.

I was taken aback.

This earth god was an extremely alert and dutiful immortal. He led us to the doorway to Lotus Bud Courtyard and then retreated. Si Ming the Star Prince signaled politely that I should go ahead, which I did, transforming back into mortal form and following Ye Hua in through the entrance. Holding so many immortals at once would no doubt make Lotus Bud Courtyard an auspicious spot for a long time to come.

Phoenix Nine was sitting under a lamp, looking miserably deep in thought. She was obviously reflecting over the events of that day and feeling ashamed of the way she had yelled in front all those officials and concubines. She did not appear the slightest bit disturbed to see three immortals appearing before her; she just looked over to the courtyard's outer building and shouted, "Yu Dang, I have guests, bring tea—"

I used a hand to cover her mouth. "Phoenix Nine, snap out of it!"

She gave a jolt and started to shake. When she saw who I was, she threw her arms around me, and with a sob in her voice, she said, "I really shamed myself today, Aunt Bai."

"Luckily Honorable Concubine Chen is just your borrowed mortal body," I consoled. "She's the one this shame will fall upon."

Phoenix Nine shook her head, still buried in my arms. "I've ruined the emperor's destiny too. I've been thinking it all through very carefully. When I jumped off the boat and into the water to rescue the emperor, I noticed that the girl who'd been dragged into the river by the giant golden-winged Peng bird could swim. If I hadn't meddled by diving in, she could have rescued the emperor, and the two of them would have still had their destiny intact.

"I had been planning to return to Qingqiu after today. The emperor is not fond of Honorable Concubine Chen, and soaring up to the sky tonight wouldn't have caused him any great distress. But by saving the emperor, I've meddled in his destiny, and when the emperor lost consciousness today, he was holding my hand the whole time. You didn't see the way he looked at me when he awoke. It was with such deep affection it made me want to cry."

"Perhaps you misinterpreted the look," I interjected. "You'd been in the water a long time yourself. Your eyes might have been full of water."

Phoenix Nine lifted her head, her eyes full of sadness. "He told me he wanted to promote me too."

I said nothing, just patted her on the back.

Si Ming the Star Prince came over, carrying a cup of cold tea. "Are you saying that Emperor Dong Hua has fallen for you?" he asked excitedly. It was only then that Phoenix Nine saw the other two in the room, the other two immortals no less.

I glanced at Ye Hua, who was sitting to the side drinking tea. "This is Ye Hua, Sky Emperor of the Ninth Sky," I said to Phoenix Nine.

Phoenix Nine kept her eyes steadfastly upon Si Ming, staring at him for ages with a bleak expression on her face. "Si Ming, what a terrible destiny you've written," she exclaimed.

I was unimpressed by Phoenix Nine's blatant disregard for Ye Hua and threw him an apologetic smile. He smiled back at me and continued calmly and unhurriedly to drink his tea. Si Ming seemed offended by Phoenix Nine's comment about his terrible destiny. It was akin to telling a top scholar they were unlearned, or standing in front of a courtesan and saying she had a plain face.

Si Ming offered her the cold tea, the corners of his mouth twitching. "There were some flaws in my initial writing of the emperor's fate. But since he has started to fall in love with you, I must now request you continue playing out the role of the woman in the destiny notebook who the emperor was meant to fall in love with. Dong Hua was keen for a love calamity to play a big part of his mortal life experience. Originally this was the role of the woman who fell into the water, but after all that has happened, I must ask you to step into this role."

"Why me?" Phoenix Nine asked in anguish. "I have fully repaid my debt to Dong Hua now. Let me get this right, Si Ming. Not only are you not going to help me to escape this situation, you are actually going to make me stay here and create a calamity for Dong Hua? Si Ming, you are really dishonoring our years of friendship."

Si Ming took his cup, placed the lid on it, and swished around the tea inside. "It's just as you've said. You were the one who ruined the emperor's destiny. Forcing you to create a calamity for the emperor is compensation. If you refuse, imagine what Dong Hua will think when his mortal life comes to an end and he returns to his immortal form and hears you confess what you did. It will be too late to ask for his forgiveness then."

"This has nothing to do with Phoenix Nine," I blurted out. "I was the one who altered Yuan Zhen's destiny, which led to all this . . ."

Si Ming put down his teacup and stood up. He gave me a respectful bow and said, "There are some things you may not understand, Your Highness. In destiny we talk in terms of causality. All things are linked, and one thing results in the development of another. Phoenix Nine was responsible for what happened to the emperor. The fact that she has become caught up in this affair, and used the two lives incantation magic as well, means that if the emperor's destiny is to change drastically, she will definitely experience magic backbite. The method I have just suggested is the only way to avoid this."

I looked at Phoenix Nine with a deep sense of sorrow.

Phoenix Nine dropped miserably back into her chair, poured herself a cup of tea, and took a sip, looking doleful. "So how am I to create this calamity?" she asked Si Ming.

She had accepted her fate.

"All you need to do is to be sweet to the emperor and win his heart. When the emperor has fallen deeply in love with you, you need to trample over his heart, again and again and again. That's it. Your work will be done."

Phoenix Nine shuddered. I shuddered too.

"When the time comes, I will choose you some play scripts that will show you how to, um, trample all over a loving heart," Si Ming said.

Phoenix Nine laid her head and chest down on the table and started to sob.

I heard a eunuch outside announcing the emperor's arrival. I stroked Phoenix Nine's head, filled with sorrow on her behalf. Leaving her there like that, Ye Hua, Si Ming, and I got up and walked out through the wall.

They escorted me back to Purple Bamboo Garden. On the way, Ye Hua put his arm around me and said, "I've got some more business to deal with. You head back to Qingqiu tomorrow, and I will meet you there in a few days." Once he said this, he turned on his heels and was gone. Si Ming explained that they needed to rush back to rejoin the empress's Flat Peach Conference.

I stood there for a while, thinking that there had been something so familiar about standing there with Ye Hua, his arm around me, but I could not work out why. It felt as if Ye Hua had been living in Qingqiu for such a long time already, and from what he had just said, he did not sound as if he had plans to leave any time soon. How long was he actually going to stay? I thought about it until I felt drowsiness hit, and scratching my head, I walked inside to sleep.

CHAPTER TWELVE

Midmorning the next day, I crawled out of bed, feeling extremely rested. I went over to say farewell to Yuan Zhen's mother. She was sad to see me go, but aware of my status as a supreme being, she knew she could not make me stay. She simply sighed a couple of times before bidding me farewell.

This diversion meant that it was nearly noon by the time I got back to Qingqiu.

Not much had changed there in the two months I had been in the mortal world. The mountain was still a mountain, the lake still a lake. Mao the Sun Prince was still treating the area with extreme kindness, and the sun was not too strong, not too weak, but just right.

Mystic Gorge was standing at the entrance to the foxhole.

"I'm back. It must have been relaxing having all this time without me ordering you about," I larked.

Mystic Gorge gave a muffled laugh and surprised me by saying, "But didn't you get back yesterday, Your Highness? You're about to undertake a serious new mission. Why are you talking as if you've only just arrived back from the mortal world?"

I felt momentarily too stunned to speak. "I have only just arrived back from the mortal world," I said eventually.

It was Mystic Gorge's turn to turn pale. "In that case, who was it that came here y-y-yesterd . . . ?" he stuttered.

My heart gave a lurch, and I started to tremble.

If someone had been posing as me so convincingly that even Mystic Gorge, with all his spiritually cultivated energy, was unable to tell us apart, it could only have been one person . . .

I closed my eyes. Xuan Nu. Very well. I had not gone looking for trouble with her over the last seventy thousand years, so what had she been doing in Qingqiu?

I took a deep breath and said, "It must have been Xuan Nu you saw here yesterday." Mystic Gorge stared straight ahead, biting his lips so hard they turned white.

"What was she doing when you saw her?" I asked when I saw how strangely he was acting.

With a quiver in his voice, Mystic Gorge said, "W-w-w-when she came to see me yesterday, sh-sh-she told me she'd found a new way of preserving Mo Yuan's immortal body and asked me to bring him to her. I-I-I thought it was you, Your Highness, so I w-w-went to Yanhua Cave and carried out Mo Yuan's immortal body. His Little Highness Ali had just woken up from his afternoon nap and was really happy to see you. No, I mean, he was happy to see the woman he thought was you. And sh-sh-she . . . took off with him too."

My heart gave a huge lurch. I grabbed Mystic Gorge by the collar. "Are you saying she's abducted Master and Ali?"

Mystic Gorge stared at me, his face pale. "I was the one who gave her Mo Yuan's immortal body, Your Highness. Punish me however you see fit. I deserve to die."

The sky boomed with thunder, a bolt of lightning struck down through the billowing clouds, and the Kunlun fan I had not used in over five hundred years appeared in the lake before me. I saw my crimson eyes reflected in the seven-foot fountain of water that spurted up from it.

"Oh, fan of mine, you are going to taste some blood today," I said with a laugh.

"Your Highness!" Mystic Gorge called hoarsely from behind me. I turned around.

"All I'm going to do is fight a battle and bring back Master and Dumpling, don't be worried," I reassured him. "Boil me a pan of water and leave it out. I will be sore and tired by the time I get back and in need of a wash."

I took out my length of white silk and tied it tightly around my eyes, cast a spell, leaped on a thick black cloud, and headed straight for the Purple Light Palace. From ancient times, the most profoundly evil members of the Demon Clan had been given the sky punishment of having only stillbirths. Legend had it that one she-demon was so evil and murderous that three of her babies died in a row. Later she thought of a way around this punishment. She used magic to keep the soul of her dead baby alive and then killed a young immortal and transferred her dead baby's soul into his body, thus bringing her baby back to life. Ten thousand years after the Demon Clan Revolt, Zhe Yan came to see me in Qingqiu and mentioned in passing how Li Jing's wife had had a stillbirth.

Xuan Nu, I thought to myself, *if you have the guts to lay one finger on Mo Yuan's immortal body, I will inflict a bloodbath upon the Purple Light Palace. Do not think for one second that our clans' friendship will stand in my way.*

Seventy thousand years ago, the Purple Light Palace had been extremely well guarded, but there was no one at the gates today. It seemed like an invitation for a funeral.

I was not the same person I had been seventy thousand years ago, the one who needed Mo Yuan to sneak into the palace in the dead of night to rescue me, and I gave a bitter laugh. The Kunlun fan in my hand seemed restless. I brought it to my lips. "Can you smell the blood?" I asked it.

I entered the palace and found Xuan Nu sitting upright on a gold couch in front of her Floating Shadow Palace, looking extremely smart and well dressed, flanked by two lines of demon soldiers. "Bai Qian, it's been seventy thousand years. I trust you have been keeping well since last we met," she said with a laugh. "I heard His Majesty Li Jing mention that Si Yin was actually a girl, and I had a strong feeling it would be you. The first time I met Si Yin in Mount Kunlun, I was astonished. No one apart from you has ever looked that much like me."

I gave a placid smile. "I imagine you are trying to amuse me, Empress," I said. "This isn't actually how you look. My memory has always been good, and I still remember your former appearance. You can't have forgotten, can you? Zhe Yan from the Ten-Mile Peach Grove has been rather idle of late. If you really have forgotten, I could ask him to come and help jog your memory."

Her face went from red to white. She gave a chuckle. "Whatever happens, today you are going to die. There's no room in the world for anyone who looks like me. Yesterday when I managed to get my hands on Mo Yuan's immortal body and your son, I knew it was just a matter of time before you arrived. I've been waiting for you. I knew you must have been preserving Mo Yuan's body, even without the Jade Soul. And you didn't disappoint me," she said, clicking her tongue in admiration. "Your only transgression was to keep me searching so long. But you've kept Mo Yuan's body in excellent condition, and I am delighted my son will soon be in possession of such a fine body. Bai Qian, I will honor your meticulous service by allowing you a quick and easy death with minimal suffering." With that, the gold couch rolled back, and the two rows of demon soldiers started surrounding me.

"Let's see what you've got," I sneered.

The sky boomed with thunder, and the Kunlun fan leaped from my hand. Soon we were surrounded by howling winds. The Kunlun fan started to grow, and soon it was three feet tall. I leaped up and grabbed it as the demon soldiers came at me with their weapons.

The fan moved in a circle, shielding me from all their swords, spears, and clubs. I brandished it again, knowing that each move meant life or death. It had been a long time since the fan had been in a fight, and it was giving everything it had. It stabbed through the flesh of one body after another, pools of blood dripping onto the ground.

Many of the demon soldiers put up a good fight. They wielded their weapons at cunning angles to try and reach me, and I only just managed to avoid being stabbed. I still had the upper hand, but there were far more of them, and we fought from noon until the sun set in the west. Most of the demon soldiers had been killed or injured under my fan, and only three were left fighting. I had a surface stab near my shoulder blade, and the white silk cloth had been torn from my face during the battle.

My eyes were my weakness, and Xuan Nu suddenly brought out a pearl that dazzled with a golden light. It glinted with such brightness that my eyes felt like they were being cut out with a knife. I lost focus, and a sword came at me and stabbed me in the chest. Xuan Nu gave a loud laugh. "If His Majesty were at the palace today, you might have had a chance at staying alive. But unfortunately for you, he is away on a hunting trip. Oh dear, it's distressing to see you covered in injuries like this. Why don't you call to be rescued?" She turned to her solider and said, "Hu Na, kill her for me."

Dying here without even having set eyes on Mo Yuan's body seemed absurd. The pain in my body would be nothing compared to the pain in my heart. The sword had gone in through my chest and out through my back. Hu Na, the demon solider who had stabbed me, was looking very pleased with himself. Complacency caused him to let his guard down, and I managed to grab his sword. Fiercely brandishing the fan, I cut his head off before he even knew what was happening.

The golden light was still shining toward me, forcing me to keep my eyes closed. I managed to pry them open in time to see a figure flitting past. Xuan Nu, who had been talking so excitedly, now fell silent. The last two demon soldiers were putting up a good fight, but they had no more backup and were fighting against a fan that was thrilled to be drinking so much blood and was only just getting started. In no time they had become the fan's sacrificial offerings.

Xuan Nu lifted up her pearl, her hand shaking. "Don't come any closer," she said. "One step closer and I will destroy Mo Yuan and your son." At some point during all this fighting, two ice chests, one large and one small, had been placed behind her. Mo Yuan lay in the big one, while the small one contained Dumpling. Everything appeared bloodred through my injured eyes, but even through this red sheen, I could make out Mo Yuan's pale face.

I stopped in my tracks, placing the fan on the ground to support me. "What have you done to Ali?" I asked, full of rage.

She was still trembling, but was starting to look a lot calmer. "He's in a deep sleep," she said, leaning against the ice coffin. "But you move one step closer, and I can't be held responsible for what happens."

I gave her a forceful stare, and the blood flowed faster down from the corners of my eyes. "Draw the sword from your chest and slide your fan over to me," she said haughtily. I said nothing, just continued to walk toward her, supporting myself with the fan. "I told you not to come any nearer," she said in a panic. "Move any closer, and I will stab your son to death."

She had a dagger in her hand. I felt the corners of my mouth twitch. "When I came to the Purple Light Palace today, I didn't expect to come out alive. Go ahead and kill him. Kill him, and then I'll avenge his death by killing you. I've been looking after Mo Yuan's body for seventy thousand years, but still he hasn't returned, and I'm bored with living. I will accompany Ali through to the underworld and make sure that he doesn't get scared. You and me, we've both been alive for so long now. We shouldn't still be taking this life-and-death stuff so seriously."

She was getting very flustered. "You're crazy!" she cried. "You've gone completely crazy."

I wiped away the blood flowing from my eyes. Yes, I was a bit crazy, I decided, but not too crazy. This woman standing before me had abused my master and threatened my relatives. How could I just let that go? I had to kill her with my Kunlun fan, here and now.

The Kunlun fan was angry, and when it was angry, the world shook. The fan had sipped its fill of blood and was raring to go. The sky above the Purple Light Palace was filled with thunder and lightning. The heavy downpour of rain washed all the blood on the floor into one filthy red river.

Xuan Nu had become hysterical. "You can't kill me," she screamed. "If you kill me, His Majesty Li Jing will raze Qingqiu to the ground. How can you implicate all your kingdom's subjects?"

I smiled, baring my teeth. "We'll both be dead by then. Who cares what happens after?

"If you really are concerned about what happens after your death, I would focus on the future Sky Emperor coming after your Demon Clan to obliterate them. It's his only son you've abducted and are planning to kill. Believe me, with his temperament he could very well destroy your clan for revenge."

She seemed to be having trouble responding, and I decided not to give her the chance. The Kunlun fan had stored up enough energy, and it flew out of my hand with a magnificent flash of lightning. At that moment, I saw a figure streak in front of Xuan Nu, and deflect the Kunlun fan's powers back at me.

Once she had recovered herself, Xuan Nu grabbed at the sleeve of the figure and in a faltering voice cried out, "Your Majesty, Li Jing!" Once the Kunlun fan had been initiated, it had the strength to kill, and if blocked when soaring through the air like this, its rebounding force would be even more ferocious. I had used up all my powers and did not have the strength to dodge it. Gritting my teeth, I closed my eyes. I supposed there were worse ways to die than perishing under the force of your own powerful weapon.

No sooner had I closed my eyes than I felt myself being grabbed and lifted out of harm's way. I turned around to see Ye Hua, who had arrived just in time, although if he had come slightly earlier, I would have been in better shape than I was now.

Ye Hua was standing there, his face pale, his lips puckered, and his pupils, usually so still, surging with fury. The lapel of Xuan Nu's white robe had been dyed bright red by the blood from my face. Outside the immortal barrier, the Kunlun fan had incited a heavy rainstorm. Raindrops the size of tender dates crashed down onto the immortal barrier, and a huge rain mist splashed up. Ye Hua gently wiped the blood from my face, saying, "Qian Qian, tell me, who hurt you?"

I shifted my position and said, "They've all been stabbed to death. I was just about to stab the only survivor when her husband appeared and blocked my weapon. Oh, can you hold me more gently please? I'm in a lot of pain."

Li Jing stood opposite us with Xuan Nu in his arms still. He jerked his head up and looked at me in astonishment. "Si Yin?" he said with incredulity.

Xuan Nu shuddered from within his arms. She looked over, and her eyes opened wide in fright. "It's Mo Yuan!" she muttered.

She had mistaken Ye Hua for Mo Yuan.

"It hadn't been my intention to see you again so soon," I told Li Jing, each word causing me pain. "You're very skilled, Demon Prince. You nearly killed me just then."

He dropped Xuan Nu and rushed over, but Ye Hua's immortal barrier stopped him from getting any closer. I looked so hideous with all my injuries that he had to look very carefully before recognizing me.

I had cast a magic spell to summon the Kunlun fan, which was back in my hand now. I gave an admiring sigh. "Demon Prince, what a good choice you made marrying this empress. In that terrible battle seventy thousand years ago, I was not too badly injured, but today I have had a proper taste of your wife's ruthlessness."

Li Jing's face was whiter than mine, even with all my blood loss. "Si Yin, Your Majesty Prince . . . w-w-wha . . . what's going on?" he asked nervously.

Ye Hua loosened his grip on me, and in a calm voice he said, "Demon Prince Li Jing, this is your Purple Light Palace we are all in. I was just about to ask you that same question."

"You're asking the wrong person," I turned to Ye Hua to say. "It was his wife, Xuan Nu, who abducted my master and your son. She's the one you should be asking. Don't worry. Dumpling hasn't been harmed."

"He's your son too," Ye Hua said quietly.

My stepson, and in a way my son, I supposed, so against my better judgment I said, "Yes, my son too."

"Your son?" Li Jing asked in astonishment.

I nodded.

His eyes lit up and then went dark. "You . . . you . . . you," he kept repeating but was unable to say any more. He turned to look at Xuan Nu. Ye Hua looked at her too. Seeing both of them looking at her, I turned my eyes to her as well.

When Ye Hua had arrived, he had thrown a bolt of lightning and split her pearl into pieces. She was kneeling down next to Dumpling's ice chest now, and seeing Li Jing look at her, she started to panic. "Your Majesty, Your Majesty, our son can finally return. Look, I've found him a proper body. I always knew Mo Yuan's body would come in useful. You should have given that bitch Bai Qian the Jade Soul when she first came to the Purple Light Palace demanding it. Oh, but who would have thought she'd be able to look after Mo Yuan's body so well without it?

You used to be jealous of Mo Yuan, Your Majesty, but you don't need to feel that way anymore. From now on he's going to be our son . . ."

"Shut up!" Li Jing shouted.

"Your Majesty!" Xuan Nu exclaimed in bewilderment. "Have I said something wrong? Wasn't that the reason you wouldn't give that bitch Bai Qian our Jade Soul? Because you were jealous of Mo Yuan? But he will be our son now. Ah yes, you still don't know who Bai Qian is. Bai Qian from Qingqiu and your old flame Si Yin are one and the same."

Ye Hua's hands were trembling.

I struggled out of his arms, and propping myself up with the Kunlun fan, I stepped outside his immortal barrier. "Just you try it, Xuan Nu. Try to insult my master one more time. Try to insult me," I sneered. "My master has the most highly revered immortal body, and I have been using my own heart blood to keep it alive for the past seventy thousand years. Your son is not worthy of such a valuable and precious body."

Li Jing turned around violently, his eyes crimson. He took a couple of steps toward me. "Heart blood? Are you saying . . . ?"

I took a step back, and with venom in my voice, I said, "What did you think back then, Demon Prince? That I wouldn't be able to preserve my master without your Jade Soul? You should listen to what your wife has to say. I am Bai Qian from Qingqiu, and I used to be a nine-tailed white fox. Ask her to tell you what powers the blood of a nine-tailed white fox has."

I pointed to my chest, which still had a sword running through it, and gave a deep laugh. "My master's immortal body was so badly injured that he needed to be fed a whole bowl of heart blood every night for three months. I was badly hurt in that battle too, and I was scared that removing all that blood from my heart might kill me. I thought that the two of us were still friends, and so I grasped the nettle and came to ask if you would lend me the Jade Soul. And what was it you said to me, Demon Emperor Li Jing?"

"I didn't know how badly hurt you were, Si Yin," he said hoarsely. "Si Yin, I really didn't know . . ."

I wiped the rainwater from my face and pointed at the ice chest containing Mo Yuan and laughed. "Do you know how I managed to sustain myself while extracting blood from my heart all those months? If you consider me a good goddess, it is because I still have a sense of gratitude and know how to repay a debt. My master looked after me for twenty thousand years and saved me from countless mishaps. If I didn't repay this debt to him, I would not deserve to be called a *goddess*. I was completely helpless. After I'd extracted heart blood for the seventh night, I lost consciousness. If Mother hadn't found me in time and transferred me half her cultivated spiritual energy, Si Yin would have disappeared without trace. You remember what I said back then, about me and the Purple Light Palace being bitter enemies? Until now, I've thought about how hard this friendship between the God and Demon Clans has been to build and decided not to make an enemy out of you. I hope you don't think it was because I was afraid of you."

Li Jing looked disconsolate.

I had been speaking with so much force I had aggravated my injury. I did not feel too bad while I was speaking, but when I stopped to catch my breath, the pain became unbearable.

I was just suppressing a cough when Ye Hua rushed over and took hold of my arm. I had not noticed, but while I had been rehashing the past with Li Jing, Ye Hua had rescued Mo Yuan and Dumpling from the ice chests and brought them over to where we were. He drew a circle of immortal energy around them to protect them and stood them up behind us.

Seeing Mo Yuan and him together, they looked even more similar, from their hair to their clothing. It was only Mo Yuan's paleness of face that distinguished them.

Li Jing stared at me for a long time before saying, "That's not what happened, Si Yin. I spent a long time looking for you after you left, and I've never stopped searching for you these last seventy thousand years, not for one moment. I've thought about it long and hard, Si Yin, and Xuan Nu was correct in what she said. The reason I didn't give you the Jade Soul back then was because I knew you'd use it to save your master, and I was jealous. Si Yin, I've never stopped loving you."

I recoiled in shock when I heard this. I stared at him and sighed. "Li Jing, I don't believe you when you say you've never stopped loving me. You are always pursuing things you've lost or can't have. But as soon as you have them, you no longer cherish them."

Tears welled up in his eyes. He gave a bitter laugh and said, "Are you just saying that to shift the responsibility for our breakup onto me and make yourself feel better? You never really loved me, did you? That's why you let me go so easily when I met Xuan Nu. You were already bored with me by then, weren't you?"

The blood and vigor that I had been fighting to keep down started to surge up once more. "You were the one who wronged me!" I sneered through gritted teeth. "You were the one who hurt me! Did you expect me to have the magnanimity to marry you and share you with Xuan Nu? And now you're claiming it was my fault. You saw how vulnerable Xuan Nu was and how in need of your pity. But even though I was a boy at the time, my heart wasn't made of stone. The way you both treated me was cruel. Where were you when I was drinking away my sorrow and dealing with those horrendous nightmares? What were you and Xuan Nu doing then?"

Li Jing went white.

I leaned against Ye Hua's arm, coughing so much I could hardly breathe. Behind me Ye Hua sneered, "Demon Prince, don't get caught up trying to settle past mistakes. We need to discuss the debt your empress has incurred today. Should we make it a public debt or a private one?"

When Li Jing failed to respond, Xuan Nu spoke up, her voice shaking. "What do you mean private or public?"

Ye Hua looked at Li Jing and, in a serious tone of voice, said, "If it's private, Li Jing, you will have to skin your stupid wife and pull out her tendons, and her soul will be reincarnated as an animal and get lost in the sea of suffering. Only this way will my indignation be eased. If it's public, then our Sky Clan will call out the sky troops, who have been sitting around for years, itching for a battle, and we can see which clan's army has been training hardest."

Xuan Nu took a deep breath. She staggered over to Li Jing in the heavy rain, wrapped her arms around his leg, and lifted her face to him. "Please save me, Your Majesty!" she implored.

Li Jing looked at her and said, "You are a fool."

"Are you really going to skin me and pull out my tendons?" she asked in a shrill voice. "Have you f-f-forgotten all I've done for you? Would you have ascended so easily to the Demon Throne without me? And now you're actually considering . . . Your Majesty!" she implored. "The Sky Clan won't send out the troops. He doesn't have the authority. He's only heir to the throne. The Sky Clan will never agree to send out the troops over a girl . . ."

Ye Hua altered his grip on me. "I wouldn't be sending the troops out just over a girl. Mo Yuan is a highly revered Sky Clan god, Bai Qian is a goddess and the Sky Clan's future empress, and Ali will probably inherit my position in the future. All three of them have suffered enormous shame and injustice at your Purple Light Palace today. Do you really think that the Sky Army will take that lying down?"

Li Jing ignored Xuan Nu, who was clinging to his leg. "Xuan Nu has always been slightly crazy," he said, looking dazed. "There's no way she would have done such a terrible deed otherwise. Please, Prince Ye Hua, be lenient with her."

"Qian Qian, do you think we should be lenient?" Ye Hua asked me softly.

He loosened his grip on my body, but I found it too painful to speak. I had wanted to add a word or two, but I felt too exhausted. All I could do was shake my head emphatically.

"Prince Ye Hua, it's very kind of you to treat this bitch Bai Qian so well," Xuan Nu said with a laugh. "But were you aware she was having an affair with her master?"

I was filled with rage, and was just about to stagger toward her and give her a slap across the face, but Ye Hua sent a bolt of lightning in her direction, saving me the trouble. Li Jing was no longer protecting her, and the bolt blew her back ten feet. She tumbled onto her gold couch and spat out a mouthful of blood.

"I never usually hit women," Ye Hua said. "Qian Qian said that your faces were very similar, but I am unable to see the likeness."

I left Ye Hua's arms and walked over to Xuan Nu, supported by the Kunlun fan. I looked into the face that was so similar to my bloody face and gave a little laugh. "I didn't really care about my appearance when I let you take my face. But whenever I see your face now, it makes me feel miserable."

She shrunk back in fear. "W-w-what are you going to do?" she stuttered. "T-t-this is the way I've always looked, you . . . you mustn't take away my face. Invite Zhe Yan here if you want, I-I-I'm not scared . . ."

I already had the fingers of my right hand pinched together. I laughed in astonishment. "Invite Zhe Yan to do what? I was just having a joke with you before. Do you think he's the only one in the Four Seas and Eight Deserts who can perform face-changing magic? I've been sitting idle for the last seventy thousand years. I developed a sophisticated technique for the craft during that time.

"If you're to be skinned and have your tendons pulled out, I would prefer it not to be with my face on your body." I gathered up my strength and chanted a spell, pinching my fingers together to release it. A dazzling white light shone out, and Xuan Nu looked over at me in a trance.

I leaned forward and patted her face before pulling a mirror from my sleeve and giving her a look. "Look at your face now," I said in pleasant voice. "Isn't it marvelous? This is what you used to look like. Perhaps you'll remember now."

Li Jing stood to the side, muttering, "How can she look like this? How is it possible?"

Xuan Nu gave a sudden loud shriek. I looked around and saw that she had ripped her own eyes out. "No! No! No!" she screamed hysterically. "This isn't how I look! This isn't me!"

Her face was dark with blood. Li Jing was at a loss for words. I shook my head, and with a sigh I said, "She was always very highly strung." I turned to Ye Hua and said, "I always found her original face to be very delicate and pretty. I never understood why she was so obsessed with mine."

Ye Hua looked at me through dark eyes and, holding me close, turned to Li Jing and said, "Do as you see fit, Demon Emperor.

"Qian Qian, can you walk by yourself?" he whispered gently in my ear. I thought about it and then shook my head. I saw a circle of soft light in front of me and fell into a deep sleep.

CHAPTER THIRTEEN

There was a very rigorous set of rules for those studying at Mount Kunlun. You always got up at seven in the morning and you extinguished your oil lamp and slept before midnight.

Being on good terms with First Apprentice meant that when Master was called away from Mount Kunlun, I occasionally got away with skipping a class or two under his watch, giving me an extra hour or two in bed. If I was lucky, I could sleep until eleven, but that was the absolute latest. I kept up this habit for so many years that it had stuck and was still with me seventy thousand years after graduating. Even in the winter months when I was feeling lethargic, I could never stay in bed past nine.

This meant that despite the tumult at the Purple Light Palace the day before, and the fact that my injured body and limbs ached so much it felt like my heart was being lashed with a cold whip, I was still wide-awake at the usual time. Finding myself back in my own carved bed, in my own room, in the foxhole, I gradually started to feel calm again.

I had passed out the day before and did not see how Ye Hua managed to carry Mo Yuan, Dumpling, and me all back to Qingqiu, although with cultivated spiritual energy, it was unlikely to have posed him too much of a challenge.

Sensible Mystic Gorge must have taken Mo Yuan's body back to Yanhua Cave. I was worried that he might not have placed Mo Yuan in his preferred sleeping position and made up my mind to go and check on Mo Yuan once I was out of bed.

I shifted my position, straining my chest injury, and it hurt so much it made me breathe in sharply. I saw something on my quilt shifting slightly in response to my movements, and I looked down to see pair of eyes gazing at me, filled with adoration. The owner of these eyes was lying on the edge of my bed, his face flooded with warmth and happiness.

Shining eyes looked up at me and a voice gently asked, "How . . . how are you feeling now?"

I nudged myself cautiously toward the middle of the bed, saying, "I had a good sleep and seem to have recovered most of my energy."

I was a goddess. My immortal body had been through a number of calamities and hardships over the past one hundred forty thousand years and was stronger than most. I could recover from most injuries fairly quickly, but not this quickly. I told this fib because I had found myself at odds with the person sitting next to me for some time now and worried that if he knew how vulnerable I was, he might take advantage and attack me, probably finishing me off.

I had known this character since Zhe Yan had first introduced him to Fourth Brother to use as his steed. Zhe Yan had come back from his hunting trip in the Western Mountains with Bi Fang the bird, who was now sitting before me, smartly dressed. Initially after being appointed as Fourth Brother's steed, Bi Fang and I had been on good terms, and he would often carry me on his back to the peach grove to eat peaches and collect wine.

And then one day, he stopped carrying me. It was only a thousand years later that I started to understand his reason. He had taken a shine to Phoenix Nine and felt hostility toward me because Phoenix Nine and I were together so much.

I had not wanted to get into an argument with him about his irrational jealousy. But it became very bad, and most days he would find something to spar with me about. I would end up getting riled as well usually, and that was how it continued. Because of this, his sudden disappearance had actually left me feeling secretly quite pleased.

The curtains were wide open, and the ray of sunlight shining through, while not extraordinarily strong, was dazzling enough to cause a stabbing pain to my poor eyes. Bi Fang rushed over to the window, saying, "Would it better if I closed the curtains?"

It threw me to hear him sounding so meek, and I was unable to respond with any more than "Hmm."

He closed the curtains and returned to the bed to tuck in the corners of my quilt. He leaned against the side of the bed and asked with affection if I wanted some water. Even Mystic Gorge was not this attentive and considerate.

I was actually quite thirsty, but I found Bi Fang's behavior confusing. While he was pouring me a cup of tea, I suddenly realized what was going on.

"Fourth Brother?" I asked with a somber smile. "You're Fourth Brother, aren't you? I've just been in a battle and my magic powers are weak. You knew I wouldn't be able to see through your transforming magic, so you dressed up as Bi Fang to trick me. Oh, very good! You're spot-on with his appearance, but you haven't quite mastered his personality. Haven't you seen how dismissive Bi Fang is toward me?"

The figure in front of me froze halfway through pouring the tea.

He turned to me, a strange look on his face. "I've not undergone any transformation. I really am Bi Fang," he said. "My master and His Highness have gone to the Western Sea on business. I was bored over in the peach grove on my own, so I thought I'd come here to see how you were."

I was taken aback, and my lips trembled as I tried to form a smile. Giving a forced chuckle, I said, "Oh, you avian folk! You can be rather detached. Different from us mammals! Please don't take what I just said to heart . . ."

His face was expressionless as he just brought my tea over and lifted it up to my mouth so I could take a sip. He looked at me solemnly for some time before saying, "I would have risked all my cultivated spiritual energy if I'd been there with you. I wouldn't have let them put a scratch on your body."

"We are all from the same foxhole. We're family. You're right. We should be there for one another," I responded awkwardly. "If you are ever in a fight, Bi Fang, you can be sure that I'll be there to cheer for you."

I'll be there to cheer for you felt like it had fallen rather short.

"In fact, I would fight to the death for you," I added with a cough, noting happily that my expression of loyalty now exceeded his.

He leaned over and said, "Bai Qian, how long are you going to pretend that you don't understand? You must know that I've come to Qingqiu because I care for you deeply. Are you saying these things just to make me angry?"

I was dumbstruck.

My goodness. I had heard how loyal feathered creatures could be. It was not possible to see unless they fell in love, but once in love, they stayed in love. And if one fell in love with you, he would love you until the day he died. Caring for my niece as he did, Bi Fang's avian tradition should have meant that he would love her through thick and thin. When and how, in that case, had he developed feelings for me?

"You and that Sky Emperor heir have been engaged for a long time, and I have been forced to hide the way I feel," he explained. "But this huge calamity befell you, and he was unable to keep you safe. And I've heard he keeps a concubine in his Sky Palace. I've been gone all this time thinking things through, and I've come to the conclusion that he's not qualified to look after your heart and soul. I'm not happy for you to be given to someone like him. I . . ."

The door creaked open before he could finish his sentence.

Ye Hua stood in the doorway, ashen faced, holding a bowl of medicinal soup with steam billowing off it. I gave a confused sigh. This debt of gratitude passage had suddenly turned into a romance passage. This really was an extremely unconventional turn of events.

Bi Fang threw a glance toward Ye Hua, but said nothing more.

Ye Hua put the bowl of medicinal soup on the desk, and because Bi Fang was sitting at the side of the bed, he sat down silently on the bench next to the desk, a frosty expression on his face.

For a time the room was extremely quiet. It gave me a moment to take stock of what Bi Fang had just said: that because of my engagement with Ye Hua, he had been hiding his true feelings toward me.

He had been hiding his true feelings extremely deeply, and for the last ten thousand years, I had not had a clue. I did not return Bi Fang's sentiments, but recalling his words filled me with happiness.

Being jilted by Sang Ji, followed by the Sky Emperor's sky decree, had well and truly messed up any chance of a romantic life I might have had. I spent the best years for enjoying romance all on my own, having a much duller time than most immortals of that age. It must have looked as if I simply did not enjoy venturing out, but actually it was because what had happened had bothered me so much. Bi Fang's confession caused a release of all the soreness and sensitivity I had accumulated over the last fifty thousand years.

I knew I could not satisfy Bi Fang's wishes, but I decided to let him down gently and with minimal pain. I thought it through before hesitantly starting to speak. "I have been engaged to marry into the Sky Clan for a long time and have only just found out about how you feel. Which means that you and I . . . well, you and I were never meant to be. Hearing you say you care deeply for me filled me with joy. But things, things follow an order, don't they?"

Bi Fang's eyes were shining. "If you agreed to be mine, I would be willing to offend the entire Sky Clan," he said, glancing at Ye Hua. Through the swirling steam of medicinal soup, I noticed Ye Hua's face turn nastier than words could describe.

Ye Hua was completely justified to look so appalled. Being made to sit there while his future wife talked through romantic feelings with another man was as preposterous as it was insulting. Bi Fang and I were being completely up-front and open, however. Ye Hua had just happened to walk in at the wrong moment, and I was not going to snub Bi Fang just because he had. After all, Bi Fang and I went back a long way.

After thinking it all through, I turned to Ye Hua. "Why don't you go outside for a moment?" I asked pleasantly. He ignored my request, just stroked the edge of the medicine bowl, his face devoid of expression. Bi Fang moved closer to me.

"Just tell me, do you want to be with me or not?" he asked softly. Sitting this close to me right in front of Ye Hua did seem very audacious.

"As you know, I concern myself with etiquette. Since I am engaged to marry into the Sky Clan, I won't do anything that could cause trouble between Qingqiu and the Ninth Sky. I appreciate the sentiment, however, and I am extremely moved. But you and I were never meant to be. It would be for the best not to bring this up again. If your feelings for me don't fade, I suggest you continue to hide them. I know how your heart feels, and I will never forget it."

My words had been impeccable, flawless, leaving both Bi Fang and Ye Hua with their pride intact.

Bi Fang stared at me blankly and then sighed. He tucked in the corners of my quilt once more before turning to leave.

Ye Hua continued to sit by the desk, his face obscured by the steam wafting up from the bowl of medicinal soup.

● ● ●

I had not slept enough to feel completely recovered. And this conversation with Bi Fang had made me feel at once surprised, happy, afraid, and nervous and set my recovery back somewhat. I was still thinking about going to Yanhua Cave, but Ye Hua seemed to have stationed himself in my room now, which was going to make it tricky. I needed to think of a way to get rid of him. In a listless voice, I said, "Oh, could you pass me my medicine, please? I've suddenly started to feel a bit drowsy. Once I've taken it, I'd like to sleep for a while and leave you to get on with your work."

He gave a murmur of assent and brought over the bowl. They say good medicine always tastes bitter, which must have meant his medicine was excellent, as it was the most bitter I have ever tasted. I knocked it back, and feeling the bitterness travel from the top of my scalp to the tips of my toes, I gave a full-body shiver.

Ye Hua took the empty bowl and placed it on a stool beside me. He did not appear to be leaving; instead he leaned over and looked at me, saying, "Every time you want to get rid of me, you use the excuse that you're feeling tired. Surely you can't be feeling drowsy at this hour?"

I gave a start.

He was right, it had been an excuse, but it was the only time I had ever used it with him, so what did he mean *every time*?

I was still turning this over in my mind when he came over and slipped his arms around my waist. Due to my injuries, I had subconsciously reverted back to my original form to heal. A fox's body is very different from that of a person with their distinct waist and limbs, but Ye Hua impressed me by deftly feeling out my fox waist.

"Qian Qian," he said in a slow, husky voice.

"Mm?" I replied. He was too busy holding me to say anything more. It was a while before he managed another sentence.

"Did you mean what you just said?"

I was confused. Everything I had just said had been intended for Bi Fang's ears, nothing to do with him. That question would have been much more appropriate coming from Bi Fang.

He buried his head, and I heard what sounded like laughter, but carrying a sense of utter helplessness. "You're letting me put my arms around you and hug you like this, and all the time I've been living in Qingqiu, you've refilled my teacup and played chess with me. Is it all just because of our engagement? If you were engaged to another man, would you . . . ?" He held me even tighter and sighed, but did not continue with what he had been saying.

I felt a wave of shock pass through my heart. I found his question strange. Was it not obvious? If we had not been engaged, how could he have ever come to stay with me and taken advantage of these intimate moments? If when he had first come to stay in Qingqiu, Mystic Gorge had chased him away with a stick, how could he ever have entered the foxhole and been given a room, not to mention my clearing out Third Brother's room for him to use as his study? He had been treated extremely solicitously.

This was the first time since getting to know Ye Hua that I had seen him get worked up by anything. It was strange to witness his weak side.

"I'm not just being good to you because of our engagement," I said with an awkward laugh. He stiffened and lifted his head to look at me, his eyes sparkling. His long stare started to make me feel uncomfortable. I gave a cough and said, "All the time you've spent living in the foxhole, you have been working hard in the day on those official documents, and on top of that, you have been cooking for us too.

"I am extremely moved by all you have done for me, and I can say with my hand on my heart that I will never forget it. As the folk saying goes, kindness involves give and take. You throw over a peach, and I throw back a pear. If I have no pear, I will throw you a loquat fruit instead. If I were engaged to another man, it wouldn't necessarily be like it is with you. And I wouldn't necessarily want to drink tea and play chess with him."

I sensed that this had been the right thing to say. I imagined that caring for each other like this was how people stayed happy in long marriages. But when Ye Hua heard what I had said, his eyes darkened. I did not understand why he looked so dejected, and not wanting to make matters worse, I kept my eyes up on the top of the bed frame. My thoughts returned to Yanhua Cave and how I would have to set up a new restriction at the entrance.

Ye Hua buried his head deep into my shoulder. "I've never cooked for anyone apart from you," he said.

I patted his back with my paws and nodded. "Your cooking is excellent. Find the time to cook for your mother and father. Oh, and your grandfather too. That would be the embodiment of filial behavior."

He ignored me and said, "I haven't done these things just because of our engagement. And I didn't move to Qingqiu just because Ali was missing you."

"Ah." I was finally understanding. "Cooking is your hobby. It's a good hobby, extremely useful."

He held me tighter still, but continued to ignore what I was saying. "Qian Qian, I love you," he said.

I sat there in a daze, my eyes opened wide in shock. What, what, what had just happened? I would not have been more surprised if the sky had just fallen in.

I always thought of my love destiny as an obstinate old tree that had been hacked away at for thousands and thousands of years and never given a chance to flower. Could this obstinate old tree finally be starting to bloom, and with a double lotus no less? Ye Hua lifted his head and looked at me intently. "What are you thinking?" he asked.

I was still in deep shock and not sure how to respond. I finally managed to take a breath and say, "This . . . this isn't a joke?"

He gave a faint smile and said, "I've never been more serious in all my life. It's possible to have a long marriage without affection, but with you I'm looking forward to nurturing a long marriage full of affection."

His intense words made my flesh tighten. From within the shock and fear, I found a clear moment to think it all over. I really had no idea that he had been feeling this way.

I thought back over everything that had come before: all the things we had done together came flashing before my eyes. I wondered if his feelings were true, and if so, whether I could see the signs. I was blushing furiously, but fortunately I was still in my original form, and the fur on my face hid my bright-red cheeks.

But I swear on my honor, my intentions toward him had always been completely decent. Even though we were engaged and would become husband and wife in the future, we would be the kind of husband and wife who were good friends. I never had other designs on him.

I was full of respect for Ye Hua and admiration of his character. But I viewed him the way a member of the older generation views one from the younger generation, full of care and concern. But romantic involvement, it seemed somewhat . . . well, somewhat . . . Ye Hua was looking at me in a strange way. He said nothing, just continued to stare.

The way he was gazing at me was making me uncomfortable. I paused, swallowed, and said, "Mother once told me that after a couple has been married a while, the romance and affection tend to wane. Over time, being together makes you more like relatives. I already feel as if you are my relative, so perhaps we can simply skip the middle part?"

My heart, once broken by Li Jing, had healed nicely, but a scar remained. It had taught me that love with the wrong person was no good. If I had been forty or fifty thousand years younger, we might have had some fun together; even if it had ended in more heartbreak, I could still have sought comfort in the fact that I was young and naive about life. But I was old now, and had no interest in any of that. Ye Hua was still very young, though, and even though I hankered after quiet, peaceful days, that did not mean that they had to be inflicted upon him too.

I had spoken very articulately and clearly before, and Ye Hua's lack of a response emboldened me further. After thinking a while, I decided to share my thoughts with him. "You're at the age where you should be having passionate love affairs and getting your heart broken. Take advantage of the fact that your love for me hasn't rooted itself too deeply yet. There is still time to pull it out if you do so quickly. When you get to my age, you'll understand. When you've lived as long as I have, your interest and enthusiasm for love wanes.

"Just as the higher you climb the colder you feel, the older you get the more you suffer the ups and down of love. Oh, it was the Sky Emperor's decree that brought us together, but I've always felt that this engagement has been unfair on you. You mustn't be too upset about it, though. Once we're married you can get yourself a couple of beautiful young concubines too."

Once I had said this, I felt as if a big stone had been lifted from my chest. I was speaking in a very calm and subdued manner.

I had to be the most magnanimous empress the Four Seas and Eight Deserts had ever seen. Even if our age difference did disadvantage Ye Hua, he should be lighting incense and giving praise to have ended up with such a generous and understanding wife.

He did not look as happy as I had been expecting. In fact he had gone deathly pale. "Are you speaking from the heart?" he asked, staring at me.

"Yes, I'm speaking from the heart. I couldn't be more sincere," I told him calmly.

Now we were on the subject of concubines, I imagined that he must be after some assurance but did not wish to ask outright. His pursed lips had become even more tightly puckered, and the light in his eyes was starting to fade.

I had become more tolerant with age, but one thing I had learned was that where feelings were concerned, there was no room for ambiguity. I kept my composure and continued to talk with sincerity. "In a thousand years I would still give you the same answer. It's for the best if the two of us keep our marriage pure and honest.

"Passion and love are not necessarily good for a couple. If some day in the future you wished to take a concubine, it would make things more complicated. Now is the right time. You need to set your sights on the long term. What I'm saying might not make sense to you today, but one day you'll take a shine to some immortal and wish to take her back to the Xiwu Palace as your concubine. That's when you'll understand what I've been saying here today."

He was quiet for a moment. "Are you, are you saying these things just to upset me?" he asked slowly.

My heart gave a jolt. He was ardent in his love for me, and though they had been meant with the kindest of intentions, I could see that my words had been hasty and insensitive.

I said nothing. I just sat there under his gaze, not knowing what I could say to convince him. I decided this needed to be handled delicately after a little more thought.

He held me in his arms. "I love you. Just you. I'll never love another," he said hoarsely. He paused a moment before muttering something else that I did not hear properly.

Oh, what a troublesome and stubborn fellow he was!

Even after saying words so intense that they made the top of my head tingle, Ye Hua still did not show any signs of leaving. He just helped me to lie down and tucked in all four corners of my quilt. I was badly injured, but not so weak that I needed his help to lie down. But he looked so sorrowful, and I did not want to make things worse, so I just lay there quietly and let him tuck me in.

When he had finished with the quilt, he took the medicine bowl from the stool and put it on the table. He picked up a cup and poured himself some cold tea. He leaned against the bedpost and said, "I've taken Ali back to the Sky Palace. He's had a shock, but it's not too serious. He just needs a couple of days to recuperate. I was planning to bring you back to the Sky Palace with me. His Revered Highness Ling Bao has a sky spring at the Shangqing realm that will really help speed along your recovery." He frowned and said, "Bi Fang is dead set against me taking you, but if you agree, he can't stop you. You lie here and rest now, and we'll head to the Sky Palace tomorrow morning."

I had heard of His Revered Highness Ling Bao's sky spring, and it sounded wonderful. Injuries like mine that normally took a month to heal could be fully healed after soaking in the water of the sky spring for a couple of days. I was lucky: Ye Hua's prestigious position would allow me access to the spring pool.

Ye Hua closed his eyes and rested quietly. I still needed to get to Yanhua Cave to look in at Mo Yuan. "Don't you have any documents to work on today?" I asked.

He half opened his eyes. "Nothing too urgent. You said you were tired, so I thought I'd lie down with you and hold you as you sleep." My mouth twitched. Had he not realized I'd been making an excuse? He gave me a meek smile and said, "What, not tired anymore?"

I felt frustrated. "Yes, I am tired. Really tired," I said through gritted teeth.

Ye Hua's general philosophy was not to put off until tomorrow what you could do today. Since living with me in Qingqiu, he had spent most of his time in the study with these documents of his that kept him so busy that he barely had time to pause for breath. Despite all the drama we had been through, Ye Hua's official, Jia Yun, did not seem to be in the position to cut him any slack. These official documents were still raining down from the sky as heavily as ever.

When you took yesterday's pile of documents and added them to today's batch, it looked as if poor Ye Hua probably would not have a moment's sleep all night. He was obviously not lying in my bed just to stifle me, but to have a rest and revive his own spirits.

When mortals in the mortal world did seriously bad deeds, they were beheaded as a punishment. Before they were beheaded, they would always be given a good meal, which they could eat in comfort before meeting the guillotine. Likewise, I imagined that Ye Hua needed a nice rest to recover his energy before returning to his study to deal with those two days' worth of documents. So I resigned myself to a nap, planning to wait until he had taken his rest and left before transforming back into human form and going off to Yanhua Cave.

I did not imagine that my scheme would fail. I really was running on limited energy, and in only a few minutes, my head started to feel fuzzy and unfocused.

Half between sleep and waking, somewhere between floating and sinking, I had a dream.

It was a dream I had been trying to have for tens of thousands of years with no success. And today I finally had it.

I dreamed of Mo Yuan.

CHAPTER FOURTEEN

I spent the first thousand years after Mo Yuan's soul passed waiting, feeling anxious and upset. Each night I hoped that I might dream of him so I could ask him when he was coming back. Each night before I went to sleep, I would make sure this question was in my heart. I would think it over five or six times so that the words were firmly in my mind. I was afraid that seeing Mo Yuan in the dream would overwhelm me with emotion and cause me to forget my question. But I never had this dream, and the idea gradually started to fade from my mind.

I had thought so hard about this old question that when I finally had the dream after seventy thousand years, the question was still so firmly in my mind that I was finally able to ask it.

The dream started with Zhe Yan taking me to begin my apprenticeship with Master in Mount Kunlun.

I had just celebrated my fifty thousandth birthday and was the same age that Ye Hua is now. Mother had given birth to four sons before me. I was her youngest child and the daughter she had always wanted. I had been born with my eye condition and was quite a feeble infant, and my family tended to fuss over me. My four brothers were given a lot of freedom and could generally do as they pleased. But not me. Everything I did was strictly controlled, and the only two places I was allowed to roam were the foxhole in Qingqiu and Zhe Yan's Ten-Mile Peach Grove. I struggled on like this for twenty thousand years, and even though I grew stronger and more robust, Father and Mother continued to worry.

After my twenty thousandth birthday, Father and Mother started to get called away from Qingqiu on a regular basis, and they put Fourth Brother in charge of me. Fourth Brother was renowned for his martial arts expertise, and he appeared gentle and obedient on the surface, but underneath he could be quite a troublemaker.

I really looked up to Fourth Brother.

After Father had instructed Fourth Brother to look after me, the young boy had sat outside the entrance to the foxhole with a stick of dog-tail grass in his mouth. He looked at me kindly and said, "From now on I'll be looking after you. Any time I climb a tree and scoop up an egg from a nest, I will share it with you. Any time I go to a lake and catch a fish, it will be your fish too."

Fourth Brother and I soon became very close.

Zhe Yan had taken Fourth Brother under his wing by then, and we only needed to mention Zhe Yan's name and any trouble we had stirred up would be resolved. I scampered around Qingqiu for thirty thousand years in Fourth Brother's care without a worry in the world.

When Father and Mother returned, they started to worry about my schooling. I was their only daughter, and they wished for me to be gentle, gracious, elegant, and generous, but I was developing the opposite of all these traits.

My behavior back then did not impress Mother much. In fact it used to cause her great worry. Her main concern was that I would not find a husband. She spent a couple of weeks in seclusion in the foxhole to think things over, and one day she had an epiphany. She realized that while I might not be the most obedient of girls, I had been blessed with a pretty face and was likely to find a husband without too much trouble. After realizing this, Mother found some peace.

Her sense of peace did not last long. Mystic Gorge relayed some gossip about the daughter of the Zhu Yin family who lived in the water residence at the foot of the next mountain. Newly married little Zhu Yin had lost her mother when she was still very young, which affected her upbringing and made her quite headstrong. Her new mother-in-law disliked her and would find any little excuse to reprimand her. Little Zhu Yin could not bear being treated that way, and after less than three months in her husband's family, she returned to her family home, weeping and wailing.

Hearing how badly little Zhu Yin had suffered under her new mother-in-law and knowing the way I was destroyed Mother's newfound sense of peace, and she became increasingly distraught.

Now she was convinced that although I would probably find a husband, with my character I would probably receive at least three daily beatings from my new mother-in-law. Imagining my future torment, Mother burst into tears.

Zhe Yan visited the foxhole on one occasion and found Mother quietly wiping away her tears. She told him what was wrong. He thought it through and sighed. "That girl's character is already set in stone," he said. "You won't be able to change it now. What she needs is a useful skill. If she arrives at her future husband's household with magic that is unrivaled by anyone, she can behave with as much naivety and arrogance as she wants and no one will ever lay a hand on her."

Mother's eyes lit up when she heard this. After thinking long and hard, she decided to find me a master so that I could start an apprenticeship.

Mother was an ambitious woman. She decided that if she was going to find me a master, it better not be in vain. It would have to be the best master in the whole of the Four Seas and Eight Deserts.

She carried out research for a number of weeks before finally setting her sights on Mo Yuan, Mount Kunlun's God of War. I had never met Mo Yuan, but I was familiar with the name.

By the time Fourth Brother and I were born, there were no longer many battles being waged within the Four Seas and Eight Deserts.

The odd one would break out every so often, but these tended to be small and insignificant. Members of the older generations would occasionally talk about the great battles that stemmed from when Pangu split the sky from the earth, and yin separated from yang. They talked about the fury that shook the Eight Deserts, how the Four Seas had turned red with blood, how men had dropped like flies on the battlefield, giving up their lives so that these battles might be won. Fourth Brother and I would listen in rapt attention as they told us these tales.

Many books had been passed down through members of the God Clan, recording these ancient wars, which Fourth Brother and I would pore over, engrossed. We took frequent trips to the houses of immortal friends to borrow their books, and whenever I found a rare edition, I would be sure to lend it out to them to read too.

Mo Yuan's name was mentioned again and again throughout these books, and the sky officials who had written them were all effusive with praise for his godly bearing and military might. They commented on his mysterious crystal armor and his immortal Xuan Yuan sword and called him the undefeated God of War.

Fourth Brother and I adored him, and when the two of us were alone, we would discuss his commanding presence and military prowess as well as his amazing magical powers.

We devoted many years to carrying out this research on him. We imagined Mo Yuan as a god with four heads, one facing in each direction, eyes like round brass bells, ears as big as palm-leaf fans, a square forehead, a wide mouth, spine and shoulders as thick and broad as mountains, and arms and legs as strong and stocky as pillars. Whenever he exhaled, a hurricane ravaged the plains, and whenever he stamped his foot, the earth shook.

We had considered every aspect. We gave deep thought to how such a supreme being might exhibit his supreme agility, his supremely keen senses, his supreme powers of defense and attack. Having outlined Mo Yuan's godly bearing and military attributes, we were feeling inspired, and the two of us ran over to find Second Brother, who excelled at painting portraits. We begged him to draw a couple of portraits of Mo Yuan so that we could hang them on our walls to kneel and bow down to every day.

My strong admiration for Mo Yuan meant I was ecstatic to hear that he was going to be my master. Fourth Brother wanted to come with me, but Zhe Yan said no, and Fourth Brother stayed in the foxhole for days and days in a foul mood.

Zhe Yan and I rode on a lucky cloud for some hours before finally arriving at the foot of an immortal mountain deep in a forest. This mountain was different from the ones at Qingqiu and the ones at the Ten-Mile Peach Grove, and I was very excited to be somewhere new.

The first people we came across were the immortal children guarding the entrance to the mountain. They met us and led us into a spacious hall where a man in a black cloak was sitting with his chin in his hands and his elbows on the table and a calm expression on his rather effeminate face.

When Zhe Yan took me inside Mount Kunlun and greeted this man with girlish features with the words "Mo Yuan, it's been seven thousand years!" I felt as if I had been dealt a heavy blow. Could those slender eyes possibly see thousands of miles into the distance? Was there any chance those dainty ears could hear what was happening at all eight points of the compass? Could those thin lips emit a sound that would command people's attention? And with that meager physique, would he even be able to lift up the Xuan Yuan sword, the Eight Deserts' weapon of the gods?

I felt deceived by all those books and their claims about Mo Yuan's brilliant feats. My faith crumbled and was replaced by an overwhelming sense of emptiness. I took Zhe Yan's hand, feeling distraught.

Zhe Yan handed me over to Mo Yuan with a carefully constructed web of fabrications, all spoken with utter sincerity. "This child has no mother or father," he lied. "He was dying in a ditch when I saw him. He only had one breath of air left in his lungs, and his fur was so matted that not one hair on his body remained upright. It was only after washing him that I was able to see that he was a white fox cub. I've been looking after him for fifty thousand years now," he continued.

"He's blossomed of late and become extremely handsome, which has made him the object of bitter jealousy within my household. I've had no choice but to bring him here to you," he explained. "He has suffered greatly, and even though I dote on him, he's a naughty fellow, and I hoped you might have an idea about what to do with him."

I was surprised that Zhe Yan had managed to fool anyone with this nonsense. Listening to his lies made me feel sad and a little disturbed. Mo Yuan sat there the whole time, listening quietly.

Mo Yuan seemed to buy Zhe Yan's story, and he accepted me as his apprentice. Looking very pleased with himself, Zhe Yan bid farewell to Mo Yuan and asked me to come and see him off. As we reached the road outside the mountain, Zhe Yan issued me a word of warning: "You may have a boy's body now, but you still mustn't wash with your fellow apprentices. You mustn't allow them to take advantage. You need to retain a young woman's modesty." I hung my head and nodded.

Mo Yuan looked after me extremely well, but I continued to resent him for lacking what I considered to be a heroic appearance, and his affection meant little to me.

•••

I did not start to revere Mo Yuan until I stumbled into my first pitfall, an encounter that caused me serious injury.

It had started with Zhe Yan's wine.

Zhe Yan made wonderful wine, and doting upon Fourth Brother as he did, he would give a lot of it to him. Because Fourth Brother and I were so close, I always got to share it. I would make regular trips to the peach grove's wine cellar, and over time I developed a real fondness for it. I felt guilty for taking so much of Zhe Yan's wine, and every time I went to a banquet and was in the company of immortal friends, I would make sure to sing his praises.

Zhe Yan may have been an exceptional winemaker, but he still had room for improvement. But I was young and naive and prone to exaggeration and would often come out with boastful statements at these banquets, about how wine like his could not be found anywhere else. Naturally some other wine experts had different opinions, but if they offered the name of any other winemaker and suggested they had superior skills, it would leave me feeling completely crushed.

Mount Kunlun's Sixteenth Apprentice, Zi Lan, would often take this stance. Even now I stand by my opinion that Zi Lan was petty to argue with me like that. My other fellow apprentices would recognize my exaggerated and excessive praise of Zhe Yan as youthful swagger, and just listen with a smile. Even when they disagreed, they kept in mind that I was the youngest apprentice, and let me off the hook.

Zi Lan was different. He would pout so much that you could have hung an oil pitcher off his lips. He would give a dismissive snort, and after a lot of tutting, he would say, "It couldn't be better than the wine Master makes, surely?"

Because of my scorn toward Mo Yuan, I hated hearing people praise him, and Zi Lan's oppositional stance served to fan the flame of my fury. I started hatching a plan to get Zi Lan to admit that Mo Yuan's wine was inferior to Zhe Yan's in front of all our fellow apprentices so that I could show up Mo Yuan's incompetence once and for all.

It was a simple idea, really. All I had to do was break into Mount Kunlun's wine cellar and steal a jug of Mo Yuan's wine. I would take this wine to Zhe Yan, who could use it as a sample to make a jug that was a hundred or maybe even a thousand times better. I would bring back this jug and give it Zi Lan, who would be forced to admit its superiority.

Mount Kunlun's wine cellar was not well guarded, and I managed to sneak in and get my hands on a jar without any trouble. The underhanded nature of this operation meant that I could not very well walk back through the main mountain entrance, and so I walked through the peach grove at the back peak of the mountain instead, from where I planned to summon a lucky cloud and soar over to Zhe Yan's.

But I managed to get myself lost within this peach grove. After a long time trying to find my way out, I became exhausted and started to feel quite thirsty. Realizing I was carrying a jar of Mo Yuan's wine, I decided to sip some to quench my thirst.

After one sip I started to feel hazy. It was only a small sip, but the flavor seeped in and spread throughout my mouth. I felt it burning as it slid down my throat. Zhe Yan really would have to up his game if his wine was going to compete on this level.

Mo Yuan was indeed a skilled winemaker. Fury filled my chest. I realized there was no point taking this wine over to Zhe Yan. I sat there for a while, fuming, before guzzling down the whole jar of wine, every last drop.

My head went dizzy, and I saw stars in front of my eyes. I leaned my head against a peach tree and fell straight asleep.

I woke up in an unusual way. Not naturally with the sun or with First Apprentice shaking me awake. I was woken up by having a basin of ice-cold water poured down onto me. It ripped me from my dreams and woke me with a start.

It was early spring, and the snow was just starting to melt, and the water that hit me must have been recently melted snow. It soaked through my clothes, and I responded with a loud, high-pitched sneeze.

I saw a woman sitting on an ebony chair. She took a sip of tea from a porcelain cup, put the cup down, and gave me a cold, impassive look. Serving girls with bowl haircuts were standing on either side of her ebony chair.

The first day I had arrived at Mount Kunlun, my fellow apprentices had warned me never to incur the wrath of the girls with the bowl haircuts. Even though they had been so rude, pouring cold water on my head, as a Mount Kunlun apprentice, I was required to remain courteous. It was the serving girls of the goddess Yao Guang, who had their hair cut in this style and were often found wandering around Mount Kunlun, and so I surmised that this must be who I was dealing with.

Yao Guang was usually a gentle and mild goddess apparently, but in wartime she was known to be fierce and brutal. She had always cared deeply for Master Mo Yuan, but over the years this unrequited love had intensified, and she had moved her immortal residence near to Mount Kunlun and would send her immortal serving girls over to Mount Kunlun every few days to stir up trouble. Her aim was to rile up Mo Yuan so that he would fight with her. She thought that if he saw her military might, she might win him over.

Despite all her efforts, Mo Yuan had failed to take the bait. He instructed his apprentices to treat her underlings with extreme courtesy, and to do our best to remain patient and tolerant toward them.

Seeing the serving girls with their bowl haircuts, I realized that the woman sitting on the ebony chair drinking tea must be Yao Guang, the goddess who was in love with Mo Yuan.

She had tied me up while I was drunk and asleep, obviously hoping that this would finally be enough to rile up Mo Yuan so much that he would engage with her in battle.

Goddess Yao Guang gave her right-hand immortal serving girl a look, and the serving girl responded by giving a loud cough and starting to admonish me. "Mount Kunlun is the most pure and sacred land in the Four Seas and Eight Deserts," she said, her voice full of fury. "How did such an effeminate he-fox muddle his way inside and manage to seduce Mo Yuan?"

I was too young to have a proper understanding of the word *seduce*, and her words confused me. I emitted a sound of bewilderment.

She gave me a fierce stare. "Just look at your eyes, eyebrows, and mouth, all so ornate. Since taking you on as his apprentice, Mo Yuan has cared for you heart and soul." Yao Guang looked at me with deep hostility. "Mo Yuan has abandoned the immortal path," the serving girl continued. "And regarding him as her immortal colleague, our goddess cannot bear to see him being led astray and feels compelled to step in and offer her assistance.

"You have committed a serious misdeed, but our goddess has always been merciful," she explained slowly. "You will become our goddess's servant. You will devote yourself to the practice of cultivating spiritual energy and banish all playfulness and vulgarity from your heart. Kneel down now and give thanks to our goddess for her great generosity and grace."

I stared at them in stunned silence, unable to make sense of what they were saying. I thought it through, but the only thing I could recall ever having done wrong since coming to Mount Kunlun was stealing Mo Yuan's wine. Other than that I had always abided perfectly by the rules.

"I haven't wronged Master in any way," I said boldly. "He treats me well because an old friend told him to have mercy upon me and the miserable life I have had. By tying me up like this and throwing water over me, you have shown me that Master has more goodness in the tip of one of his fingers than you have in your entire body. I refuse to become your servant." I did not actually believe what I had just said about Mo Yuan being better than Yao Guang; I had only said these things to annoy her.

Yao Guang was so livid she started shaking. She fiercely bashed her hand against the arm of the chair. "What a stubborn boy!" she said. "Drag him off to the water dungeon and lock him up inside for three days!"

I still remember Yao Guang's eyes as she gave this order, burning red with jealousy. It had all just been a misunderstanding, but I was a child, full of youthful vigor and not used to expressing myself properly. Instead of explaining the situation and getting myself out of this mess, I signed my own death warrant and spent the next two days experiencing intense suffering as a result.

Yao Guang's water dungeon was far more sophisticated than most others. When it was empty, it was waist-height with muddy water, but as soon as you were lowered in, this water would start to rise. It would move up your body, inch by inch, until it was covering your head. Even when your head was covered, the water would not actually drown you, it just gave you the awful sensation of drowning. Had you been allowed to experience this sensation constantly, you might have become used to it over time, but after a couple of hours, the water receded, and you would be left panting wildly and waiting for the torturous process to repeat itself.

I had spent so many years being idle and lazy, and even if I had exerted all my strength, I would not have been a match for this goddess. I was helpless to defend myself and had no choice but to endure my torment.

By the time Mo Yuan found me, I had been tortured to within an inch of my life. Fortunately I still had youth and stamina on my side. Through my daze, I remember seeing Mo Yuan's solemn face as he ripped open the dark steel chain of the dungeon door with one hand. Sparks flew everywhere. He fished me out of the water, wrapped me in a cloak, and held me close to him. He turned to pale-faced Yao Guang, and in an icy voice he said, "Meet me on the summit of Mount Cangwu on the seventeenth of February, and we will settle this score."

"I wish very much to battle with you," Yao Guang said in distress, "but not like this, and not . . ."

I did not hear the end of her sentence, as Mo Yuan was already striding off with me in his arms. At the entrance to Mount Kunlun, we bumped into First Apprentice, who reached out to take me, but Master did not hand me over. He just walked alongside First Apprentice with me still in his arms.

For the first time it dawned on me that even though Mo Yuan did not have a wide mouth, his voice was still deep and resonant. Even though his arms were not as strong and stocky as pillars, he was still sturdy and powerful. Mo Yuan was tough after all.

As soon as I returned to Mount Kunlun, I fell into a death-like sleep. When I awoke, First Apprentice told me that Mo Yuan had gone to the summit of Mount Cangwu to battle with Goddess Yao Guang. Such a rare spectacle only came around once in ten million years, and Second to Sixteenth Apprentices had all gone along to watch.

"How could Master have picked me to look after you?" First Apprentice asked with a sigh. I had no idea, but I was equally dismayed at not being able to witness Mo Yuan battling against Yao Guang.

First Apprentice was an incessant talker, and after listening to him burble for a couple of days, I finally understood what a serious operation Yao Guang's abduction of me had been. After the lamps had been turned out that night and I still had not returned to my room, my fellow apprentices became anxious. They searched all over Mount Kunlun, but could not find me. After turning the place upside down, they started to suspect that I might have stirred up trouble with Yao Guang's immortal servants and been taken captive.

It had just been a guess, and they had no proof, but my fellow apprentices were all extremely worried, and eventually they decided to alert Master. Master had been about to go to bed, but as soon as he heard this news, he draped a cloak over himself, and taking First Apprentice with him, he broke into Goddess Yao Guang's residence.

Yao Guang did not admit what she had done to Mo Yuan, even when he threatened her life. Master flashed his Xuan Yuan sword at her in complete disregard of all etiquette and charged his way inside to find me.

First Apprentice tutted and gave a big sigh. "If it hadn't been for Master's courage, you would probably never have seen the light of day again, Little Seventeenth," he said with a laugh. "You were exhausted. You fainted as soon as Master brought you back to Mount Kunlun. You were having nightmares, holding onto Master's hand and yelling with such distress it was hard to listen to. We couldn't pry your hand off his.

"Master was extremely upset by the state he found you in. He patted you on the back to comfort you and said, 'Don't be scared. Don't be scared. Master will protect you.' You looked just like a little baby," he said with a chuckle. My face went red. "What did you do to offend Yao Guang so much?" he asked in bafflement. "She's known to have an evil streak, but she's never been that cruel and ruthless before."

I had thought about this carefully while I was recuperating, and thought that I had a good understanding of the whole situation. I had been about to tell him that her fury had been fueled by jealousy, but I did not think it was fair to talk about someone behind their back, so I just mumbled a couple of incoherent reasons instead.

This was what unfolded in the dream I had just had about Mo Yuan. So far what had happened in the dream was indistinguishable from what had happened in reality. But in reality, Mo Yuan had returned to Mount Kunlun the afternoon following the Cangwu battle. Yao Guang had been brutally defeated and had subsequently fallen out of love with Mo Yuan and moved far, far away. But in the dream, Mo Yuan never returned from Cangwu. Each day I would grab First Apprentice and ask, "When is Master coming back?" And First Apprentice would respond with the words "Soon, soon."

CHAPTER FIFTEEN

So much time had passed in the dream and so much had happened, but when I lazily opened my eyes and saw the sun's shadow slanting over the west, I realized I must have been asleep for only three or four hours. The dream made me feel like I had lived through another seventy thousand years, and on waking I felt like I had aged. Ye Hua had left my room by then. I lay there for a while, staring up at the bed curtain, before attempting to get down from the bed, avoiding my chest injury as best I could. While my manner of turning around and clambering out of bed could not exactly be called smooth, by the time I had all four legs on the ground and had only strained my wound a little, I felt a rush of pride at my own deftness.

Yanhua Cave was filled with a thick fog that enshrouded Mo Yuan, and I could only make out his vague shape. I cast a spell, transforming myself back into human form, and walked over to where he lay.

I had been worrying unnecessarily. Mystic Gorge had tended to Mo Yuan just as he should have, even spreading his hair out over the pillow and carefully arranging all the strands. Even with my hawk-like attention, I could find nothing to fault.

I sat down next to him and entered into a trance, looking at those eyes, unopened for seventy thousand years, that straight nose, those pouting lips. To have thought this handsome face was sissy. How young and ignorant I was when I first met him, how absurd my thinking!

Nothing scares people as much as change. It was change that had caused an image of this alluring face to freeze forever within my mind. It was seventy thousand years since I had seen him smile, but I still had a crystal-clear image of him smiling as he stood in the peach grove at Mount Kunlun's back mountain, as peach blossom petals flew gracefully through the air.

It was extremely quiet inside the cave, and after sitting there awhile, I started to feel cold. I placed his hands on my chest, but it did not stop me from shivering. I left the cave to pick a handful of wildflowers, and exchanged them with the old ones in the vase. I took the vase outside and filled it with stream water to keep the flowers fresh and placed the vase next to Mo Yuan. This added a little bit of life to the icy cave.

Sitting there I suddenly remembered how it would very soon be gardenia season. I could pick some gardenias and weave them onto the thin willow branches I had collected the year before and make a flower curtain to hang at the entrance to Yanhua Cave. Whenever the cave got cold, their floral fragrance would be released, which was certain to bring some comfort to poor Mo Yuan inside. This idea really brightened my mood.

Seeing that the sky was starting to darken, I knelt and bowed down before him. I gave the cave a final once-over and started to hurry back down the mountain.

I had been groggy earlier and had no idea who had dressed my wound for me. It had to be either Ye Hua, Mystic Gorge, or Bi Fang, but whoever it was had been very sensitive to the fact that I was a woman, even if I had reverted back to my fox form, and they had just dabbed at the blood on my body, rather than throwing me into a wooden barrel and giving me a proper bath.

I had just climbed a mountain and exerted myself further by rushing in and out of Yanhua Cave. Now I was finally able to relax. Feeling the mountain wind blowing over me, I realized I was sticky with sweat from all this toil.

There was a small lake halfway down Fengyi Mountain, and while it was nothing compared with His Revered Highness Ling Bao's sky spring, I bathed in it regularly and found its waters extremely pleasant. It took me some time to remember the way, but once I was certain of the direction, I turned around and started to head eagerly there.

I peeled off my cloak, and summoning immortal energy to protect my injury, I entered the water. The water in this lake came from melted ice, and even in this early summer evening, the cold seeped through to the depths of my heart, and my teeth started chattering. I stood still, scooping up water and wetting my body bit by bit. Once I had fully acclimatized, I started to slowly submerge myself.

I stared in fascination at two bright trails of red within the jade-green lake water reflected onto the white of my petticoat.

It was highly unlikely that there would be anyone strolling by the lake at this hour, and after a while of hemming and hawing, I decided it was safe to take off my petticoat. Before I had managed to remove it, I heard a furious cry: "Bai Qian!" I trembled to hear my name called out like that.

This voice was familiar, but it was the first time I had heard him call me by my full name. I trembled, still in shock. I had been concentrating so hard on standing steadily in the middle of the lake, and his call had distracted me, causing me to lose my balance. I toppled into the water and would have drowned if Ye Hua had not rushed into the middle of the lake and grabbed tight hold of me.

He was so tall and broad chested that once he had me in an arm-lock, he managed to press me effortlessly into his chest. My injury did not appreciate being squeezed against such a firm chest, and it throbbed with so much pain I almost threw up blood. He had not summoned any immortal energy to protect himself, and his clothes were soaked through, while his dripping-wet hair stuck to his ears.

I was pressed to him, locked in place. I was unable to see the expression on his face, but I was right up against his heart and could hear it hammering loudly against his chest.

I gave a quiet sigh of relief that I had not had a chance to remove my petticoat. He loosened his grip on me and pressed his lips against mine.

My jaw dropped from the shock, enabling him to push his tongue past my teeth and into my mouth. I stared at him through wide eyes, but he was so close that all I could see were his pupils, the blackness within them surging and turning. He could clearly see me staring in wide-eyed surprise, but it did not stop him from this intense sucking and nibbling. In no time at all, my lips and tongue were completely numb, and I could taste what I suspected to be a couple of trickles of blood.

I was choking slightly, tears pricking the corners of my eyes. I had a vague sense of déjà vu, and I felt a strange feeling I could not name moving over me in waves.

He bit gently down onto my lower lip and mumbled, "Qian Qian, close your eyes." These mumbled words refocused my mind, and I reached out and pushed him away.

My badly injured body and the confusion raging in my mind meant that as soon as I pushed away Ye Hua's support, my feet went limp and I stumbled violently, nearly falling.

He reached out and grabbed me, remembering to avoid my injured chest this time. Before I could thank him for his consideration, he was nuzzling against my shoulders. "I . . . I thought you were trying to drown yourself," he said in a deep, husky voice.

I was too shocked to respond, but also amused by his interpretation of the situation. "All I was trying to do was take a wash," I said with a chuckle.

He held me even tighter, his lips pressed against my neck, his breathing heavy. ". . . won't let you . . . not again . . . ," he said slowly, a sentence with no beginning or end.

It all felt quite surreal, and I decided it was probably not a smart time to remain silent. I said Ye Hua's name a couple of times, but he did not respond. Despite the awkwardness, I persevered, trying to bring the conversation onto more comfortable territory. "Were you not in your study working on documents? How did you end up all the way here?" I asked.

I felt his breath on my neck becoming more even. "Mystic Gorge went to bring you food and discovered you weren't there," he explained somberly. "I came out looking for you as soon as he told me."

I patted him on the back and said, "Oh, it's dinnertime, is it? Shall we go back home then?" He said nothing, just gave me a loose hug in the water. I had no idea what was he was thinking. In my experience people in love were a law unto themselves and often needed guidance from others. Not wishing to disturb him, I just let him continue to hold me.

After a while I gave a sneeze, probably reminding Ye Hua that I was injured and that it was not wise for me to soak in this cold water for too long. Half supporting and half carrying, he rushed me to the bank. He used magic to dry our sopping-wet clothes before picking up his cloak and wrapping it around me. Together we walked down the mountain.

I was feeling giddy from the kiss in the lake. I could still remember the exact way it had felt, as if something were coursing deep inside my body, surging and tumbling, something invisible, formless, intangible. It was there for moment, and then it was gone. I sighed quietly to myself.

Ye Hua walked in front on the way down. All I could hear was the soughing of the mountain wind and the occasional chirrup of an insect. My mind wandered, and I did not notice that Ye Hua had stopped until

I bumped into his back. He took a step to the side so that I could see up ahead.

I scrunched up my nose and craned my head forward to look in the direction he was indicating. Inside the dilapidated old straw pavilion at the foot of Fengyi Mountain, I saw Zhe Yan smiling lazily up at us. He had a folding fan in his hand, which was resting on Fourth Brother's shoulder.

Fourth Brother was sitting cross-legged, squinting, a stalk of dog-tail grass in his mouth. He lifted his eyes to me and said, "Why is your face so red, Little Five? Are you drunk?"

I tried to appear composed, but just as I was about to come up with some excuse, Ye Hua gave a quiet cough. Zhe Yan looked me up and down, and tapping the folded fan, he said, "The moon is as cool as water tonight. Willows grow luxuriantly and flowers fill the courtyard. Perfect conditions for a tryst."

I gave an awkward laugh, but was unable to stop myself from stealing a glance at Ye Hua. His mouth was turned up at the corners, and his eyes shone brightly behind those locks of wet black hair.

Zhe Yan and Fourth Brother had obviously not come back to Qingqiu merely to bask in the moonlight and compose poems. They explained that Bi Fang had come to see them that afternoon and told them that I had been beaten to within an inch of my life. They had not thought such a thing possible and had dashed over to see this rare sight with their own eyes.

I clenched my teeth to stop myself from speaking, but the words popped out anyway. "Last time I was beaten to within an inch of my life, I was obviously very rude and recuperated before you two had the chance to come over and have a good gawk. What terrible manners. I am badly injured, yes, but not quite hanging on within an inch of my life. I'm sorry to disappoint you both."

Zhe Yan stood there with a mindless smile on his face before eventually passing his fan to me. "Disappointed is an understatement," he said with a laugh. "Fine, fine. Since I've made you so angry, I imagine it will take a wonderful treasure to pacify you. We commissioned the Western Sea Emperor to paint this fan for you. As you can see, you have done well out of my insult."

I reached out to take the fan, bursting with joy, but emitting an indifferent humph to hide this fact. We headed back to the foxhole, Zhe Yan and Fourth Brother walking in front, while Ye Hua and I brought up the rear.

"I was surprised to see you getting so irate from just a few teasing words," Ye Hua said in a quiet, pensive voice. "Zhe Yan obviously has quite a talent."

I covered my mouth to yawn. "It has nothing to do with talent. He's much older than me, which means I am perfectly within my right to get angry with him. If it were some younger immortal who had said something to offend me, I would be unlikely to argue back, not at my age."

"I only hope you feel you could argue and discuss things with me," Ye Hua said after a moment's silence. I felt my mouth about to open for a second yawn, but I managed to swallow it down instead.

Mystic Gorge was waiting for us in front of the foxhole. It was already past nine, and most households were extinguishing their lamps and climbing into bed by now. I felt guilty to have kept him up so late worrying.

When he saw me, he started to walk over. He bowed, and his face turned from green to black. "Demon Emperor Li Jing left a calling card. He wishes to see you, Your Highness. He's been waiting in the mouth of the valley for a while now."

Ye Hua stopped walking and gave a frown. "What can he want now?" he asked.

Zhe Yan grabbed Fourth Brother by the back of the collar just as he was about to enter the cave. "The gods are obviously smiling down on us today. We have timed our trip well. We have stumbled upon what promises to be a spot of genuine drama," he said with a laugh.

I walked toward the cave without breaking my stride. "Throw the fool out," I instructed Mystic Gorge in an even voice. Trembling, Mystic Gorge said, "He's waiting at the mouth of the valley, Your Highness. He has not stepped inside."

"I see," I said with a nod. "Leave him as he is in that case."

Zhe Yan was visibly itching for drama, and my placid response was akin to stamping on the fire of his hope. But before all the embers were put out, he made a last attempt to cajole me into action. "All issues of love and hate need to be resolved. By dragging it out you are just inviting trouble. Why delay when you can seize the day? Why don't we all go down there now and settle it once and for all?"

Ye Hua gave him a cold look. I rubbed my forehead thoughtfully and said, "Everything that needs be resolved has been resolved. I have no outstanding issues to discuss with him. This is obviously a matter that interests you greatly, and if you wish to go and see him, I will ask Mystic Gorge to light you a candle."

With a swish the last sparks of hope in Zhe Yan's eyes died. He gave a disappointed sigh. "We've gone to a lot of trouble to make this trip. Would it have hurt you to provide us with a bit of excitement?"

We did not often host guests at the foxhole, and only had one regular guest bedroom, which Ye Hua was currently occupying. Big Brother's and Second Brother's old rooms had grown dusty over time. But Zhe Yan was happy to share Fourth Brother's room with him, and this seemed to go some way toward making up for his disappointment on being denied any drama.

I followed Mystic Gorge into the house to rest, but he was going to try to stay awake to wait for Bi Fang, who was still out searching for me. I kept him company for a while, but after a few yawns, Ye Hua took me by the arm and led me off to bed.

I felt very happy to see that virtuous Mystic Gorge had prepared me a large pot of hot water so that I could bathe before I slept.

Ye Hua knocked on my bedroom door the next morning and told me we should set off for the Sky Palace soon. I had taken such a long nap the afternoon before that I had been yawning nonstop by the evening, but when I actually got into bed, I had not slept very well at all, and as soon as I heard Ye Hua's footsteps, I was wide-awake.

He was already packed. I walked around my room, picking out a couple of changes of clothes as well as my new fan.

Over the years I had wandered far and wide over the Four Seas and Eight Deserts, but this would be my first trip to the Ninth Sky. This rare opportunity made possible by Ye Hua would also give me the chance to have a leisurely wander around the kingdom. Even though I was still physically injured, my fox heart was starting to feel excited.

There was only one path in and out of Qingqiu Kingdom. Whether you were soaring on a cloud or traveling by foot, you had to pass the crescent-moon-shaped mouth of the eastern valley. Ye Hua did enjoy his morning strolls, so I bowed to his preference, and rather than summoning a lucky cloud straightaway, we set off toward the mouth of the valley on foot.

The mouth of the valley was the border between the mortal and immortal worlds, and half of it was a mist of propitious vapors, the other half a haze of red dust. The essences of these two worlds had been pushing against each other for so long that the area was a constant haze of dense fog.

I could make out a figure standing within this dense fog, dressed in a silvery-purple robe. He had an extraordinarily handsome face, which showed a lot of emotion. It was Li Jing.

He looked surprised to see me. "I never thought you'd agree to see me, Si Yin," he said slowly. I was just as surprised: I had not expected him to still be there.

In the past, he had waited for me at the foot of Mount Kunlun for more than a week, but he had been nothing but an idle prince back then, and all he would have been doing otherwise was cavorting with concubines or watching cockfights and dog races at the Purple Light Palace. It was very different now that he was the Demon Clan Emperor, and I was astonished he could spare all this time.

Ye Hua stood there, his face expressionless. He glanced at me. "Zhe Yan was right about what he said last night," he said in a breezy tone of voice. "It's better to resolve things as early as possible. Just because it's resolved in your mind doesn't mean it has actually been resolved. Issues like this require both parties to come together to deal with things once and for all and make a clean break."

I gave a surprised laugh. "This is a complicated topic. You sound like you have some experience in that field." He looked taken aback, and his face went strangely pale.

I sat down on one of the marble stools set out at the mouth of the valley. Ye Hua understood. "I'm going to walk on ahead and wait for you there," he said, wandering off.

Li Jing took a couple of steps toward me and gave a reluctant smile. "I'm relieved to see that you are all right," he said. "Your injuries aren't causing serious problems, are they?"

I drew up my sleeves to cover my hands. "I'm sorry to have caused you worry, Demon Emperor," I said calmly. "This old body of mine is a hardy one. It's nothing but a few minor injuries, no lasting damage."

He let out a relieved breath and said, "Oh, that's good news." He took something from his sleeve and held it in front of me. I lifted my eyes and saw a lustrous pool of jade. It was the artifact that I had asked for and been denied all those years ago: the Jade Soul.

My fan clattered to the ground. "Demon Emperor, why are you giving me this?" I asked, lifting my head.

He gave an anguished laugh. "Si Yin, I had a lapse of judgment back then. Please take the Jade Soul, place it inside Mo Yuan's mouth. That way you'll no longer need to feed him those cups of heart blood."

I looked at him for a while and gave a laugh. "Demon Emperor, I appreciate the intention behind your kind act, but Master's immortal body hasn't needed my blood nourishment for five hundred years now. Take this sacred artifact back for the Demon Clan."

Around five hundred years ago, I had locked Qing Cang back inside the Eastern Desert Bell and slept for 213 years as a result. During that time, I had been unable to provide blood nourishment for Mo Yuan's immortal body. The first thing I did when I woke up was rush to check on him. I was so worried about what might have happened to him that my hands and feet were like ice blocks. But I discovered that Mo Yuan's immortal body was in a well-nourished state, even without my blood.

Li Jing was still holding the Jade Soul out to me, looking awkward with his hand in midair. Finally he put the artifact away quietly, with an air of disappointment. "Si Yin, we'll . . . we'll never be able to go back to how it was, will we?" he asked hoarsely.

His voice came out as hazy as the fog surrounding us. It had an ethereal quality to it. I searched deep into my memory and managed to conjure up an image of Li Jing as a young boy. He had inherited his father's looks, and his eyes had become even more concentrated in their feminine beauty, but he was much more pleasant and confident than his father. He had a constantly flushed and cheerful face.

Hearing him sound so pitiful made me much less unhappy about running into him. I thought back over everything that had ever happened between us, all those hours we had spent together, all the things we had shared. It felt as if it had taken place in another lifetime entirely. I felt calm and composed. There would be no more ripples or waves and certainly no *going back*.

I was quietly wishing for an overcast sky. I was unable to hold back from saying, "Demon Emperor, this is nothing but some unresolved issues of the heart. I have already explained that you will always be chasing after what you can't have. The only reason you are throwing yourself before me now is because having been abandoned by you, I failed to find a place to bash my head against the ground in order to end my life. Instead, I'm alive and doing well. From that you conclude that I was never really in love with you, and that's the reason you've chosen to come here today and make things complicated . . ."

The corners of his eyes had reddened, which looked dramatic against the rest of his pale face. He did not respond; he just looked at me with a serious expression.

I calmed my mind and opened my fan, running a finger along the painted peach flowers on its surface. "This is the last time we will sit down together and speak like this," I said softly. "There are a couple of things I would therefore like to explain.

"Seventy thousand years ago you gave me my first taste of love. Because it was my first experience of love, I was passive and reserved. But there was so much love flowing out of my heart. Mother always worried about my strange temperament. She thought that I was unlovable, and if it were not for our Bai family prestige, I wouldn't have a chance of finding a husband.

"But you didn't know who my family was, or even that I was actually a woman, but you started to like me all the same. Day after day you would deliver me those love poems, and you even dismissed all your bedchamber concubines. Those acts filled me with happiness and gratitude. We members of the White Fox Clan are not like most land mammals. We are much more passionate and loving, and when we find a partner, we mate for life.

"I thought that the two of us would become lifelong companions. I had thought that once I'd completed my apprenticeship, we might wed. If Xuan Nu hadn't come along . . .

254

"We both knew about the bad blood between our clans. But after we got together, I would spend my days thinking about how in the future I might convince Father and Mother to agree to our marriage. Each time I thought of a good reason, I would be filled with glee and would write it onto a piece of silk in fear that I might forget it. Before long I had a whole foot of silk covered in tiny characters. How foolish it all seems looking back at it now."

Li Jing's lips quivered.

I continued to stroke the fan. "What did you think that Xuan Nu could do for you that I, Bai Qian, future goddess of Qingqiu, couldn't? But what a huge blow you delivered me, right when my love was blazing at its strongest. I was such a wreck after you went off with her, and the pain in my heart consumed me.

"My only regret was being foolish enough to trust Xuan Nu heart and soul and giving her the opportunity to tempt you away. I was just going to slap her across the cheek, nothing more, but the way you protected her . . . Do you know how much that hurt me? And that thing you said, 'It was ridiculous of me to think I could be a homosexual . . . ,' that hurt me even more. You just abandoned me, focusing on your own happiness and pleasure without a second thought for my sadness and suffering. Not everyone lets pain and sadness show openly on their face, Li Jing. But even though I kept mine hidden, that doesn't mean it hurt me any less.

"I always thought that I would one day be your wife, but that turned out to be nothing more than a joke. Every night I'd have the same nightmare in which you would be holding Xuan Nu and pushing me off Mount Kunlun. It was during the time that I was having these nightmares that I heard how your four qilin beasts had carried Xuan Nu into the Purple Light Palace, where she became your bride, and how the wedding celebration had gone on for nine days straight. It may sound foolish, but even though I sound free and easy when I say these things, even after everything that's happened, I still have thoughts about you that I know I shouldn't.

"The Demon Clan Revolt happened soon after. Xuan Nu stumbled over to us, having suffered under Qing Cang's whip, and was carried up to Mount Kunlun. I was secretly happy, and every spare moment I would turn my mind looking for excuses for you, trying to convince myself that you couldn't really love Xuan Nu or you wouldn't have let her suffer like that. I managed to use these delusional thoughts to console myself. Later I discovered that it had been nothing but a confidence trick, that your clan had injured her just to gain our trust. Li Jing, you don't want to know my thoughts when I discovered that. Later my master passed. I gathered up every ounce of confidence I had left, and with my crushed heart, I marched into the big Purple Light Palace to plead with you to lend me the Jade Soul. You'll never understand how much courage I had to drum up to do that, or how devastated your response made me. You say you were jealous of Master and that's why you denied me the Jade Soul. But, Li Jing, you hurt me so badly. Your devotion to me was not one-ten-thousandth of that shown to me by Master. I was in Yanhua Cave, and I had lost a lot of blood. My injuries were so bad that my life was hanging in the balance. It wasn't your face that flashed through my mind, however. That's when I knew that my heartbreak was finally over. That's when I knew I was free."

Li Jing closed his eyes tightly, and when he eventually opened them again, they were completely bloodshot. "Si Yin, please don't say any more," he said, choking up.

I put away my fan with reluctance. "Li Jing, you're the only man I've loved in all my one hundred forty thousand years. But the twists and turns of time change us, and we can never go back."

He was trembling. Finally two streams of tears started to roll down his cheeks. "I've learned all this far too late," he said in an anguished voice. "You are no longer where you were waiting for me."

I nodded. There was no reason to worry about trouble from the Demon Clan in the future. As we were about to part ways, I gave a sigh. "In the future we will be like strangers," I said.

"We shall not see each other again." He bid me farewell and was gone.

The fog had cleared by then. Ye Hua was standing some way off, waiting for me. "They were obviously very sweet words, but upsetting coming from you."

I managed to force a smile.

CHAPTER SIXTEEN

There were no sky soldiers standing guard when we arrived at the Ninth Sky's southern gate, just a couple of tigers napping nearby, their orange-and-black fur sleek and shiny. With one glance you could tell that they were spirit creatures with extraordinary levels of cultivated spiritual energy.

"We may not have much defense at Qingqiu, but at least we have Mystic Gorge sitting there to watch over the place," I teased Ye Hua, tapping my fan. "Don't tell me your kingdom's most sacred realm only gets a couple of tigers?"

"The old Taoist prince is hosting an altar sermon at today's Taoist assembly. I expect they're all attending that," he said with a frown. He turned, gave a faint laugh, and said, "Qian Qian, I heard that you had regular discussions about Taoism with Yuan Zhen when you were down in the mortal world, helping him pass his calamity. I presume this means you have a deep knowledge and understanding of Taoism. The old Taoist prince has been complaining for years now about how there is no one in the sky who can rival him on the subject of Taoism and how lonely it has been standing on that high peak by himself out of everyone else's reach for so long. But now that you're here, what a wonderful opportunity for you two to hold a discussion or two."

I swallowed. "That's very kind of you," I said with an awkward laugh.

Outside the Ninth Sky's southern gate, there were boundless stretches of white clouds for as far as the eye could see, while within the gates it was a completely different story. The ground was made of gold, the steps of jade stone, the paths flanked by an emerald-green bamboo grove, and a thousand trails of propitious vapors. It completely surpassed the glitzy gold of the Water Crystal Palaces of all Four Seas. Luckily I had expected this and had tied the white silk around my head as a precaution. My eyes would have probably been destroyed by now otherwise. Every so often I heard the distinct call of a crane and the flapping of wings as one flew overhead. I gave an ardent sigh and took Ye Hua's hands. "Your family is so wealthy!" I exclaimed.

Ye Hua's face turned first white, then green. "Not all the palace quarters in the Ninth Sky are quite like this one," he explained. As we walked along, I paid close attention to the extravagant splendor of the Ninth Sky, so different from the terraced rice paddies and farmhouses of Qingqiu, although these were charming in their own way.

The few palace attendants we came across were all extremely circumspect and polite. None of them acted in the slightest bit taken aback by my strange silk-bound face. I was delighted to see them all acting with such deference as they paid their respects to Ye Hua.

I had heard that Ye Hua had been given his own government department and army to command when he was only thirty thousand years old, and it was at this time that the Sky Emperor had built him Xiwu Palace, as a gift.

Despite the fact that it was my first time coming to the Ninth Sky, I had a hunch that Xiwu Palace had not always been as dim and gloomy as it was now. It did not need anything as flamboyant as golden tiles and jade eaves, but Xiwu Palace could have done with a bit of brightening up.

By the time I had recovered my senses, Ye Hua was leading me toward the back gate. He was carefully examining the low wall near the back door, making rough measurements. He pointed to one wall and told me, "Jump."

"What?" I said in bafflement. He frowned, put his arms around me, walked along the wall to the spot he had just been pointing at, and leaped over with me into the courtyard.

Was jumping through walls what people did in the Ninth Sky rather than walking through doors? It seemed a strange habit . . . Ye Hua smoothed his sleeves, looked at me, and gave an awkward smile. "If we'd gone through the main door, it would have alerted everyone in all these courtyards of our arrival, and we would have had to put up with endless greetings and fuss. Jumping over the wall has saved us a lot of hassle."

A thought suddenly occurred to me. I tapped him on the shoulder with my fan and said, "We've arrived here very early today. It's not yet even the time that Jia Yun usually delivers your documents. I assume you will have told him not to deliver any to Qingqiu today. You wouldn't have wanted him to make a long journey for nothing. Entering through the main door would have alerted Jia Yun to your arrival, and that would certainly have given you some hassle."

I gave a chuckle. "Or to put it another way, it was very late when we got back to the foxhole last night. Did you manage to finish working on your last few days' worth of documents?"

He stiffened, and his face went red. He clenched his fists, rolled up his sleeves, and gave an awkward cough. I had been concerned about Ye Hua acting old before his time; at only fifty thousand, he seemed more serious and uptight than Dong Hua even. Seeing this display of youthful vigor came as a relief, and I gave my fan a joyful little shake.

Ye Hua lived in Zichen Palace, located next to Dumpling's Qingyun Palace. I was only planning to spend two or three days recuperating in the Ninth Sky, and since we had made this stealthy entrance and avoided all the pomp and ceremony that would normally be bestowed upon a visiting god or goddess, I did not wish to let Ye Hua go to the trouble of providing me with my own bedchamber. I was just about to bring this up meekly and explain that I would be happy to spend the next few days living in Qingyun Palace with Dumpling, but before I could say anything, he led me through into a special courtyard.

I looked up and saw a plaque hanging high above the courtyard door engraved with calligraphy characters that read "Concentrated Beauty."

"This is your courtyard," Ye Hua told me, his eyes twinkling. I shook my fan and mumbled to myself. It was only just beginning to dawn on me how extravagant they were up here in the sky. I could not help but compare it to the courtyard I had been put in during my months in the mortal world, helping Yuan Zhen through his calamity.

I would be in the sky for only a matter of days, and yet I had been provided with my own courtyard. One was a mortal emperor and the other an immortal emperor, and apart from both being emperors, they were as different as mud and clouds.

I gave a sigh and reached a hand to push the vermilion courtyard door. It creaked open, revealing a courtyard full of peach trees all in bloom. My eyes were filled to the brim with peach blossom pink. Overwhelmed by the sight, I muttered, "So you've tricked me into coming here to help the empress tend to her flat peach orchard!"

Ye Hua's expression froze, but I could see the corners of his mouth twitching. "I'm not sure exactly how big the empress's flat peach orchard is, but it wouldn't possibly fit into this courtyard. These are peach trees I planted myself two hundred years ago and have been tending ever since. This is the first time they've blossomed."

My heart gave an unexpected lurch. I stepped slowly out into the courtyard and used my fan to pick a branch of the blossoms.

The peach blossom flowers on the branch were delicate and exquisite. I was just about to put the fan away when from behind me I heard a resonant and heartrending voice calling out, "Empressss!" I turned to see Ye Hua standing on a step to the side of the courtyard, his eyes obscured by a couple of locks of dark hair. A woman stood in the doorway behind him, and I assumed she was a palace attendant from the way she was dressed. She was holding an elegant vase in one hand while clinging to the vermilion door with the other. She gazed at me, her blinking eyes full of affection, two lines of tears streaming down her face.

My hand started to shake, and the branch I was holding pinged up into the air. Half the petals dropped off it, and some came tumbling down onto me.

The woman stumbled over to me and wrapped her arms around my legs. "Empress, it's you!" she said through her tears. "Nai Nai has been waiting for you for three hundred years. You have finally returned . . ." Laughing and crying, she turned to Ye Hua and said, "That soul-binding lamp really is a sacred object—Empress hasn't changed a bit."

From her expression I realized she had mistaken me for someone else. I could not extricate my legs from her grip, but I used my hands to try and push her off me. She lifted her head to look at me, her eyes misty with tears, but behind those tears I could see pure joy.

As she reached out to touch the white silk around my eyes, I felt the need to say something. "You must have mistaken me for someone else. I'm Bai Qian from Qingqiu, not this empress of whom you speak."

This young immortal attendant, Nai Nai, looked taken aback, but she continued to hug my legs. I threw Ye Hua a helpless look, but my white silk was in the way, stopping me from communicating with my eyes, so I raised a hand and beckoned him over instead.

He came over to help Nai Nai to her feet, his eyes remaining on the peach grove in front of him the whole time. "This is Goddess Bai Qian from Qingqiu Kingdom," he said calmly. "She will be staying in this courtyard for a few days under your care. You mustn't call her Empress again. Instead you shall refer to her by her honorable title, *Goddess*."

Nai Nai, still clamped around my leg, looked in confusion first at him, then at me. I gave her a reassuring smile, but she did not react, just took her sleeves up to her tear-stained face to give it a wipe before nodding to Ye Hua's request.

I had brought along only two changes of clothes, so I did not have much to unpack. Ye Hua sent Nai Nai off to get me a bathing robe and other accessories and told me to lie down for a bit while he went to Qingyun Palace to fetch Dumpling.

Ye Hua had been extremely perceptive. He could see that my injuries were making it hard to walk and that the long trip had left me exhausted. He could also tell that I had been missing Dumpling. I felt very touched by how sensitive he was being to my needs.

Dumpling had been missing me too, it would seem. Ye Hua carried him through, and as soon as he saw me, he leaned out of his father's arms calling, "Mother," in a sweet little voice, which was delightful to hear.

The vase into which Nai Nai was sticking peach blossom branches suddenly smashed to the ground. I realized that little immortal must have been on familiar terms with Dumpling's mother. Dumpling's mother had been cut down in the prime of life, never again to experience the joys of motherhood. Her passing had allowed me the pleasure of becoming a stepmother, which was obviously a painful thing for this little immortal attendant to have to see.

What a brave and loyal immortal attendant she was.

Ye Hua said that Dumpling had been in a state of shock following the incident at the Purple Light Palace, but that it had not been too serious. I gave him a little inspection and saw that he was still as pale and plump as ever, and when he smiled, those two little dimples appeared as before. He did not look as if he had been scarred by the experience, which was a great comfort to see.

He clearly wanted to come over to me, but his father held him tightly. He struggled for a while, looking frustrated when he found he was unable to free himself. He flattened his mouth in displeasure and looked at me and pretended to cry without tears in his eyes.

I stroked his hair lovingly and said, "Mother's not very well. Let Father Prince hold you for the time being."

He blinked, his little face suddenly turned red, and he gave a little wriggle. "Ali knows. Mother's having another baby, isn't she?" he said quietly.

"What?" I asked in astonishment.

He fiddled shyly with the seams of his clothing. "That's what the book says," he explained. "That a lady isn't meant to play with children from other families when she's pregnant, in case it harms the . . ." He thought about it for a while, and struck one of his little fists against his palm as he remembered the word. "Yes, the embryo," he finished in an assured tone of voice.

My heart trembled. This little darling, a child no bigger than a garlic sprout, already knew about embryos! "Where did you lay your hands on such a book?" Ye Hua asked with a chuckle.

"Cheng Yu lent it to me," Dumpling said innocently.

I saw the veins in Ye Hua's temple start to pulse. Tut, tut, this Cheng Yu, who had soared from the mortal world, was obviously a wonder to behold, daring to defy the power of the mighty and pluck hairs from a tiger's tail. I was full of admiration.

"Why is your face so red, Your Little Highness?" Nai Nai asked, sounding confused. "Even if Goddess is pregnant, would that be so bad?"

Dumpling reached for my face and gave it a big loud kiss, saying, "I'm happy, actually. If Mother has a baby, I won't be the youngest member of the Sky Clan anymore."

"We'll have one right away after we're married," Ye Hua said after a short pause.

"If you want one then, I would be happy to oblige," I replied meekly. Ye Hua opened his mouth, but no words came out.

My reason for coming to the Sky Palace was to soak in the water of His Highness Ling Bao's spring pool. And so, after having rested and settled in awhile, I rushed off toward His Highness Ling Bao's Shangqing region.

Since I intended to bathe in his sky spring, naturally I needed to be courteous and introduce myself first and explain and why I was there.

It was not the best day to have arrived, as it coincided with the old Taoist master's Taoist assembly, and since Ling Bao was the old Taoist master's master, I was obliged to at least show my face at the assembly. Ling Bao was not inside his Jade Imperial Palace. Seven older immortal men who were waiting in the great hall told me that Ling Bao would pay me an official visit once the old Taoist master's assembly was over. I presented them with a night pearl, and eighteen immortal attendants formed two lines, their hands full of fruit, flowers, and wine, and led Ye Hua, Dumpling, and me toward the healing waters of the sky spring.

I had a basic understanding of Sky Clan rituals and knew that being led by eighteen immortal attendants was the courtesy bestowed upon gods and goddesses. A question suddenly popped into my head. I managed to keep it to myself for a while, but before long I found myself turning to Ye Hua and saying, "If I were your head concubine and I wished to soak in these springs, how many immortal officials would I have leading me?"

He stopped walking, Dumpling in his arms. "Fourteen," he said at last. "What of it?"

I held my fan and gave a melancholy sigh. "Nothing of it. I just realized that marrying you won't improve my status but will actually cause it to drop. It doesn't seem like a very good deal from that point of view."

I could see him silently grinding his teeth. "As the Sky Empress, you would be led by twenty-four immortal attendants, and we would assign you another four dexterous attendants to rub your back."

I gave an awkward laugh, followed by a deep sigh. "Well, that sounds a bit better."

The sky spring tumbled down from a man-made mountain. It was a secluded spot, and the spring water and its surrounding mist were a clear emerald blue. In the chaos before yin split from yang, there had been nothing but mist between the sky and earth, apart from this shallow blue pool.

Dumpling gave a joyful whoop when he saw the pool. He let an immortal attendant take off his little gown and cloak, and I watched his small, tender white figure as he leaped into the water. He bobbed up to the surface, where he splashed around making ripples.

Ye Hua watched him awhile before inspecting all the different types of fruit, flowers, and wine that the immortal attendants had brought along with them. "These are all fruit wines," he turned to me and explained. "Ali can be given a little, but make sure he doesn't drink too much. He's allowed to try one of each of these seasonal fruits too."

I nodded. He was both father and mother to this little boy. Not an easy job. Seeing this new side to him filled me with admiration.

He looked momentarily taken aback, but then the icy look began to thaw, and a radiant smile appeared on his face instead. He took the fan from my hand. "This fan has been painted with romantic peach blossoms, but it has not been inscribed with a poem. Why don't I take it with me now and write you an accompanying poem?

"You stay here for a while and have a good soak, and when you've finished, come by my study to find me." He gave such a bright smile that it dazzled my eyes, and before I had recovered my senses, he had taken the fan and was gone.

"Why is Father Prince going?" Dumpling asked, still splashing around in the spring pool. "Why doesn't he stay and soak with us?"

"The sky commander has a big assignment for Father Prince," I said with a chuckle. "He has to go and find out what it is."

The alcohol was too much for Dumpling, who soon became tipsy.

Ye Hua had made a point of telling me to allow Dumpling only one of each type of seasonal fruit, and assuming that the same applied to all the varieties of fruit wine, I allowed him half a jar of each. I had not imagined that he would be away with the fairies after two half jars, giving him an adorably naive and foolish smile, smiling and smiling until his head drooped to the side and he toppled drowsily back into the water.

"His Little Highness has never drunk this much before," Nai Nai piped up anxiously. "Maybe I should take him to the medicine prince's residence for an examination."

I had been drinking alcohol for more than one hundred thousand years, always from that supreme being Zhe Yan's supply of top-quality wine, and saying I was qualified to speak on the subject was a modest statement. All Dumpling had drunk was fruit wine, which was nothing more than immortal fruit stored for long enough to start fermenting. It was harmless stuff, and impossible to get drunk from, even if you consumed a lot.

The only reason Dumpling had fallen into this drunken stupor was because he had never drunk before and his tolerance was low. After he fell asleep, I calmly checked his pulse and looked him over, but found the energy circulating in his body to be stronger than my own even. Taking him to the medicine prince's residence just to dispel the effects of the alcohol would be making too much of a fuss. "It's no good to coddle boys in this way," I said, turning to Nai Nai. "There's nothing seriously wrong with him. Take him back to his room and let him just sleep it off. He'll sleep through until the middle of the night at the latest, after which he is bound to wake up naturally."

Two immortal attendants scooped Dumpling out of the water and put his clothes back on him, and Nai Nai carried him back to his palace. I ate a few pieces of fruit, drank the dregs of wine left by Dumpling, and drifted off into a hazy sleep. When I opened my eyes again, it was evening. I had really done a disservice to those poor eighteen immortal attendants, who had waited at the side of the pool for me all this time without a word of complaint. With much revived spirits, I smoothed my hair, knotted my robe, and, imagining that there would be further dazzling scenery between Yuchen and Xiwu Palaces, made the prudent decision to keep my white silk tied around my face.

Our three-month cohabitation in Qingqiu had given me a basic understanding of Ye Hua's living habits. It was at this hour he would usually drag me over to play chess with him. I imagined he would probably still be in his study. Considering that my fan would be useful for swatting away mosquitos, I decided not to go straight back to Concentrated Beauty, but to nip into his study first instead.

There was no one standing guard outside. I knocked on the door. Hearing no answer, I gave it a gentle push, and it began to open. There was no one in the outer room either, but I could tell that there were candles burning furiously on the other side of the door curtain, as I could see their shadows flickering.

I heard a low-pitched female moan from inside, and my heart gave a thump against my chest. I felt at a momentary loss, and my ears burned. I had been walking in on one tryst after another recently. I couldn't have been unlucky enough to find myself a door curtain's width away from yet another couple's boudoir activity, surely?

I tempered myself.

Ye Hua often came across as calm and aloof, but he was young, and naturally he would be hot-blooded. All the immortal attendants I had come across today had possessed delicate and charming features. Dealing with a desk full of documents night and day was obviously monotonous for the poor youngster. Lifting his head and setting eyes on a young immortal attendant with features as fine as those in a painting might well give him ideas as to how to sweeten the bitter pill of his bureaucratic drudgery.

It gave me a strange feeling.

It was a good thing if Ye Hua had shaken off that untoward way he had started thinking about me, and I should have been overjoyed. But instead I found myself feeling anxious about whether the young immortal attendant with features as fine as those in a painting was indeed beautiful enough for Ye Hua.

I considered the sage Buddhist words: "It would be better to tear down ten temples than to destroy one marriage." I pinched my ear, which was burning hot, and got ready to slip out quietly, taking such light steps that I would not disturb even a puff of cloud.

But before my right foot had even crossed the doorway, I heard Ye Hua's gentle voice calling out, "What exactly are you doing out there? Are you coming in or not?"

I rubbed my forehead and gave a quiet sigh. Even with a beautiful woman in his arms, Ye Hua could still make out some faint indistinct sound. He really was an exceptional god.

The candles behind the curtain started to leap. I did not wish to enter, but did not feel I could leave now either. "I've inscribed your fan with a poem. Come and get it," Ye Hua said.

I gave a gulp. Since he was instructing me to enter, I imagined he had to be decent. I was actually feeling curious to see what the little immortal attendant I had heard moaning looked like, so I plucked up the courage to eagerly lift the curtain and step into his study.

My instinct had not been too far off; however, it was not just one young immortal attendant on duty in the inner room, but two.

They were, though, fully clothed and on their knees, their heads lowered to the ground. The shoulders of the one on the left were shaking, as if she were lying there silently sobbing.

Ye Hua was sitting behind his desk with a big stack of documents in front of him. Next to the documents was a blue-and-white porcelain bowl of soup, with steam billowing off it. His austere expression was very different from the amorous one I had been picturing while standing outside.

I was filled with surging waves of doubt so strong that they reached the top of high mountains and filled deep valleys. I needed to retain my goddess bearing in front of these little immortal attendants, however, and so temporarily overcoming this doubt and feigning calmness, I took the fan from Ye Hua's hand. While I was inspecting his inscription on its surface, I managed to regain enough composure to ask, "So what is all this then?"

Ye Hua's handwriting was beautiful. He had written eighteen characters in two columns on the fan's surface. They read, "To winds of the east let us raise a glass, relax together and enjoy the time we pass." I had been trembling in anticipation as I opened up the fan, afraid that he might have written something too gushy.

But I was pleased with what I saw.

The room fell quiet. I lifted my eyes in curiosity and saw the girl kneeling on the right was looking at me, an expression of abject terror in her eyes.

She had beautiful eyes. In all my one hundred forty thousand years, I had never seen such beautiful eyes. Phoenix Nine's eyes were very lovely, but she was younger, and they did not show any of the sediment of time. The eyes before me seemed filled with boundless emotion, and once I had seen them, I found it hard to look away.

There was something really special about this young immortal attendant.

But her eyes were her only charming feature. The rest of her face was quite commonplace, and she was nowhere near as beautiful as Princess Green Sleeves from the Southern Sea Emperor's family.

Through trembling lips, this immortal attendant managed to call out a shaky name. I heard it clearly: it was the name of Dumpling's mother, the woman who had jumped from the immortal punishment platform.

I stroked the white silk on my face. I had been mistaken for her three times now, and I was getting so used to it I no longer felt the need to put people right. I just took a sip of tea and looked her up and down again. "You have very beautiful eyes," I told her quietly.

It was a compliment, given with sincerity, and most would be happy to hear it. The young immortal attendant kneeling in front of me was clearly different from most: she not only seemed displeased to hear my compliment, she actually fell onto the floor and lay sprawled on her side, staring at me through increasingly panic-stricken eyes.

I may not have been quite as blessed in the looks department as Fourth Brother, but I was always by far the most beautiful woman in Qingqiu. I would have expected her to be revering me for my beauty, which had not faded over these tens of thousands of years, not to become so fearful of my appearance that she fell into a crumpled heap on the floor!

Ye Hua calmly removed my white silk and pulled me over to the seat next to him. The two immortal attendants in front of us were both staring wide-eyed at my face. They must have finally realized that I looked nothing like Dumpling's mother.

Ye Hua raised his chin and addressed the two immortal attendants staring dumbly at me in a cold voice. "Princess Liao Qing, there is no longer any room for you at Xiwu Palace. Please return to the Eastern Sea tomorrow morning. Su Jin, you obviously place a great deal of importance on your friendship with Princess Liao Qing, so if you really can't bear to see her leave, I suggest you ask the Sky Emperor to issue a decree to have you both married out into the Eastern Sea. How does that sound?"

His words chilled me to the bones. Both the kneeling immortal attendants turned white.

I was shocked. I squinted at the girl on the left, who was still sobbing soundlessly. I could vaguely make out the elegant bone structure of her face, so similar to that of the Eastern Sea Emperor. She had to be Princess Liao Qing.

Which meant that the girl kneeling on the right, with the eyes that did not match the rest of her face, was the woman my unfilial apprentice, Yuan Zhen, had tried to have his way with, and who had attempted to hang herself as a result, and Ye Hua's head concubine, Su Jin.

I had found her appearance rather commonplace before I knew who she was, but now that I knew she was the reason my poor beloved little apprentice had faced all those trials and tribulations, I found her looks even more commonplace. I gave a sad sigh into my sleeve. *Yuan Zhen, oh, Yuan Zhen, what bad taste you have. You would be doing yourself more of a favor if you took advantage of yourself while looking in a mirror; you are miles more attractive than she.*

Su Jin was still looking at me, her eyes clear again, while Liao Qing was still sobbing and pleading. I could see how angry Ye Hua was. Apart from during the battle with Xuan Nu at the Purple Light Palace, I had never seen him so angry. I was intrigued, and even though I already had what I came for, I was unable to tear myself away. I picked up a teacup, filled it with boiling water, found a corner to sit down in, and calmly waited for the tea to cool.

Even when he was angry, Ye Hua was amazingly skilled at maintaining his composure. Princess Liao Qing's defense was enough to move any listener to tears, but he remained completely unaffected. He just sat there quietly, looking through his documents.

I had seen Princess Liao Qing reduced to tears by the depths of her love for Ye Hua once before, after the Eastern Sea banquet, and now, even though Su Jin was so affected by the princess's performance that she was wiping away tears of her own, I found I was able to keep my cool.

After listening for a while, I finally caught up with what had taken place and understood why Ye Hua was so angry. Earlier that evening, Eastern Sea Princess Liao Qing had made a brazen attempt to feed Ye Hua a bowl of soup she had spiked with a love potion in the hope of seducing him. Unfortunately for her, she had not picked a quality potion, and Ye Hua had smelled it while holding the bowl. She had not ended up lighting a fire in his heart as she had been hoping, but had ignited flames of fury instead.

The desk immortal who ground Ye Hua's ink had been standing by his desk at the time and had witnessed the whole thing. She had rushed to fetch Head Concubine Su Jin to adjudicate the proceedings, in line with Sky Palace regulations. I was impressed with Su Jin's display of tolerance, which seemed to go above and beyond. When she learned that Liao Qing had tried to seduce her husband with a love potion, she had not shown the slightest resentment or anger, but had actually pleaded clemency for the princess. Such a generous attitude could make her a model concubine of the entire Four Seas and Eight Deserts.

I had come in to collect my fan during a break in their drama. As soon as I worked out what had happened, I was no longer interested in staying. There were far more interesting things to do than watch this pair kneeling on the floor and wailing. Mortal world plays had similar plots but were less subdued and better written.

My tea was the ideal temperature to drink. I finished it in a couple of swigs, picked up my fan, and made to leave.

Just as I was about to make my escape, Princess Liao Qing wrapped her arms around my leg. "Empress, I didn't know who you were last time we met, but you helped me then, and I will always remember that and be grateful. Now I'm pleading for you to please help me one more time."

I turned silently to Ye Hua. "Since Princess Liao Qing has knelt before me to ask me to help, I feel obliged to give a few words of advice, if you will permit me."

Ye Hua lifted his head from his documents, looked at me, and said, "Be my guest."

I gave a sigh. "Princess Liao Qing is not the only one at fault here. You knew from the start how she felt about you, and you brought her back to the Sky Palace anyway. I appreciate that you wanted to repay the favor you owe her by helping her to avoid marrying the Western Sea's second prince and giving her space to think before returning to the Eastern Sea, but she was not to know that was your thinking. She was obviously hoping that your affection toward her would grow. She saw how upright and honorable you have been acting toward her, and so she eventually took it upon herself to make the first move."

It was hard to read what Ye Hua was thinking from his eyes. He looked at Liao Qing with indifference and said, "You told me that all you wanted was to work as a serving girl at Xiwu Palace and you would be completely satisfied."

"Do you think you can believe anything told to you by a girl in love?" I said with a yawn.

Liao Qing had cried so much that her face was barely recognizable. I tapped the edge of my fan and said, "You listen to an old lady's words. You'd be better off going back to the Eastern Sea." Then I took a couple of steps back to free myself from her grip. I straightened my clothes, and before she had a chance to react, I picked up my fan and slipped from the room.

I had gotten as far as the threshold of the outer room before Ye Hua caught up with me and pulled me back. I turned around to look at him. He let go, and we stood there shoulder to shoulder. "It's dark outside. Will you be able to find your way back to your courtyard?" he asked.

I looked around and said, "I'm sure I'll be able to find it," but my words sounded full of doubt.

He was silent awhile before saying, "I'll walk you back." I heard Liao Qing sobbing from the inner room, behind the curtain with the flickering candle.

The two of them must have tired themselves out completely with all that fuss. They could use the time while Ye Hua accompanied me to have a rest and recover their energy, so that they could give him an even more spirited display later.

Even though I was temporarily removing Ye Hua from the scene so that he could act as my guide, I imagined I would not be taking him away from these serious back palace matters for too long. I led him out without too much of a sense of guilt.

The moon was frost colored, and a cold wind was blowing.

Ye Hua was quiet along the way, save for the occasional warning about tree branches or stones that could trip me. He took me down an uneven path, and because of my eyes, I had to keep my focus on where I was walking, which prevented me from talking.

I had been feeling quite tired anyway, and by the time we had walked the whole path, I felt even more depleted. Arriving at the front entrance to my courtyard, all I wanted was to dive into my room and flop down onto the bed.

But I had just reached the threshold when Ye Hua grabbed me again.

I lifted my head pitifully and said, "You don't need to take me any farther. I know the way from here."

He was slightly taken aback by my comment, but laughed all the same. "If this courtyard were any bigger, you would probably end up getting lost in it and might not even manage to find your way back to your room. I know this about you by now." He paused, staring at me with a serious expression. "I actually wanted to ask you something. Why did you persuade Princess Liao Qing to go back to the Eastern Sea just then?"

I covered my mouth to give a half yawn. "Didn't you want her to go back to the Eastern Sea?" I asked.

His eyes went dark. "That's why you advised her to go back, because it was what I wanted?" I rested my fan on my elbow and said nothing.

There was a slight hint of aggression to Ye Hua's voice. I was not sure if it would be better for me to be sincere and nod or to be insincere and shake my head, or whether I would be best off to just look unruffled and unreactive. I did not have much experience with situations like this, even at my grand old age. The immortals I spent time with tended to be cheerful and easygoing.

I had never really understood youngsters who had grown old before their time, and Ye Hua, the epitome of these, had been acting very unpredictably of late, almost as if he had been bewitched, making him even more unfathomable. I had no idea what answer he wished to hear.

Before I could decide how to reply, he had his head in his hand. "So that's how it is?" he said with a bitter smile.

By the time an immortal obtains my amount of cultivated spiritual energy, enough to enter the realm of god or goddess, they naturally need to be familiar with the ways of the world. They do not need to know everything, but they need to partially understand how to read people's faces. With a quick glance at Ye Hua's face and the bitter smile upon it, I realized how full of resentment he was feeling, and how mistimed my silence had been. I should have responded to his question.

As soon as this dawned on me, I smiled at him to try to make up for it. I looked at his frosty face and began awkwardly, "Of course I hadn't forgotten my promise to help you find a couple of beautiful concubines. But you need to choose them wisely, or you will just end up drifting apart, which will cause you nothing but trouble. Since Eastern Sea Princess Liao Qing isn't to your liking, there's no reason for her to continue living here."

I rested the fan against my elbow again, tapping it as I frowned. "And she's a scheming princess. Today she tried to feed you love potion.

Who knows what astonishing stunt she might try to pull tomorrow! The back palace should remain as tranquil and free of drama as possible."

Ye Hua was silent for a long time, a strange expression on his face. "I shouldn't have asked you something like that," he said in a flat voice. "When I pulled you into my study just then, I was hoping to rouse a little jealousy out of you. I was not expecting you to just sit there, enjoying the spectacle."

My heart gave a loud thump. Goodness. I thought he had called me in just to collect my fan. I had not imagined for one second that might have been his intention.

He lifted his head and glanced at me briefly. I could read neither sorrow nor joy on his face. He continued speaking in that same flat tone of voice. "Bai Qian, do I not hold even a small place in your heart? Is it all taken up by him? How long are you willing to wait for him?"

I felt a tug on my heartstrings, but I was not sure why.

Ye Hua bid me farewell with a grim expression on his face. When he had gone, I walked through to my room without rousing Nai Nai and lay down.

I had felt overwhelmingly tired before, but lying on my soft and cozy cloud bed now, all I could do was toss and turn, turn and toss, unable to sleep. All I could think of was the tug I had felt on my heartstrings, while Ye Hua's grim facial expression continued to hover in my mind. Finally I entered a daze and then started to drift off to sleep.

CHAPTER SEVENTEEN

I was woken in the middle of the night by someone tapping on my door.

Because I was in a strange new bed, I had not been sleeping very deeply, and as soon as I heard the tapping, I lifted myself up, draped a cloak around myself, and went to answer the door.

Nai Nai was standing under the cool starlit sky, her eyes were bloodshot, and she was carrying the still-sleeping Dumpling in her arms.

Her brow unfurrowed slightly when she saw me. "Yesterday you said that His Little Majesty would wake in the early hours, but it's the early hours now, and still he shows no signs of waking," she said in a panicked voice. "And his little face has been getting redder and redder. I am so sorry to disturb you, Goddess, but I'm very worried."

I was halfway awake now. Nai Nai entered my room and lit a candle while I carried Dumpling to the bed. I moved my hands around his body and felt relieved to find that he was cooling down.

Children tended to have low alcohol tolerances, but Dumpling's was much lower than I expected. I saw Nai Nai looking apprehensive still and offered her a reassuring smile. "Most little children who gets tipsy on fruit wine wake up in the middle of the night, and that's what I assumed would happen to Dumpling. He actually looks like he'll sleep through until early tomorrow morning. The fact that his face is rosy is a good sign. It shows that the alcohol is being flushed out. You mustn't worry too much."

Nai Nai let out a loud sigh.

When I saw how red her eyes were, I felt a surge of tenderness toward her. "I don't think you should take Dumpling back with you. You haven't had a wink of sleep, have you?"

She gave an embarrassed smile.

As a merciful goddess, I did not like the idea of Nai Nai being deprived of sleep for the rest of the night too. The two of us undressed Dumpling, covered him with a cloud quilt, and moved him into the middle of the bed. I gave Nai Nai a kindly smile and said, "I will transfer immortal energy across to him at intermittent points throughout the night. He's certain to wake up tomorrow as his boisterous Dumpling self. When he does, he will need some stodgy sticky-rice porridge to fill his stomach. Go and have a good sleep, recover your energy, and when you wake up tomorrow morning, make that porridge and bring it over."

Nai Nai hesitated before saying, "But if His Little Majesty is here with you, you won't be able to get to sleep."

I patted Dumpling's face. "Look how deeply he's sleeping now. We could make him into the shape of a ball and roll him back to Qingyun Palace and he wouldn't be the wiser. He won't disturb my rest."

Nai Nai giggled, bent down to curtsy to me, blew out the candle, and made a deferential exit.

There was nothing seriously wrong with Dumpling, but he was sweating profusely. From his face it was obvious how deeply he was sleeping, and he did look a little the worse for wear. I brought over a basin of water and cast a magic spell to warm the room slightly. I took the cloud quilt off him, stripped him completely, and wiped him down.

I tended to him from two in the morning until Mao the Sun Prince took his post.

I did not get a wink more sleep, but for this I had no one to blame but myself. As I was putting Dumpling's clothes back on him item by item, it dawned on me how much work it was having a child, and the admiration I felt for Ye Hua reached new heights.

I had just finished getting Dumpling ready when Nai Nai arrived with the porridge, and I had not yet had the chance to carry out the washbasin. Nai Nai looked at the basin on the ground in surprise before kneeling down, taking the white cloth, twisting the water out of it, and taking the basin out to empty the water.

By the time she returned, I had finished giving myself a wash and was having a taste of her porridge, which was delicious. Knowing that little children could be fussy when it came to food, she had used a little sugar to sweeten it. Telling her to go back so she could wake early to make the porridge had been a ploy; I had not really thought that Dumpling would wake up this early.

Since Dumpling was not yet awake, he was unable to appreciate this bowl of delicious, sweet porridge. I looked pityingly at the bowl in front of me, certain that if porridge could think, it would be mulling over all the hardship it had suffered, being tossed around the wok and stewed for hours on end, all so that it could be sitting on this table, piping hot in this bowl. To let it get cold and go to waste seemed a terrible shame.

I gave a disgruntled sigh.

Nai Nai pursed her lips and smiled. "Since His Little Majesty is still asleep, it would be a shame for the porridge to get cold, and you haven't had any breakfast yet. If you would care to try your little serving girl's cooking, please go ahead."

Since she had offered, I did not feel I could say no, so I accepted with a laugh. I had just finished it when the eighteen immortal attendants who had stood in wait while I soaked in the water the day before made their dignified entrance into Concentrated Beauty. The two at the front were carrying trays of breakfast treats, while the other sixteen carried fruit, flowers, and wine, the same as yesterday. I gave a silent sigh. His Highness Ling Bao treated his guests with true Sky Kingdom hospitality, extreme kindness with no expenses spared.

I had eaten my breakfast by then and was about to tell the immortal attendants with the breakfast trays to take them away, but seeing all those cakes, I had second thoughts and asked them to leave the trays in my courtyard for Dumpling. He had been asleep for a day and a half and would need some food once he woke up. I left Dumpling in Nai Nai's care and joined the procession of lively immortal attendants and headed toward Ling Bao's sky spring for another day of soaking.

Most Ninth Sky roads were decorated with curious-shaped rocks and huge, sprawling man-made mountains. These enhanced the look of the area, but made the roads difficult to travel down.

I stopped walking when I heard two gossiping immortals mentioning Princess Liao Qing.

I had returned to my room last night before the matter between her and Ye Hua had been concluded, and although I had been bored by the way in which the drama involving Liao Qing and Su Jin had been playing out, I was still curious to hear how it had ended. It was like reading half of a predictable play script, you have guessed how it ends and could forgo the second half, but the possible ending turned over in your mind, compelling you to read on just to see if you were right.

"I knew when I first saw Liao Qing from the Eastern Sea that she wasn't happy with her lot," one of these work-shy immortal attendants said. "And sure enough, look what happened yesterday."

"I'm not sure exactly what she did wrong. I went to ask Red Mandarin Duck, who was on duty with the prince last night, but she wouldn't say, and actually scolded me for asking," said the other.

"It has to be something really bad if the prince wants to send her back to the Eastern Sea," the first one said. "Our empress went to beg on Liao Qing's behalf last night apparently. She spent hours kneeling down in the prince's study."

The second one gave a heartfelt sigh. "Oh, she didn't really need to do that. But she is such an exceptional empress, so beautiful and kind. I can't understand why the prince is so dismissive of her. He hasn't been to visit her once since I've been working at the empress's palace. And that awful incident with the Northern Sea ba snake's good-for-nothing son. The Sky Emperor was livid, but when Snow Candle ran to Prince Ye Hua's study to tell him what happened, I heard he didn't even bat an eyelid."

Now it was the first one's turn to give a loud sigh. "I know that as serving girls we shouldn't be talking like this, but our empress is the prince's head concubine, yet he acts as if she doesn't exist. He's so cold toward her. Our empress doesn't have it easy, she really doesn't."

The second one responded, "Now the prince has been bewitched by that nine-tailed fox from Qingqiu. I've heard that this is something they're very good at. She is the prince's future wife, but they're not married yet, and she already has him twisted around her little finger. Who knows what it will be like once they're actually married! He's so infatuated with her that he's been spending all his time in Qingqiu. The empress was terrified this affair would consume his mind and he would completely abandon all his official duties, so she sent her immortal attendant Qing Hua to Qingqiu to give him a friendly reminder about his sky duties. And how did they repay her concern and effort? By booting this attendant out of Qingqiu!"

The first one gave another sigh. "Oh, our empress is so kind and compassionate. I'm scared of the suffering this Qingqiu goddess is going to unleash upon her."

The two of them were silent awhile. The eighteen immortal concubines standing with me on my side of the wall seemed to have practically stopped breathing. My two at the head of our procession were about to pass through the rocks, but I raised my fan to stop them.

They looked at me anxiously, and I responded with a pleasant smile.

The two immortal attendants on the other side of the rocks were obviously in excitable moods, and their period of silence, a time in which they were reflecting on the depth of their devotion to Su Jin, I imagined, was only short-lived. I remembered being that age and predicted that after this pause in the conversation, they would return to the topic of the nine-tailed white fox and her bewitching ways.

I had not lived in vain all these years; sure enough, the first little immortal attendant to speak again started by saying, "You must have heard that the Qingqiu goddess is one hundred and forty thousand years old."

The other gasped. "Really? One hundred and forty thousand? D-d-doesn't that make her an old lady? The prince is ninety thousand years younger. She is so much older than him—old enough to be his grandmother. How shameless she must be. I know they are engaged, but still. Trying to ensnare the prince at her age. It's obscene!"

"Yes, it is, it is," the first replied. "She is old and shameless. She must have used magic to bewitch the prince. I just hope that the prince sees through her sooner rather than later and comes to understand how devoted our empress is and comes back to her."

Their conversation trailed off at this point. Presumably this was a topic they had been over again and again.

I had been interested to hear the gossip about Liao Qing but had unwittingly stumbled upon Su Jin's girl servants telling tales about me behind my back instead. The tone of their conversation had been very snarky, and had I heard myself being discussed like that back when I was Little Seventeenth in Mount Kunlun, I would have dealt with them so severely that even their parents would have had a hard time recognizing them.

Luckily for them I had devoted seventy thousand years just to the practice of spiritual cultivation and had reached a state of selflessness and egolessness. Nowadays I viewed worldly matters the way one might view clouds floating in the sky, and naturally I was keen to avoid clashing with these two. Instead I beckoned over the two immortal attendants from the head of our procession, the ones who had been about to pass through the rocks. I covered my mouth with my fan, and in a quiet voice, I said, "I recall that gossiping about gods and goddesses is forbidden by the Sky Kingdom regulations?"

The two immortal attendants looked surprised, but they both nodded. They both started jabbering at once. "Those two immortal attendants must have a death wish to risk inciting the wrath of gods and goddesses like that. We will definitely report them and have them disciplined in accordance with the sky regulations."

I gave a cough. "My wrath has not been incited," I said. "You hear things like this being said every so often, and while it isn't very pleasant to listen to, neither will it cause any lasting harm." I closed my fan and patted them both on the shoulders. "I understand that rules are rules," I said kindly, "but you two were too obtrusive back there. You shouldn't interrupt people in the middle of a gossip like that. Can you imagine how ashamed and humiliated the two of them would have been had you actually passed through the rocks back then? Since they have been violating the Sky Kingdom regulations with their behavior, sooner or later they are certain to get caught and will be disciplined, but until then, why not let them continue to gossip freely? If they behave like this again in the future, please go ahead and report them, have them punished. These two immortal servants seem to be too spirited and irresponsible for their current positions. I suggest that they be reassigned to more suitable ones."

The two immortal attendants nodded their agreement to everything I said and went off to deal with the reassignment of these two attendants, while the other sixteen immortal attendants stayed with me.

Soaking in the sky spring was dull without Dumpling playing beside me in the water. Two of my immortal attendants took out lutes and started to play, which passed an hour or two. But even if their musical abilities had been exceptional, they could not compare with Mo Yuan. When I first heard their music, I found it enchanting, but after a while it started to grate, and the first opportunity I got I told them to put their instruments away.

I continued to bathe but found myself becoming increasingly bored. I imagined that having something to read might make the time go by quicker, so I put my clothes back on and told my attendants to stay put while I returned to my courtyard to get a couple of books.

I was just about to push open the door to Concentrated Beauty when it was thrust open from inside. There was Ye Hua, the deeply sleeping Dumpling cradled in one arm, while his other hand rested on the door frame. Ye Hua did a double take when he saw me standing there and his brow furrowed.

The first time I had seen Ye Hua in the Eastern Sea Water Crystal Palace, he had looked like an unkind and cold youngster. Since getting to know him, I had not really seen that side of him again. Instead, his smile regularly made me feel as if there were a spring breeze on my face, and had actually made me forget about his inherent coldness. But his current facial expression quickly reminded me, and I gave a big shudder.

His pupils were dark. "Ali appears to be drunk," he said somberly. "I've asked around and discovered that he's been asleep since yesterday. Can you tell me what's been going on?"

I looked at the rosy-cheeked Little Dumpling in his arms. "I let him have half a jar too much wine yesterday and he got drunk," I said calmly. "That's all."

He frowned. "He got so drunk that he slept straight through until now? Why didn't you tell me, or take him to the medicine prince's residence for an examination?"

"You shouldn't pamper children in this way!" I exclaimed. "I used to steal wine from Zhe Yan when I was a child, and I slept for four or five days straight once. Father and Mother never took me for a medical examination. And Dumpling's a little boy. If you pamper him like this, he'll turn into a little wimp."

Ye Hua was quiet for ages. He walked over to me. "You haven't been here to raise Ali," he said hoarsely. "You see him as nothing more than a stepson. You've never loved him like an actual mother. Would you be speaking like this if he was your actual son?"

I was stunned. As soon as my brain caught up with my ears, I felt my blood running cold. In the past I had heard people talking about their hearts turning cold, but I had never known what it actually felt like, until now.

I may not have ever been a mother, but I knew that even if I were I would definitely not fuss over my child like that. The fact that Dumpling's real mother had jumped off the punishment platform when he was still so small was a tragedy, and it was terribly sad that most of his life had been spent without maternal love or care. That was one of the reasons I felt so wholeheartedly devoted to him. And that was why it was such a shock to have my devotion called into question like this.

I shook my sleeve at him behind his back. "How could I have ever given birth to such an adorable and lively child?" I said with a sneer. "Sadly the amazing woman who gave birth to Ali jumped off the immortal punishment platform many years ago. During my apprenticeship at Mount Kunlun, I practiced the Taoism of freedom and flexibility, but I didn't reach the Western Paradise, and I never obtained a bodhisattva's heart, which obviously means that I lack the kindness to care properly for Ali. Compassion and kindness are qualities that your head concubine seems to embody, Prince Ye Hua, why not get her to bring up your precious child from now on? Don't let him suffer under my inadequate care any longer."

I saw his back stiffen. "Stop saying things just to make me angry," he said eventually. "That wasn't what I meant." And with that he strode off to the medicine prince's residence with Dumpling in his arms.

I watched him walking away, feeling utterly hopeless. I was just about to step inside the courtyard when Nai Nai came rushing out, her eyes bloodshot.

She looked at me as if I were a compassionate bodhisattva from the Western Paradise. She grabbed me by the sleeve, and with a tremble in her voice, she said, "Did you see who just left the courtyard?"

"What's wrong?" I asked gently, rubbing my forehead.

Two shiny tears splashed down from the corners of her red eyes. "It's my fault, Goddess. It's all my fault," she said through choked sobs. "You are so good to His Little Majesty, and if my last mistress was still alive, she would be filled with appreciation too. If His Little Majesty had fallen into Su Jin's hands and been hurt because of me, I would n-n-nev . . ."

She jabbered on for a while, but I did not have the foggiest idea about what she was saying. Her sentences made no grammatical sense, and there was no logical order to what she was saying. I tapped the fan to stop her. "Let's skip over the unnecessary detail," I advised kindly. "You said something about Dumpling falling into Su Jin's hands and being hurt. What did you mean?"

My advice gave her a focus, and she started telling me what had happened in a coherent way, speaking with much more clarity and fluency than before. It transpired that Head Concubine Su Jin had led four palace attendants to my courtyard this morning. She told Nai Nai that she had been taking a morning stroll when she had sensed some inviolable godly energy that she had followed all the way to Concentrated Beauty. She decided she had to pay a visit to the owner of this inviolable godly energy and greet Dumpling at the same time.

Aside from the fact that no immortal in the Four Seas and Eight Deserts had godly immortal energy that was not inviolable, I was generous-hearted enough to accept the slightly incongruous compliment. I did not know how long the drama between Su Jin, Ye Hua, and Liao Qing had played out in the end, but the fact that she had woken up early this morning with the energy to walk all the way to my place was impressive.

Nai Nai explained that Ye Hua had banned Su Jin from seeing Dumpling and did not let her near Concentrated Beauty either. As the model concubine of the Four Seas and Eight Deserts, she had always abided by the rules, but for some reason today she had disobeyed two at once. Nai Nai had been unrelenting, and refused to let Su Jin into the courtyard, which was an extremely courageous way for a lowly immortal attendant housekeeper to deal with the Sky Palace's head concubine.

Nai Nai managed to defend Concentrated Beauty, and eventually Su Jin gave up and left with her tail between her legs. After tending to Dumpling, Nai Nai had gone to the back courtyard to fetch some water. When she returned, Dumpling was nowhere to be seen, and she thought Su Jin must have come back to steal him away. She had been rushing out to give chase when she bumped into me.

I gave her a reassuring pat on the shoulder. "It was Ye Hua who carried Dumpling off, nothing to do with Su Jin. You don't need to worry."

Nai Nai had described fending off Ye Hua's head concubine the way one might describe fending off a plague of rats. I turned the story over in my head and fancied I understood what was going on. The most probable explanation seemed to be that Nai Nai's former mistress had had a run-in with Su Jin before jumping off the immortal punishment platform.

Ye Hua seemed to treat Su Jin very badly.

Suddenly I understood. "The reason Dumpling's mother jumped from the punishment platform has something to do with Su Jin, doesn't it?" I wondered out loud, interrupting Nai Nai.

Nai Nai's face turned white, and she fell silent. "The Sky Emperor issued a decree that expressly forbids us from discussing this matter," she said at last. "The Sky Emperor sent all the immortal attendants who knew about the incident to an immortal mountain far away from the Sky Palace."

I deduced that Su Jin had perhaps not always been the model concubine she was today. That to strive for favor, she might have actually forced Dumpling's mother off the punishment platform.

Dumpling was three hundred years old, which meant that Dumpling's mother had jumped off the punishment platform in the last three hundred years. Such a major incident and so recently would naturally have caused a big uproar. It was five hundred years ago that I had been injured by Qing Cang and had fallen asleep for three hundred years. The fact that I could not recall hearing any mention of such an incident in the Ninth Sky since waking concurred with what Nai Nai had said about the Sky Emperor suppressing it.

This generation's Sky Emperor was kind and just. He obviously looked upon Su Jin with fond nostalgia from the time she had been his concubine and had decided to put this measure in place to protect her. It was this measure that allowed Su Jin to retain the reputation of model concubine that she enjoyed today.

Oh, what bloodthirsty happenings.

Despite disruptions from Ye Hua and Nai Nai, I did not forget that the reason I had come back to Concentrated Beauty was to look for some books.

The Sky Palace was such a conventional and orderly place that all I had been expecting to find on the bookshelves was a few Buddhist scriptures and some Taoist texts about physical and spiritual cultivation. The fact that I was willing to pick one of these showed how driven to boredom I was feeling. I was extremely surprised to find some play scripts on the shelves, and I picked out a couple and had a flick through. They were not ones I had ever read, and they looked fairly intriguing. I turned reticently to Nai Nai and gave her a smile. "Your former mistress had very good taste."

I was just about to take these books back to the sky spring with me when the main courtyard door started to creak open.

I lifted my head and saw the model concubine from Ye Hua's back palace standing there behind the threshold, a barely perceptible smile on her face.

I sighed to myself. She must have been acting the model concubine for too long and found it emotionally and physically draining to be openly flouting Ye Hua's orders as she was today.

The model concubine saw me, stooped down, and gave a curtsy. "Big Sister, I passed by to see you some time before, but unfortunately you were out. I was going to the sky spring to pay my respects to you there, but then I heard that you had returned to Concentrated Beauty, so I ran all the way over and, Big Sister, how delighted I am to have finally caught up with you . . ."

Her words sounded earnest, but I could tell she was not telling the truth about running over: her face was composed, she did not have a drop of sweat on her, and her breathing was even.

Having only just heard her two serving girls gossiping, I felt slightly disarmed. And hearing her call me Big Sister irked me and destroyed the calm state I had worked hard to return to. In no time at all, I was feeling irate and flustered once more.

I had never liked being addressed as Big Sister, which was what Xuan Nu used to call me when we were young. Xuan Nu had been both a thorn in my side and a thorn in my heart for so many years now, and as soon as the model concubine said it, I felt the thorn digging its way in deeper, making me feel instantly distressed.

I used to be arrogant and stubborn when I was young, but the last ten thousand years devoted to spiritual cultivation had been time well spent, and it had gradually allowed me to become calmer, more subdued and demure. It meant that even though I was distinctly unimpressed with the model concubine standing before me, I was able to put my play scripts in my pocket and in a curt voice ask her, "If you've been so eager to pay your respects, why didn't you do so when you saw me last night?"

The smile on her face froze.

There was a marble table under the huge peach tree next to me, surrounded by two or three marble stools. Sensing that this conversation with her might drag, I walked over to the table and sat down.

I saw her stiffen. She stood there for a while, her back completely straight, before she smiled and said, "Sky Palace etiquette is somewhat different from etiquette elsewhere. A discreet praise must follow the appropriate degree of ceremony to show sincerity to the person being praised.

"According to Sky Palace etiquette, I should have come to praise you as soon as you arrived at the Sky Palace, Big Sister. But the prince did not inform me of your arrival, and when I saw you for the first time yesterday evening, I did not know who you were. It was a failure of etiquette on my part, and I hope you won't take offense. This morning I intended to come to pay my respects and give praise to you first thing, but I was delayed. I have dishonored you by coming so late, and I am truly sorry."

She was a good speaker, and her explanation was flawless. No wonder she had earned herself the title of model concubine of the Four Seas and Eight Deserts. But hearing her call me Big Sister over and over again like that was starting to make me feel dizzy.

I rubbed my forehead and lifted my fan. I gave her a nod and said, "I have just arrived here, and I don't have a thorough understanding of the Ninth Sky regulations yet. I'm intrigued to see them in action, however, so as you're here, why not cut to the chase and praise me."

"But I've just praised you," she said, looking startled.

I had never heard anything like it. I turned and gave her a careful look up and down. The only thing I could imagine she might mean was that stooped posture when she came in and that barely perceptible curtsy. Surely an insignificant imperial concubine did not think this was an appropriate way to praise a goddess with one hundred forty thousand years of cultivated spiritual energy?

I felt extremely disgruntled, but being a generous immortal, I did not wish to quibble about the finer points of meaningless etiquette. Instead I swallowed down my disappointment, looked at her solemnly, and gave a nod. "Oh, you've already praised me, have you? That's a very convenient and accessible method of praise you've adopted . . ."

Before I had even finished my sentence, the model concubine fell to her knees. She had been standing courteously to the side this whole time, apart from when she had a slight fold over her waist, which she considered to be offering praise. Now she had her hands clenched together and her upper body against the floor. As she was in this position, I saw the hem of a cloak flash past the doorway.

The corners of my mouth started to twitch. I gave a cough and said, "And what are you doing now?"

The model concubine lifted her face, on which I saw elements of both strength and softness. "When I praised you just now, it was following the etiquette of the head concubine praising the empress," she explained in an anguished voice. "Now I am praising you in gratitude. You have been looking after little Ali these last few months, Big Sister, and for this I cannot thank you enough.

"Ali lost his mother when he was still so young, and as you surely know, he has mistaken you for her, probably because of the way you cover your face, just as his birth mother used to do. I hope you will continue to look after him. The prince was deeply in love with Ali's mother, and when she jumped from the punishment platform, he jumped off after her. By the time the Sky Emperor rescued him, he had only one breath left in his body, and his cultivated spiritual energy was almost completely depleted. He spent more than sixty years in his Zichen Palace in a deep sleep.

"If it hadn't been for Prince Ye Hua's mother taking Ali to his bedside each day, and Ali calling out 'Father Prince' over and over again, Prince Ye Hua may never have woken up. You see all these peach trees, Big Sister? The prince planted them all in Concentrated Beauty

Courtyard after he woke up in order to cherish the memory of Ali's mother.

"The prince has spent the last two hundred years in a state of complete joylessness. The fact that you look so similar to Ali's mother shows how fated you and he are. I am praising you like this in the hope that you and the prince might soon be married, so that you can bring comfort to his half-dead heart."

I looked at the model concubine in shocked silence. This declaration of hers had obviously been intended to upset me. If she wished to tell me that I was nothing but a substitute for Dumpling's dead mother, she should have just come out and said it directly.

Instead she was talking in this roundabout way. By praising me so lavishly and prostrating herself too, she had attempted to make her provocative words sound kinder, more natural and considerate.

I knew very well what she wanted me to take from this, but sadly for her, I was not going to rise. And I certainly was not about to have a furious argument with Ye Hua over whether the only reason he loved me was as a replacement for Dumpling's mother.

This model concubine had not had an easy time. Even with her being so deeply and devotedly in love with Ye Hua, he only treated her with contempt. If it were a play, it would be a romance involving a husband who did not love his concubine. He had a heart made of steel, and no matter what she did, he remained unmoved. Behind her husband's back this poor, loving concubine would cry her eyes out.

Half out of misery, half in order to upset her rival in love, she brought up the romantic past of the man she cherished, but all she ended up doing was upsetting herself, while her rival in love remained unaffected. It was quite a pitiful sight.

I stood up and walked over to her, tapping her on the shoulder with my fan. "I know you are after Ye Hua, but don't imagine that everyone else wants the same as you. As a little immortal, you shouldn't try to be too clever. Oh, there is something else I feel I must mention.

All the immortals throughout the Four Seas and Eight Deserts praise me in accordance with Qingqiu ceremonial etiquette. If you wish to praise me properly, you must bathe, fast, and light incense for three days beforehand, and for three days after, you must perform three ceremonious kneelings and nine kowtows. It is rather a cumbersome form of etiquette, but even your husband, Ye Hua, abides by it, which I appreciate. What I don't appreciate is having insignificant, low-status immortals praising me by simply cupping their hands together and thinking that's all there is to it. From now on you must tell me in advance if you wish to praise me, and do so in a formal manner following the Qingqiu ceremonial etiquette. If you are unable to abide by this, fine, but I would appreciate you not bringing up the Sky Palace regulations in front of me again. And one more thing, I am the youngest of my mother's children, and I am nobody's big sister, and anyway you are too young to address me like that. In terms of ceremonial hierarchy, it would be more appropriate for you to call me *Goddess*."

By the time I had finished with her, I was in a much better mood. My eyes happened to drop to the floor to where her hands were, and I saw they were clenched into tight fists. This young girl had given an almost flawless performance, but inside she was still full of youthful vigor.

I tutted and sighed. I beckoned for Nai Nai, walked around the model concubine's prone figure, and headed back to the tranquility of the sky spring.

I did not know how Ye Hua really felt, and after hearing Su Jin's words, I started to feel quite down. Ye Hua had been so deeply in love with Dumpling's mother. If I was right and Su Jin had made Dumpling's mother jump off the punishment platform in order to destroy her rival in love . . . then wouldn't cold-faced, cold-mannered Ye Hua have attacked Su Jin? I was so focused on this train of thought that I actually asked the question out loud. Nai Nai, who was standing next to me, said, "Goddess, your guess is absolutely right. He did once attack her."

She hesitated a moment before starting to explain. "It was not long after the prince had woken up from his long sleep. He was feeling physically weak, dispirited, and listless. He spent his days alone in his palace, ignoring everyone, even His Little Majesty. The prince's mother, Empress Le Xu, was incredibly worried, and she asked for me to come and comfort him. Whenever I spoke of my former mistress, the prince would become visibly moved.

"A fortnight after the prince had woken up again, the Sky Emperor arranged for a sedan chair to carry Su Jin into Xiwu Palace. There was a gentle breeze that day, and the sun was shining brightly, an auspicious day by any account. Empress Su Jin was not welcomed into Xiwu Palace, however. I saw with my own eyes as Prince Ye Hua grabbed his sword, his face completely expressionless, and used it to stab her in the chest. It looked like a fatal stab, but unfortunately the Sky Emperor arrived just in time to whisk her away, thus saving her life.

"Since then it has been as you have witnessed. She was returned to Xiwu Palace under the Sky Emperor's protection, but the prince has nothing but disdain for her, treating her as if she is nothing but a container for my former mistress's eyes. Some of her immortal attendants feel very sorry for her, but as far as I'm concerned, you reap what you sow."

"Eyes?" I asked in disbelief.

Nai Nai gritted her teeth. "My poor suffering mistress had her eyes taken out."

I was quiet as I thought over everything I had just learned. When it came to strange happenings like this, I usually felt the need to dig deeper and find out the whole story, but for some reason I felt resistant this time. I gave a loud sigh.

Nai Nai's eyes had turned red again. "I used to be very naive, as was my mistress. After all this happened, I realized how difficult it had been for Ye Hua to ensure that my mistress had a safe and peaceful existence in the Sky Palace, and how much strain it had put on him to keep her safe and looked after. Empress Le Xu told me that the prince thought he could protect my mistress better if he hid his true feelings about her.

"He hid his true feelings from all the sky immortals, including my mistress. But he didn't manage to hide them from the one person he was actually trying to deceive: the Sky Emperor."

As soon as she said this last sentence, her face turned white. She suddenly realized what she had done, and with quivering lips, she said, "I have been incredibly indiscreet."

She had said a lot, but the first part had been quite incoherent, and the last part had not made much sense to me, so I was not sure how indiscreet she had actually been. I felt a complex knot of emotions forming inside me.

I was just leaving Concentrated Beauty with this tangle of feelings still inside me when I felt a gust of propitious vapors flutter toward my face.

Of all the immortals in the Four Seas and Eight Deserts, there were only four or five with immortal energy as outstanding as this, and of these four or five, the most outstanding was the one with the refined interests and the even more refined tastes: Zhe Yan.

And that was exactly who I now found standing next to the wall of Concentrated Beauty, pulling up his sleeves and laughing as he watched me.

I was too surprised to speak.

When Su Jin had been lavishing that excessive display of praise on me earlier, I had seen the seam of a cloak flash past the doorway, and glancing up, I had thought it might be Zhe Yan, but assuming he was still with Fourth Brother in Qingqiu, I had dismissed that idea and had thought no more about it. But the gaudy cloak I had seen earlier had indeed been his.

I had lost my temper with Su Jin and ended up speaking to her in an impolite manner, which, looking back, had been at the expense of some of my goddess decorum. The fact that Zhe Yan had witnessed the whole exchange made me blush with shame.

When he had finally stopped laughing, he took a couple of steps over and said, "I haven't seen you lose your temper for a long time. It was a very opportune moment to have been eavesdropping on you. Fourth Brother used to complain that taking you to Mount Kunlun had been the wrong decision. As soon as you started studying magic there, you lost all your spark, all that childlike energy you had when Fourth Brother was taking care of you. From what I have seen today, however, it looks as if not all hope has been lost."

I was one hundred forty thousand years old, which would make me a doddering old lady in mortal terms. If I was still as naive and spirited as when I was a young girl . . . the thought was too terrifying to imagine.

I had accepted my old age and had a reasonable understanding of the impact of age on bearing. Zhe Yan, on the other hand, had never accepted his age and would never accept my wisdom on the subject.

I gave him the response he was looking for. "I'm not fond of Ye Hua's head concubine," I explained with a meek little shake of my fan. "I've always appreciated alert and inspired young immortals, but this one is too alert and inspired, coming over here trying to be so clever. I really don't enjoy behavior like that, and as a member of the older generation, I felt she needed to be given a slight dressing-down. I didn't really lose my temper. You're making it sound worse than it was."

He gave a little laugh. Zhe Yan never used to laugh this much. He had been acting very pleased with himself of late. But he did seem to have everything he could possibly want, and it made sense that he would laugh more.

"Ye Hua only brought me to the Ninth Sky yesterday," I said once he had stopped laughing. "Why have you rushed over to see me so soon? Surely you haven't come all this way just to eavesdrop on my conversations?"

He gave a cough and tried to hide a smile. He swept his eyes up and down over Nai Nai, who was still standing beside me. Nai Nai proved herself worthy of her long residence in the Ninth Sky and perceived that she ought to be making herself scarce. After she bent down to praise Zhe Yan, she said, "I will go on ahead to the sky spring and wait for you there, Goddess."

I nodded.

Zhe Yan had never been one for tact, and as soon as Nai Nai had wandered off, he put on an exaggeratedly solemn facial expression. I was so shocked by his impersonation that I immediately started shaking. Three hundred years ago when I first woke from my deep sleep and discovered Master's body had remained nourished, even without my heart blood, Zhe Yan had done this same impersonation. Furrowing his brow and adopting this grave expression, he had knocked his hand against Mo Yuan's ice chest and told me the most comforting words I could ever imagine hearing: "It looks like Mo Yuan might be about to return." But my joy was short-lived; he had been making it up.

Now as I stared at his narrow eyes in a daze, new hope started to take root in my heart. But I was filled with fear that this hope would also be short-lived. Having learned my lesson, I was quick to pour cold water over the leaping flames of hope.

I heard a hiss as the flames in my heart were extinguished. I calmly pulled my clenched fists up into my sleeves, and in a flat voice, I said, "Keep me hanging on if you wish. I'm in no great rush to hear it anyway."

He stopped his impersonation and gave a casual laugh. "If I told you that Mo Yuan was about to wake up, would you still be in no great rush?"

On hearing Zhe Yan's words, my poor fox heart felt as if it were on fire, and it leaped out of my chest and into my throat. I heard my own voice sounding hoarse as I said, "You're . . . you're lying to me." I heard myself sobbing as I said it.

He stared, and reined in his smile. I saw waves of lines appear on his forehead. He came over and patted my back. "I promise I'm not playing around with you this time, little girl. I've spent the last couple of days on business in the Western Sea with Fourth Brother. I saw the Western Sea Emperor's oldest son when I was there and sensed something a bit strange about his immortal energy. I performed soul-chasing magic and discovered two souls inside his body. One was his, and the other . . ." He paused, and lowered his voice to say, ". . . belongs to your master, Mo Yuan."

I lowered my head and stared at the embroidery on my shoes sticking out from under my skirt. "How do you know that the Water Emperor's son's soul belonged to Mo Yuan?" I asked dumbly. "Supernatural mortal-world stories have plots like that, but it turns out that the man is actually pregnant. Perhaps the Western Sea Emperor's oldest son has been concealing the fact that he's expecting a baby from his parents?"

My head had been lowered, and there was now a mist in front of my eyes, which stopped me from being able to see Zhe Yan's expression clearly. I just heard him sigh and say, "With soul-chasing magic, it is possible to find the source of a soul. The second soul in the Western Sea's oldest prince's body was sleeping deeply. I followed it to its source and discovered that it was being nurtured by the spirit power from shattered pieces of itself, which it had managed to fit back together. Ask yourself, who in the Four Seas and Eight Deserts could possibly take a soul that was fragmented to the point of being unrecognizable and use the spirit power from its own scattered pieces to reconstruct itself as a whole new soul? Only Mo Yuan, of course.

"He is the oldest legitimate son of Father of the Universe, who brought me up too. Growing up alongside Mo Yuan, I'm naturally very familiar with his immortal powers. You told me that before Mo Yuan became dust flying, he asked his seventeen apprentices to wait for him. At the time, I assumed he had said this just to give you all hope, not wishing for all of you to feel too sad. Even though he was always true to his word, I couldn't believe he could possibly survive something like that. When I discovered this soul sleeping deeply within the body of the Western Sea's oldest prince, I was filled with admiration. Never in his life has Mo Yuan disappointed his nearest and dearest. That is the sign of a truly outstanding man. He has already spent seventy thousand years reconstructing his soul. Some fragments of it are still scattered, and it will take a little longer before his soul is complete and ready to return to his body. He needed to tap into someone else's immortal power when he slowly nursed himself back to health. Once that process is complete, he will be able to return to his own body and wake up properly. That must be why Mo Yuan's soul inhabits the body of the Western Sea's oldest prince. He is resting there while he recuperates. Unfortunately, the prince is not a very physically robust immortal, and he is finding it hard to produce enough spiritual energy for his own self-cultivation, as well as that needed to nurture Mo Yuan, and his body is getting weaker by the day. The fact that Mo Yuan's soul has housed itself inside such a feeble body means that it will take him seven or eight thousand years longer to recuperate. Having verified that it was indeed Mo Yuan, I planned to come and tell you straightaway. But when I arrived in Qingqiu and saw how badly injured you were, I decided to keep it to myself for a while in case you got upset. You've had a whole day to bathe in the sky spring now, so I imagined you must be more or less recovered."

This torrent of words entered my ears, but my brain was too crammed to make sense of them. The words tumbled around my head like a wok of rice porridge being stirred. I felt so confused it was as if my mind had taken a wander far away from the Ninth Sky, leaving me in a state of bewildered confusion.

I was about to be granted the wish I had been making for seventy thousand years. I just stood there for a long time in a state of complete disbelief, feeling as if I were choking. Suddenly I saw a hole in Zhe Yan's story. "B-b-but if M-M-Master is using the Western Sea's oldest prince's immortal energy to recuperate, how will he ever repay the large debt he incurs?"

Zhe Yan gave a cough. "I'm sure Mo Yuan had his reasons for choosing the Western Sea's oldest prince," he said slowly. "Either this prince or a member of his clan must have owed Mo Yuan a favor, and this is their repayment."

He took hold of my shoulder, lifted my chin, and gave a frown. "Little girl, are you crying?"

I dabbed at my face, and sure enough my hand came away wet. My knees buckled, and I knelt down onto the ground, grabbing pathetically at a corner of his sleeve. "I . . . I'm so w-w-worried that this is just a delusion," I sobbed.

CHAPTER EIGHTEEN

As soon as I heard what Zhe Yan had to say, I lost all desire to stay in the Ninth Sky. Although I was upset with Ye Hua, he had done me a huge favor by arranging for me to use the sky spring to heal my injuries, and leaving without saying good-bye would have come across as extremely ungrateful. But rushing over to find him now would look like I was the one backing down. In the end I decided to leave him a letter thanking him sincerely for the care he had shown me over the past two days. As soon as it was written, I strode out the Southern Sky Gate with Zhe Yan, and we made our way hurriedly down from the sky.

At the moment Mo Yuan was nothing but a sleeping soul in the body of the Western Sea's oldest prince, but I was still anxious to see him. The eagerness with which I was rushing toward the Western Sea made me feel like a mother bird from a mountain forest waking early to search for insects and flapping its wings triumphantly, a fat juicy worm in its beak, as it soared back to the nest to feed its chicks.

We traveled for a couple of hours on a cloud before we reached the Western Sea. Zhe Yan soon became bored and spent the whole time chattering in my ear. Luckily for me he and Fourth Brother had been getting on famously of late, which saved me from having to listen to those same old dull things that Fourth Brother had allegedly disgraced him by doing and saying.

The subject of today's chatter was the Western Sea Emperor's family secrets. I sat solemnly on the cloud and listened in rapt attention.

Of the four Water Emperors, it was the Western one that had left the least impression on me. I had always assumed this was because I had spent so long inside Qingqiu, ignoring the comings and goings of the immortals of this younger generation.

But from what Zhe Yan was saying, these last two generations of Western Sea Emperors had indeed kept low profiles, and their clan had lacked presence within the Four Seas and Eight Deserts. This low-profile Western Sea Emperor had somehow inadvertently become part of an extremely high-profile event.

Mo Yuan had borrowed the body of the Western Sea's oldest prince, De Yong, to house his sleeping soul while he recuperated.

This process had started more than six hundred years ago. De Yong, who had never been particularly robust, had started to feel increasingly weak and listless. None of the medicine masters from the Western Sea Water Crystal Palace could work out what was wrong. A lot of time and effort was spent in vain trying to nurse him back to health.

They pleaded with the Sky Palace's medicine prince to pay a visit and give his diagnosis. He arrived accompanied by two immortal children and carried out a thorough examination of De Yong. Twisting his beard, the medicine prince prescribed two types of medicine for his patient, but all these did was prevent De Yong from coughing up blood.

Before the medicine prince left, he ushered the Western Sea Emperor into a quiet corner and explained that De Yong was not suffering from a physical illness, and as a medical doctor he was unable to offer further assistance.

When he heard that even the medicine prince was unable to help, the Western Sea Emperor was overcome with grief and indignation. He sat there with bloodshot eyes, pondering it for a long time before coming up with a plan. He decided to design a notice seeking a doctor. He would write this notice in bright, shiny characters and post it all over the Four Seas and Eight Deserts. He wrote that any man who could cure the illness of the oldest prince of the Western Sea would be recruited as the boy's head concubine, while any woman who could cure it would become the head concubine of the second prince.

Yes, that jogged my memory. I had heard rumors about the Western Sea's oldest prince, De Yong, being homosexual. The Western Sea Emperor had been so anxious and in a rush that he had not given careful thought to the content of this notice. There certainly were plenty of capable people under the sky who were homosexual, of whom Li Jing's father, Qing Cang, was one, but there were also a large number who were not. This notice was not very well thought through in that it was likely to scare away capable people who were not homosexual and did not wish to become the oldest prince's head concubine. It was some time before the emperor realized the problem with his notice, but by then the damage had been done.

The Western Sea Emperor found a large crowd of more men than there were drops of water in the Yellow River standing outside his court in response to the notice. They flowed in wave after never-ending wave. Sadly, despite the solid learning and talent of these men, none possessed the key to cure his son's illness.

Mo Yuan's soul was very deeply hidden, in a realm beyond that transcended by immortal magic, and none of these men could see the second soul nesting in De Yong's body, siphoning off a portion of his immortal energy each day.

Ever since then, De Yong had been suffering, becoming less and less like an immortal each day that passed. The Western Sea Empress was completely distraught over her eldest son's languid appearance and spent her days weeping before her husband. The Western Sea Emperor was equally troubled.

But heaven never closes off every path. De Yong's younger brother, Second Prince Su Moye, was on good terms with Fourth Brother, and they often ate and drank together. After Fourth Brother had found Bi Fang in the Western Mountains and returned to the Ten-Mile Peach Grove, he and Zhe Yan had a huge argument, and he stormed off to the Western Sea Water Crystal Palace to find Su Moye to drink away his annoyance with.

He had arrived at the Western Sea Water Crystal Palace that time to find a gloomy atmosphere hanging over the place. Su Moye drank more than usual, and soon started slurring his words. Slouching against Fourth Brother's shoulder, he explained the whole sorry state of his family affairs. He talked and talked, holding nothing back. As soon as Fourth Brother learned of the plight of Su Moye's household, he felt full of compassion. He offered to see if he could get Zhe Yan to come over and help.

Zhe Yan had made very clear his position as a "mysterious god who has shunned the three unwholesome roots and retreated from the world, who has refined interests, and even more refined tastes," and in normal circumstances, he would have refused to get embroiled in a situation like this one. But he also wanted to keep Fourth Brother happy. So he humbled himself by rushing over to the Western Sea. That was when he discovered the wonderful news fulfilling my deepest wish: that Mo Yuan was soon to wake up.

Zhe Yan gave me a playful look. "Before your fourth brother and I left the Western Sea, we told the group of young immortals there that we would be sending an immortal envoy to personally assist De Yong's recovery. For Mo Yuan's soul to have a smooth recovery, De Yong's body requires careful attention."

What he was saying made sense, except for one detail. "But you don't have an immortal envoy at the peach grove, do you?" I asked with a frown.

He gave a free and easy laugh. "When the Eastern Sea Emperor held his son's one-month banquet, I heard that a palace attendant arrived with a piece of white silk wrapped around her face. She gave the emperor some of my peach blossom wine as a celebratory gift and claimed to be an envoy from the peach grove.

"This palace attendant also said that she was Prince Ye Hua's younger sister. A couple of old immortals have spent weeks in the Ninth Sky making discreet inquiries about this but have so far failed to come up with anything about this mysterious little sister of Ye Hua's. These same immortals went over to the Eastern Sea Emperor to make sure they had heard correctly and were told that it had not been a female palace attendant after all, but a boy dressed as a girl. This boy was in a homosexual relationship with Ye Hua and had been pretending to be a girl and telling people he was Ye Hua's little sister to keep their relationship under wraps."

The corners of my mouth started to twitch. "What a hilarious story for the Eastern Sea Emperor to have come up with. Hilarious and ridiculous!" I said, forcing a laugh.

I was very grateful to Zhe Yan for the opportunity to personally nurse the Western Sea prince back to health, thus allowing me to repay my debt to Mo Yuan. But having to go to this homosexual prince's bedside disguised as a boy rather decreased that gratitude. I was starting to feel sorry that Fourth Brother had not been present at the Eastern Sea Emperor's banquet to stop me from offering up Zhe Yan's name as I had.

Zhe Yan glanced across at me. I looked up at the sky and transformed myself into a boy's image, although my face was still obscured by that piece of white silk four fingers wide.

Just sitting on the cloud and waiting to arrive at the Western Sea felt like torture. With an air of stern godly authority, Zhe Yan led me into the sea. We were swirling through the water for a while before finally arriving at the magnificent palace residence, in front of which a crowd of young Western Sea immortals had gathered to greet us. It was an extravagant display with all of them dressed in splendid attire.

Even though Zhe Yan had referred to me as just a little immortal envoy, the fact that a god as respected and worshipped as he had led me personally all the way to the Western Sea earned me a lot of respect, and the Western Sea Emperor treated me very well. Zhe Yan was cordially invited to sit down and rest his feet at the most important seat within the great hall. Fine tea leaves were steeped for him while he was waited upon by a great gathering of palace attendants bearing trays of fruit.

Seeing that Zhe Yan was taking a rest, I naturally decided to join him.

Some tens of thousands of years ago, Second Brother had become fascinated by literature and would often bring poems about love and heartbreak from the mortal world to discuss with me. One of these poems was written by a mortal who was commonly recognized as being extremely talented, but highly lacking in morals. I cannot recall the whole poem, but two lines stuck in my mind: "Nearing your hometown you grow more timid, you dare not ask questions about the place you love."

Second Brother provided me with a thorough explanation of this poem. Apparently the poet had wandered far from his hometown and had received no news from home for many years. On returning, his heart had been like an arrow focused on the target, but as he approached, he had become fearful, too nervous to ask for news of his household because of what he might hear. These two lines brilliantly revealed both the yearning and the foreboding in this talented poet's heart. I had not agreed with Second Brother's analysis. I was unable to grasp how a poet could be filled with such yearning for home and yet stop in his tracks when he was so near. It had sounded like a complete contradiction to me.

It was only now that I realized the profound implication of these two lines and came to appreciate the talent of this mortal poet, because sitting in the great hall of the Western Sea Water Crystal Palace, about to return to the one my heart had been yearning for, I was filled with extraordinary fear. I was both impatient to see Mo Yuan's soul and terrified at the prospect.

Zhe Yan did not rest for long. He took a couple of sips of tea with his eyes closed before explaining to his host that he had important matters he needed to attend to. He said these words with such godly authority and sternness that even though the Western Sea Emperor obviously wished him to stay longer, he did not press the matter. He called for a group of little Western Sea immortals to see Zhe Yan out, some at the front to clear the path and others to walk behind. In this formation, the bustling throng made its way out of the palace.

Having seen Zhe Yan off, the Western Sea Emperor started to look nervous. He said a courteous word or two to me before taking me to see his oldest son, De Yong. I was taking deep breaths, my whole body feeling taut from the tension and fear. I was terrified that when I actually came face-to-face with De Yong, I might be so overwhelmed with emotion that I would perform some serious breach of etiquette.

I had naively thought that since Mo Yuan's soul inhabited the Western Sea's oldest prince's body, the prince would radiate an energy that would give me a sense of affection and familiarity. I felt certain that his physical appearance would in some way reflect its association with Mo Yuan's soul. But as soon as the palace attendants pushed open the doors of the Western Sea's oldest prince's Fuying Hall and I followed the

Western Sea Emperor inside and saw De Yong sprawled on the bed, his hair in disarray and a blank look in his eyes, my heart sank.

The young invalid lying on the bed had delicate features and was incredibly fragile-looking. He looked nothing like Mo Yuan. The immortal energy surrounding his body was weak and lackluster. It was hard to believe that this body could possibly contain the soul of the most powerful and influential god in the whole of the Four Seas and Eight Deserts. Mo Yuan must have been sleeping very deeply, as he had not allowed De Yong the slightest benefit from the association. He had not passed on a hint of his strong and calm immortal energy.

The Western Sea Emperor stood to the side of his son's sickbed, prattling away earnestly. He told his son that the immortal prince standing by his bedside, surrounded by a thousand trails of propitious vapors, was an apprentice who had come highly recommended by His Godliness Zhe Yan. That they were putting his health in this immortal's hands. That this chronic illness that had gone untreated for all these hundreds of years was going to be given to this immortal to cure. And De Yong should act with extreme gratitude and be cooperative.

I suddenly realized that this "immortal prince" referred to me. Useless old me. The Western Sea Emperor was extremely garrulous. He continued to ramble, while De Yong and I regarded each other in silence. De Yong's young serving girl brought in an embroidered, drum-shaped stool and placed it by De Yong's bedside so I could sit down to take his pulse. I took hold of De Yong's wrist, my hand trembling. His pulse was not too weak nor too strong, not too sluggish nor racing, not too light nor too heavy, it was just as Zhe Yan had said: completely normal.

"What can you tell me about my son's illness?" the Western Sea Emperor asked, rushing over.

I forced a smile. "Can you take everybody out of this hall for a while please?"

I was dismissing this crowd of idlers so that I could perform soul-chasing magic and look for Mo Yuan's soul. Soul-chasing magic was a delicate procedure, and until you had cultivated enough spiritual energy to rise to a god or goddess rank, no matter how outstanding your immortal powers, you would not be able to chase down a soul. Implementing this magic required a hundred-foot radius of pure and calm energy, which would be disturbed by people standing around.

De Yong, who had been staring into space since I entered the hall, swept his eyes lightly over me. I gave him a pleasant smile, held my hand out flat, and gave him a karate chop. De Yong opened his eyes wide, swayed from side to side, and fell lopsided across the bed.

It had been many years since I had practiced soul-chasing magic, but luckily I still remembered the words of the accompanying incantation. I drew some spells out on my hands, and a ball of dazzling white light spread across the hall. This white light tapered into a silver beam, which landed on De Yong's smooth forehead, where it appeared to vanish. I took a deep breath. My soul dived gingerly out of my body, followed the silver beam of light, and slid slowly inside De Yong's primordial spirit. This was an extremely meticulous piece of magic, and even a momentary lapse in concentration could cause the soul of the person performing the magic to fuse with the primordial spirit of the person receiving it.

De Yong's primordial spirit was flooded with a pure silver light, but because the light was so pure, it felt like being surrounded by darkness. I spent a long time wandering around directionless within his primordial spirit, unable to find the place where Mo Yuan was sleeping. I searched back and forth, back and forth.

I was just about to retreat and apply another type of soul-chasing magic when I heard some familiar music wafting over. It was calm and melodious, desolate and refined. I could still remember the song from the closing ceremony of Xuan Ming the Winter God's Taoist assembly when Mo Yuan had played this ancient Buddhist melody on the guqin.

My heart gave two hammer-like beats. I focused all my energy and ran in the direction of the music.

I stumbled on the way, nearly tripping, and the sacred Buddhist melody screeched to a stop. I reached out a trembling hand to touch the thing I had tripped on and found it soft to the touch. I felt a barely perceivable wisp of immortal energy crawling up my finger, winding itself around my hand, getting tangled between my fingers. I could not cry, but I felt the corners of my eyes stinging. My eyes and my head both felt filled with emptiness. The fragile little thing I was touching . . . was Mo Yuan's soul.

The twists and turns of time had reduced Mo Yuan's soul to this. Master Mo Yuan, the Four Seas and Eight Deserts' one-and-only God of War. Mo Yuan, with his strong fighting soul, now so weak he was dependent on this pathetic wisp of immortal energy to keep him going.

No wonder De Yong looked nothing like Mo Yuan.

But it was all going to be fine, because Mo Yuan had finally returned. Zhe Yan had not been lying to me. Mo Yuan, whom I felt closer to than to my own father even, had finally returned.

I had spent too long in De Yong's primordial spirit, and it was starting to get choppy and producing waves. It would not be wise to delay for too long. Although I had not been able to see anything through the silvery white emptiness, I had knelt down before Mo Yuan's soul. With my heart filled with a mix of anxiety and joy, I had bowed down before him twice before following the energy of primal chaos back into the outside world and carefully leaving his body.

Once I had been released from the soul-chasing magic, De Yong started to wake.

He opened his eyes and looked at me in surprise. "Why are you crying?" he asked. "Please don't cry just because you haven't managed to cure me. If anyone should be crying, it should be me. Please don't cry on my account. I've been this way for so long now, and it doesn't even bother me much anymore."

I touched the white cloth around my eyes, and sure enough my fingers came back wet. The choppiness and the waves in his primordial spirit must have caused tears to drop from my eyes. I cast a spell to dry my dampened white silk cloth. "I'm crying tears of joy," I said with a sheepish smile.

He frowned. "There I was thinking how softhearted you were, and feeling sympathy and sadness because of the sorry state of my health. Surely my suffering isn't making you joyful!"

"Of course not, of course not," I hurriedly replied. "The reason I'm happy is because I know a cure." I patted his shoulder, smoothing out the creases in his gown. "You are not to worry. I am feeling tentatively happy, but I will not feel completely happy until you're completely better."

Zhe Yan was right. If Mo Yuan's soul was relying on De Yong's frail body, it would take him at least another six thousand years before he could return to his own immortal body and wake up properly. But if we could borrow the Sky Emperor's soul-binding lamp, we could use it to piece together all the fragments of his scattered soul and repair it completely. After that, I could transfer to him half of the spiritual energy I had been cultivating over the last one hundred forty thousand years. With these measures, he might actually wake up quite soon.

In all my years, I had never set eyes on the Sky Clan's soul-binding lamp, but I had read accounts of it in the classics. According to these records, the soul-binding lamp was created by Father of the Universe during the age of primal chaos and could bind the souls of both immortals and mortals.

If the soul of an immortal had been fragmented, but the pieces not completely dispersed, all you needed to do was to light the soul-binding lamp and let it burn next to the bed of the person in question for three days, and the scattered bits of soul would come together as new. The lamp was even more effective when it came to mortals. Even if the mortal had turned to dust flying and flames dying, all that was needed was something that had their breath on it, which would be placed on the lamp and left to burn for a while. Once the lamp recognized this mortal's breath, it would slowly start to absorb every particle of this mortal's energy within a thousand-mile radius. Once it had absorbed all this mortal's energy from between the sky and earth, it would start to copy the mortal's soul, producing an exact replica.

I cast a spell to put De Yong to sleep and left Fuying Hall, where I discovered the crowd of idlers I had banished earlier lined up anxiously against the wall. I could not see the Western Sea Emperor among them. Before I had to ask anything, a perceptive young palace attendant at the front of the queue leaned over and bowed to me, saying, "An important guest has just arrived. The Water Emperor went to the great hall to greet him. If there is anything I can do, Immortal Prince, no matter how trifling, you only have to say the word and I will do my best to assist you."

So the Western Sea Emperor was welcoming another distinguished guest. He must have been feeling extremely honored. Zhe Yan and I were a god and goddess who were renowned for our outstanding glory, and by gracing his Water Crystal Palace with our presence, we had already done a lot to brighten his realm. But having the good fortune of receiving another distinguished guest as well, what were the odds? I imagined that such a coincidence would happen only once in ten thousand years.

I did not have anything to ask of her. All I wanted to do now was go back to the Ninth Sky to find the Sky Emperor and ask him if I could borrow the soul-binding lamp. My current alias did not provide me with a high enough status to just come and go from the Western Sea Water Crystal Palace as I pleased. First, I would have to find the Western Sea Emperor and explain face-to-face that I was leaving. Since these palace attendants had shown themselves to be so helpful, I picked two at random, asking one to lead me to the great hall where the Western Sea Emperor was greeting his guest and the other to stay behind and wait on De Yong.

There were two long lines of young Western Sea immortals extending out from the entrance to the great hall. They were standing in deference with their heads bowed. I saw their faces and recognized them as the same immortal attendants who had been present when the Western Sea Emperor had greeted Zhe Yan and me earlier.

From the number of attendants present, I deduced that this new guest was not above Zhe Yan in status, but that his level of office was probably much weightier. I waited anxiously. A moment later two palace attendants came out dressed in garish colors and led me into the great hall.

The distinguished guest was a man I was still rather annoyed with. Heir to the Sky Throne: Prince Ye Hua.

He was sitting on a carved red sandalwood chair when I walked in, supporting his chin with his hand. He looked wan and wore a slight frown, his face paper white. He was in the same clothes he had been wearing this morning, his off-duty attire, and just like in Qingqiu, his hair had not been bound, just fastened in a ponytail with a black silk band.

I looked around the great hall but could not see the Western Sea Emperor. All the things that Ye Hua had said to me earlier as he had been cradling Dumpling flooded back, making my blood boil. I gave an indignant snort, spun on my heels, and started to storm out.

I had six or seven paces on him, but as I was striding away, I felt some wind blowing behind me, and before I knew it he had grabbed me.

He grabbed me with an extremely heavy hand. I found it unimaginable that he would have the gall to restrain me like this without a second thought for the one hundred forty thousand years of spiritual cultivation I had so bitterly undertaken to ascend to my goddess rank.

He had caught me off guard when he grabbed me, and I stumbled and fell back, landing straight in his arms.

I had enough immortal energy to bump him three or four paces back, until he was pressed up against the huge crystal pillar in the center of the great hall. He clung to me obstinately, his lips pursed tightly and his eyes like raging dark pools.

His hands were extremely strong, and I struggled for a long time, unable to break away. I considered using some magic to free myself, but he got me in an armlock and moved up against me, pressing me tightly against the wall.

My wandering mind was brought right back to my body by a sharp pain in my neck. No! Yes. He was actually biting it. And his teeth were sharp! This position gave him the complete upper hand, and I was powerless to fight back.

His lips and tongue wandered over my neck, and his breathing became heavier. My heart felt calm, but my body was trembling. I felt overcome by some strange emotions. I was still struggling to free my hands, but not so I could push him away. My hands felt as if they had separated themselves from my control, and all they wanted to do was grab him and hold him tight.

I heard a voice in my head. It sounded as if it came from thousands of miles away, over mountains and oceans, and was only faintly discernible. "If I had nothing at all, would you still want to be with me?" a man asked. A girl chuckled in response. "What do you actually have, aside from the sword resting in the corner?" she asked. "And all the sword is good for is chopping firewood to roast wild beasts. And yet I'm still here, am I not?"

These disembodied voices caused chaos in my mind. My body felt as if it had been invaded, from the top of my scalp to the tips of my toes. My heart overflowed with what felt like thousands of years of pent-up desire. This desire kept me locked to the spot, unable to move.

He used one hand to undo the front of my gown while his hot lips moved across my collarbone and down my chest. There was a deep three-inch knife scar from where I used to feed Mo Yuan my heart blood for all those seventy thousand years.

His left hand, which was holding both of my hands, stiffened slightly, but gripped me even tighter as he glided his lips around the scar on my chest. I raised my head and gave a muffled moan. I suddenly felt a stabbing pain in the place he was kissing me, which was even more painful than when I used to stab myself there.

This pain caused me to regain some lucidity. I felt physically drained, and all I wanted to do was slide down the crystal pillar.

Eventually he released my hands, and I instinctively went to slap him across the face. He intercepted my hand and dragged me back into his arms. His right hand ventured inside the front of my gown, and he pressed it against my chest. His face was still as white as paper, although his eyes were burning brightly.

"Bai Qian, do I have any place at all in your heart?" he asked.

He had asked me this same question twice already, but I never knew how to respond. Of course he had a place in my heart, but I was not sure if his understanding of this was the same as mine. Being on my own for the last few days, I had quietly contemplated the place he did hold. I had thought about it for a long time, but it had always ended up giving me a headache.

The hand he had pressed against my breastbone gradually went from scalding hot to ice-cold, and that burning brightness left his eyes, and they became filled with darkness instead. He took his hand off my chest and said, "You've waited such a long time for his return. Now he's back, of course you cannot give yourself to another. I've been deluding myself."

I lifted my head sharply and looked at him. "How do you know about Mo Yuan's return?" I was not sure exactly what he was saying, or how Mo Yuan's return related to the place he held in my heart.

He turned and looked toward the outer hall. "Zhe Yan told me the night before we returned to the Sky Palace," he said flatly. "I bumped into him when I was out looking for you in Qingqiu and we had a chat. I knew you were planning to come to the Sky Palace to borrow the soul-binding lamp so that Mo Yuan could wake up sooner." He paused before asking, "What will you do once you've borrowed the lamp?"

Zhe Yan seemed to have told him everything. I rested a hand on my forehead and sighed. "I plan to go to the Eastern Sea island of Yingzhou to pick some immortal grass so I can transfer him seventy thousand years of my cultivated spiritual energy. He'll be able to wake up faster that way."

He turned his head sharply, his dark eyes looking even darker against the pale white of his face. He regarded me for a while, before enunciating every word carefully and saying, "You. Are. Crazy!"

Every immortal's energy is unique, so when cultivated spiritual energy is transferred between immortals, the accidental transfer of too much could disturb both sets of immortal energy, leading to chaotic cultivating practice and demonic tendencies.

Immortal grass helped by purifying immortal energy. To transfer seventy thousand years of my own cultivated energy across to Mo Yuan without harming both of us in the process, I would need a small amount of immortal grass. I would extract seventy thousand years of my own cultivated spiritual energy, mix it with immortal grass, and refine it into a pill that I would then give to De Yong. If it all went according to plan, within three months Mo Yuan would wake.

Because of this function, Father of the Universe used to worry that immortal grass would lead young immortals into bad cultivating practice, and so he destroyed all the immortal grass growing in the Four Seas and Eight Deserts, except for that growing in Yingzhou, which he kept guarded by the four ferocious beasts of Yingzhou.

When Father of the Universe's body returned to the primal chaos, these four ferocious beasts took charge of half of Father of the Universe's godly power, making them even more ferocious. I still remember Father going to Yingzhou to get Mother some immortal grass before she came to Yanhua Cave to transfer half her cultivated spiritual energy across to me. He came back from the island covered in injuries.

It was hard to find any immortal in the sky or earth with as much cultivated spiritual energy as Father, but even he had been seriously harmed in his struggle against these beasts. Ye Hua was right: my plan to go there was crazy, and I envisioned that I too would return with serious injuries that would take some time to heal.

There had been two or three footsteps between us, and as soon as he released me, I leaned against the big pillar without moving. He lifted one hand and managed to keep me trapped against the pillar. All the brightness had left his eyes. He gnashed his teeth and said, "You would even give your life for him?" He was the one keeping me trapped, but from his facial expression, you would think it was the other way around.

I found it strange what he had said. If I were unable to get the immortal grass from those four ferocious beasts, I would simply turn around and flee: it was not a question of losing my life. If I was unable to get hold of the grass and I had to look after Master's body for seven or eight thousand more years instead, then that was what I would do.

But looking at Ye Hua's pale and solemn face, I suddenly realized the problem. Any serious injury would be on top of the seventy thousand years of cultivated spiritual energy I would have just lost, which would take twenty or thirty thousand years to reestablish.

Within this time period it would be impossible for me to receive the eighty-one wildfires and nine sky lightning bolts that were a customary and essential part of the Sky Emperor and Empress's traditional accession to the Sky Throne. I had never heard of a Sky Emperor succeeding to the throne without his empress succeeding with him.

I coughed and lifted my head to look at him. "So why don't we just walk away from this agreement, abandon it and move on."

"What are you saying?" he asked, swaying. I pushed his hand away, fumbled about for a teacup on the table, and gulped down the tea.

"This whole mess had nothing to do with you," I heard my voice saying. "It was Sang Ji who wronged me and shamed Qingqiu. The Sky Emperor wanted to gloss things over for both our families and so he made this extremely unfair agreement. But this time it is me who is calling off the engagement. Let's both go our separate ways, put this behind us, and speak no more of who owes who."

Ye Hua was facing away from me. He remained completely still and silent.

"Come to my room tonight," he said eventually. "I have the lamp here with me." Without turning around to look at me, he walked across the hall, nearly bumping into the other crystal pillar near the entrance.

"Be careful," I called out nervously.

He steadied himself and put his hand on his forehead. "All this time I have just been deluding myself," he said faintly. "If we start charting how much I owe you, and you owe me, we'll get so knotted up we'll never be able to untie ourselves."

CHAPTER NINETEEN

I stood in the great hall feeling dazed and desolate.

I picked up a cup of cold tea from the table and took a couple of sips to wet my parched throat before taking a series of haphazard steps out of the hall.

Half of the young Western Sea immortals who had been standing in those two lines outside the hall had been dispersed, walking ahead of Ye Hua, I assumed, clearing the path. The other half I saw clattering along in the direction of the Western Sea Water Crystal Palace's main entrance.

It looked as if another guest had arrived.

I grabbed an attendant from the end of the procession and asked what was going on. She looked at me with an aggrieved expression and said, "A visitor from afar has arrived, and the Water Emperor's officials are going to greet him."

Today the Western Sea Emperor seemed destined to receive visitors. Nothing would surprise me anymore, not even if the Buddha from the lotus seat of the Western Paradise showed up. Due to the low profiles kept by these last two generations of Western Sea emperors, they had not received much attention from my generation of immortals. Receiving one distinguished guest after another like this was clearly an honor for them, and likely to increase their social standing no end.

Because Ye Hua had the soul-binding lamp with him, I no longer needed to travel to the Ninth Sky, which was one thing off my mind at least, but oddly enough I did not feel as relieved as I had expected. Ye Hua's solemn figure flashed again and again before my eyes, until I felt the strings of my fox heart start to tighten.

The two immortal attendants who had led me into the great hall dutifully led me back to Fuying Palace. When I had seen De Yong earlier, his complete dissimilarity to Mo Yuan had brought up a range of complicated emotions inside me, and when we arrived back outside his palace door, I decided against going in to see him again. Instead I found a young attendant to take me straight to where I would stay.

The Western Sea Emperor had a reputation for being a little bit hopeless. He certainly had none of the refinement of his Eastern Sea counterpart. There were two buildings to the east of the Fuying Palace, one toward the inner palace, called the Inner House, and the other toward the outer palace, called the Out House.

I found that I had been unlucky and would be staying in the Out House.

The flowerpot on the stool inside and the tea implements on the table were made of shining white porcelain, and even the immortal servants waiting on me were dressed in dazzling white. Looking up, my eyes were filled with this vivid white, and seeing the crowd of young immortal servants rushing around before my eyes in this color, I started to feel so dizzy I could bear it no longer, and I ordered them all outside to pull up weeds.

The Out House fell silent, but the silence only served to make my heart feel more desolate. Just as I was being confronted by this sense of desolation, I heard a squeak from behind the curtains and lifted my eyes to have a look.

It appeared that the distinguished guest that half the young Western Sea immortals had raced to greet was not the Buddha from the lotus seat of the Western Paradise after all. I poured out a cup of tea and called out, "Fourth Brother, come and have some tea!" He leaped inside and looked me up and down before taking the cup I was offering and having a sip.

His eyes were twisting in confusion when he said, "What are you doing living in an Out House, and why on earth are you disguised as a boy? What has happened to morals and decency!"

I glanced up at the rafters and said, "Zhe Yan made me dress like this."

Fourth Brother snorted out his tea. He wiped the corners of his mouth with his sleeve. "Dressing like that is not actually a bad look for you," he said, keeping a straight face.

Usually when Fourth Brother came to the Western Sea, it was to drink with the Western Sea Emperor's second son, Su Moye. But the reason he had rushed all this way today was not to see Su Moye, but me, his little sister.

He had wanted to go with Zhe Yan to the Ninth Sky to find me, but Zhe Yan had not let him. Instead he had waited in Qingqiu, and when Zhe Yan still had not returned, he realized Zhe Yan must have escorted me straight to the Western Sea. Fourth Brother decided to come straight over to find me, and pay a call on Su Moye at the same time.

He sat in the white wooden armchair and, with his head tilted, said, "I just came to see if you were settling in all right here. You can rely on Zhe Yan to make sure things run smoothly. What's wrong, though? You look as white as a sheet. Mo Yuan is about to return, shouldn't you be jumping for joy?"

I lifted my hand to my face and tried to look joyful. "Of course I'm full of joy," I said. "I'm bursting with joy, but in my own quiet way."

"So why do you look so distracted?" he asked with a frown.

I rubbed my face and laughed awkwardly. "It must be because I've just performed soul-chasing magic and haven't had the chance to recover properly yet."

The look that he flashed me was as intense as a flare. I gave another awkward laugh. "And on top of that, this morning Ye Hua and I had a row." During the long time he had spent in Zhe Yan's company, Fourth Brother had honed his skills in the bad habit of digging for gossip, and when it came to spreading gossip, it was a case of the student surpassing his master. Zhe Yan was the expert, while Fourth Brother had become the expert of experts.

I did not think that the argument Ye Hua and I had engaged in over Dumpling could be considered gossip worthy, but if I did not give him something, he would be pestering me all afternoon. I weighed it up and decided that for a quiet life, I would throw him a couple of bones. I took a sip of tea to wet my throat and cherry-picked parts of the Ninth Sky argument to tell him.

He slouched in the chair, his ears pricked, listening eagerly. When I had finished, he sat there awhile before lifting his head and giving me a strange smile. "You've always thought that as a member of the older generation, you should be showing tolerance toward those who are younger than you, and even when young people say foolish things that offend you, you try not to get worked up and argue with them about it. When it comes to this argument with Ye Hua you've just described, while you are my beloved sister, and so naturally I side with you, logically speaking, I think Ye Hua is the one in the right. Ali is a young child. You gave him enough alcohol to inebriate him for hours and hours, during which time he didn't wake up once. And you never thought it worth sending someone to let Ye Hua know?

"The Sky Clan is good at fighting, but their medicinal magic has always been lacking. Seeing his precious son in a drunken stupor must have terrified Ye Hua. How was he to know if there would be any lasting damage? And then this child's stepmother just off and leaves. If he weren't a bit angry, I would call him a saint."

He paused and then leaned over the desk to stroke my head. "You usually just make a joke and laugh off things like this, but this experience seems to have really rattled your cage. You even took it out on his main concubine. I must say that as your brother, I admire your pluck, but I'm also wondering whether your strange behavior couldn't be caused by . . . jealousy, could it?"

Hearing that gave me a start, and my head suddenly filled with a flashing white light. For the last two days, from when I had left Qingqiu for the Ninth Sky, every so often I had been feeling this tug on my heartstrings. I knew that I was acting with more impatience than usual. My run-in with Su Jin had left me feeling extremely uneasy. I had found Ye Hua's criticisms of me extremely hard to listen to. I had spent the whole day feeling distracted and anxious. *Can it be, can it really be that I am jealous? Is this how jealousy feels? Have I been feeling jealous this whole time without being the slightest bit aware?*

The teacup dropped from my hand and clattered to the floor. Fourth Brother leaped up and clapped his hands together. "You *are* jealous!" he said, nodding.

I felt completely dazed. I looked anxiously toward Fourth Brother. "No, it's not possible," I protested. "I'm ninety thousand years older than him. If I'd got moving quicker, he could be my grandson, or my great-grandson even, that is how much older I am. I've always felt that this arrangement was unfair to him. I was even willing to give him a couple of beautiful concubines. And the day before yesterday when he declared his feelings to me, I did not find myself palpitating with eagerness. I have some experience with romance, and if I truly felt for him, I would have experienced some eagerness when he declared his love for me, surely?"

Fourth Brother's eyes were shining brightly. "He's actually declared his love for you? Ah, he's fallen for the cub I raised, what good taste!

What very good taste." He chuckled for a long time before adding, "You shouldn't worry about age. Father is fifteen thousand years older than Mother. As long as you both look like a couple, which I would say you do. What you've just told me about giving him some concubines reminds me of a time Zhe Yan was very keen to help find me a wife. Look how long he's been doing that, without any success whatsoever." He gave a giggle. "He doesn't think there's any goddess in the whole of the Four Seas and Eight Deserts who's worthy of me, apparently."

He gave my shoulder a knowing pat. "Palpitating with eagerness is obviously a wonderful feeling, and naturally a period of great passion is fantastic, but as a woman you should be more sensitive and conscious of your romantic feelings. They are not always spelled out that brightly. Even though you are my little sister, I have to say you have always been quite emotionally unaware. Even though you are an excellent goddess, when it comes to matters of the heart, you are quite frankly inept. The way I see it, the type who would have you palpitating with eagerness would be too passionate and too dramatic for someone like you. Someone as unaware as you needs the feeling of eagerness to flow in a constant steady stream, not a gush of water."

The veins in my forehead pulsed.

He picked up a teacup off the desk and turned it around between his fingers, smiling. "Mystic Gorge said that Ye Hua has been living in Qingqiu for four months already. It may be a little early to ask this, but would you feel sad if he no longer lived in Qingqiu? No, with you being so unaware, it would probably take you ten thousand years to work out the answer to that. I'll put it another way. If he were to leave now, what would you miss about him?"

I could feel the veins in my forehead start to pulse again. The first few days after Ye Hua had moved to Qingqiu, I had found his presence there quite odd. But my thinking was that after the marriage, we would have to live together sooner or later, and it was better to just go with the flow.

Being dragged off for those daily walks. Him cooking while I stoked the fire. Sitting next to him, cracking sunflower seeds and reading my play scripts while he read over his documents. Playing a couple of games of chess in the evening. I thought that after we married, we would spend many, many nights that way and had gradually become very accustomed to our routine. It had only been four months of days like these, but now that Fourth Brother had made me ponder it, I could not really remember how I had spent my days before Ye Hua came to live in Qingqiu.

My heart felt heavy.

Fourth Brother gave a laugh. "Once Mo Yuan has recuperated, we will arrange a meeting between Father and the Sky Emperor and ask him to start the arrangements for your wedding. Your wise brother sees that you have a lot of love in your heart for Ye Hua. Fate must have finally opened his eyes and aimed his red phoenix star at you. It may be moving silently, but I can see it. Don't get yourself in too much of a muddle. Ye Hua has made the first move by declaring his feelings. If he were to go back on his word, I am sure you would feel . . ."

I was sitting upright with my ears pricked waiting to find out how I would feel if Ye Hua were to go back on his word. But all Fourth Brother did was put the teacup back on the table with a clatter and say, "The way you are acting right now has really set my mind at ease. I shall head back now." With that he leaped out the window, and with a whoosh, he was gone.

I thought back over Fourth Brother's words. They echoed through my heart, causing ripples on the lake that had remained perfectly still for the last tens of thousands of years. Fourth Brother had hit the nail on the head: although I had thought a lot about giving Ye Hua these beautiful concubines, I had looked at a large number of immortal girls his age and had not seen a single one that I had deemed worthy of him. If I had indeed fallen for Ye Hua . . .

At one hundred forty thousand years old, I felt as if the longer I lived, the more I regressed. I had fallen for a man ninety thousand years my junior, one who should by all rights have been calling me Old Ancestor. I paced around my empty lodgings, fretting, huffing, and puffing, but still I could not come up with a solution.

I lay down on the bed in my clothes, but my heart still felt uneasy. Lying down did not make me feel any calmer, and as soon as I closed my eyes, Ye Hua's pale face appeared in the vast darkness before me.

I turned it over in my mind, back and front, wondering if it would be possible to reassess what I had said to him about calling off our engagement and instead wait to see how things panned out. Although it gave me a headache to think about the strange words he had said that afternoon, I decided to let it go and not argue with him. Tonight I would display my goddess demeanor. I would go to his place to collect the soul-binding lamp, and while I was there I would drop all pretenses and talk to him openly and honestly.

That night I found my way to the bedchamber where Ye Hua was staying. He was sitting on a marble stool in the courtyard, drinking wine. There was an aventurine wine jar on the marble table next to him, and a further seven or eight jars lying in a jumble on their sides under the table. The nearby coral reflected off these jars, shining with a brilliant lustrous green light. Yesterday when Dumpling had been drunk, Nai Nai had sighed and sighed about how His Little Majesty must have taken after his father when it came to alcohol.

He gave a start when he saw me and lifted a hand to his temple. "I assume you've come to collect the soul-binding lamp," he said, standing up. Once on his feet, he started swaying. I reached out a hand to support him, but he gently waved it away. "I'm fine," he said calmly.

The Western Sea Emperor had provided him with a magnificent bedchamber, and the table at which he was sitting was a hundred paces from the inner hall. His face was completely devoid of expression, but several shades paler than when I had seen him last, and when viewed against the jet-black of his loose hair, his cheeks looked rather sallow. He turned and started walking toward the hall, and I followed three or four steps behind.

He was walking steadily now, as if it had been another man swaying before. He was walking slightly slower than usual and raising his hand every so often to rub his temple. He did look slightly drunk, but Ye Hua even got drunk with quiet composure, very much in keeping with the rest of his personality.

There were no waiting attendants in the hall. I sat down on a chair and lifted my face to meet his lifeless gaze.

His eyes were sharp and beautiful, and filled with total darkness. When he was not smiling, they looked very cold, but naturally still filled with that Ninth Sky majesty.

Although I was good at judging people's moods from their words and gestures, I was not usually very good at reading eyes. Today was different, however, and the two of us looked at each other for a long time, which allowed me to see through the coldness and into the dejectedness and misery.

His gaze shifted to the side, and he was quiet for a while before muttering something softly. I stared blankly at the tung oil lamp that had suddenly appeared in his hand.

"So this is the soul-binding lamp?" I marveled. "But it looks so ordinary."

He placed the lamp in my hands, and with a calm expression, he said, "Put it at the head of De Yong's bed for three days and make sure it doesn't go out during that time. All the pieces of Mo Yuan's soul should come back together. The flame in this lamp needs to be carefully protected the whole time. Don't be tempted to use immortal energy to protect it to make life easier for yourself."

He dropped the lamp into my hand, and a circle of familiar energy rushed toward me. It was tinged with red dust, more like mortal energy. I had never had any mortal friends, and so it surprised me how familiar this energy felt. I nodded at his warning, saying, "Of course. I will be extremely careful with it."

"I am worrying unnecessarily," he said at last. "You're always extremely diligent and careful where Mo Yuan is concerned."

As a sacred Sky Clan artifact, the soul-binding lamp had been enshrined and worshipped by Sky Emperors of the past. Having so many conventions meant that the Ninth Sky was extremely strict, and its regulations were always rigidly upheld. I was slightly puzzled by the fact that even though the old Sky Emperor was still alive, Ye Hua, currently only heir to the throne, had this precious lamp in his possession.

The Sky Palace was very different from Qingqiu and even the Purple Light Palace. Their regulations were strictly adhered to, and their clan's sacred artifacts never freely lent out. If I were to go to the Sky Palace to meet with the Sky Emperor and ask to borrow this sacred lamp, it would wipe the Ninth Sky's debt to Qingqiu clean off the abacus. The fact that Ye Hua had lent me the lamp like this touched me deeply. I turned to him, holding the lamp. "You've done me such an enormous favor," I exclaimed. "I worry that this must have incurred you quite a loss. If there's anything you want in return, all you have to do is say. I will grant you any favor I am able."

He sat in the chair opposite me, looking tired. He gave a faint frown and said, "There's nothing I want."

His expression pulled again at my heartstrings. Before Fourth Brother's lecture, I could not really explain these strange occasional tugs I had been feeling. But after Fourth Brother's revelation, I had started to think he might be right and explored my own emotions further. I was already beginning to expand my awareness of how I felt.

The soul-binding lamp was in my hands now. Should I turn around and leave, or stay there and straighten things out with Ye Hua? Perhaps he did not wish to talk, and would rather be left alone there?

I hesitated as I thought it through. "Is there really nothing you want? If so, I will leave now."

He raised his head sharply and looked at me, his face calm. "You want to know what it is that I want?" he said slowly. "It's the only thing I have ever wanted." He looked at me, his face immutable. "Only you."

I started to tremble. What was happening to me tonight? Hearing those romantic words did not make me feel nauseated, instead they moved me, as did the expression on his face. He was handsome at the best of times, and when he said beautiful things like that, who could possibly have resisted him? Under his deep gaze, I heard some words escape my mouth.

It took me a moment to realize what I had just said. When I did, I wanted to drop down into a deep pit and be buried in the center of the earth.

The words that had escaped my mouth had been "Would you like to spend a night of intimacy with me?"

I recovered my wits before Ye Hua had recovered his. With my face flame red, I packed away the lamp and went to leave, but Ye Hua came over before I got to the doorway and was holding me from behind.

I lifted my head to the rafters, wanting to just fall down dead from the shame. The alcohol fumes surrounding Ye Hua gave me spell after spell of dizziness, and he held me so tightly that it made all my regret disappear. All I felt was a brilliant peach blossom haze, as if my soul had left my body. My soul might actually have left my body, because I followed up with more audacious words.

"It's rather indecent to just do this in the doorway. Shall we just move to the bed?" I cast a spell and changed my body back into its female form . . .

• • •

I woke up in the middle of the night with my head in such a confused state it felt as if someone had replaced it with a big wok of rice porridge. Ye Hua must have cast a spell to shield some of the night pearl's glow. He had me in his arms, holding me tightly against his chest, and my face was resting against his long scar.

I thought back over our night of union, but all I could remember was the fluttering of the bed curtain. After all the physical excitement, I had floated into a hazy sleep in which I vaguely remember him saying, "If I only have you completely this one time, if only for tonight, even if you are just doing it to get the soul-binding lamp for Mo Yuan, I still have no regrets." I think that was what he said. I did not hear his words clearly, and because of those strange, disjointed voices and hallucinations earlier, I no longer completely trusted my own brain.

Unfortunately, being with him like that did not give me the kind of clarity that the beautiful women in my play scripts experienced, and for the first time I wondered if these mortal-world plays painted an overly simplistic picture.

Ye Hua was fast asleep still, but after waking suddenly like that, I was unable to drift back off. As I ran my hand down his chest scar, I suddenly remembered something I had heard.

There was a rumor that three hundred years ago, the Shark Clan from the Southern Sea had sent their troops out to revolt, vying for independence. Unable to hold them off, the Southern Sea Water Emperor sent a letter to the Nine Skies, pleading for his help. The Sky Emperor put Ye Hua in command of the army he sent to quash the unrest. But the Shark Clan had fought with unexpected bravery and ferocity, and during this Southern Sea battle, Ye Hua was almost killed.

I had remained in Qingqiu for so long without leaving that I knew little about this event, and it was only today that I was reminded of it. When I finally awoke from my great slumber following the battle with Qing Cang, Fourth Brother had mentioned it a couple of times, wringing his hands in anguish each time he recalled it, a pained expression on his face. "Can you believe that Shark Clan, revolting like that without rhyme or reason? This younger generation of immortals is becoming increasingly unruly. The Shark Clan was such a fine specimen of immortals, and because of this their entire clan has been destroyed. But they almost turned the young Nine Skies heir into dust flying and flames dying, and they paid the price."

Sometimes Fourth Brother's incessant chatter used to exhaust me, but it was thanks to him that I knew a few things about Ye Hua's impressive military might. Any battle waged in the Four Seas and Eight Deserts over the last twenty thousand to thirty thousand years in which Ye Hua was in command, the troops seemed invincible, obliterating everything in their path. Ye Hua's almost fatal blow at the hands of the Shark Clan had come as a shock to everyone, Fourth Brother in particular.

Ye Hua woke up as I was pondering all this. He looked down at me. "Why are you awake?" he asked quietly. "Aren't you tired?"

I had never been good at keeping my questions in my head. I stroked the prominent scar on his chest before my question inevitably popped out.

He clung to my arm, and his voice floated over, sounding desolate. "Please don't mention that battle. Their whole clan was destroyed, and I didn't get what I wanted. Both sides ended up suffering greatly."

"You nearly died in the Southern Sea," I said, giving him a bright smile. "You should be happy that you survived. What else did you want?"

"If I hadn't thrown the fight, do you think there was a chance they would have been able to harm me?"

A loud boom resonated from within my head.

"Thr-thrown the fight? You put your life at risk on purpose?"

He clasped my arm tightly. "It was just to trick the Sky Emperor," he explained.

"So you were trying to feign death?" I said, thinking I understood, before starting to feel confused again. "But why would you want to lose your reputation as the undefeated-in-battle heir to the Sky Throne? Why on earth would you want to feign death?"

For a long time he said nothing, and I started to wonder if he might have drifted off to sleep once more. But he suddenly looked down at me, and in a bitter voice he said, "I never knew what envy felt like until I felt it for my second uncle, Sang Ji."

His alcohol tolerance was obviously not as good as I had thought. He had consumed four or five jars of wine earlier, and while he had seemed fairly clearheaded earlier, he was now talking as if he were drunk. He was not usually a big talker, but as soon as he had mentioned the Sky Emperor's second son, Sang Ji, the floodgates opened, and a barrage of words flooded out. I imagined that all those jars' worth of wine must have finally reached his head.

During this ramble he revealed a surprising piece of gossip about the way in which Sang Ji and Shao Xin had eloped, and I listened with rapt interest. I lay in his arms, listening in fascination, racing ahead, trying to fill in the gaps in his story, and ending up quite confused.

All I had known previously was that after stealing Shao Xin away, Sang Ji had gone to the Sky Emperor's court and knelt down before him. He had made such a fuss about the affair that before nightfall the whole of the Four Seas and Eight Deserts knew about it. This had been extremely humiliating for our Qingqiu clan and had enraged Father, Mother, and my older brothers. But before hearing Ye Hua talk about it, I had been unaware of all the twists and turns that had led up to this pivotal event.

Sang Ji was utterly in love with Shao Xin, and taking her to the Ninth Sky was a grand gesture of his deep affection. Sang Ji had always enjoyed the benefits of being the Sky Emperor's favorite son. He thought that if he expressed his true love for Shao Xin, he could win over his father, who would give the devoted young couple his blessing.

But instead Sang Ji's declaration of his affection for Shao Xin provoked catastrophe. The Sky Emperor refused to give his blessing and felt extremely humiliated by the fact that his second son had fallen in love with a ba snake. Not only this, his son's actions had also caused terrible humiliation for the Qingqiu goddess and were likely to have repercussions for the friendship between the Sky Clan and the Qingqiu Nine-Tailed White Fox Clan.

The Sky Emperor was not yet aware that his son had been brazen enough to leave a letter in the foxhole, breaking off the engagement. He was still hoping that for the sake of these two clans' friendship, he might be able to resolve things, covering up the hornet's nest that his second son had stirred up. One bright and clear afternoon, the Sky Emperor came to a decision. He grabbed Shao Xin, who doting Sang Ji had ensured had been treated very well in the Ninth Sky up until that point, and locked her up in the demon tower.

Sang Ji was extremely upset when he found out what his father had done. He rushed to the Sky Emperor's bedchamber and knelt down outside it for two whole days, until his knees were covered in bruises. All he had managed to get out of the Sky Emperor was that the little ba snake was just a good-for-nothing demon spirit who not only had the audacity to seduce the Sky Emperor's second son, but had also caused huge waves during peacetime. According to the sky regulations, her punishment should have been having her spiritually cultivated energy destroyed and being banished to the mortal world, never to rise back up as an immortal.

Sang Ji was just a prince and powerless against his father's awe and majesty. He had no idea how to save Shao Xin. He reached such depths of despair that he eventually threatened to kill himself. He begged to be allowed to go down to the mortal world with Shao Xin so that the two of them could be together. He was willing to sacrifice his life to be with Shao Xin, turn to ashes and dust if that was what it took to be alongside her.

Sang Ji's declaration was so full of desperation and melancholy that all in the Ninth Sky who heard it would start to weep. But the Sky Emperor, being the Sky Emperor and the head of the Sky Clan, had his ways of dealing with things, and he destroyed Sang Ji with a few simple words.

"If you wish to take your life, I won't stop you," he said. "But it will leave me with the life of your little ba snake in my hands. Go ahead and destroy your own soul, but know that as soon as you have turned to ash flying and flames dying, I will devote myself to tormenting your little ba snake. I will inflict so much pain and suffering onto her that she won't know whether to beg for her life or the sweet release of death."

Sang Ji was still in a complete state, but he made no more mention about dying in the name of love; he just sat in desolation in his palace. The Sky Emperor was relieved to see that Sang Ji had finally calmed down, and his mind moved away from dealing with this unfortunate event and on to new matters. As soon as his back was turned, Sang Ji, who had only been acting desolate and resigned, took advantage of a loophole. He burst into the Sky Emperor's court and knelt down before him, causing such a hullabaloo that in no time at all everyone between the sky and earth knew what had happened.

It was at that point Zhe Yan and my parents had come up to the Ninth Sky, seeking justice. If Sang Ji had not turned this into such a public and high-profile matter, the Sky Emperor could have quietly dealt with Shao Xin as he wished without anyone being any wiser. But now everyone was talking about it, and while the Sky Emperor had every right to exclude Shao Xin from any special favors within the Sky Palace, she had not done anything that could justify him punishing her with death. The Sky Emperor had his hands tied. He had no choice but to release Shao Xin and banish Sang Ji, thus allowing the two of them to be together.

"Sang Ji asked for clemency and received it," Ye Hua explained. "It was a rocky road, but in the end he got what he wanted. The Sky

Emperor still doted on him, but there was no longer any question of him being heir to the Sky Throne. He was free from the shackles of that title. He had earned his freedom, his utter freedom."

I hugged his arm and gave a yawn. "What about you?" I asked.

"Me?" he said at last. "When I was born, seventy-two multicolored birds spiraled around the rafters and a hazy light shone over the East for three whole years. Mo Yuan was the only other god whose birth was marked with such honor and respect. The Sky Emperor saw the unprecedented glory surrounding my birth and named me heir to the throne straightaway, although it was only when I turned fifty thousand that I was given my official heir ceremony. All the time I was growing up, I knew that Bai Qian from Qingqiu would one day be my wife."

I had not been aware that his birth was such a spectacle. "Were you not curious about me when you were younger?" I wondered out loud. "What would you have done if you hadn't wanted me as your wife?"

He was quiet and hugged me even tighter. "If it hadn't been Bai Qian from Qingqiu I'd fallen in love with," he began slowly, "I would have tricked the audience of pedantic old sky immortals into thinking I had turned to dust flying and flames dying and left the Three Realms and the Five Phases to find a completely new place to live happily and nurture my love."

All this talk was making me dazed and sleepy. I gave an admiring sigh about the lucky way that things had worked out. "Fortunately you did fall in love with Bai Qian from Qingqiu," I said, pulling up the cloud quilt, finding a comfortable position in his arms, and falling back asleep.

Halfway between sleep and waking, I suddenly heard him say, "Qian Qian, if anyone tried to seize your eyes and left you unable to see, would you be able to forgive them?"

I was thrown by the oddness of the question. "There's no one in the whole of the Four Seas and Eight Deserts who would dare to try it!" I said flippantly, feeling confused.

He was silent for a long time. Just as I was drifting back off, he said, "What if that person was me?"

I touched my eyes, still very much within their sockets, feeling completely thrown by his crazy words. I hugged his arm. "I am afraid it would mean the end of our relationship," I said casually.

"You really don't remember, do you?" he said.

"Remember what?" I asked, not understanding the grave tone in his voice.

"A long time ago, before I had been officially named heir, I was sent to the mortal world to slay a red-and-gold-flamed lion beast," Ye Hua said. "I was able to slay it, but I was badly wounded. So badly, in fact, that I turned into a small dragon. While recovering, I found a small thatched hut on Junji Mountain and fell into a deep sleep. When I awoke, I saw a woman with a beautiful face. She wore white clothes, and for many weeks she cared for me as a dragon. At night, while she slept, I would turn into a human and hold her in my arms."

Ye Hua paused. I thought he might be worried that I would be jealous of this woman, but strangely I was not. His words seemed to stir something in my mind, but I said nothing, and he continued.

"One day while I was with her on Junji Mountain, she brought home a crow and kept it as a pet along with me. I couldn't bear having to share her attention, so when her back was turned, I changed back into a man, summoned a cloud, and returned to the Ninth Sky. But I couldn't stop thinking about her, so I set a plan in motion." Ye Hua paused again, but still I said nothing. My mind was clouded with strange thoughts, but I couldn't make them out.

Ye Hua spoke again. "I cast a barrier around the mountain so no one from the Ninth Sky could see, and then I returned to her, this time as a man. I cast a spell on myself so it looked like I was gravely wounded. I appeared in front of her, and she did her best to save me. I let her nurse me back to health even though I had been fine all along. When I had healed, I told her that I must repay her for her kindness.

She asked me to repay her with my body, and we were married in the mortal world."

Ye Hua fell silent.

"Go on," I said before I even realized it. It felt like I was in a trance. I felt no jealousy. I wasn't even surprised at Ye Hua's trickery. All of it seemed so strangely familiar.

"I had fallen in love with this woman. I did not wish to be heir anymore. I wanted to stay on the mountain with her. This scar," Ye Hua said as he ran a finger down the scar from the battle against the Shark Clan, "is the result of my deception of the Sky Emperor. When the Shark Clan revolted, I was dispatched to fight against them. I let their chief gravely wound me to make it look like dust flying and flames dying. My plan was to make the Sky Emperor believe this and then return to the mountain to be with her. But while I was gone from the mountain fighting the Shark Clan, she ran away, breaking through the barrier I had cast that shielded us from the eyes of the sky realm. The Sky Emperor saw that she was pregnant with my child. There was no way to escape our fate. I abandoned the plan to feign dust flying and flames dying. The Sky Emperor summoned her to the Ninth Sky to have my child, but I was wary of him after the way he had treated Shao Xin and Sang Ji. I had to be very cold to her. I couldn't let the Sky Emperor know that we were in love."

Ye Hua spoke calmly so as not to upset me, but I was strangely numb.

"What happened to her?" I asked.

"The Sky Emperor could not be fooled," Ye Hua said. "He sent me away to fight, and then . . ."

"And then what?" I said. "And what does this have to do with someone taking my eyes?"

"Qian Qian . . ."

I felt him shudder against my chest.

"What was her name?" I asked.

Holding me even tighter, he said, "Sleep well."

I waited for him to say more, for him to explain, for the buzzing in my mind to quiet, but he said nothing more. Eventually I closed my eyes and the world went black.

That night I had a dream. I was aware it was a dream as I was having it. In this dream, I was standing on top of a mountain that was lit up with a brilliance of peach blossoms. The flowers were all fully open, rising and falling over the contours of the mountain in long, unbroken stretches. It was just as marvelous as Zhe Yan's Ten-Mile Peach Grove. Within the depths of these glorious peach blossoms, there was a little thatched hut, and the clear sound of birdcall could be heard nearby.

I took a couple of steps up ahead and pushed open the door of the thatched hut. Inside I saw a girl dressed in white standing behind a seated man in black, combing his hair in front of an old bronze mirror. They both had their backs to me. I could see their vague reflection from within the mirror, but they were shrouded in a dense mist, which obscured their faces.

"I've found somewhere where the two of us can live," the man said. "It's not a place of green hills and clear water, however, and I'm not sure how much you'll enjoy living there."

"Can we grow peaches there?" the girl asked. "As long as we can grow peaches, I don't mind. We can use the wood from the peach trees to build our house, and we can eat as many peaches as we want. But aren't you happy on this beautiful mountain? And you've only just finished repairing our hut. Why would you want us to move?"

Immortal energy radiated out from the man, while the girl, obviously a mortal, had none. Their voices were familiar, but because it was a dream, the whole experience was fragmented, and I could not work out how I recognized them.

The man was silent awhile. "The soil is different there, and I'm not sure that we'll be able to grow peaches. But if you want peaches, we'll find a way."

The girl was quiet a moment before suddenly leaning forward and throwing her arms around the man's shoulders. He turned around and gazed at her for a while, stroking the hair on her temple with his slender fingers and then kissing her there.

They were kissing with such passion that they seemed to blend into one. I was still trying to get a clear look at their faces, and because I knew it was just a dream, I did not try to avert my eyes. I just watched this kissing couple with wide eyes as they made their way onto the bed, despite the fact that it was the middle of the day and the sun was shining brightly outside.

Suddenly I found myself looking at a different scene.

I gave a sigh. I was dreaming after all.

The setting of this new scene was the mouth of a peach grove. "Whatever happens, you must not step off this mountain," the man in black urged the girl in white. "You are pregnant with my child now, and you could be easily tracked down. If that were to happen, things would become very difficult for us.

"I'll be back as soon as I have done what I have to do. Oh, and yes, I've thought of a way for us to grow peach trees." As soon as he had finished saying this, he pulled a bronze mirror out of his sleeve pocket and placed it in the girl's hand. "If you feel lonely, call my name into this mirror, and I will speak to you if I can. But remember, whatever happens you must not step outside this peach grove or off the mountain."

The girl continued nodding until he disappeared. She gave a quiet sigh and said, "We bowed down and praised the great pool in the Eastern Desert when we married, but still he has not taken me back to meet his family. I feel as if I am just his mistress. Still having to run around hiding after I am pregnant with his baby is no way to live." She shook her head and went inside.

I shook my head too. This relationship of theirs would be no different from those between immortals and mortals since the dawn of time; it would not end well.

As soon as the girl went into the house, the scene in front of me changed again. It was still the same peach grove I was seeing, but most of the peach blossoms had withered, and all the branches and twigs were bare. A waning moon hung in the sky. It was a very desolate scene. The girl in white was holding her bronze mirror and calling something. All I could see was an indistinct blur of her features and her lips opening and closing, but I could not hear what she was saying.

The girl suddenly stumbled outside of the hut. My heart gave a lurch. I had completely forgotten I was dreaming. I hurried outside along with her. "Don't you remember, your husband told you not to leave the peach grove?" I warned. Unable to hear me, she just continued to run wildly.

A thick immortal barrier had been placed a hundred feet outside the peach grove, and it should have easily kept a mortal like her contained. But she ran through this immortal barrier, and without the slightest effort, she slipped past it, as if it were not there at all.

Ferocious bolts of lightning suddenly came down from the sky.

I woke in terror.

I opened my eyes to see the room flooded with bright morning light. I was on my own, and the soul-binding lamp had been placed by the head of the bed.

I discovered that I was not in Ye Hua's bed after all, but on my own in the Out House. Ye Hua really did know how to take care of things.

Two brightly dressed immortal attendants came over to wait on me and give me a wash. I already felt very clean, however, and realized that I did not need a bath. Ye Hua must have washed me himself before leaving this morning.

Waking to see the bright morning sunlight shining onto the brilliant white of my room, I felt an unprecedented sense of clarity. And I had another realization.

I remembered a scene from one of my play scripts. The daughter of a government official was traveling back to her hometown to visit family, but on the way she ran into a burly bandit who wanted to take her back to the mountains with him and make her the bandit chieftain's wife. I was quite taken with this burly bandit, whom the play script described as marvelously adept with a double-headed ax and much more gifted than the scholars who could not go two moments without quoting Confucius.

This virginal official's daughter despised her bandit captor and told him she would rather die than submit to him. But by the next scene, this same well-brought-up and unsubmitting virgin was entering the hibiscus net with a young scholar who had jumped over the wall to see her. I realized that these beautiful girls did not go into the hibiscus net with just anyone. Neither did they engage in the act of love to receive clarity. These beautiful girls knew how much they adored these scholars before they let anything happen with them.

It had been me who had seduced Ye Hua last night. Earlier on in life, love had dealt me a bad hand and been the cause of much anguish, but now I was starting to be interested in it again. In Ye Hua's arms, I had felt complete.

Fourth Brother was right: I had transcended the age gap and fallen in love with Ye Hua. You could not choose whether or not you fell in love. I felt relieved that I had not managed to find any female immortals of marriageable age within the Four Seas and Eight Deserts who I had deemed worthy of becoming Ye Hua's concubines.

Seeing that Ye Hua and I were in love, there was no reason to cancel our engagement. I decided that I would go to Ye Hua's palace between taking breakfast and going to Fuying Hall to light the soul-binding lamp and ask him if he would be willing to be the first Sky Emperor to succeed on his own and have his empress join him on the throne later.

I imagined that he would be receptive.

I ate my breakfast, feeling extremely pleased with myself, and strode past Fuying Hall and all the way to Ye Hua's bedchamber.

Good luck never seems to last for long, however, and I found myself being turned away at the door. "The prince returned to the Sky Palace early this morning," explained the two immortal attendants guarding his hall.

Being heir to the Sky Throne was not easy, and Ye Hua had an endless pile of documents to work on each day. He had rushed over to the Western Sea yesterday, and obviously had some urgent matter that he needed to rush back for.

Understanding that his role was a very demanding one, I thanked these two immortal attendants and made my way back toward Fuying Palace, feeling dispirited.

I cast a spell to put De Yong to sleep and carefully lit the soul-binding lamp. It burned by De Yong's bedside for three days, and I sat beside him, watching over him this whole time. Each day, the Western Sea Empress would send a couple of her servants to poke their heads around the door, terrified that I might have killed her son. Luckily each time this happened, the Water Emperor's guards managed to block them at the door and send them away again.

The crowd of immortal attendants in the hall walked around as if in the presence of some deadly enemy. Usually they would be clamoring to serve De Yong, but now not one of them dared to come within three feet of his bed, and when they walked past, they did so with extreme light-footedness, terrified of making a sudden movement and snuffing out the soul-binding lamp's flame.

Sitting beside De Yong as he slept was extremely boring, and the energy emitted from the soul-binding lamp as it burned sent me into a bit of a trance. I asked an immortal attendant at the side to bring me a plate of nuts. I started shelling the walnuts she brought over and removing the kernels, an activity that helped to keep my mind calm and focused.

After three days of keeping watch, a large mound of walnut shells had piled up in front of De Yong's bed. My eyes were red from fatigue, and because I had been staring at the soul-binding lamp for so long, when I closed my eyes, all I could see was just leaping flames.

De Yong slept constantly for three days, during which time he recovered a lot of energy, and when he woke up, he was feeling extremely reinvigorated. He said that he had not felt so alert for six hundred years, and he soon became overexcited. He clamored about how he wished to go for a swim in the Western Sea and enjoy the scenery he had not had a chance to view for the six hundred years of his illness. Fortunately he could see that I had been through a lot in the last three days and was reasonable enough not to force me to go with him.

Mo Yuan's soul had obviously reformed by now. My next move was preparing for my trip to Yingzhou to obtain some immortal grass. There was nothing in particular I needed to get ready for this trip, but I did need to recover my physical strength. I returned to the Out House and told my immortal attendants to keep the door closed to any visitors. After thinking about it, I decided to place an immortal barrier on the room too. I dived into bed and fell straight into a deep slumber.

I slept for five or six days straight.

When I finally woke up, I removed the immortal barrier. I decided I would go to see the Western Sea Emperor to ask for a few days' leave. I opened my door and gave a jump of fright: two immortal attendants were kneeling down right outside. They looked as if they had been kneeling there a long time, and looked shocked to see me. "The immortal prince has awoken!" they said quickly. "His Godliness Zhe Yan has been in the great hall waiting for you for the last two days now."

I gave a start.

I seemed to be everyone's favorite person these days; in fact, I could not remember ever having so many visitors. Fourth Brother, Ye Hua, the Eastern Sea Emperor and his wife, and now Zhe Yan for the second time. I could not imagine what he might have come to tell me this time.

I walked in front while the two immortal attendants scrambled to their feet and staggered after me. As I walked down the stairs, Zhe Yan lifted his head and looked at me. He smiled and beckoned me over, saying, "Come and sit down here." I slowly walked over and sat down, dismissing the immortal attendants who had accompanied me by telling them to go outside and pull up weeds. I fumbled for a cup of tea from the table and took a small sip to moisten my throat. Zhe Yan looked me up and down and said, "From your appearance, I imagine that Mo Yuan's soul must be fully reformed.

"The day before yesterday, I refined a pill and have come here just to give it to you. I think it could be rather useful." As he said this, he produced a shiny white pill, which he placed in my palm. I took the pill up to my nose and sniffed it, detecting the faint scent of immortal grass.

I stared at him in speechless disbelief. "D-d-did you refine th-th-this pill with your own cultivated spiritual energy? D-d-did you know I was planning to transfer spiritually cultivated energy to Mo Yuan?" I looked him up and down carefully. "You went to Yingzhou to pick this immortal grass and managed to return without even a scratch from the four ferocious beasts?"

He covered his mouth with his sleeve and gave a cough. "Oh, were you planning to transfer your own spiritually cultivated energy to Mo Yuan? I didn't know. You lost a considerable amount of your immortal energy during your battle with Qing Cang, so luckily we can use this pill I refined instead. I'm not sure you have enough spiritually cultivated energy to spare and still call yourself a goddess." He turned the teacup in his hand and said, "I was brought up by Father of the Universe. I am unable to repay the kindness he showed by nurturing me as a child. He left behind two children, the younger of whom is no longer. Anything I can do to help the older one, I will gladly."

They were light words, but said with a lot of emotion. With moist eyes I took the pill and thanked him.

He acknowledged my thanks, but said nothing. I gave a sigh. I sat beside him in silence, holding the pill.

He glanced at me, looking as if he wanted to say more, but then deciding not to. He forced a smile and said, "I should go. Pick a day when De Yong is feeling full of energy and give this to him. He might find it very strong, so you should stay near to keep an eye on him."

I nodded and watched him leave the hall.

De Yong had been full of energy recently, and the Western Sea Empress was overjoyed. Because she was happy, the Western Sea Water Emperor was happy too, and so was everyone else in the whole of the Western Sea. But De Yong was still weak, and giving him a strong pill that contained tens of thousands of years of Zhe Yan's cultivated energy was likely to put him back to bed for the rest of the month.

I decided to allow De Yong some more time to bound around and enjoy himself before sending him back to bed. While De Yong was out enjoying himself, Fourth Brother's drinking buddy, Su Moye, invited me for a drink or two.

After I decided De Yong had enjoyed himself sufficiently, I personally administered Zhe Yan's pill to him. De Yong was very weak, but not quite as weak as Zhe Yan had feared, and he was in a coma for only seven days after taking this pill.

His mother sat by his bedside, with tears streaming down her face this whole time. I assured her that this was just a side effect of the strong pill he had taken on his weak body, but she would not hear this, and whenever she looked at me, her face was full of fury.

I was keen to escape from that glaring face, but she was extremely anxious about her son and the possibility of him suffering a setback while I was not at hand to help. She pleaded with her husband to make me stay and sit with her by De Yong's bedside.

There was no way I could refuse a face-to-face request from Western Sea Emperor. I had to just bite my lip and agree. She spent these days sitting by the bed, filled with sorrow for her son. I started shelling walnuts, but the look of infinite grief and sadness she gave me made me lose enthusiasm for the activity. I had nothing to occupy me, and those seven days were extremely bleak and desolate.

On the evening of the seventh day, De Yong recovered from the heavy dosage and woke back up. I was the only one in the room at the time. His mother had been there until very recently, but after watching over him for seven whole days, all the suppressed rage toward me had been redirected into a sorrow so intense that it had affected her breathing. She had fainted and been carried out by her husband.

I approached De Yong to see how well the pill had been absorbed. Just as I was approaching the edge of his bed, he grabbed my hand. He had a strange expression on his face. "Have you been by my side, looking after me this whole time?" he asked.

I nodded. "How do you feel now? Are you in any pain?" He did not respond.

"I heard that you were a homosexual. Is that true?" he said with a frown. I was impressed with the Eastern Sea Emperor: this rumor had spread all the way to the Western Sea.

Whenever I tried to talk myself out of tricky situations, I always ended up making them worse, so I decided not to try. Instead, I pulled back my hand, and in a calm voice I said, "I heard that you were homosexual too, Your Majesty."

"Correct," he said, raising an eyebrow. "But you're not my type."

I reached out a hand to check his pulse. "You're one of those feeble scholar types. If I'm not your type, I imagine you must go for someone more like Ye Hua."

Ye Hua was the best looking of all the male immortals I knew. Although he was facially very similar to Mo Yuan, that calm, cold expression of his gave him a look of strength. De Yong was refined and sentimental: I imagined that he would identify himself as a gentle type and that he would probably go for manly men, and I hazarded a guess that Ye Hua would be his type. By asking this question, I was hoping to deflect any further questions about my own orientation and preferences.

As soon as he heard the name, his face went bright red, and he quickly looked away.

My heart gave a thump, and the hand I was taking his pulse with started to tremble. "So y-you do like Ye Hua?" I asked.

He turned to me. "Things like this cannot be forced," he said with embarrassment. "You have looked after me extremely conscientiously, and for that I am most grateful. If my palace attendants had not alerted me to your affections, I would not have guessed that you had this intention toward me. Before I was aware of your feelings, I felt comfortable in your care and had no reservations. But b-b-because of that rumor about you and His Majesty Ye Hua, I cannot help feeling negativity toward you. How life can make fools of us sometimes. It is only now that I've realized your true feelings are for me. I'm sorry that I am unable to reciprocate your affections. I feel as if I have let you down." He paused and gave a sigh of distress. "I read about a situation like this once a long time ago, in a play script my brother, Su Moye, brought me to read. I could never have imagined a situation like this happening in reality." He gave an emotive sigh and said, "Immortal Prince, is it true about you and His Majesty? Does His Majesty Prince Ye Hua resist his homosexual urges?"

I was completely taken aback by what he was saying, and it took me a while to grasp the homosexual love triangle that De Yong was describing. The corners of my mouth twitched. I smiled through clenched teeth and said, "Yes, he does resist them. I have tried everything, but still he resists. I set my sights on the next best thing, and started to pursue you instead."

His face flushed red before the blood drained from it, turning it white.

I had known that Ye Hua had the kind of face that provoked peach flower feeling in girls, but I had not imagined that the same might be true for men too. Fourth Brother was right when he said that we were living in strange times. I decided it would be for the best if I stopped Ye Hua from visiting the Western Sea in the future.

De Yong's pulse was steady and his energy calm.

Wanting to be completely sure, I decided to perform another round of soul-chasing magic, to be certain that Zhe Yan's immortal energy was doing what it should inside De Yong's body: protecting and nurturing Mo Yuan's soul.

De Yong's experiences did not seem to have taught him anything, and again I used the side of my hand to give him a karate chop, knocking him out. Because it was the second time I had performed soul-chasing magic on him, I had no obstacles to entering his primordial spirit this time. Nor did I need any Buddhist melodies to guide me. The journey to find Mo Yuan was a smooth one.

The last time I had been inside here, all I had seen of Mo Yuan's soul was that faint wisp of immortal energy nursing it. This time it was a huge surge, and I was unable to get anywhere near him. There was no way that such strong immortal energy could have been refined from mere tens of thousands of years of spiritual cultivation.

Mo Yuan was obviously just about to wake up. But . . . the immortal energy nursing Mo Yuan . . . this energy was surging yet calm, restrained yet majestic, and so familiar, but it was not Zhe Yan's. My heart turned icy cold. I finally understood what Zhe Yan had wanted to tell me when he had hesitated before giving me the pill. I finally understood why he did not have a single scratch on his body from his trip to Yingzhou.

Zhe Yan had never actually been to Yingzhou. He had never roused the anger of those ferocious beasts guarding the grass. He was not always the most upright of people, but he never lied and he never took advantage of others. He had clearly wanted to tell me the truth about this pill: how it had been refined by Ye Hua. Why then had he hidden this from me? It couldn't, it couldn't be . . .

I forced myself to calm down and retreated from De Yong's primordial spirit. I stumbled out and grabbed the teacup from the table next to me. Before I had a chance to take a sip, I started to cough up blood. My soul was undulating wildly.

My heart was beating rapidly and my legs felt weak. I leaned against the table and slid to my knees, my teacup smashing to the floor. De Yong stroked his head and sat up in bed in shock. "What's happened to you?"

I forced a smile, and placing a hand on the table, I managed to pull myself up. "Your illness is much better. You no longer need me to nurse you. Please explain to your father that I have some urgent business to attend to and that I've had to return to the peach grove."

CHAPTER TWENTY

I soared on a cloud through the resplendent, rosy-red clouds gathered above the Western Sea and up into the Ninth Sky. I tumbled off my cloud once on the way, and by the time I arrived the Southern Sky Gate, I was in a bit of a state. The two sky soldiers standing guard there stopped me courteously.

I looked down at myself and realized I looked more than a little disheveled. Showing up at the Ninth Sky in this state was certain to bring dishonor upon Qingqiu. I was so anxious to see Ye Hua that I saw no option but to offer up Zhe Yan's name again, posing once more as his immortal envoy. Zhe Yan had sent me to pay my respects to the heir to the Sky Throne, His Majesty Ye Hua, I explained.

These two sky soldiers were extremely cautious in their handling of affairs. Politely they asked me to wait while they went to Xiwu Palace to announce my arrival. Although I was still burning with anxiety, my heart was soothed by the fact that they were taking news of my arrival to Xiwu Palace rather than Lingxiao Palace, where serious matters were handled. Since this was the case, I imagined that Ye Hua had not suffered any major misfortune.

A short while later, the sky soldiers returned, followed by a young immortal attendant who led me inside. This immortal attendant looked familiar, and after a while I recognized her as the one who worked in Ye Hua's study.

Her eyes opened in wide surprise when she saw me. Working in Ye Hua's study had obviously given her a fair idea of the ways of the world, and although her eyes were round as pancakes, she managed to keep her jaw steady. She straightened her clothes, bowed to me, and took the lead, cautiously and conscientiously showing me the way.

There was a warm and gentle wind, and I smelled the faint scent of lotus flowers. "How has the prince been recently?" I asked quietly as we were nearing Xiwu Palace. "What is he doing at the moment?"

The little immortal attendant turned around. "His Majesty is very well today," she said with deference. "He has just finished a meeting with three Star Princes, and now he is waiting for you in his study."

I nodded.

Less than half a month ago, he had lost tens of thousands of years of cultivated spiritual energy, and yet today he was sitting calmly in his study, conducting palace business. It seemed rather too quick a recovery.

The little immortal attendant led me to the doorway of Ye Hua's study before politely taking her leave.

I eagerly pushed open his study door, stepped excitedly over the doorway, and enthusiastically lifted up the curtain of the inner room. I managed to carry out this series of keen movements without a hitch, but my agitated heart meant that I was not really looking around me, and I knocked over two antique plant pots in the courtyard, making a huge crash.

Ye Hua raised his head from the pile of documents on his desk and gave a faint smile. He rubbed his temples saying, "Did you come here today just to demolish my study?" His desk was spread with documents and laid out with open books.

He did not look as pale as he had the last time I had seen him at the Western Sea Water Crystal Palace, but he was visibly thinner.

I was no longer the ignorant young girl I had once been. The years had taught me that if someone is intent on keeping something bad from you, they will manage to keep it hidden.

I rushed over to him and reached for his wrist to check his pulse. He suddenly stopped smiling. He dodged my hand and took hold of my lapel. "What's this?" he asked with a frown.

I lowered my head to look. "Oh, it's nothing. I was performing soul-chasing magic on the Western Sea's oldest prince a couple of hours ago. I was careless and strayed from my soul and coughed up a bit of blood."

He stood up, picked up a cup, and turned around to fill it with tea. As he was pouring he said, "I know you are devoted to looking after Mo Yuan, but you must make sure you look after yourself too. We don't want Mo Yuan waking up and you falling immediately unwell."

He was still facing away from me. Looking at his back, I said, "Can you guess what I saw when I climbed into the primordial spirit of the oldest prince of the Western Sea?"

He turned around and handed me a cup of tea. "Mo Yuan?" he said, tilting his head.

I took the cup, and with a sigh, I said, "Tell me about the four ferocious beasts guarding the immortal grass in Yingzhou, Ye Hua, what do they look like? I know it was you who refined the pill that Zhe Yan brought me. How much cultivated spiritual energy do you have left in your body?"

The hand he was holding his cup in stopped in midair, but his facial expression did not alter. When he had recovered from his shock, he gave an understated smile and said, "Oh. Yes. You're correct. It was me. The Sky Emperor sent me to visit the Eastern Sea a little while ago, and when I was passing Yingzhou, I suddenly remembered that you wanted a couple of stalks of immortal grass, so I went there and plucked some for you.

"Those beasts guarding the grass weren't as ferocious as everyone makes out. If they were a bit brighter, I might have captured one and brought it back for you to train to amuse yourself and help pass the time."

I could still remember the state Father had been in when he came back from Yingzhou, covered head to toe in wounds. "How much cultivated energy did it cost you?" I heard myself asking dryly. "And why did you get Zhe Yan to lie to me when he came over to deliver the pill?"

"Oh?" he said, raising an eyebrow. "That's the first I've heard about that! Didn't Zhe Yan tell you that I was the one who refined it? I shouldn't have trusted him with this matter," he added with a laugh. "He's decided to use the situation to his advantage obviously, to steal my thunder. My level of spiritual energy is actually higher than most immortals," he explained as he rifled through the documents on his desk. "A while ago the Sky Emperor transferred some of his over to me too. Refining that pill was nothing."

I looked at his right hand, right up inside his sleeve. "I've been watching you," I said gently. "You have added the tea leaves to the cups, poured the water, and shuffled through your documents, all using only your left hand. Why don't you give your right hand some exercise too?"

His left hand stopped still, hovering above the documents.

He paused for only a short time before he continued flicking through the papers. "I was a bit careless when I was getting the immortal grass, and one of the beasts managed to bite me. My right hand is slightly injured, so it's easier for me to just use my left at the moment. It's nothing serious, though. The medicine prince has had a look, and said that in a month or two, it'll be as good as new."

If I were his age and he mine, I might well have believed his nonsense. But over the years, I had learned to know when I was being deceived.

He had told me that the Sky Emperor had transferred some cultivated spiritual energy over to him, but there was no way that the Sky Emperor would have done this without good reason. It must have happened after he had dived off the immortal punishment platform and lost so much cultivated energy he nearly died. That was the only circumstance in which I could see the Sky Emperor transferring over his own supply of cultivated energy. It was the same as seventy thousand years ago when Mother rescued me.

And the Sky Emperor would have transferred only enough cultivated spiritual energy to make up for that lost; it would not have exceeded the amount Ye Hua had cultivated over the fifty thousand years he had been alive. From the immortal energy circling Ye Hua, I estimated that he must have lost an average immortal's forty or fifty thousand years' worth.

He told me that the ferocious beast had bitten his right arm, but it had been only a minor injury and would be fine after he had given it a chance to rest. All the ancient gods knew how tenacious these beasts were, and generally if they bit into something, they tended to swallow it down skin, bones, tendons, and all. It was strange to hear being bitten by one described as just a minor injury.

These lies he was telling seemed intended to comfort me, and not wanting to disappoint him, I ignored the tugging of my heartstrings and let him think that he had managed to deceive me. I let out a loud sigh of relief, and said, "Oh, that's good to hear. You've really put my mind at rest."

"There's absolutely nothing to worry about with me," he said with one eyebrow raised and a smile on his face. "It's the Western Sea's oldest prince you should be thinking about. He took that pill fairly recently, and his condition could still be unstable. I think you'd be better placed back there, in case there are any complications with him."

This was clearly a tactful way of asking me to leave. He had been looking fine before, but now he was starting to look peaky. He had been putting on a show of strength, but was obviously not able to keep it up for too long.

I decided to allow him his dignity and pretended that I suddenly remembered something important I had to do. "Oh dear. How could I have forgotten that!" I blustered. "I need to hurry back down right now. Please take good care of yourself, mind your injury."

Having to say these words upset me. I decided to go back to Qingqiu to question Zhe Yan and find out exactly how bad Ye Hua's injury actually was. I charged back over there only to find that Zhe Yan was not at Qingqiu.

Fourth Brother was sunning himself on the grass outside the fox-hole, a stalk of dog-tail grass in his mouth. "Zhe Yan went back to the peach grove a few days ago," he explained. "He told me he'd done something he was feeling very ashamed about. It has been a long time since he's felt any shame, and he was nursing an exceptionally guilty conscience. He said he needed to go back to the peach grove to recover."

I uttered a few curses, and feeling bleak and wretched, I hopped onto another cloud and shot off toward the Ten-Mile Peach Grove. I found Zhe Yan next to the Jade Pool behind the peach grove mountain. It was midday, and the sun was still high in the sky. Zhe Yan's mouth was clamped tightly shut. I waited for him to take the initiative and tell me about the matter with Ye Hua. It was only after midnight, when the moon was high in the sky, that he eventually came out and admitted it.

He explained that it had happened a couple of weeks before, on the twenty-second of June. He and Fourth Brother had been moon gazing in the bamboo forest outside the foxhole when two immortals had suddenly descended. These immortals had been sent under the command of the Sky Emperor. They had made this urgent trip to the Qingqiu Valley to ask him to come to the Ninth Sky to save someone's life.

It was usually the medicine prince who presided over medical matters in the Sky Kingdom, but since the Sky Emperor had sent his people thousands of miles asking for Zhe Yan personally, he had assumed that none of the medicine being prescribed by the medicine prince was helping. Zhe Yan was not on the best terms with this generation's Sky Emperor, but he knew that it was always wise to take the opportunity to have the Sky Emperor owe you a favor. He agreed to these visiting immortals' deferential invitation and went back up with them to the Sky Kingdom.

On arriving in the Ninth Sky, Zhe Yan discovered that the person the Sky Emperor had sent his people thousands of miles to save was none other than the Bai family's future son-in-law: Ye Hua.

He had examined Ye Hua and found that while he was not beyond help, neither was he in a very good state. The Taotie had completely bitten off his right arm, and all he had left was an empty sleeve and twenty thousand years of cultivated energy.

At this point in the story, Zhe Yan started to get choked up. "Your husband-to-be is so young, but he's always so sensible and well organized. A couple of days before he departed, he sent a note to the old Sky Emperor, explaining that the immortal grass growing in Yingzhou was in violation of the immortal laws and gave a long list of reasons why it should be destroyed. He asked the Sky Emperor for permission to travel to Yingzhou and remove every last blade growing there. After thinking it through carefully, the Sky Emperor granted him permission.

"Two days after Ye Hua arrived in Yingzhou, the Sky Emperor received the news that the area had sunk into the Eastern Sea, which both pleased and reassured him. But when Ye Hua returned the next day, he was in this grievously injured state. The Sky Emperor chastised himself for overestimating his grandson. He should have provided the boy with a couple of good helpers to assist him in warding off the ferocious beasts keeping watch over the immortal grass.

"The Sky Emperor assumed that Ye Hua's spiritually cultivated energy had been depleted by this encounter with the four ferocious beasts. It was when Ye Hua secretly entrusted that pill to me that I found out that even though the beasts had been responsible for his missing arm, they had not caused him any other damage. With four swipes of his sword, he slayed them all.

"The reason Ye Hua looked so unwell was due to the fact that having picked the grass, he used all of his cultivated spiritual energy to light the furnace to make that immortality pill. I've given him medicine for his physical injuries, and you mustn't worry, he will recover over time. His arm is gone, but it isn't a completely lost cause. I have fitted him with a new arm, and although he can't use it yet, within the next ten thousand years, it will gradually develop its own life force, and he should be able to use it."

The moon looked like it was hanging askew from the tree branches. It was big and round and cool.

Zhe Yan gave another sigh and said, "He didn't trust anyone in the Sky Palace. That's why I had to be the one to bring you your pill. As your husband-to-be, he wanted to help you repay your debt to Mo Yuan. He told me to hide this from you because he was scared of how doctrinaire you can be. He thought that if you knew that the pill had cost him over half his cultivated energy, you would refuse to use it.

"Oh, and he thought you might be worried too. I've never thought of you as a careful type. I would never have imagined that after giving De Yong the pill, you might leap back into his primordial spirit to ensure it was working. But I still have a lot of admiration for Ye Hua, how responsible he is and how sturdy." He gave another sigh, and in a voice full of regret he said, "Being able to slay those four ferocious beasts like that, and at only fifty thousand years old, his future prospects are limitless. What a pity to see all his pure spiritual energy dissipated away like that."

I was feeling quite choked up too, and my heart was very heavy.

Zhe Yan asked me if I would like to stay over at the peach grove. I thanked him for his kind invitation, but declined. I asked instead for a big handful of health recovery and energy supplement pills, and with the clear moon up above me, I climbed onto a cloud. Zhe Yan had already given Ye Hua all the treatment he could, and he tried to convince me to stay in the peach grove, saying there was nothing else I could do to help his recovery. But I just wanted to be there to look after Ye Hua. Even if there was nothing particularly useful I could do, I just wanted to be there by his side, tending to him.

I cast a spell and turned myself into a moth to avoid the sky soldiers and napping tigers at the Southern Sky Gate. I spent a long time trying to remember the way to Ye Hua's Zichen Palace and eventually flapped my way through the gates.

Zichen Palace was in complete darkness when I arrived. I fell to the floor, accidently knocking over a stool, which landed on its side with a loud clunk. The palace was immediately flooded in light. I saw Ye Hua sitting up in bed, wearing a white silk gown, giving me a curious look. I had only seen him wearing his black cloak, and seeing him in this flimsy white silk gown, well, it did something to me. And his jet-black hair hanging loose, oh yes, that did something to me as well.

He stared at me for a while and then frowned. "Aren't you meant to be looking after the oldest prince of the Western Sea?" he asked. The way he was frowning had a strong effect on me too.

I gave a nervous laugh. "De Yong is just fine," I said calmly. "When I was down there tying up the loose ends of this Western Sea affair, I started thinking about your injured arm. I worried that you might find it difficult to hold your teacup steady when you're pouring hot water, so I decided to come back and help look after you."

He gave me an even more puzzled look, followed by a slight smile, and then shifted over to the edge of the bed saying, "Come here, Qian Qian."

His voice was so deep that it made my ears turn red. "That's probably not a good idea," I said with a cough. "Why don't I go to Dumpling's bed and squeeze in there with him instead? You have a proper rest, and I'll come back over and see you tomorrow." I turned around, about to slip out, but before I had got past Ye Hua's door, the entire hall descended into pitch darkness. I lost my footing and knocked over that same stool again.

Suddenly Ye Hua was behind me with his arm around me. "Now I can only hug with one arm, so if you don't like it, you can always struggle free," he said.

In the past when Mother was instructing me on how to be a good wife, she had mentioned a husband and wife's boudoir etiquette, and this situation in particular. She explained that when a girl first became a wife and her husband came to her seeking pleasure, she should delicately push him away at first. That way he would see her as a restrained girl to be cherished.

I had thought that my little cough had been a delicate yet clear expression of refusal. But it seemed that Ye Hua had not taken it very seriously. Unfortunately Mother never taught me what to do if this recently married girl's husband did not accept her delicate refusal, and how she might continue to maintain the impression that she was a restrained girl to be cherished.

Ye Hua's loose hair brushed against my ear, tickling it and making me flustered. I quietly turned around and returned his hug. "If I stay, do you agree to stay on your half of your bed?"

He coughed, and smiled. "With your lithe figure, you won't take up half the bed."

I gave him a coy little push and fumbled for the edge of the bed. I hesitated before deciding to take off my cloak. I lifted up the corner of the bed quilt and lay down inside. I retreated toward the wall and pulled the cloud quilt over, covering myself. I waited until Ye Hua had joined me in the bed before retreating even farther against the wall.

He used his one able arm to hook me and nimbly pulled back the cloud quilt covering my body. He took hold of a corner of the quilt and yanked it toward him, whipping it off me completely.

Although it was a midsummer night in early Lunar July, it was chilly in the Ninth Sky. I put my cloak back on. If I spent the whole night like this, it would not be me looking after Ye Hua the next morning, but rather him looking after me.

Maintaining my dignity was not something that overly concerned me. I nudged a bit closer to him and closer still. He turned around to face the edge of the bed, and I moved in closer still.

I continued moving toward him. He turned back around facing me, and I nudged myself right into his arms. He hugged me with his left hand, saying, "Would you rather spend the night sleeping soundly in my arms with the quilt over you, or hunched in the corner without the quilt?"

Slightly surprised, I said, "We can both sleep hunched in the corner with the quilt over us." As soon as I said this, I wondered if there was something wrong with my brain.

Hugging me, he gave a quiet laugh. "Not a bad idea."

We spent the night cuddled up, a pair of lovebirds squeezed up against the wall. It may have been a bit squished, but I slept very soundly leaning against Ye Hua's chest. Within my sleepy haze, I thought I heard him say, "You know, your personality is exactly the same as before. You still can't accept anything from others."

I gave some vague answer from within my dreamy state. Seeing him had given me partial reassurance, and I slept so soundly that I cannot remember what my response was.

In the middle of the night, he started to cough violently, and I was woken up with a jolt. He crept quietly out of bed, tucking the quilt back in at the corners for me, and then hurriedly pushed open the palace doors and went outside. I listened carefully to his coughing fit outside the palace hall. He was obviously trying to cough quietly, and if not for my sharp fox ears, and the attention I was paying, I probably would not have heard him. I stroked the place in the bed next to me where he had just been lying, a sudden welling of sadness in my chest.

He spent some time calming himself down outside before returning to me. I pretended to be asleep, obviously quite convincingly, as he pulled back the quilt and lay back down without seeming to be aware that I was awake. I could smell the faint salty scent of blood. I lay against him, and once I sensed that he had fallen back to sleep, I nuzzled into his arms and reached out an arm to hug him. I was overcome by sorrow, such deep sorrow. And with that in my heart, I gradually drifted off.

The next day when I awoke, I could not see any sign of his illness. I almost started to doubt all the sorrow, joy, worry, and concern I had felt the day before and wondered if the whole thing had been no more than a haunting dream.

But I knew that it had been no dream.

Being with Ye Hua had made me start to really miss Dumpling. I had heard that there was a religious assembly to be held on Spirit Mountain over the next few days, where Gautama Buddha would be hosting a forum to spread Buddhist teachings and enlighten all beings. Cheng Yu would be taking Dumpling to attend these activities.

I was concerned that the religious atmosphere in the Western Paradise would be too austere for a boy Dumpling's age and that he might get quite bored, but Ye Hua disagreed. "He's only going to the

Western Paradise so he can eat Spirit Mountain sugarcane. And anyway, Cheng Yu is there to look after him. Even if the other immortals behind the altar get so bored they fall asleep, Ali will be just fine."

I decided he knew what he was talking about. Ye Hua's complexion had not yet returned to normal. Zhe Yan had told me that his right arm had been bitten off completely and the new arm was not yet functional. Every time I saw it, I felt hugely upset, but I knew I had to keep it to myself. Meanwhile he acted as if he was not the slightest bit concerned. News of his injury had reached all the officers, from the highest-ranking Ninth Sky Emperor to the ninth-rank immortal officers, and as a result, over the last few days, no one had come to bother him with trifling matters, leaving him unusually carefree.

I was worried about Ye Hua's injury and wanted to stay near him for the time being. Concentrated Beauty was a fair distance from Zichen Palace, not as near as Qingyun Palace, and besides, I felt strange staying where Ye Hua's first wife had lived. I decided to move in with Dumpling at Qingyun Palace for a while. It probably violated some Sky Palace regulation or other, but understanding that I was from a wild place like Qingqiu, the immortal attendants let it pass and made me up a bed in Qingyun Palace.

I got out of bed very early for the first few mornings and braved the predawn darkness, using my hands to guide me all the way to Ye Hua's Zichen Palace. Once there I would help him dress and we would eat breakfast together. Because I had not woken up this early for many tens of thousands of years, I gave the occasional sleepy yawn as we were eating.

A few mornings later, I had just managed to pry myself from sleep and prepared to make my bleary-eyed way over to Zichen Palace. But when I opened my eyes, I suddenly saw Ye Hua there, propped up in bed beside me, reading a book. My head was resting on his immobile right arm while his left arm held a scroll of marching combat tactical deployment diagrams. He saw that I was awake and turned the page, saying, "It's not light outside yet. Sleep some more. I'll wake you when it's time to get up."

I am ashamed to say that from that moment forth, I no longer had to fumble my way through the darkness to his palace each morning. Instead, he was the one to rise early and come into Dumpling's palace, and as a matter of course, breakfast was relocated to Qingyun Palace too.

Those Sky Palace days were spent in a similar way to how we had spent our time in Qingqiu. Following breakfast, we would take a walk together and then head to his study, where we would brew two pots of tea. He would get on with his things, while I would get on with mine. When night fell we would play a game or two of chess by the flicker of candlelight.

Every so often the medicine prince would visit Xiwu Palace, but he never said anything in front of me. Running into him reminded me of Ye Hua's injuries, and so I did not much enjoy his visits. Apart from that, I found everything very pleasant. I was at the age that I no longer had clear access to memories from my youth, but I knew that being with Li Jing had never given me the happiness and wholeness that I was experiencing now.

Despite my advanced years, the lack of peach blossom experience in my younger life meant that I had all these romantic sentiments and notions: things I had read in poems that I had stored up and never had a chance to do. Now that these feelings had been stirred up inside me, I allowed myself the occasional daydream about how it would feel to wander under the moonlight with Ye Hua or frolic amid the flowers together.

But Xiwu Palace was much higher up than the moon, and if the two of us had wanted to moon gaze together, we would have to do so by looking down past our feet. If we were lucky we would see the moon, but we would have no chance to bask under it and have its soft light shine down onto our bodies, creating a hazy, dreamlike mood. So lofty activities like composing poems under the moon were out of the question; I had to just swallow down my disappointment and give up on the notion. Luckily when Ye Hua and I took our strolls, we would pass many different types of flowers and shrubs, so we had more or less frolicked in the flowers.

When Ye Hua used to drag me off for our early morning walks back in Qingqiu, our circuit of the pond and the bamboo forest near the foxhole mainly consisted of him asking me what I wanted for lunch. We would discuss what we were going to eat in great detail, and when we passed Mystic Gorge's thatched hut, we would call out for him and give him a list of ingredients to get us.

Ye Hua did not have to worry about cooking for us in the Sky Kingdom, so now when we strolled, Ye Hua would ask me about the play script I had read the day before instead. Usually I raced through these frothy books, seeing them as nothing but a way to pass the time, and as soon as I had finished one, I would forget everything about it, including the female protagonist's name. All that I was left with was a vague idea about what kind of story it had been.

But since Ye Hua had started taking an interest, I became more attentive when reading these scripts, making sure that I would be able to recount the story for him the next day. After a few days of retelling these stories as we strolled along, I decided I had a talent for it.

On the seventh of July, the Spirit Mountain's Buddhist assembly came to an end, and that meant Dumpling would be on his way back to the Sky Palace. There was a cool breeze blowing that evening, and the fragrance from the osmanthus flowers on the moon that had opened early this year floated all the way to the Ninth Sky.

I sat with Ye Hua in the Jade Pool pavilion. There were a few lanterns hanging up inside, and a tung oil lamp had been placed on the marble table. Ye Hua was holding his pen in his left hand and drawing a tactical deployment diagram under the lamplight.

I had studied tactical deployment for twenty thousand years during my Mount Kunlun apprenticeship and was proud to have excelled way beyond my results for Taoist studies, Buddhist studies, and all the other studies I detested and finished at the top of the class. But whenever I saw a tactical deployment diagram nowadays, it did not just give me a headache, but an allover body ache. I sat for a while admiring the way Ye Hua held his pen before leaning to the side of the pavilion bench, closing my eyes, and letting my mind wander.

As soon as I closed my eyes I heard a clear, melodious child's voice floating over from the distance. "Mother! Mother!" Dumpling was calling. I stood up and looked. Sure enough there he was, wearing a lustrous jade-green tunic and hauling what looked like a rather heavy cloth bag over his left shoulder.

The weight of the cloth bag made him walk in a zigzag path. When Ye Hua saw him, he stopped working on his diagram and walked over to the pavilion steps to have a look. I got up from the pavilion bench and strolled over to watch too. "Mother!" Dumpling shouted out again from a hundred or so paces away. I called out in response.

He lowered his plump little body and squatted down so that he could slowly and carefully lift the cloth bag off his back and onto the ground. He lifted a little hand and wiped the sweat from his face, shouting, "Mother, Mother! Ali has brought you some sugarcane from Spirit Mountain. I chopped it down myself!

"I chose the biggest and thickest sugarcane to chop down," he added, giving a proud giggle. He turned around and grabbed the top of the cloth bag so that none of the sugarcane could fall out, and straining his whole body, he dragged it step by step up to where we were.

I was about to go and help him, but Ye Hua stopped me. "Let him bring it over himself."

All my attention was on Dumpling, and I did not even notice that he was not alone until I saw a figure flash out from behind a bush of some flower I have forgotten the name of. This person was carrying a cloth bag as well, only his was much smaller than Dumpling's.

He took a couple of steps toward us, and under the soft, glowing light of the lantern, I saw his beautiful little pale face staring across blankly.

"Cheng Yu, Cheng Yu, this is my mother," Dumpling shouted from behind. "See, isn't she beautiful?"

So this beautiful pale face belonged to Cheng Yu, the god who dared to defy the power of the mighty and pluck hairs from a tiger's tail.

Cheng Yu stood there staring blankly at me for ages. Then he reached out and pinched my thigh. While I was grimacing from the pain, he turned to Ye Hua. "Your Majesty," he said tentatively, "may I please touch the empress?"

Ye Hua gave a cough. I was startled. Cheng Yu wore a broad gown with wide sleeves, a man's attire, but his voice was soft and gentle, and the flesh of his chest rose and fell in a very unboyish way. I had done my fair share of cross-dressing over the years, and my wisdom and experience told me that this Cheng Yu was actually a girl.

Before Ye Hua had a chance to respond, Dumpling had huffed and puffed his way over. He stood in front of me, defending me from Cheng Yu. He raised his head in a defiant way and said, "Didn't Third Grandfather cure you of this bad habit? Why do you have to touch everything new and interesting you come across? My mother belongs to my father. He's the only one who can touch her. You're not allowed."

Ye Hua chuckled, while I gave a cough.

Cheng Yu's face turned green, and sounding aggrieved, she said, "She's the first goddess I've ever seen. What would be the harm in just touching her?"

Dumpling gave a disgruntled snort. Cheng Yu, still sounding aggrieved, said, "I'll just touch her once and only for a second, surely you couldn't object to that?" Dumpling continued giving a series of disgruntled snorts.

Cheng Yu pulled a handkerchief from her sleeve and used it to wipe her eyes. "I soared up to the Sky Palace to be an immortal when I was still so young. His Third Majesty works me so hard, and I am constantly tired. I have so many years of dreariness ahead with nothing to look forward to. The only wish I've ever had was to see and to touch a goddess. It's such a modest wish. How cruel Si Ming has been to keep me from satisfying it."

She looked so miserable you might have thought her parents had just died. My brain was turning. I assumed the person Cheng Yu had called His Third Majesty was the same person Dumpling had just called Third Grandfather and that it must be Sang Ji's younger brother and Ye Hua's third uncle, Prince Lian Song.

Dumpling's mouth flattened in annoyance. He looked first at me, then at his father, hesitating for a while before saying, "Okay, you can touch her, but only once."

Ye Hua glanced at Cheng Yu, and then returned to the marble table to continue with his tactical diagrams. Before he picked up his pen, he issued the soft words: "Not only do you have the gall to take any liberties with my wife in front of my face, you also trick our son into giving you permission. You've really surpassed yourself this time, Cheng Yu."

Before she had even touched the seam of my robe, Cheng Yu's excitedly extended hand dropped obediently back down to her side.

Dumpling dragged his heavy cloth bag all the way up into the pavilion, and he stood there with a serious expression on his face as he unfastened it. It was indeed filled with sugarcane, cut into sections. He picked out a particularly succulent section and handed it to me, then picked out another just as succulent for his father. But Ye Hua was holding the pen in his left hand, and because his right hand had no function, he was unable to take the sugarcane.

Dumpling walked slowly over and stood on tiptoes so that he could wrap his arms around his father's lifeless right arm. He wrinkled his nose, and two teardrops splashed down his cheeks. "Isn't Father's arm better yet?" he asked through his tears. "When will Father be able to hug Ali again?"

I tried to hold back my own tears. Zhe Yan had said that Ye Hua's new arm would take at least ten thousand years before it gained function. Ye Hua had hidden this from Dumpling, and from me, acting as if everything were fine and it were nothing important. I had been playing along with his story by pretending that I was not that bothered with it either.

He had lost his right arm for me, so from now on I would be his right arm. Ye Hua put down his pen and scooped up Dumpling with his left arm. "I can hug you just as well with one arm, see? Crying at the drop of a hat like that is not a good way for a boy to behave, is it?"

He glanced over me, and with a faint smile he said, "I always thought there was something sweet about having a beautiful woman worrying about you, but your worry has a bitter flavor. I've felt a bit of sensation in this arm over the last few days. You mustn't worry so."

I sighed to myself while pretending to look overjoyed. "I know your arm will be better in no time, but will it ever be as nimble as before? You're so good at drawing portraits, it would be a real pity if you could no longer draw them because of this and Dumpling and I had to go and get ours drawn by someone else."

He lowered his head and gave a laugh and placed Dumpling back down on the floor. "I've always been better with my left hand anyway. Even if my right hand doesn't fully recover, it won't stop me from doing anything. Why don't I sketch a portrait of you both now to prove it?"

My mouth flattened in surprise. He was exceptional enough to have been chosen by the Sky Emperor as his heir. Even more amazing than his military prowess was the fact that he could draw with his left hand!

Cheng Yu, who had been sitting to the side, looking docile and dejected this whole time, now waltzed over saying, "Empress, you are so extraordinarily elegant, no ordinary painter would dare to lower his pen and paint you. Only His Majesty Prince Ye Hua is talented enough to capture your fine goddess's bearing. I shall bring out some paper, a pen, and a drawing table."

Cheng Yu was good with her words and knew how to use them to make people happy. Her compliments about me obviously pleased Ye Hua, who lifted his hand to grant her permission.

Cheng Yu rushed back and forth like a gust of wind, bringing back ink, paper, a pen, an ink stone, a pot to rinse the brush, and a drawing table. I took Dumpling in my arms as instructed by Ye Hua and sat at the pavilion bench. I saw Cheng Yu sitting at the side with nothing to do and so I beckoned her over with a smile. I invited her to sit down beside me and told Ye Hua to draw her with us.

Dumpling wriggled in my arms.

Ye Hua gave a slight raise of his eyebrows, but said nothing. As he lowered his brush, he looked at me and gave a faint smile. The jet-black sky behind him was reflected in this smile, and under the soft candle-light, it seemed to radiate with the brilliance of the whole universe. My heart trembled, and warmth spread out from my ears.

Despite having no movement whatsoever in his right arm, Ye Hua moved with ease and elegance as he spread his ink. I felt pleased with myself for choosing such an excellent future husband.

After what felt like a very short time, Ye Hua finished his picture.

Dumpling had fallen asleep in my arms by then. Cheng Yu went over to Ye Hua to have a look at what he had drawn. She was not bold enough to express her anger, but her voice carried a strong sense of disappointment. "I've been sitting here all this time, and the only part of me this enlightened sage prince has drawn is my sleeve," she wailed.

I carried Dumpling over to take a look too. Ye Hua's left-handed capabilities were indeed not far behind those of his right. Once I told Second Brother about this, he was certain to want to befriend Ye Hua.

My walking back and forth disturbed Dumpling, who started to wake up. He looked at me through blinking eyes before slipping down from my knees. He looked at the painting and said, "Wow! Wow!" a couple of times, and then, "But why aren't you in the picture, Cheng Yu?"

Cheng Yu gave him a sorrowful glance. She looked so pitiful that I felt compelled to go over to her and put a hand on her shoulder. "Ye Hua has been a bit physically useless recently," I said to comfort her. "His hand must have become tired after all that sketching. You must forgive him."

Cheng Yu covered her mouth and gave a cough. "Ye Hua is physically useless?" Ye Hua had been just about to rinse his brush, but now it froze in midair, and I saw the carved white jade pen with the purple plume in his hand snap in two.

Oh dear, I have said more than I should have.

Dumpling gave Cheng Yu a silly, naive look. "What does *physically useless* mean?" he asked. "Does it mean Father can carry Ali, but not Mother?"

I gave a chuckle and took a step back. It was not a very steady step, and suddenly sky and earth turned upside down for me. By the time I had regained my balance, I found I had been hoisted up onto Ye Hua's shoulders.

I was in shock. "Put away the drawing table and take Ali to bed in his chamber," Ye Hua breezily instructed Cheng Yu. Cheng Yu nodded as she gathered up her sleeves. Dumpling covered his eyes with his hands and shouted out, "Pervert! Pervert!" over and over again until Cheng Yu, looking mortified, reached out a hand and covered Dumpling's mouth.

When we had been in the Western Sea Water Crystal Palace, Ye Hua had been very attentive and gentle with me, but for some reason he was rougher this time.

He put me down on the bed, my head resting against his unstable right arm, while he held me firmly with his left. He searched out my mouth, gave a quiet laugh, and then bit me. He did not bite me hard, but I did not feel he should be allowed to take advantage like that, and I was about to bite him back, but his lips had moved over to my ear by then . . .

He took my earlobe in his mouth and sucked it with such fervor that it began to ache. He bit it gently, and my whole body suddenly started to tingle. I heard myself humming like a mosquito.

When he heard me, his lips slipped off my ear. He came across an obstacle: my red skirt. This skirt had been given to me by Second Brother's wife when she had stayed in the foxhole. She had told me that it was a very special skirt because of the kind of silk it was made from.

I knew very little about clothing and fabric, all I knew was that this skirt was very difficult to put on and even more difficult to take off. But despite the fact that he had only one functioning hand, Ye Hua still managed to slip my skirt off me with the greatest of ease. In the blink of an eye, it was in his hand, being waved around and cast to the floor.

He removed the rest of my clothing with the same ease and fluidity, but when it came to undressing himself, he was extremely clumsy. I could not bear to watch him attempt it all by himself and sat up to help. He gave a laugh. He leaned over as I was taking off his robe and ran his lips down my neck. I lost control of my body. The strength drained out of my hands, and the most I could do was give his clothing an aimless yank to the side.

I was impressed with my ability, however, because a couple of tugs and I had managed to remove all his clothes too.

He buried his head in my chest, sucking the area around my knife scar, sometimes softly, sometimes hard. That knife wound had healed five hundred years ago, and I no longer had sensation in the area, but for some reason, by kissing me delicately there, he brought me out in head-to-toe pins and needles. It felt as if a cat were scratching my heart.

I put my arms around his neck, and his loose, silky black hair slipped over my skin. As I moved, his hair swept over me. I lifted my head and panted. He put his lips to my ear and asked, "Are you uncomfortable?" His voice was full of gentle affection, completely different from the action of his hands, which were applying strong pressure as they worked their way down my spine.

His hands, usually so cold, were exceptionally hot today. The parts of me he touched felt like sizzling cakes just out of the wok, crunchy enough to snap to bits with one bite. He moved his lips to my jaw, nipping at it gently. I pursed my lips and held my breath to stop myself from panting. I felt as if something inside me was rapidly growing roots and sprouting shoots and might suddenly burst up into a towering tree. And all this tree wanted to do was to hold Ye Hua, to wrap itself tightly around him.

His lips moved around my jaw and to my mouth. He kissed me softly for a while before biting my lower lip, which caused my teeth to part. I was too overcome with desire to restrain myself. I kissed him back passionately and preemptively slipped my tongue into his mouth. He seemed surprised at first, but then the hand caressing my lower back started to rub deeper. I was so filled with desire I was trembling and completely forgot to move my tongue. By the time I had recovered my wits, he had pushed his tongue into my mouth.

I felt overwhelmed with excitement and wondered how much longer I could handle this teasing buildup of his. When he next withdrew his tongue from my mouth, I could not stop myself. "I want you now!" I murmured. Hearing these slow and sultry words coming from my own mouth gave me a jolt.

He gave a surprised laugh and said, "My hands aren't very steady, Qian Qian. You'll need to move farther up the bed."

I loved how deep his voice was. It felt as if I had fallen into a trance. My head was chaotic as I did as he had said and moved farther up the bed.

When he entered me, I lost control of what my hands were doing, and my fingernails dug into his back. He gave a muffled groan and then moved his mouth next to my ear. "Tomorrow I'm going to trim your nails," he panted.

Afterward, I lay back in Ye Hua's arms. He was on his side, playing with my hair, looking lost in thought. I still felt as if my head were full of rice porridge being stirred around, and my brain felt as confused as ever.

I lay there in confusion for a moment before suddenly remembering something very important.

Fourth Brother was not completely wrong in his assessment of me: every ten thousand years or so, I could be very unaware. I had come to the Ninth Sky to look after Ye Hua, and despite spending all this time with him, I had completely forgotten the important thing I had to tell him.

I turned around to face him, pressing myself against his chest. I looked straight into his eyes and said, "Do you still remember what I told you in the Western Sea about wanting to cancel our engagement?"

His body stiffened. He lowered his eyes and said, "Yes, I remember that."

I leaned over and kissed him, the tip of my nose touching his. "I wasn't aware of what I really felt back then. Please don't take what I said to heart. We are in love—of course we shouldn't call off the marriage. When I was sitting in the Western Sea with nothing to do, I started to think of a suitable day and came up with the second of Lunar September. It is a good day to build, a good day to slaughter livestock, a good day to hold a ceremony, an all-around suitable day, really. Would you like me to meet with your grandfather to ask if we could organize our wedding for that date?"

He raised his eyes sharply, his jet-black pupils reflecting half of my face back at me. He looked at me for a while before speaking in a hoarse voice. "What did you just say?" he asked.

I thought back over everything I had just said but did not think I had in any way overstepped the mark. I wondered whether Sky Palace regulations dictated that Ye Hua should be the one to meet with the Sky Emperor and decide on a date for the wedding. Perhaps it had been improper of me to suggest being the one to meet with him?

I stroked his face and said, "I didn't think it through properly. It would obviously be much more suitable coming from you. Or if you'd rather not, I could talk to Father and Mother and ask them to approach the Sky Emperor. After all, our marriage is going to be a big affair. Perhaps it would be better to let them be the ones to discuss it."

As soon as I finished what I was saying, I gasped, finding it hard to breathe, and realized he was smothering me in a ferocious hug. He realized he was being too forceful and held me to his chest more gently. "Tell me again what you would like us to do." he said.

I was slightly taken aback. Had I not just explained that very clearly? I was just about to repeat myself when I suddenly wondered if Ye Hua was doing what I thought he was doing and deliberately trying to make me tell him words of endearment.

His loose jet-black hair was all mixed up with mine. His eyes were the same jet black as his hair, and as deep as ponds. Within the bed curtain, I could smell the faint fragrance of peach blossoms. I felt my face redden as expressions of love rose up through my throat. I was biting them back when I fell under some enchanted spell, and before I knew what was happening, out popped the words "I love you. I want to be with you forever."

He said nothing.

Qingqiu women are always very direct and sincere: we call a spade a spade. But Ye Hua had grown up in the constrained and conservative atmosphere of the Ninth Sky, and I wondered if he might have found my words too frivolous and brazen?

While I was getting into a spin about this, he remained silent, but then he suddenly turned and pinned me down and moved his body on top of mine. I moved my arms out of the way and threaded them around his smooth back. He was holding me so tightly that I could no longer tell where my body ended and his began. As he bit my earlobe, he quietly said, "Qian Qian, let's have another baby."

I heard a deafening rumble as all the blood rushed to my ears. My ears were burning as if they had just been dipped in fresh chili oil. I knew that there was something incongruous about this sentence, but I could not for the moment work out what.

We kept each other awake all night, and it was only when Mao the Sun Prince came on duty that we finally fell into a deep sleep.

When I woke up, the bedchamber was dark and Ye Hua still deeply asleep. I was happy because waking up before him gave me a chance to have a proper look at him.

I got a little closer and put my face up to his so that I could see him clearly. His face was like that of my master, Mo Yuan, but I had never thought of him as Mo Yuan. Looking at him now, I saw subtle differences between their appearances. Mo Yuan's eyes were not as dark as Ye Hua's, which were like ancient pools of deep, calm water.

I had always felt reverence for Mo Yuan's solemn and dignified face, but recently, looking at Ye Hua's face had shown me elements that gave me a feeling of excitement.

I spent a while gazing at his face from close up like this before finally dozing off again. When I awoke, I thought he was still fast asleep, and turned around to have another look at him. He stretched out a hand and dragged me back into his arms, making me jump. "You're welcome to carry on looking at me," he said, his eyes still closed. "But once you're finished, lie back into my arms for a while. It's not as warm against the wall as it is in my arms."

My ears turned red. I gave an awkward laugh and said, "You had a mosquito on your face. Um, I was just about to get it for you, but you scared it away when you started speaking."

"You still have the energy to swat mosquitos off me, that's impressive," he said, and pulled me forcefully to him. "Shall we get up or sleep more?"

One of my hands was next to his shoulder, and I made sure not to press too hard against it while I stroked his nose with my other hand. "I want to sleep some more, but I'm feeling too sticky. Can we get an attendant to bring us a couple of pails of water and have a wash before going back to sleep?"

He got up, threw on some clothes, and left the bed to request the water. After our passionate night, it looked as if Ye Hua's injuries were more or less better. I felt extremely reassured and wondered if I should reduce the dose of health recovery and energy supplement pills I had been sneaking into his tea.

My engagement to Ye Hua had been set out in writing by the Sky Emperor, who had sent us a few small gifts, but we were not yet officially betrothed. I started to plan it in my head. I had chosen a suitable day. Now I needed Father to meet quietly with the Sky Emperor and try to move things forward, ask him to make our betrothal official, and choose a day. Of course, it was the second of September I had my heart set on.

Ye Hua's lack of cultivated energy concerned me. I worried that he would be unable to handle the great tradition of the nine thunders and eighty-one wildfires when he succeeded as Sky Emperor. This had been the traditional way that a Sky Emperor and Sky Empress succeeded to the throne since ancient times. My intention was to marry him soon and suffer the thunders and wildfires on his behalf.

Although my run-in with Qing Cang had considerably reduced my own supply of cultivated energy, I was certain I could cope with the sky thunder and wildfires. The only problem that needed addressing was how I could fool Ye Hua into staying inside; he was less naive and easy to deceive than I had been at his age.

After bathing I thought about this a lot, and then gradually drifted back off to sleep.

I had been thinking that these matters would all just naturally fall into place, and I should just go along with them. I had no idea what Ye Hua was about to reveal, that his words when he woke up would turn my whole plan on its head.

He gathered me up in his arms and told me glumly that the second of September would not work. We would have to wait for another two months until we got married.

This was because he was required to go down to the mortal world for two months to experience a calamity.

This calamity was his penalty for slaying the four ferocious beasts in Yingzhou.

Although it had been under the command of the Sky Emperor that Ye Hua had gone down to Yingzhou to destroy the immortal grass growing there, the Sky Emperor had not given him instruction to slay the four ferocious beasts left behind by Father of the Universe. Since Father of the Universe had returned to the primal chaos, everything he had ever used, all his crockery, and even his chipped cups had been taken up to the Ninth Sky by members of the Sky Clan, where they were treated as sacred objects. And these were just bits of pottery he had eaten and drunk from, they could not be compared with four ferocious beasts that had been endowed with half of his godly powers.

Ye Hua had performed a noble service by destroying Yingzhou's immortal grass and thus earned himself a lot of virtue. But by killing the four ferocious beasts that had been protecting the grass, he had committed a serious misdeed. When weighed against each other, the demerits outweighed the merits. There was nothing for it: he was bound for the mortal world to suffer his punishment.

Fortunately, of all those billions of mortal lives in the universe, the mortal life the old Sky Emperor had chosen for Ye Hua was in a world that had a completely different timescale from that of the immortal world of the Four Seas and Eight Deserts, and a day in our realm was equal to a whole year in theirs. This meant that although Ye Hua was to experience a whole sixty-year reincarnation calamity, he and I would only spend a little over two months apart.

Even though I knew it was only for a couple of months, I could not bear the thought of being apart from him. I could not say when it was that my feelings for him had grown so strong, but I experienced it as sweetness mixed with sadness.

I had been hoping to marry Ye Hua soon, and the fact that we would have to wait left me feeling bleak.

"Can you wait for me for two months?" Ye Hua asked.

I used my fingers to work out the timing. "You will go down into the mortal world at the beginning of Lunar August, and you will be in your reincarnated form for a little over two months. That means we could move our wedding to October. October is known as the little spring. There will be an abundance of peaches and plum blossoms. That does not sound like a bad time for a wedding." Thinking more about the calamity, I grew concerned.

"I will need to wait only a couple of months for you, but you will experience it as a lifetime. Has Si Ming let you see the destiny he has written for you?"

I had been given the opportunity to read the destiny Si Ming wrote for Yuan Zhen and had been extremely impressed by his writing.

Shao Xin had entrusted me with the task of going down to the mortal world and altering Yuan Zhen's fate and interfering with the big drama Si Ming had gone to all that trouble of arranging, preventing it from playing out properly. I was not sure whether he held a grudge toward me over this or not. What if he used Ye Hua to get back at me by arranging a love triangle? My whole body went cold, and I gave a huge shudder.

Ye Hua chuckled and kissed my forehead. "Si Ming isn't responsible for my fate when I get to the mortal world. After discussing it, the Sky Emperor and his senior advisers ordered Si Ming to leave the page of my destiny notebook blank. How my fate unfolds will be completely up to my own actions."

I relaxed slightly, but to ensure that nothing could go wrong, I asked one thing of him. "I know you'll drink Si Ming's Forget River Water from the Netherworld when you return from this calamity, but even still, you must not get married when you're down there."

He said nothing. After a moment's hesitation, I said, "I'm not worried about anything else, really, just that you . . . well . . . just that this reincarnation calamity punishment might tug you into some peach blossom experience. I'm not very tolerant when it comes to things like this. I hate getting sand in my eyes."

He used his fingers to brush the hair from my eyes. Stroking my face, he said, "There's not even the shadow of a peach flower, and you're already feeling jealous?"

I gave an awkward cough. I had faith in Ye Hua's love for me, and if he were to be reincarnated with a memory of me in his mind, I would not have been feeling so anxious. But this strange rule existed that before an immortal was sent down into the mortal world for a calamity, they had to drink a large cup of water from the Forget River, which made them forget every single thing that had come before. It was only after they returned to their immortal form that they would remember the details from their old life.

He scooped up my hair and gave a laugh. "If I were to get embroiled in a romance with someone else, what would you do?"

After thinking about it, I decided it was time for some serious words. I fixed him with a somber look. "If that were to happen, I would come down to grab you and steal you back to Qingqiu, where I would imprison you in the foxhole. I'd be the only person you'd see. When you ate it would be just with me, when you read it would be just with me, when you drew it would be just with me. I would keep you locked away, and I would be the only person you would ever see. I don't care if you would be comfortable with that arrangement or not. I would be comfortable with it, and that's what counts."

I put myself in his shoes to think about it further, and added, "Yes, I would be comfortable." His eyes were blazing with light. He used a hand to brush the hair from my forehead and kissed the bridge of my nose. "From the way you're talking, it sounds like you're really planning to come down and steal me back," he said earnestly.

CHAPTER TWENTY-ONE

On the fifth of Lunar August, the mid-autumn festival celebrations were held. The osmanthus flower wine that had been fermenting in Guanghan Palace was ready to drink, and Chang'e the moon goddess arranged for jars to be delivered to all the palaces. I warmed up the jar that had been brought to Xiwu Palace, and Ye Hua and I had a couple of glasses together, which served as his farewell drink.

My plan had been to go down to the mortal world with him so that I could stay close by and watch over him, but Ye Hua would not hear of it. He was insistent that I go back to Qingqiu and wait for him there. He was probably afraid that I would use magic to protect him down there, opening myself up to my own magic backbite.

I started scheming. I would pretend to return to Qingqiu to put Ye Hua's mind at rest, but as soon as he drank the water from Forget River and transformed into his mortal form, I would come out of the shadows and follow him down.

That was how it was when you loved someone: their well-being was all you thought about, if they were fine, you felt fine. That was the amazing thing about love too: when you held someone in your heart, any hardship or wrong you experienced felt like nothing but a sweet torment.

Si Ming the Star Prince told me where I would find Ye Hua. Ye Hua was being reborn into a distinguished family who lived south of the Yangtze River. This family had an excellent, longstanding literary reputation, and for two generations the males had held senior temple positions.

Si Ming spoke with enthusiasm and clicked his tongue admiringly. He explained that his years of writing destinies had shown him that children from households like this one were certain to follow in their family's footsteps. In Ye Hua's case, this would mean using his writing ability and sharp mind to rise to a powerful position in government. Ye Hua had such remarkable writing skills in his actual life and such abundant work experience that in his reincarnated form, he was certain to excel.

At the same time, I was well aware that in the mortal world, aristocratic families like this one tended to be extremely conservative. They raised their offspring strictly and rigidly, giving them extremely dull childhoods. Their children grew up to be similarly strict, rigid, and dull, completely different from the bright and lively rural children, who grew up scampering around the countryside.

Ye Hua did not have a very lively character to begin with, so I did not nurture much hope of his reincarnated form being given one. I did worry that growing up in a family like this one would be a boring and lonely experience for him.

Ye Hua was reborn as the first grandson in the prestigious Liu family, and he was honored with the name Liu Ying Zhao Ge. I was not very taken with this name, finding it long and pretentious and nothing like his fine-sounding immortal name, Ye Hua.

I returned to Qingqiu and picked out four or five sets of clothes, which I bundled up. I poured myself a cup of cold tea to moisten my throat and then raced my way over to Zhe Yan's Ten-Mile Peach Grove, where I planned to brazenly ask for more pills.

I was halfway there when I ran into Zhe Yan racing toward me on a cloud, followed closely by Fourth Brother astride Bi Fang.

They all stopped in front of me.

Fourth Brother's eyes were radiating light. "Fifth Cub, it looks as if you are about to be granted the wish you have nurtured for all these years. We've just rushed back from the Western Sea. De Yong spent all last night tossing and turning, and this morning Zhe Yan performed soul-chasing magic on him to see what was going on and discovered that Mo Yuan's soul was no longer inside De Yong's primordial spirit. We are just on our way to have a look inside Yanhua Cave. Mo Yuan has been asleep for seventy thousand years. I believe he's chosen today as an auspicious one to finally wake up . . ."

I was completely dumbfounded. When I finally recovered my senses, I found I was grabbing Fourth Brother's hand. "M-M-M-Master has woken up?" I managed to stammer. "He's actually woken up?"

Fourth Brother gave another nod and then frowned. "Put your bundle down on the cloud," he said.

I had known that Mo Yuan would wake up within three months. I counted on my fingers and worked out that it had been only two months since I had given De Yong that pill. Mo Yuan had woken up so quickly? Could it actually be happening?

I had hidden out in Qingqiu for the last seventy thousand years. Although I had not witnessed any massacres or old dynasties being replaced by new ones, I had seen Qingqiu's great pool suffer 779 droughts, and I had seen Yehou Mountain, which moves by one foot every hundred years, shift from beside the Zhu Yin cave household to beside Father and Mother's foxhole. Seventy thousand years was half of my lifetime. I had sacrificed half of my life to achieve just one thing: to wait for Master to wake up again. And now, he finally had.

Zhe Yan gave a low sigh. "So young Ye Hua didn't expend all that cultivated energy in vain."

I nodded, the corners of my eyes stinging.

Fourth Brother smiled. "Zhe Yan told me about what Ye Hua did. What a genuinely kind person. But how unfortunate for you. You've only just managed to repay your debt to Mo Yuan and you incur this one to Ye Hua. You repaid your debt to Mo Yuan by giving blood from your heart for seventy thousand years. How will you possibly repay the forty thousand years of cultivated energy you owe Ye Hua?"

I pulled out my fan and used it to shield my stinging eyes. "Ye Hua and I will be husband and wife soon. As far as I'm aware, married couples in love don't quibble over who owes whom."

Zhe Yan stepped back onto his cloud and gave a laugh. "You sound thoroughly enlightened," he said. Bi Fang offered his breezy congratulations, and I accepted gratefully.

Zhe Yan and Fourth Brother took the lead, while I turned my cloud around and followed after them. I decided that I could delay my visit to Ye Hua for a while. When I first went to Mount Kunlun to start my apprenticeship, I was extremely rebellious, and even though I was his apprentice, it did not come naturally to me to act piously toward Mo Yuan. By the time I had matured and understood my filial duties, he was already lying in Yanhua Cave.

I could barely contain my joy. Now that Mo Yuan was awake, I wanted to go straight over and show him that his youngest apprentice had matured, become calm and composed, and learned how to take care of others.

As Mo Yuan's apprentice, I had been in the form of a boy. I was just about to turn myself back into Si Yin, but Zhe Yan lifted a hand to stop me. "With Mo Yuan's cultivated spiritual energy, he must have seen through your disguise a long time ago. He knew full well that you were a girl, he just didn't want to expose your lies out of respect to your parents. You don't really think you managed to pull the wool over his eyes for twenty thousand years, do you?"

I put away my fan and gave a laugh. "You're right. Mother's magic might have been good enough to fool my sixteen fellow apprentices, but I always thought it was far-fetched to imagine that I could have fooled Master."

The three of us traveled in a line until we were almost halfway up Fengyi Mountain, where I jumped down from my cloud and raced ahead, the mountain laurel scent entering my nose in fragrant bursts.

I ran through the clear August air and straight into Yanhua Cave.

At the far end of the cave was the fog-shrouded ice chest where Mo Yuan had taken his long sleep. At this critical moment, my eyes started to mist. I gave them a rub, the back of my hand and my fingertips coming away damp.

I saw the faint outline of a figure sitting on the ice chest. I staggered a few steps nearer and saw that this person was none other than . . . Master Mo Yuan. He was finally awake after all those years of sleep. He was facing the vase of wildflowers I had picked for him. His expression and posture were exactly the same as seventy thousand years ago, and seeing them again made me want to weep silent tears.

My fellow apprentices and I used to have a roster for sweeping Mo Yuan's room, and I had gotten into the habit of placing a bunch of seasonal flowers in a little vase inside his room when it was my turn. Mo Yuan would always look at them closely and give me an appreciative smile.

Being on the receiving end of this appreciative smile always made me feel very proud. I had startled him by crashing into the cave, and he turned his head. He raised a hand to support his cheek and gave a faint smile. "Little Seventeenth? Is that really you? Yes, it is, isn't it! Come over and let Master see you properly. Let me see how you've turned out after all these years."

I tried to walk steadily, but my heart was pounding like a drum, and the rims of my eyes felt hot. I ended up stumbling over, crying out "Master!" in a shaky voice. My cry contained a huge array of emotions, but mostly it was pain mixed with joy.

He reached out a hand to me, saying, "Why do you look as if you are about to cry? Oh, and what a lovely skirt!"

Zhe Yan wafted away the mist in the cave and stepped inside, followed by Fourth Brother. "You've been asleep for seventy thousand years, Mo Yuan," Fourth Brother said with a smile. "You've finally woken up today."

Yanhua Cave was chilly. I gave a sneeze, and Fourth Brother dragged me outside, Zhe Yan and Mo Yuan strolling out after us.

Apart from Ninth Apprentice Ling Yu, whose life Mo Yuan had saved, all the other Mount Kunlun apprentices had fathers with important positions in the Sky Clan. After I had run off with Mo Yuan's immortal body, these apprentices were said to have spent several thousand years trying to find me before their families called them back and they moved on with their lives.

Recently Fourth Brother had taken a low-key trip over to Mount Kunlun to have a look around and had returned feeling disheartened. Mount Kunlun's once flourishing population had been reduced to Ling Yu with a couple of young immortal servants who had stayed behind to look after the place. It was a sad state of affairs.

I did not know whether I should mention Mount Kunlun's demise if Mo Yuan were to ask. I fretted about this the whole way back to the foxhole. But surprisingly, Mo Yuan's first question was on a completely different topic. He sat down in the foxhole, and Mystic Gorge brewed a pot of tea and brought it over.

While I was pouring us both a cup, Mo Yuan turned to Zhe Yan and asked, "All these years I've been asleep, you haven't seen a boy who looks just like me, have you?"

The ceramic teapot in my hand tilted, spilling most of the water out onto Fourth Brother's knees.

Fourth Brother smiled at me through gritted teeth and good-naturedly wiped away the water.

All these years there had only been one person in the Four Seas and Eight Deserts who looked like Mo Yuan: my husband-to-be, Ye Hua.

At first I had found it strange that Ye Hua and Mo Yuan had the same face, but I had not thought that they were connected. I had just assumed that this was what an attractive man's face looked like and Ye Hua, being supremely attractive, would naturally look the way he did.

But the way Mo Yuan was talking made me start to question this. Perhaps these two were connected, and connected quite closely.

I pricked up my ears to listen. Zhe Yan gave a short burst of laughter and glanced at me, saying, "There has indeed been someone who matches that description, and your little apprentice here happens to be on rather familiar terms with him."

Mo Yuan turned to look at me, and my face flushed. I was like a girl who had gotten married to her sweetheart without asking the consent of her custodians, while Zhe Yan was like the local gossip who had blurted out the details of my romance right in front of these custodians. Mo Yuan was a father figure to me, and I found the whole thing extremely embarrassing.

Zhe Yan kept glancing at me, his gaze so intense that his eyes looked as if they were about to get a cramp. I forced myself to keep calm and composed. "Master, it does sound like you could be talking about my future husband," I said with a giggle. "Yes, the future head of the Sky Clan." Another giggle.

Mo Yuan's teacup stopped in midair. He lowered his head and took a sip to moisten his throat. He composed himself and then in a quiet voice said, "Well, he certainly has good taste in brides. What is your betrothed's name? And when was he born?"

I told him.

He calculated using his fingers and then took a calm sip of tea. "How have you managed to get your hands on my twin brother, Little Seventeenth?" he asked.

"What?" I said in a thunderstruck voice.

I glanced around and saw that I was not the only one looking shocked. Zhe Yan and Fourth Brother, who were usually much more aware of what was going on, both looked as if they had been struck by bolts of lightning too.

Mo Yuan turned his teacup around in his hand and said, "It's no wonder you're all so surprised. I only found this out myself when Father of the Universe passed away. My mother only gave birth to one baby, me. But in the womb, I had a twin brother."

Mo Yuan explained that the problem had started when his mother, Mother of the Universe, became pregnant with him and his brother. It was the year that the four poles fell and the nine kingdoms crumbled. Mother of the Universe had worked hard to repair the four large pillars holding up the sky, but it impacted upon the health of her unborn babies, and she had been able to give birth to only one healthy baby, the bigger one. Father of the Universe felt that they had let their youngest son down badly, and he obstinately held on to the little soul that would otherwise have flown out of the world and vanished. He raised it inside his own primordial spirit, waiting to see if he had the fate and fortune to create an immortal embryo for his son, so that he could wake up and be reborn. Father of the Universe used half his magic to create this immortal embryo, but still his son's soul did not wake up. Father of the Universe decided to turn this immortal embryo into a dazzling golden egg instead, which he buried at Mount Kunlun's back mountain, to be dug up once his son's soul awoke.

But as fate would have it, Mother of the Universe and Father of the Universe returned to the primal chaos before their son's soul could wake up. Before Father of the Universe passed away, he explained the situation to Mo Yuan. He separated his son's soul from his own primordial spirit and entrusted it to Mo Yuan's care. Mo Yuan placed his brother's soul in his own primordial spirit, just like Father of the Universe had, and nurtured it there. Much time passed, but Mo Yuan's twin brother still failed to wake up.

"It must have been when I offered up my primordial spirit to the Eastern Desert Bell that he finally awoke. I think he must have collected up all the pieces of my scattered soul, and put them back together again, as I don't know how else I could have managed to wake up. I have a vague recollection of a child sitting by my side for seven or eight thousand years, repairing my soul. He'd managed to repair half of it when a golden light shone right into the cave where we were, carrying him away. After he left, I continued the work of repairing my soul. It was not easy, and it took a long time. You say he's heir to the sky throne, which leads me to think that a Sky Clan lady must have wandered into Mount Kunlun, found the golden egg that Father of the Universe buried, and swallowed it. His immortal embryo must then have taken root in her abdomen. That must have been the point when the golden light shone in and took him away."

Zhe Yan gave an awkward laugh. "When Ye Hua was born, seventy-two multicolored birds circled around for eighty-one days, and a haze of smoke hung in the eastern sky for three years. Learning that he is your twin brother, it is no wonder."

Learning this news felt like being struck by lightning. I had never imagined that this might be my future connection to Mo Yuan. As I listened to him explain his relationship with Ye Hua, I entered the calm state that follows a great shock. The fact that they were twin brothers seemed obvious now, given the way they both looked.

• • •

Mo Yuan wished to go and meet Ye Hua. He had just woken up and needed a couple of years of confined rest before he would be fully recovered. I did not think he was in a fit state to go rushing off to the mortal world and imagined that so doing would have a negative impact on his recovery. I went against the natural inclination of an apprentice always to be honest with their master and thought up an excuse to stall him. I promised that once his injuries were better, I would bring Ye Hua over to meet him.

Despite its spiritual energy, Yanhua Cave was very cold and not a suitable place for Mo Yuan's recuperation. He was intent on returning to Mount Kunlun, to the cave at the back mountain where he had always done his confinement in the past. I was not keen for him to see the sorry state that had befallen Mount Kunlun, but paper cannot wrap fire: he was going to have to find out this upsetting truth at some point. Deciding that it would be better for him to come to terms with it sooner rather than later, after a couple of rounds of tea, I accompanied him back to Mount Kunlun. Zhe Yan and Fourth Brother, having nowhere special they needed to be, decided to come along too, as did Bi Fang.

With Fourth Brother astride Bi Fang and the remaining three of us on lucky clouds, we soared toward Mount Kunlun, the place that Fourth Brother described as astonishingly different from how it was in the past.

I was certainly astonished by the sight of it.

All the way down from the entrance of the mountain, we saw crowds of little immortals. Some were standing, others squatting or sitting, and there was a circle of swirling purple-and-green mist covering half the mountain in radiant, mystical beauty. This immortal energy steamed and billowed, making it obvious to all present that it was indeed an immortal mountain.

During the twenty thousand years I had been studying magic at Mount Kunlun, it had always been a rather understated place. How had it become so lively?

Bi Fang retracted his talons and dropped down, Fourth Brother still astride him. Fourth Brother approached a little immortal who looked honest and gentle. He cupped his hands together, and giving a deferential bow, he inquired about what was going on.

"I couldn't really tell you," the little immortal said through rapidly blinking eyes. "I just came out to get some soya sauce, and on the way I heard the news that mystical breath had been seen swirling around the top of the next mountain for the past three or four days. I heard that a large number of immortal friends had gathered to see what was happening, so I rushed straight over to have a look too. As you can see, it was well worth the trip. This mystical breath . . ." He clicked his tongue in admiration. "Well, it is not like any mystical breath I've ever seen before. It's just so beautiful. I've been sitting here watching it for two days now. Get down from your bird and let him pull up worms while you watch the spectacle with us. I guarantee a feast for the eyes. There's a space here next to me. I can squeeze up and we can watch it together."

Fourth Brother thanked him for his kind offer before excusing himself and walking quietly back to where we were. "It's nothing," he said with a cough. "They're just admiring the grace and majesty of Mount Kunlun and have traveled far and wide to give praise."

Zhe Yan hid half his face behind his sleeve and also gave a cough. With a playful smile, which spread all the way out from the corners of his eyes to his brows, he turned to Mo Yuan and said, "Mount Kunlun is an immortal mountain that rose from a dragon's backbone. Perhaps the mountain sensed your imminent return and became so excited it started puffing out mystical breath to greet you with, attracting the attention of these ignorant little immortals from nearby."

Mo Yuan kept his composure, but I could see the corners of his mouth twitching.

• • •

The five of us decided to make ourselves invisible to enter the mountain so as not to disturb the little immortals watching the spectacle from the mountainside. Ninth Apprentice was extremely conservative, and the prohibition at the entrance of the mountain was the same as it had been for tens of thousands of years. He had kept everything just as it was.

I thought Ling Yu would be the only apprentice we would meet today, but as soon as we entered the mountain door, I looked ten paces ahead and gave a jolt of surprise. My sixteen fellow apprentices were standing there in two lines, one line on each side of the foot-wide stone path. They were dressed in the robes they had worn back then with their hair tied in topknots.

The Shorea tree that the two Buddhas from the Western Paradise had brought over when they came here once for tea was still standing in the courtyard. My sixteen fellow apprentices were standing solemnly under this Shorea tree, their arms folded in front of their chests, looking as if they had been standing in wait like this for the past seventy thousand years.

It was First Apprentice whose eyes were first to go red. He fell with a thump to his knees, and in a shaky voice said, "Ninth Apprentice shared the news a few days ago. We knew that mystical breath had been seen soaring into the sky above Mount Kunlun and that every so often a dragon's groan could be heard. Even though we didn't know exactly what it meant, we all traveled through the night so we could be here. We suspected that it might be the felicitous sign that Master had returned, but none of us could quite believe it. We were standing in the hall just now when we sensed your immortal energy hovering outside the entrance to the mountain. We hurried out, but we weren't quick enough to greet you at the entrance. Master, you've been gone for seventy thousand years, but you've finally returned." After he had finished his speech, he broke down in tears. His face was the same, but it had aged a lot. His sadness infected the others, and all fifteen apprentices knelt down one after another and burst into tears. Sixteenth Apprentice Zi Lan's body was wracked with silent sobs.

Mo Yuan lowered his eyes. "I've made you wait for a long time. Please rise, all of you. Let us go inside and talk."

Our reunion started with all the apprentices sobbing loudly. Once they had finished crying, they talked about how their carelessness had led to the disappearance of Little Seventeenth, Si Yin.

On hearing the name Si Yin, First Apprentice became so grief stricken that he was almost unable to breathe. I was Si Yin. It was me who had added medicine to their food so that they would sleep deeply enough for me to steal Mo Yuan's immortal body and flee through the night, away from Mount Kunlun. He did not mention my misdeed, just kept repeating how careless he had been and that my disappearance was all his fault. He had spent all these years looking for me without ceasing, but he had heard not a whisper of me and imagined I must have met with disaster. First Apprentice was meant to be responsible for keeping an eye on all the younger apprentices, and failing in his duty filled him with shame. He begged Mo Yuan to forgive his carelessness.

I had been leaning against Fourth Brother, but when I heard First Apprentice's words, I rushed forward to come clean. "I haven't met with disaster! I'm standing right here!" I explained, the rims of my eyes red. "I'm just wearing a different robe, that's all. I am Si Yin!"

The group of apprentices turned to me and stood staring stupidly. First Apprentice tumbled to the floor, and when he eventually crawled back up to his feet, he came over to hug me. He wiped away his tears, and sounding distraught, he said, "Ninth Apprentice always said that we all had subconscious homosexual tendencies. When the Demon Clan's second prince came to abduct you, I beat him up so badly that I quashed this tendency in him. But it was already too late for you. Poor Little Seventeenth, not just a homosexual, but a cross-dresser too."

Fourth Brother let out a chuckle. "First Apprentice, have a look at my face," I said sorrowfully, holding back my tears. "Can't you see I'm not male?"

Tenth Apprentice pulled First Apprentice off me. "You never used to bathe with us, Little Seventeenth, was that why?" he asked awkwardly. "Have you been a girl all along?"

"Yes, she's a *la-dy*," Fourth Brother said. I stamped on his foot.

When they had finished talking about me, the apprentices moved on to discuss their accomplishments over the last seventy thousand years.

My sixteen fellow apprentices had been a rough-and-tumble bunch when they were younger, and I had followed their example. I no longer climbed date trees or waded in rivers to fish, but they had taught me how to hold cockfights and cicada fights, to race dogs, play games, eye beautiful girls, drink alcohol, and appreciate erotica: all the things pleasure-seeking young men did, I learned to do too. Behind Master's back, I did whatever I wanted, thinking of myself as one of those tragic romantic lost characters.

My sixteen fellow apprentices were at least partially responsible for the bad path I ended up on. But this same bunch had somehow managed to transform themselves into a group of respectable and accomplished men. When Old Fate had been writing their destinies, he had obviously fallen asleep halfway through.

But I was happy that it had all worked out so well for my fellow apprentices, and hearing about all their successes was clearly very gratifying for Master too.

But then I started to ask myself what I had I achieved during this time, and I felt a sense of gloominess travel up my spine.

Fourth Brother had taken out a pen and sat to the side, scribbling down notes from what everyone was saying for the records. From time to time he would clap his hands and shout, "Legend! Legend!" Alongside my feeling of gloominess, I also started to feel a bit lost.

"You are a lady, and ladies don't need achievements in the same way men do," Tenth Apprentice said to comfort me. "All my younger sisters wanted was to do was marry into good families. Marrying into a good family is a perfectly good achievement, Seventeenth Apprentice."

Sixteenth Apprentice gave a laugh. "At Seventeenth Apprentice's age, she's probably been married for years. She must even have a few children by now. When are you going to introduce your fellow apprentices to your husband, by the way? I'm very curious to see the kind of man someone like you has ended up with!"

These words were like a punch right in the gut. I wiped the sweat from my forehead and gave a bleat of laughter. "You are too kind," I said. "I am actually getting married the month after next. Naturally you will all be invited to celebrate with us."

Mo Yuan had been sitting to the side throughout these conversations, his eyes raised as he listened. As soon as I said the words "celebrate with us," I saw the cup in his hand tilt and half his tea spill onto the floor. I rushed over to clean it up, while Zhe Yan gave a cough.

Ninth Apprentice Ling Yu had kept Mount Kunlun spick-and-span. After Fourth Brother had been away from the foxhole for a couple of months, his room had usually gathered half an inch of dust. It had been seventy thousand years since I had set foot on Mount Kunlun, and yet the room in which I slept as an apprentice did not contain a speck of dust. I lay in my old bed, feeling slightly ashamed, and then turned around to face the other side.

Sixteenth Apprentice Zi Lan was in bed in the next-door room. He knocked on the wall, saying, "Seventeenth Apprentice, are you asleep?"

I gave a loud sigh out my nose to show I was awake still, but the sound was not much louder than a mosquito's buzz, and I was not sure that he had heard, so I added, "No, I'm not asleep yet!"

It was a moment before his voice floated through the wall, saying, "You have suffered greatly on Master's behalf over these last seventy thousand years."

My impression of Sixteenth Apprentice was someone who always criticizing and challenging me. If I said east, he would feel obliged to say west, and if I talked about something I liked, he would have to smear it in the mud. Hearing these words made me suspicious, and I wondered whether it really was Sixteenth Apprentice. "Is this really Zi Lan?" I asked in a high-pitched voice.

He was quiet a moment and then gave a snort. "It serves you right that you've remained unmarried all these years!"

It was Zi Lan after all! I gave a chuckle, deciding not to enter into an argument with him. I lay back on the bed and turned to the other side. I'd lived to this grand old age, and I had done many things I regretted, but lying on my narrow Mount Kunlun bed, I felt as if none of them really mattered. The moonlight shone down gently, although there was no particular scenery outside for it to illuminate.

News of Mo Yuan's momentous return quickly spread. By early the next morning, everything that flew in the sky, all that crawled on the land, anything with a spiritual root had heard the news that the ancient God of War had returned.

According to the rumors going around, Mo Yuan was wearing a gold-and-purple crown on his head, his mysterious crystal armor on his body, and locust boots on his feet, with the Xuan Yuan sword in the hand of one arm and a beautiful girl on the other. On the sixteenth of August, he had landed majestically down on top of Mount Kunlun. The whole mountain range shook three times, and all the beasts and birds had looked up to the sky and called out, while all the fish had bobbed to the surface of the water and wept for joy.

There was not much truth to this account, and when we heard it, my sixteen fellow apprentices and I were shocked almost to the point of tears. The gold-and-purple crown, mysterious crystal armor, locust boots, and Xuan Yuan sword were all parts of Mo Yuan's signature attire and had been on display at Mount Kunlun's great hall for the last seventy thousand years for his apprentices to bow down before. After pondering who this beautiful girl on his arm might be, Fourth Brother and I decided that it was probably me.

This outlandish rumor spread far and wide, and soon every immortal, god, and goddess in the Four Seas and Eight Deserts had heard it, and wave after wave of them arrived at Mount Kunlun to pay their respects to Mo Yuan.

Mo Yuan had been planning to go into confined recuperation the day after returning to Mount Kunlun. However, due to this influx of immortal visitors, his plan had to be put on hold for a number of days.

There was nothing out of the ordinary about most of the young immortals arriving to praise him. First and Second Apprentices led some of them over to Mo Yuan so they could say a few words, while others just had tea in the front hall, where they rested a while before heading off. It was the young immortal who arrived at noon on the third day who was somewhat unusual.

This young immortal was wearing a white robe and had a gentle and quiet manner and a kindly face. When Mo Yuan saw him, his usually placid face did a double take. The young white-robed immortal was lucky enough to be given an audience with Mo Yuan, but he did not bow or pay homage, he just raised his beautiful soft eyes and said, "It's Zhong Yin, do you remember? I haven't seen Your Godliness for a long time, but your spirit has not changed at all. I have come to Mount Kunlun on my older sister's behalf. She appeared to me in a dream last night and told me I should come here and deliver a message. My sister . . ." He gave a smile. "She told me to tell you that she's been very lonely on her own."

I beckoned for Seventh Apprentice's young immortal servant who was standing nearby and told him to offer Zhong Yin a cup of tea.

Mo Yuan said nothing. He just rested his cheek in his hand, leaning nonchalantly against the armrest of his chair.

Zhe Yan glanced at Mo Yuan and then looked at Zhong Yin. "Brother Zhong Yin, you must be having a little joke with us," he said, not unkindly. "Your older sister, Lady Shao Wan, turned to dust flying and flames dying more than one hundred thousand years ago. How could she possibly have come to you in a dream?"

Zhong Yin blinked sweetly and said, "Your Godliness Zhe Yan, I think you may have misunderstood me. I have come to deliver the words of my older sister—I have no other agenda. I was not going to come, but my sister looked so unbearably miserable in the dream, and so I undertook this long and arduous journey to Mount Kunlun. Your understanding is that my sister had turned to dust flying and flames dying and therefore should not be able to come to me in a dream. But His Godliness Mo Yuan also turned to dust flying and flames dying, but he has returned now. My sister may have turned to dust flying and flames dying, but who knows where her soul has actually scattered? It is not beyond the realm of possibility that she has sent me this dream message, surely?"

As soon as he finished speaking, he bent his body and gave a bow before leaving the great hall. Mo Yuan got up from his seat and strolled over to the back courtyard without a word. I was about to go over to see what was wrong, but Zhe Yan stopped me. Second Apprentice walked over, looking upset. "Master has just gone off. What are we going to do about all the other immortal friends who have come to offer praise?" he asked.

Zhe Yan looked disconsolately up at the sky and said, "Lead them all through to the front hall for a cup of tea, and when they've had it, lead them outside."

I had always thought that Master Mo Yuan must have a history. Even though he did everything with such precision, I was right: he did have a history, and from what this white-robed Zhong Yin had to say, it sounded like it had been rather a violent and turbulent history. I started to feel anxious. I decided to act the filial apprentice by going first to the front hall to greet the young immortal Zhong Yin and then to Mo Yuan's room to comfort him.

When I knocked on Mo Yuan's door later that evening, he was sitting in front of his guqin in meditation. Dusky candlelight shone onto his face, showing the years and all his experiences within them. I stood anxiously in the doorway. His eyes moved up from the guqin to me, and he gave a faint smile. "Why are you just standing in the doorway like that? Come inside, please."

I walked quietly over. My intention had been to comfort him, but I stood there for a long time, and nothing came out. I was mystified by the matter that the young immortal in the white robe had mentioned, but it sounded like it had involved romantic heartbreak. And if that were the case, how would I even begin to comfort Mo Yuan?

My thoughts had just started to run away with me when I heard a few scattered guqin notes. Mo Yuan's right hand was resting on the strings as he plucked randomly. "I see your mind still wanders as it used to. Some things don't change, not even after tens of thousands of years," he said.

I rubbed my nose and gave a laugh. I walked closer to where he was, and with a gentle, comforting tone of voice, I said, "Master, people generally aren't reborn after they die. Zhong Yin has probably been missing his sister, and that's why he had his dream. You mustn't take it to heart."

He looked surprised. He lowered his head and plucked a little more at the strings of the guqin before saying, "Was that the only reason you came around tonight?"

I nodded.

There was another chaotic series of guqin notes and then the music came to a stop. Mo Yuan lifted his head and looked at me squarely for what felt like a long time before asking, "Do you truly love him?"

This question caught me off guard. I felt awkward discussing a matter like this with a member of the older generation, but never a shrinking violet, I rubbed my nose and answered with sincerity, "I do love him. Truly and utterly."

He turned away, gazing out the window for the longest time before saying, "I'm so glad to hear that. I can relax in that case."

He had a strange expression on his face this evening. Was he worrying that I might not make a good wife, that I might create an unhappy marriage for myself? When I realized that was what it must be, I cheerfully reassured him by saying, "Oh, you mustn't worry, Master. Ye Hua is a good man, and the two of us are in love. I truly love him, and he truly loves me back."

Mo Yuan did not turn around. "It's getting late. You should go back to your room to rest," he said calmly.

Mo Yuan rarely came to the great hall after that. I had gone there to comfort him, but after leaving his room, I realized that I had brought him no comfort whatsoever. I felt rather ashamed of myself. He obviously needed to come to terms with what had happened on his own, without others sticking their noses in.

If I was not able to see Mo Yuan, I decided that the least I could do was dampen the fervor of some of the young immortals who had traveled here to praise him. Their persistent eagerness was beyond belief. And the longer they stayed, the more tea they drank, and their used teacups were stacking up higher and higher in the front hall.

Fourth Brother guessed that they were all competing with each other for the honor of who could stay at the revered deity Mo Yuan's residence the longest and drink the most tea there. It was just like when Fourth Brother and I were small and used to hold competitions over who could pick the most peaches at Zhe Yan's or who could drink the most alcohol. We decided that our only option was to put up a series of posters informing all the young immortal coming to Mount Kunlun to offer praise that each of them would only be offered one cup of tea and no refills of water. Frustratingly enough, this did nothing to dissuade the little immortals, who continued to fill the hall.

I spent twenty days on duty in the front hall, during which time I began to think of myself as master of the tea ceremony. On the night of that twentieth day, I had finally had enough. I dragged Fourth Brother out into the middle courtyard under the date tree, and asked him to cover for me while I escaped to the mortal world for a few hours to check on Ye Hua.

The dates on the tree were already thumb-sized, but they were still green and not ripe yet. Fourth Brother picked a couple and held them in his palm. "Why are you being so secretive about this? Are you worried that your fellow apprentices will make fun of you if they find out where you're going, tease you about being a woman in love?" Fourth Brother could be very intuitive, but this was not one of those times.

My secretiveness had nothing to do with my fellow apprentices. I just did not wish to worry Mo Yuan with the fact that his twin brother was currently down in the mortal world experiencing a calamity. If he found out, he would certainly want to go down and make sure Ye Hua was all right, and the dusty air in the mortal world would not help his recuperation. Fourth Brother's interpretation showed that he thought that women were easily embarrassed, even women who had reached my grand old age. It made me feel strange to realize that I was actually much more thick-skinned than he realized.

Fourth Brother pointed at me and said, "If I allow you a few hours in the mortal world, I will not get a moment's sleep tonight. I will give you one hour. Ye Hua has only gone to the mortal world for a minor calamity, and nothing bad is going to happen to him. The only reason you're going down is because you're being clingy."

I managed to maintain my composure, although my ears went crimson. I had not chosen a good time to ask this favor of him. I had forgotten about the spat between him and Zhe Yan in the corridor earlier that afternoon. But an hour was long enough for me, so I thanked Fourth Brother and strode quickly off the mountain.

He threw the two dates he had been holding into the lily pond. "If you are not back within an hour, don't be surprised if I come down myself and drag you back," he said breezily.

Mount Kunlun had been bathing under the bright Milky Way when I left in the dark of night, but when I arrived in the mortal world, it was daylight, the azure sky stretching on for miles and miles. I dropped down outside a little private school and made myself invisible. The sound of reading drifted over. "'Shu Xiang went to visit Han Xuanzi and Shu Xiang congratulated . . . '"

I walked in the direction of the voice and saw a delicate-faced child sitting at the back of a classroom. He would have been quite an exceptional-looking mortal child, but he looked juvenile and unformed, incomparable to Ye Hua. However, his cold, indifferent facial expression was identical to Ye Hua's.

He finished reading, and the teacher at the front of the classroom opened his eyes and looked at the textbook in his hand. "Liu Ying, stand up and explain that section to the rest of the class," he said. The child with the cold expression got to his feet. My heart started to tremble. My eyesight was slightly better in the mortal world than in the immortal realms, and I could see that this child was indeed Ye Hua's reincarnation. I knew I would be able to recognize him.

He went through the passage line by line, explaining it carefully and logically, as the teacher twirled a strand of his long beard and gave regular praise and words of encouragement. I watched Ye Hua in his classroom, looking extremely clever but also utterly charming. I stood outside the school's window frame and waited until classes were over for the day.

Ye Hua's two book servants helped him pack away the things from his desk, and they all left together. I followed behind them, about to make myself visible, but wondering the best way to approach them and strike up a natural conversation. I hesitated awhile, unsure of what to do. While I was running through different options, I heard a whistle as two objects came hurtling past me. Without thinking, I waved my sleeves, and the two stones flying past immediately changed direction and crashed against the trunk of an old willow tree at the side of the road.

Ye Hua turned around when he heard the commotion, and three or four young scoundrels cursed him and started running away. As they ran they sang out a taunting rhyme: "Fire can harm, ice can harm, young Liu Yang was born with only one arm. Misdeeds in past lives cause this life's repercussions, reincarnation hears no discussions. Young Liu Yang may do well at school, but his body is nothing but a broken tool!" I heard a roaring in my head, and I lifted my eyes to look at Ye Hua's right arm.

The Sky Emperor, that utter wretch! Ye Hua was his own grandchild. How poisoned his heart must be to reincarnate his own flesh and blood and not even give him an able body! Ye Hua's right sleeve was hanging by his side, completely empty.

Ye Hua's two book servants rallied around him, defending him loyally, and were about to chase after those little scoundrels, but Ye Hua stopped them. The bullies looked familiar. I thought about where I had seen them before and realized they had been in Ye Hua's classroom with him.

As someone who was similarly unacademic, I understood the mindset of this group of young scoundrels. They were obviously falling behind in their studies, and seeing a prodigy like Ye Hua made them feel intense jealousy. They had every right to their feelings of jealousy, but only if they stayed away from Ye Hua and felt them from a distance. Making up a malicious taunt like that and singing it in front of him was too much. Oh, those little scoundrels. Later in life when they were suffering and feeling hard done by, they would realize what they had done, and how awful they had been.

Ye Hua stroked his empty sleeve with his left hand and gave a slight frown, but said nothing. He just turned around and carried on down the road. It was agonizing to see him like this, but I could not risk making myself visible here now; all I would do was scare the life out of them. I had to just bite down on my bitter rage, push it into my chest.

I followed him around from dusk until nightfall, but I never found the right time to appear before him in my true form. His two book servants were constantly by his side, and I was starting to find their presence extremely irritating. At nine that evening, Ye Hua eventually crawled into bed. His servants helped him undress and waited on him until he fell asleep. Once he had drifted off, they extinguished his candle, and giving a yawn or two, they headed off to their own beds.

I summoned my energy and released myself from the invisibility spell. I sat beside Ye Hua's bed, using the moonlight to take a closer look at him before reaching out over the quilt and nudging him awake. He gave a little groan, turned around, and sat up a little. "What's happening?" he asked in a fuzzy voice. When he saw that it was not one of his book servants speaking to him, but a stranger, he gave a start. He stared at me in disbelief and then closed his eyes and lay back down, mumbling, "Oh, I must be having a dream."

My heart trembled. I gave him another hasty shake to wake him, and before he could say anything, I cut in with the question, "So do you recognize me?"

I knew that he did not really recognize me and that thing he had just said about still dreaming, rather than asking me who I was, had probably been because he was still half asleep. But I was hoping so much that he would recognize me, so I asked him again.

Sure enough, he responded by saying, "No, I don't remember you." He frowned, the sleepy haze finally lifting. He paused for a while before saying, "So I'm not dreaming?"

I pulled a night pearl the size of a dove egg from my sleeve to offer more light. I took his hand and used it to stroke my face. "Does this feel like part of a dream?" I asked with a smile.

He went red.

I gasped in surprise. Could Ye Hua in his reincarnated form really be this shy?

I moved a bit closer to him, and he leaned away, his face growing even redder. I had never seen this side of Ye Hua before, and I found it intriguing. I shifted closer and closer, and he inched farther and farther toward the wall, where he cowered, his pale little face bright red by now. Working hard to maintain a look of calm composure, he said, "Who are you? And how did you get into my house?"

Seeing Ye Hua's coy shyness brought out my teasing side. I covered my face with my hand, and adopting a listless voice, I said, "I'm a little immortal from Qingqiu Kingdom, sir. I dropped down for a visit to the mortal world a couple of days ago. During that time, I saw you and have come to greatly admire you and have been unable to think about anything else. I have been pining away for you, and I have become wan and thin. I have come here tonight to declare my feelings in the hope that you might feel the same." After I had finished my speech, I looked up at him shyly. While I had been saying these words, I was cringing so much my body tingled, but the way I was looking at him seemed to be having an effect.

He looked at me in disbelief before burying his crimson face in his sleeve and giving a cough. "But, but I'm only eleven years old," he said.

The hour Fourth Brother had granted me was already up. I found reincarnated Ye Hua much more interesting than Ye Hua in his immortal form. It would seem that the Liu family knew a lot more about raising children than the Sky Emperor who reigned over the whole of the Ninth Sky. I started to feel slightly more relaxed that Ye Hua was not going to get into too much trouble down here.

Before I left, the two of us exchanged tokens of affection. I gave him the pearl bracelet that he had given me when I had gone down to help Yuan Zhen through his calamity. This bracelet would help to keep him safe. I was unable to stay with him throughout his time there, but knowing he was wearing this bracelet, I would worry about him less. He took off the jade pendant from his neck and fastened it around mine. I leaned over to his ear and reminded him one last time, "You really must not marry anyone else. I will pay you a visit when I can, and when you are old enough, we shall marry." He went red in the face, but he gave an earnest nod.

I had told Ye Hua that I would go and visit him when I had time. But I became extremely busy back in Mount Kunlun and did not find a moment to go back down.

Mo Yuan had decided that he would start his confinement in seven days. Zhe Yan wished to refine some pills for Mo Yuan to take into his cave with him to aid his recuperation. He designated me as his assistant. I spent days going back and forth between the medicine room and the pill room, and I did not even find enough time to sit down and wet my throat with a cup of tea.

By early on the second of September, we had refined the pills, which we placed inside a jade bottle to give Mo Yuan, with the instruction that he take them into the cave. Mo Yuan entered the cave, looking pale and unwell. He said nothing to his other apprentices, but he asked me one question: "Is Ye Hua good to you?"

I told him honestly that he was. And with that, Mo Yuan nodded and walked into the cave.

After Mo Yuan went into confinement, the flow of young immortals who had come to praise him finally stopped. I went outside to count the tea plants left on the mountain and saw that they were all bare. Every leaf had been plucked and used.

Fifteen of Mo Yuan's apprentices said farewell and returned to their own posts and lives, each leaving one immortal child to assist Ninth Apprentice in looking after Mo Yuan. I also said farewell to Ling Yu and left the mountain alongside Fourth Brother and Zhe Yan.

I climbed down from Mount Kunlun and flew down to the mortal world. In my estimation, Ye Hua would be seventeen or eighteen by now, a magnificent and prosperous age for mortals. I wondered what the boy who had been eleven only six days ago would look like at this age.

It was with excitement that I dropped lightly down just in front of the Liu family mansion.

I scoured every inch of their household grounds but could see no sign of Ye Hua anywhere. My excitement started to wane.

I came out of the Liu family house full of disappointment. After looking in every nook and cranny, I decided to make myself visible. I strolled up to the front gate and asked the young servant standing guard where Liu Ying Zhao Ge was. I was told that he had taken the civil service exams and done incredibly well and been sent off to work as an official for the heir to the mortal throne.

The little serving boy at the Liu residence spoke with great emotion and lofty sentimentality. "Our little lord is a rare prodigy, a rare prodigy. He was admitted into the imperial college when he was just twelve. Five years ago the emperor's grandfather developed the civil service grace exams. Our young lord took the exam just to have a go and see what would happen, but he ended up getting the top results in the country. He entered the Hanlin Academy, rose rapidly up through the system, and has already become a high-ranking government minister for the Ministry of Revenue. Oh, a rare prodigy, a rare prodigy indeed."

I was not so interested in what office Ye Hua held, but I was happy to now know where I could locate him. I summoned all my energy, cast a spell, and leaped onto a cloud, rushing off toward the heir to the mortal throne's palace.

CHAPTER
TWENTY-TWO

I found Ye Hua in the back garden of his government minister residence. He was wearing black satin off-duty clothes and sitting opposite a girl in white, drinking wine and admiring the thick haze of peach blossoms in the tree above them.

The girl in white must have said something, as he lifted his wine goblet and gave her a wide smile. She immediately gave a demure bow.

His smile was warm and gentle, but I saw excitement in his eyes. It had only been six days since I had last seen him, but he seemed to have completely forgotten about our love tokens. Could he really be such a rascal? I felt the jealousy well up, and I was just about to go and ask him to explain himself when suddenly I heard a voice behind me. "It's been a while since I've seen you, Goddess. I would like to use this opportunity to pay my respects."

I turned around in surprise.

The invisibility spell I had used only prevented me from being seen by mortal eyes, but immortals still could see me. I saw Su Jin standing in front of me, dressed in simple clothing. "What are you doing here?" I asked in surprise.

She looked at me squarely, gave a slight bow, and said, "The prince is all on his own in the mortal world, experiencing his calamity. I was worried he might be lonely, so I created a mannequin in imitation of someone he has been thinking a lot about and placed her down here with him to keep him company. I've been invited to the Western Empress's mother's tea ceremony today, and I decided to stop off on the way to make sure this mannequin was looking after the prince properly."

I stopped and turned to stare at the woman in white with Ye Hua. I had not given her a proper look before. Now I could see she was just a mannequin encased in human skin. "You're very kind," I said in a flat voice, groping for my fan.

"You must know who this mannequin is modeled on?" she asked, giving me an eager look. I tilted my head and looked the girl in white carefully up and down, but nothing about her appearance jumped out at me. There was a strange expression on Su Jin's face. "I imagine you must have heard the name Su Su?" she said.

My heart trembled. Su Jin seemed to have been leaping from strength to strength recently. The two of us had only just met, but already she knew exactly where to aim for my weakest spot. Of course I knew the name of Dumpling's mother, the woman who jumped from the immortal punishment platform, Ye Hua's beloved first wife. Since I had become aware of my feelings for Ye Hua, I had been careful to put all the hearsay I had heard about Dumpling's mother out of my mind, hiding it all in a box that I had locked with three different keys, promising myself never to open it back up, as to do so would lead only to unhappiness.

I was not Ye Hua's first love, a fact that filled me with regret and dismay each time I thought about it. That was the way our fate had been dealt, however, and there seemed no point in complaining. Sometimes it was important to just acknowledge bad luck and move on. Love was never a smooth ride.

"You don't need to be concerned, Goddess," Su Jin said when she saw my expression. "The prince is currently in mortal form. He can't tell that it's a mannequin sitting in front of him, transforming his dreams into reality. There is no way he'll continue to feel affection for a mannequin once he returns to his immortal form, even if she does look like Su Su."

Was this her way of telling me that the prince had already fallen in love with this mannequin? I gave a laugh and said, "Aren't you scared that Ye Hua will want to punish you when he returns to his immortal body and remembers the way you tricked him?"

Her face stiffened, and she forced a smile. "All I've done is create a mannequin, which I positioned in the marketplace in front of his house. If he weren't interested, they would have just walked past each other and gone their separate ways. But the prince fell in love with her as soon as he saw her and invited her back to his house. If in the future he decides to blame me for that, I will just have to accept it."

I felt an ache in my chest. I stroked my fan and said nothing. "It seems that some people become imprinted upon each other's bones," she said, giving a soft smile. "Even after drinking the Netherworld's Forget River Water, an impression remains. As soon as he turned around and saw her, he fell in love with her all over again. Yes." She paused, and when she spoke again, her words were slow and deliberate. "Goddess, you must know that for the last three hundred years, the prince has been using the soul-binding lamp to gather up Su Su's energy?"

It was as if someone had suddenly struck a gong inside my head. I felt so shaken up that I no longer knew where I was. Violent waves rose up through my chest. Prior to this, Ye Hua had actually been trying to recreate Su Su? Six days ago I had sat beside his bed and asked him if he remembered me, and he said no.

Six years later he comes across a girl in the marketplace who he should not have had any recollection of and he brings her back to his house. The fact that he did not recognize me but had a sense of her proved that his love for Su Su was greater than his love for me. Suddenly all three locks on the box sprang open and the contents poured out. It seemed to be only because wearing my blindfold, I looked slightly similar to his first wife that Ye Hua had gradually fallen for me. Nothing made sense any longer. My brain became chaotic, and I felt a painful throbbing in my heart.

But even throughout this mental torment, I managed to retain my goddess bearing and dignity in Su Jin's presence. "You clearly know a lot about love, and even though you are Ye Hua's head concubine, you are aware that he is not fond of you," I said with calm composure. "I imagine that you've had to lower your expectations considerably to deal with his constant rejection of you over the past two hundred years. You are meticulously calculating for someone your age and have obviously gone to a lot of trouble to create this mannequin for Ye Hua. It is fine with me if she keeps him company. In fact, it will save me the trouble. In fact, if in the future Ye Hua gets angry with you for deceiving him, I will be sure to put in a good word."

The smile froze on her face. For a long time she did not move a muscle. But then the corners of her mouth started curling upward, and she said, "Thank you very much, Goddess."

I waved a hand at her, saying, "It would not be prudent to show up late to the Western Empress's mother's tea ceremony."

Su Jin lowered her head and gave a deferential kowtow. "In that case I shall now take my leave."

Once Su Jin had gone, I turned back around to look at the scene behind me and saw Ye Hua and the mannequin still drinking together. A couple of peach petals floated down from the tree and landed in Ye Hua's hair. The mannequin stretched out a pale hand and gently brushed them away. She lifted her head and gave Ye Hua a shy smile.

Ye Hua took a sip of wine, but said nothing. My head throbbed in agony.

Fourth Brother often used to say that it was as if the muscles in my fox brain had not developed properly, because everything I did was sloppy and haphazard. Father and Mother had been lucky enough to stop me from meeting with any serious misfortune, but on a few occasions I did bring shame to my Nine-Tailed White Fox Clan. I actually thought that Fourth Brother had probably brought more shame upon the clan than me, but because he was older, I decided not to quibble.

It was only now that I realized that Fourth Brother had been right: I was sloppy and haphazard and often did not think things through. The first time Ye Hua declared his feelings to me, why had I never thought to wonder why—when he could have any female immortal in the whole of the Four Seas and Eight Deserts—he picked me? Later when I started to reciprocate his feelings and the two of us had fallen in love, I had never thought to ask him this important question.

If he did like me only because I reminded him of Dumpling's mother and saw me only as a replacement for her, what was the difference between being with me and being with this mannequin he was currently drinking wine with? I knew that developing a grudge against a dead woman was pathetic, but when it came to love, it was impossible to feign high-mindedness to appear dignified.

I was unable to put out the evil flames in my heart now. I rubbed my temples. I needed to lay out all these matters and consider them carefully. I cast a spell, climbed on a cloud, and made my way back to Qingqiu in an utter state of confusion.

That evening I brought out the soul-binding lamp and held it under a night pearl to inspect it properly. It had been with De Yong at the Western Sea all this time, boosting his energy levels and aiding his recovery. After Mo Yuan had woken back up, Zhe Yan had gone to collect it and brought it back to Qingqiu, where it had remained ever since. Ye Hua had not asked for it while I was up in the Ninth Sky, and it had slipped my mind to return it.

Under the white light of the night pearl, I saw the soul-binding lamp ignited with an unimpressive flame, not much bigger than a bean sprout. Who might have guessed that coiled inside this ordinary-looking lamp was three hundred years of one mortal's energy.

The more I thought, the heavier my heart became. I did not trust everything Su Jin had to say, but it corroborated what Nai Nai had told me. From all these fragments, I managed to piece together the whole story and could see that it was true: for the last three hundred years, Ye Hua's feelings for Dumpling's mother had remained as deep as the ocean. All the love in his heart was for one woman, and although she had been dead for three hundred years, his love for her was still very much alive. Did his love for her just shift to me when he met me?

The more I thought about this, the more the vigor of the evil flames in my liver and gallbladder burned, and one grievance after another welled up in my heart. I loved Ye Hua because he was Ye Hua. It had nothing to do with him looking like my former master; I had never seen him as a Mo Yuan replacement. If I had, I would have been extremely reverent and polite toward him and always on my best behavior.

Since my love for him was genuine, I had hoped the same of his. If he was only with me due to my resemblance to Dumpling's mother, who he was missing, pining for, and unable to get over, I wanted nothing to do with it.

"Would you like me to bring you some wine, Your Highness?" Mystic Gorge asked quietly from outside.

I gave a silent nod.

The wine that Mystic Gorge brought in for me was new wine and had not been left long enough to mature. The masculine yang energy had not had the chance to bond with the softer, earthier, feminine yin energy, and it left a dry and spicy sensation in my throat. It burned so much that I started to feel light-headed, and my mind filled with greater confusion. Mystic Gorge must have noticed how unsettled I was looking and had intuitively known to pick out a bottle of something really strong for me.

I drank until the soul-binding lamp in front of me started to look like ten soul-binding lamps, at which point I decided I might have had enough. I stood up, stumbled over to my bed, and fell down upon it. Despite my dizziness, I did not manage to sleep. I was constantly aware of something bright and shiny on the table. It was dazzling me so much, it was no wonder I could not sleep. I sat on the edge of my bed, squinting at it, and realized it was the lamp. I realized that the lamp must have . . . it must have rebound something.

I thought and thought, but I could not work out what it was.

The bright lamplight made me feel as if there was something pressing down against my chest. I felt too weak to crawl up out of my bed, so I attempted to blow out the lamp from where I was. No matter how much I huffed and puffed, I did not manage to extinguish the flame. I thought about casting a spell to extinguish it, but I could not think what the right spell might be. I cursed silently and cast any old spell and sent it in the direction of the lamp and whatever it was rebinding. There was a loud crack as the lamp seemed to smash to pieces.

After all that exertion and effort, everything started spinning. I fell straight down onto the bed and into a deep coma-like sleep.

I slept solidly for two days, and as I slept, many memories returned to me.

I realized that when Qing Cang broke out of the Eastern Desert Bell five hundred years ago and I used everything I had to lock him back up again, it was not as Mother and Father had told me; I had not just slept peacefully in the foxhole for the following 212 years. Instead Qing Cang had sealed off my immortal energy and dropped me down onto Junji Mountain in the Eastern Desert.

Without knowing it, all this time I had actually been Su Su. Dumpling's mother. The mortal who jumped from the immortal punishment platform.

I had often wondered to myself why the calamity by which I had soared up to the rank of goddess had been such a benign one. I had fought a battle with Qing Cang, slept for 212 years, and woken up a goddess. On waking up in the foxhole three hundred years ago, I had been astonished to find that my primordial spirit had changed from a shining white light to a shining gold light and had assumed it to be a favor bestowed upon me by Old Fate. I had been grateful that Old Fate was such a benevolent being.

I had no idea that my battle with Qing Cang had merely been a prelude to my official calamity that sent me soaring up to the goddess rank. It had not just been true love I lost, but also my eyes. If Qing Cang had not sealed off my primordial spirit, when I jumped off the punishment platform I would have lost all my spiritually cultivated energy too.

Old Fate always knew exactly what he was doing. *Benevolent? Benevolent? Like hell he was benevolent!* I finally understood why in Qingqiu, Ye Hua had often looked like he wanted to say something to me, but had then stopped himself. I understood that strange thing I could vaguely recall hearing him say the night we stayed at that mortal world inn: "I both wish you would remember and hope you never do." It had not been a dream or a hallucination. It all made complete and perfect sense. Ye Hua had wronged me back then and he had let me down badly.

He might never understand why I had left Dumpling behind and jumped off the punishment platform.

An avalanche of past memories suddenly came tumbling back into my mind. Those agonizing days from three hundred years ago felt as raw as if it had all happened yesterday. I did not care to think about what he had done and not done and for what reasons in order to protect me when I was an ordinary little mortal; neither was I in the right state of mind to think.

When I woke up from this dream, all I remembered was those three years of lonely nights spent in my courtyard, as gradually all hope was destroyed. I felt overwhelmed by these feelings of desolate sadness. For those three years, I had been so helpless and so full of sorrow.

I realized that in this frame of mind, it was going to be difficult to marry Ye Hua in October, but I knew I still loved him. Three hundred years ago, he had completely confused and disoriented me, and now he was doing it again. It must have been karmic retribution from something in my past. I still loved him—I could not control what my heart felt—but the events of three hundred years ago were like a barrier I was unable to move past. I could not forgive him for what he had done.

Mystic Gorge brought me some water to wash with. He regarded me for a moment before saying, "Your Highness, would you like me to bring you some more wine?"

I put my hand to my face to wipe it, and it came away completely wet.

Mystic Gorge brought in more wine. During my last drinking session, I had polished off seven or eight jars, which I had assumed to be Fourth Brother's entire reserve. There had obviously been much more in the thatched hut than I had thought, as Mystic Gorge suddenly materialized with another five or six jars.

I would drink until I passed out. As soon as I awoke, I would drink more. I drank and slept, drank and slept, spending three or four days in this tedious cycle. On the fifth day, I woke up at dusk to find Mystic Gorge sitting in my room, frowning anxiously at me. "You have finished all the wine from the cellar now. It's time you started taking care of yourself, Your Highness."

Mystic Gorge was extremely worried about me. There was nothing wrong with me physically; I just lacked energy. I was not as bad as Phoenix Nine when she was heartbroken, as after a few drinks, she was usually vomiting bile. I had enough practice in wine drinking to have developed a good tolerance.

Without any strong liquor to soak it in, I started to regain some clarity of mind. Within this semi-lucid state, I remembered something important that I needed to keep in mind no matter what. My eyes were still in Su Jin's eye sockets. I needed to get them back.

Su Jin had taken advantage of my vulnerable state in my love calamity and stolen my eyes. Now that my calamity was over, I did not think it was appropriate for her to still be walking around with them. The thought of my eyes in her face gave me a real sense of unease.

I called for my Kunlun fan and stood in front of the mirror, making myself look more presentable. My complexion was not in a good state, and so as not to disgrace Qingqiu, I decided to open a tin of rouge and apply a small amount to my cheeks.

Glowing with radiance, I traveled up to the Ninth Sky. I cast a spell to slip past the sky guards and sky soldiers at the Southern Sky Gate and made my way to Changhe Hall in Xiwu Palace: Su Jin's residence.

As a model concubine, she enjoyed a very comfortable life, and she was reclining on the royal bed with her eyes closed when I entered. When I was in front of her, I made myself visible, causing the immortal attendant who had just entered to serve her tea to give a startled yelp. The model concubine's eyes flicked open, and she gave a little jolt of alarm when she saw me. "Goddess, you have scared me by arriving like this," she said, although the calm and relaxed way she turned around and lay back down on the bed did not make this look to be the case.

I sat down at the side. She put on a big smile and said, "I'm trying to work out why you've come here. I imagine it must be to inquire about the prince's recent situation. If you wish to hear about the prince . . ." She paused, and her smile became even bigger. "Su Su is looking after the prince very well in the mortal world, and he is looking after her extremely well in return."

The nasty smile on her face looked strange against her kind, twinkly eyes. I stroked the surface of the Kunlun fan and tried to show tolerance in my face. "Well, in that case it's obviously a good thing that she's there with him. It really puts my mind at rest to have you here to take care of Ye Hua. The reason I have come here today is because now it's my turn to take care of you."

She looked at me with suspicion, and I responded with a poised smile. "You have been using my eyes for the last three hundred years, Su Jin. Have you been enjoying them?" I asked.

She raised her head sharply, and I saw her face flush bloodred before turning a peachy pink, then going deathly white. I watched with intrigue as she passed through all these different shades.

"W-w-what did you just say?" she warbled.

I unfolded my fan, and with a laugh I said, "Three hundred years ago, I underwent a love calamity and lost my eyes. You were the one who stole them. After thinking it all through carefully, I decided to come over and get them back. So, would you like to be the one to do the honors, or shall I do it for you?"

She took two steps back and bumped into the armrest of the royal bed, although she did not seem to notice. "Are you . . . are you Su Su?" she asked, her lips trembling.

I extended my fan fully, and with a hint of impatience creeping into my voice, I said, "So which of us is going to cut them out then, you or me?"

She twisted her sleeves, her eyes expressionless. She gaped a couple of times, but no words came out. After a long time she made a sound, something between a laugh and a sob. "That girl . . . she was obviously a mortal. There's no way it could have been you."

I picked up a cup of tea from the table, strong and steaming. "What difference does it make if she was a mortal or a goddess?" I asked. "Just because I was transformed into a mortal three hundred years ago and was unaware of what was happening to me does not give some insignificant little immortal the right to take my eyes and trick me into jumping off the immortal punishment platform."

Her legs went weak, and she crumpled to her side. "I . . . I . . . I . . . ," she began, but never got any further with the sentence. I went over and stroked her eye sockets. "I was lucky enough to have been given some good wine recently," I said softly. "Unfortunately I drank a little more than I could handle and my hands are still a bit shaky. It will probably hurt a lot less if you carry out the procedure yourself."

Just as I was about to lower my hand, she gave a bloodcurdling shriek. I erected an immortal barrier in front of Changhe Hall to prevent any immortal children or palace attendants from entering. She was panicking so much that her pupils had become pinpricks. She grasped wildly at my hands, saying, "You can't . . . you can't . . ."

I patted her face and said, "Three hundred years ago, you used to pretend you were weak and gentle. You were always putting on that act. You didn't allow me to see anything but your weak and gentle side, did you? When Ye Hua cut my eyes out, he said that what was owed must be returned, but we both know the real story. Since you were the one responsible for my eyes being cut out of my face and transferred into your own eye sockets, give me one reason why I should not take them back right now. Do you think the fact that you have been using them for the last three hundred years gives you ownership of them?"

I brought my hand down to her eyes and did the deed. She gave a bitter cry. I leaned in toward her ear and said, "The Sky Emperor dealt quietly with what happened three hundred years ago. And what has happened today will be dealt with quietly too. You have now repaid your eye debt, but you still owe me for making me jump down from the immortal punishment platform. To pay this debt, you can either jump down from it yourself or you can find the Sky Emperor and tell him you would like to be transferred to the banks of the Ruo River, where you can use your puny supply of immortal power to guard Qing Cang in the Eastern Desert Bell, and you will never return to the Sky Kingdom."

She seemed to have gone into cramps. The agony must have been unbearable. I had experienced something similar, and being a mortal at the time, I had suffered all the more. She could hardly breathe from the pain, but she managed to force out the words, "There's no way I will . . ."

There it was: the end of this weak and gentle pretense. I had forced her to show her true colors. I lifted her blood-drenched face and gave a laugh. "Oh? Would you rather I went to the Sky Emperor and told him myself? But I'm the kind of person who says one thing one day and a completely different thing the next. If I end up talking to the Sky Emperor, who knows what I'll end up telling him."

I felt her go stiff under my hand, and she curled up into a ball to deal with the pain. I recited a Buddhist mantra: "Good karma, bad karma. The natural law of retribution."

Bi Fang had disappeared again, and Fourth Brother had gone after him, leaving Zhe Yan alone in the Ten-Mile Peach Grove. He was shocked when I handed him the bloody eyeballs. He held them up to the sun to inspect them. "It's been three hundred years, but you've finally found your eyes! It's a miracle! But you drank my medicine back then. How can you remember your past heartbreak? It's another miracle!"

Because these eyes had been taken from an immortal body, they would need to be implanted within forty-nine days or they would lose their function.

Zhe Yan was extremely curious about what had happened. He had assumed that my eyes were lost for good. He had no idea that they had been put into someone else's face and that one day they might be returned to me and fitted back into my eye sockets.

I forced a smile.

He looked at my face and realized that I did not want to talk about what had happened. He gave a cough but respected my wish and asked no more questions.

Zhe Yan explained that it would take a few days for the impure energy to be eliminated from my original eyes. He would wait until that had happened before carrying out the procedure to replace them with my current eyeballs. I gladly agreed and decided that while I was there, I would help myself to a couple more jars of wine from his back mountain cellar before getting onto a cloud and soaring back to Qingqiu.

I spent the next few days in a drunken stupor. I made two requests of Mystic Gorge: to keep a close eye on what Ye Hua's head concubine was up to and to seal off the Qingqiu Valley to visitors; I wished to see no one.

Zhe Yan's wine was much stronger than the stuff Mystic Gorge had been hoarding, and I got so drunk that night that I actually vomited up bile. My head ached to the point where I considered taking up a sword and slashing my own forehead open. But feeling like this had its benefits: as soon as I closed my eyes, everything started spinning, and there was no longer room in my head to think about anything else.

Mystic Gorge urged me to pace myself, take a couple of days off drinking, or at least to take more care of myself. But the heartbreak I was experiencing now was different from that in the past, and without getting drunk I had no means of sleeping. While I was blind drunk, I was oblivious to everything, although I had slightly more lucid spells during which I vaguely remembered Mystic Gorge coming over to talk to me.

He said many things, most of which were irrelevant, but two things he said stuck in my mind. The first was that the head concubine had gone to the Sky Emperor, presenting a letter requesting to leave the Sky Palace and move to the banks of the Ruo River, where she could cultivate spiritual energy by keeping guard over the imprisoned Qing Cang. The Sky Emperor was touched by her generous offer and granted her permission to do this.

The other news he gave me was related to Ye Hua's mortal world calamity. Despite drinking water from the Forget River, which should have brought complete amnesia about the past, he had retained a strong belief in the supernatural and spent his whole life searching for the immortal realm of Qingqiu. He rose to the rank of prime minister but never married, and when he turned twenty-seven, he became depressed, grew ill, and died. His final request to his domestic servants was for his body to be cremated and his ashes buried along with a pearl bracelet he had kept on his person throughout his whole lifetime.

I cannot remember whether I cried when Mystic Gorge told me this. If I did shed a tear or two, I was not sure exactly why I was crying. I had drunk so much that I could not work out what I was feeling.

This was still the case a few days later when Mystic Gorge rushed into the foxhole with the news that Prince Ye Hua had been waiting in the mouth of the Qingqiu Valley for seven days now and wished to see me.

Mystic Gorge had followed my orders not let anyone in, even Ye Hua. But after seven days, Ye Hua still showed no signs of leaving, so Mystic Gorge decided to come and tell me and ask me for specific instructions about what I wished him to do.

My brain, unused for so long now, started to turn again.

Ye Hua had become ill in the mortal world and died at the age of twenty-seven, and naturally, following his mortal funeral, he would return to his immortal life.

My chest suddenly flooded with pain. I pressed my hand against my heart and slid down the table as my legs turned to jelly. Mystic Gorge came over to try to help me up, but I would not let him.

I leaned against a table leg and looked up at the rafters. I wanted to see Ye Hua. I wanted to ask him about all that had happened three hundred years ago. Had Su Jin betrayed him by marrying the Sky Emperor and broken his heart so badly? Was it in this wretched heartbroken state that he had met and married me in my mortal form?

Had he ever truly loved me? Was it really for my own good that he left me alone and miserable in the Sky Palace for those three years? Had he been in love with Su Jin while he was in love with me? And if so, how deeply? If Su Jin had not tricked me into jumping down from the immortal punishment platform, would he have married her? Was the deep affection he seemed to have for me now nothing but repentance for how he treated me before?

The more I thought about it, the worse my thinking got. I put my hand over my eyes, and it came back completely wet, water trickling between my fingers. What if he said yes? What if his answer to all these questions was yes?

I worried I would be so upset I could actually end up killing him. Mystic Gorge regarded me anxiously. "Are you going to go out and see him, Your Highness?"

I inhaled deeply. "No, I'm not. Tell him to leave Qingqiu and never come back. I'm going to visit the Sky Emperor tomorrow to call off the engagement."

Mystic Gorge returned sometime later. He stood there quietly for a moment before saying, "His Majesty does not look very well. He has been standing in the valley for seven days and nights now and has not moved an inch this whole time."

I glanced at him, took a sip of wine, but said nothing. He hesitated before saying, "His Majesty has asked me to give you a message, Your Highness. Apparently you told him that if he were to have a romance in the mortal world, you would capture him and bring him back to Qingqiu and lock him up. Apart from talking to a girl who looked identical to you in your mortal form and inviting her to his house, all he did was tend to his sick mother. He was not inspired with even a bud of peach blossom feeling. He wonders if the promise you made to him in the mortal world still stands, the one about marrying him when he grew up?"

I hurled a wine jar across the room. "Of course it doesn't stand!" I cried out involuntarily. "None of his pack of lies stands! Get out and get rid of him too. I have absolutely no desire to see him."

But even in the depths of my sorrow, I knew that it was not that I did not want to see him. But something was blocking my heart, and I did not know how I could possibly see him.

I did not end up going to the Ninth Sky the next day to cancel the engagement as I had stated. I decided to wait until I was in a better mood for it, which I suspected could take some time.

The next day, the one after that, and the one after that, Mystic Gorge reported that Ye Hua was still standing in the valley and that he had not moved an inch. I screamed that if he mentioned Ye Hua one more time, I was going to beat him back into his tree form and leave him like that for ten thousand years. He finally stopped bothering me with these reports.

I was not drinking so much alcohol anymore. Since finding out that Ye Hua was standing outside Qingqiu, drinking only served to make me more clearheaded and alert. The more alert I became, the deeper my pain, and the deeper my pain, the less able I was to sleep.

To rub salt on an already sore wound, I woke up one morning at the height of this misery and sensed big waves running through the immortal power I had used to seal Qing Cang within the Eastern Desert Bell five hundred years ago.

My heart gave a sudden lurch. This really was the darkest of times. It had been one thing after another recently, but all that came before paled in comparison to this. Qing Cang had obviously found a way of continuing to cultivate spiritual energy within the bell, and he was about to break out of it once more.

I gave my face a quick wash and sent Mystic Gorge off to the Ten-Mile Peach Grove to tell Zhe Yan what was happening and that I needed his help. Five hundred years ago when Qing Cang made his first attempt to break out of the bell, I was forced to stop him and lock him back inside. Our battle had caused grave damage to the bell, and I had been forced to use half my cultivated spiritual energy to repair it.

I tried to work out how much spiritual energy I had left and whether it would be better to launch a savage attack or to try to take him by ruse. I had enough self-awareness to know that I was no match for him either way.

Qing Cang was not a benevolent being at the best of times, and regaining his freedom after so many years of being locked up, he was likely to go berserk and ignite the most destructive weapon the Four Seas and Eight Deserts had ever seen, reducing the universe to a pile of cinders.

This realization made the romantic problems that had disturbed my sleep so much seem ridiculous. I pulled out my Kunlun fan, jumped to my feet, and set off toward Ruo River. I did not have time to wait for Zhe Yan; I needed to go straight there and try to hold Qing Cang back myself first. I could not risk him detonating the bell.

I was not surprised to see Ye Hua in the valley. I knew he was still waiting there and that I would have to pass him on my way out of Qingqiu. I closed my eyes and brushed past him, feigning indifference, but he reached out and grabbed hold of my sleeve. His face looked haggard, exhausted, and eerily pale.

Every moment was crucial, and I had no time to waste with him. I turned my head and used my fan to chop off the part of my sleeve in his grasp. He heard the sound of material ripping and looked up in surprise. "Qian Qian!" he called out in a hoarse voice.

I turned back to face the front, ignoring him, and continued speeding toward Ruo River. When I glanced back, I saw he had jumped onto a cloud too and was following me.

For years after, I often thought back to this moment and wished that I had just said something nice to him. Anything. But all I had done was give him a cold look. And said nothing.

I looked down at the monstrous white waters of Ruo River and up at the heavy black clouds pressing down from above. The tower-like structure of the Eastern Desert Bell stood on the bank of Ruo River. It was swaying and rumbling, causing the entire area to shake. There was no sign of Su Jin, who was supposed to be guarding the bell, and I imagined that all the commotion must have frightened her away into hiding.

Through the layers of clouds, I could partially make out the head of the earth god in charge of Ruo River's wild lands. This earth god and I had been destined to meet five hundred years before too. He was hiding in the clouds, anxiously watching the restless Eastern Desert Bell, and I could just make out the top of his head. He turned around when he saw Ye Hua and me approaching and hurriedly bowed down before coming over.

"Your Highness, you've arrived!" he said in a panic-stricken voice. "The immortal prince of Ruo River has gone to the Sky Palace to ask for army assistance, and he has asked me to wait here. Qing Cang's anger is extreme this time. The immortal prince's Ruo River residence has been shaking, as has my earth god temple . . ." He was still babbling on when the bell was lit up by a huge blast of white light, inside of which we could just make out the outline of a person.

I uttered a silent curse and was just about to jump off my cloud when this figure suddenly turned still. Ye Hua approached from behind and hooked his leg around my ankle to trip me. He recited an incantation to freeze me and whipped out a special trap that he used to bind my hands and feet. I was completely stuck. I could see that Qing Cang was moments away from breaking out of the bell. "Let me go!" I screamed in panic.

Ye Hua ignored me. He pushed me toward the Ruo River earth god with a simple message. "Look after her, and whatever happens, don't let her fall down off this cloud." He gave his left hand a turn, and in it appeared a double-edged sword, flowing with cold light. I saw him take the sword and move toward the blustering winds. He got off his cloud and headed straight for the silver light ribboning out of the Eastern Desert Bell. I felt as if the sky had just fallen in.

I opened my mouth a few times, but no words came out. An agonizing wind blew into my eyes. As Ye Hua was heading toward that silver light, I heard my voice come out sounding completely devoid of hope. "Earth God, please release me," I was saying. "You have to think of a way to release me. Ye Hua is going to die if he does this. He only has a tiny amount of cultivated spiritual energy left. It's suicide what he's doing!"

The earth god mumbled something about how ingenious the trap Ye Hua had used to bind me was, and there was no way he could spring it open. There was also something strange about the incantation Ye Hua had used to freeze me, he explained, and he could not undo that either.

It was pointless wasting energy on asking him for help. If I was going to get out of this bind, it would have to be by my own means. I focused all my energy and managed to lift my primordial spirit up out of my body. I had not imagined that this trap Ye Hua had set was not just a physical immortal lock; it was actually gripping my primordial spirit, and despite all my desperate attempts to escape, it continued to keep me held tight. From my tear-blurred eyes, I saw the silver light spreading out from all four sides of the Eastern Desert Bell, while the thunder and lightning from Ye Hua and Qing Cang's battle carried all the way up to the sky. The earth god created a puny little immortal barrier to surround the two of us, stopping me from being injured by the evil energies.

It was a serious trap that Ye Hua had bound me with. I was dripping with sweat by the time I managed to free myself from his body-freezing incantation, but however hard I tried, I could not release myself from the grip of his trap. The earth god and I sat together between the twilight sky and the dark earth. "Your Highness. It's still not safe for us here, and I'm not sure how long my immortal barrier will last," he whispered. "Shall we move a little farther away?"

I heard my own despondent-sounding voice give a breezy, "You go. I'm going to stay here with Ye Hua."

I was still bound by the trap at this point, and completely useless. There was nothing I could do for Ye Hua, but I still wanted to stay with him and look over him.

I had never seen Ye Hua with a sword before, nor had I ever thought about what he might look like holding one. I had heard about his excellent swordsmanship, however. The sword in his hand was the Qing Ming sword, and I had heard his immortal admirers saying that whenever he pulled Qing Ming from its sheath, the entire Four Seas and Eight Deserts started to tremble.

The first time I heard this, I assumed it was just young people exaggerating. But now I was witnessing the Qing Ming sword's movements for myself: its turning, flying, and curling. The bit about the entire Four Seas and Eight Deserts starting to tremble was a slight exaggeration, but I was indeed dazzled by its splendor. Thunderous gases spooled out of the sword as it moved, and my eyes started to feel like they were being ravaged by its glare.

The two fighters were locked so inextricably in combat that it was hard to tell where one ended and the other began. I was too high up to see who had the upper hand, but I knew that Ye Hua was unlikely to be able to hold out for very much longer. I just hoped he could last until Zhe Yan arrived, or until his grandfather dispatched his hopeless troop of sky soldiers and commanders.

Sand and stone flew through the air over the Ruo River banks, and soon the whole sky was filled with earth. I suddenly heard Qing Cang give three lengthy laughs, followed by a long cough. "You may have overcome me, but I will never surrender to you," he said. "If it wasn't for my old injuries, and all the energy I expended getting out of the bell, there's no way a novice like you could have defeated me."

The thick smoke and dust gradually dispersed. Ye Hua's sword was standing on the ground, and he was kneeling on one leg and using it to prop himself up.

Trembling, I turned to the earth god and said, "It's safe on the ground now. Hurry up and get us down from here . . ."

Just as the earth god was taking down his immortal barrier, the Eastern Desert Bell gave an explosion of bloodred light. I could not work out what was happening. Qing Cang had just been defeated; how could he possibly be controlling the bell still?

Ye Hua raised his head sharply. "What have you done to the bell?" he asked in a deep voice.

Qing Cang was lying in the dust. "You want to know how I managed to ignite the bell without even touching it?" he said weakly with a laugh. "I've devoted seventy thousand years so that I could link my life to the bell's. If I die, the Eastern Desert Bell ignite. I am about to die, so it looks as if you'll be coming with me, along with all the other immortals from the Eight Deserts . . ."

I watched in wide-eyed horror as before Qing Cang had even fin-ished speaking, Ye Hua threw himself into the ball of bright-red hellfire. I heard a heart-wrenching scream. *But whatever happens, Ye Hua, you must not . . . you must not leave me here on my own.*

The moment Ye Hua flew into the red hellfire resulting from the ignition of the Eastern Desert Bell, the powerful trap binding my hands and feet loosened, and I was released. I immediately understood two things: firstly, that a powerful trap like this obviously ran on its owner's supply of cultivated spiritual energy, and secondly, that when this owner had no more spiritual energy, the trap was no longer able to bind.

This hellfire had turned half the sky bloodred and filled the banks of Ruo River with thick demon energy. I gathered up all my remaining cultivated energy and sacrificed it to the Kunlun fan, which crashed toward the Eastern Desert Bell. The bell's body shook. I peered into the red light, but I could not see Ye Hua.

It sounded as if evil soul eaters were rising up from beneath the earth. The sound became more intense, like the approach of a thousand soldiers and ten thousand horses now: it was the Eastern Desert Bell's chime of lament.

The red light flickered and went out, and a black figure tumbled down from the top of the bell.

I staggered over to catch him, the impact causing me to stumble back a couple of paces and land on the ground. I placed his head in the crook of my arm and looked down at his pale face. His eyes were black, and blood trickled down from the corner of his mouth. His long cloak was soaked with blood.

"I always thought it was strange how Ye Hua only wore black," Zhe Yan had once said. "And that one time we drank wine together, I asked him about it. I always thought it was because of how much he liked the color. But Ye Hua responded by holding his wine cup still. 'Well, it's not exactly a pleasing color,' he said at last with a laugh, 'but it is useful. If you are ever stabbed and bleeding profusely, it stops you from seeing the blood. You could think that you just knocked over a vase of water and got soaked through. If you can hide the fact that you've been badly injured, your loved ones will not feel as concerned, and your enemies will not feel soothed.'" When Zhe Yan had told me this, I had felt pleased that somber Ye Hua had finally learned to tell a joke. It was only now I realized he had been completely serious.

Three hundred years ago, when I was turned into naive and helpless Su Su, I thought that I loved him from as deep as my bone marrow. After losing my memories and returning to Bai Qian from Qingqiu, Ye Hua and I started getting close again. He told me that he loved me, and I gradually started to love him back. I thought that it was true love.

I could not forgive him for cutting out my eyes and putting me in the situation where I had been forced to jump off the punishment platform. I could not forgive him for saying that he loved me again and again only because of the debt he owed from before. I could not forgive him for never understanding me.

I had been alive so long, and when it came to love, I had learned to be selfish and unreasonable, and I could not bear having so much as a grain of sand kicked up into my eyes. But for my last two lives, I had been placed by his side. My two great love affairs had both been with him, and I realized now that I had not understood him either.

When Mo Yuan had sacrificed his primordial spirit to the Eastern Desert Bell seventy thousand years ago, he had spat a hundred times more blood than the trickles seeping from the corners of Ye Hua's mouth. Ye Hua's cultivated energy was incomparable to Mo Yuan's, so why was there so much less blood?

I lowered my head and gave him a sharp bite on the lip. I used the tip of my tongue to pry his mouth open, ignoring how much it made him tremble, and stuck it into his mouth to have a probe around. I could feel hot, thick liquid trickling down from his mouth to mine. His eyes were getting darker.

As Bai Qian, I had been allowed to enjoy only a couple of months of being in love with Ye Hua, our time together in the Ninth Sky, during which we had shared only a couple of nights of intimacy.

He pushed me away with his one good hand and started to cough heavily before spitting out a large mouthful of blood that was such a bright red that it made my eyes go blurry. That push must have taken the very last of his energy, because he slumped to the side after that, the only movement his chest rising and falling.

I crawled over and put my arms around him. "Are you planning to swallow it all down?" I asked. "How old are you? Even if you are weak, I won't think any less of you."

He was trying hard not to cough. He attempted to lift his hand, but could not manage. Even speaking was too much effort for him, but he still tried to maintain his composure and give a calm "I'm fine. It's not a serious injury. I'll be just fine. You—you mustn't cry."

I was holding him in both arms and unable to wipe my face. I just looked into his eyes and said, "You just offered your primordial spirit to the Eastern Desert Bell. I've never seen anyone except Mo Yuan escape when they've done that, and even Mo Yuan slept for an entire seventy thousand years. Don't lie to me, Ye Hua, you're dying, aren't you?"

His body stiffened. He closed his eyes and said, "I heard the news about Mo Yuan waking up. You and he are obviously meant to be together. You'll make each other very happy. He'll look after you well, even better than I could. I can rest assured. You must forget about me."

I gave him a look of disbelief.

Time seemed to stop. He suddenly opened his eyes, panting, and said, "If I die, I won't be able to tell you that, Qian Qian, you are the only one I have ever loved. You must never forget me. If you dare forget me, I, if you dare . . ." His voice gradually faded, but he managed to utter, "Then what will I do?"

I leaned in close to his ear and said, "Ye Hua, you mustn't die. Just hang in there. I'm going to take you to find Mo Yuan. He'll know what to do." His body was starting to feel heavy in my arms.

I moved my mouth over to his ear and yelled, "If you dare die on me, I'll go straight to Zhe Yan's and get him to feed me his special potion so that I forget you ever existed. I'll spend my days with Mo Yuan, Zhe Yan, and Fourth Brother, and I will be happy, never even knowing who you were."

His body trembled. He managed to pull his mouth into a smile and said, "If that's what you want." Those were his final words in this life: "If that's what you want."

CHAPTER
TWENTY-THREE

I sat in a mortal-world teahouse, watching a play.

It was three years Ye Hua had been gone. Three years since the Ruo River battle, Qing Cang's death, and Ye Hua sacrificing his primordial spirit to the Eastern Desert Bell and his soul flying away. My Kunlun fan had taken on half my immortal energy and crashed itself against the Eastern Desert Bell, again and again, causing the bell to chime out in lament for seven whole days and nights.

According to Zhe Yan, by the time he had rushed over, Ye Hua had already breathed his last. I sat beneath the great bell with his body in my arms. I was covered head to toe in blood. I had set up a thick immortal barrier around the two of us and was letting no one come near. The Eastern Desert Bell tolled its lament for seven days, summoning all the immortals of the Eight Deserts, who gathered at Ruo River. The Sky Emperor sent fourteen immortal men down from the Ninth Sky to collect Ye Hua's body. They stood outside my immortal barrier, pelting it with bolts of lightning and using rumbles of thunder to try to weaken it, but they did not manage to make a crack.

Zhe Yan had begun to think that I might stay on the bank of the Ruo River, holding Ye Hua like that for the rest of my life. Luckily the Eastern Desert Bell chimes reached so far and wide that they interrupted Mo Yuan in his confinement, and on the eighth day, he ventured out.

I had absolutely no recollection of any of this. The only thought running through my head was that Ye Hua was dead, which meant that I was dead too. Lying on the Ruo River bank, holding him for the rest of my days, sounded like the best option. Even though he would never again open his eyes, even though the corners of that mouth would never again rise up into that calm smile, even though he would never lean in toward my ear and call my name in that deep voice of his. Even though none of these things would ever happen again . . . at least I would still be able to see his face and know that he was there beside me.

I do not have a clear memory of Mo Yuan arriving. Just the vague recollection of sitting beneath the Eastern Desert Bell, my head empty, completely oblivious to anything from the past, when suddenly I saw Mo Yuan frowning at me from the other side of my immortal barrier.

My heart, which had felt as dead as fallen leaves, suddenly stirred. For the first time since all this had happened, I realized I was still alive. I saw that Mo Yuan was there and thought that he must know a way to save Ye Hua. He had suffered the same calamity after all. He had sacrificed his own primordial spirit to the Eastern Desert Bell and lived to tell the tale. If there was any way to save Ye Hua, to hear him say the name Qian Qian again, I could easily wait seventy thousand years; I could happily wait seven hundred thousand years.

I dismantled my immortal barrier, intending to pick up Ye Hua's body and bow down to Mo Yuan, plead for his help. But when I tried to stand, I discovered I had no energy. Mo Yuan strode over and looked at me. "Put him in a coffin," he said somberly. "Let Ye Hua leave with dignity."

Mo Yuan went back to Mount Kunlun, and I took Ye Hua's body to Qingqiu, followed closely by the fourteen immortal men from the Ninth Sky. As far as I was concerned, Ye Hua was mine, and I was not about to hand him over to anyone. This formation of immortal men waited at the entrance to the valley for half a month before going back to the Ninth Sky with their tails between their legs and reported their failed mission to the Sky Emperor.

The following day, Ye Hua's father and mother traveled to Qingqiu. His mother, who had looked pleasant and docile, was so angry she was actually shaking. She wiped the corners of her eyes with an embroidered handkerchief that was already soaked through and said, "It was only today that I discovered you and that mortal Su Su are one and the same. What did my son do wrong to have been planted next to you twice in one lifetime? He loved you as Su Su with all his heart. He was even planning to abandon his heir role for you. It was the Sky Emperor who arbitrated on your debt with Su Jin and decided that you needed to pay her back with your eyes. He also sentenced you to three months of lightning strikes, to be delivered once you had given birth. You only had to suffer the loss of your eyes in the end, though; Ye Hua took those lightning strikes in your place. But you had to go and jump off the immortal punishment platform. My son jumped off the platform after you. When you jumped off, it was part of your calamity and it allowed you to soar up and become a goddess. Ye Hua on the other hand . . . Well, after jumping, he slept for sixty years straight. Now, three hundred years later, he has turned to dust flying and flames dying, also your fault. My son has not had one moment's happiness since meeting you. He has done so much for you, and what have you done for him? And yet you are now laying claim to his body, without a qualm of conscience? Even in death, you want dominion over him, over his corpse. I ask you one question, what right have you got?"

My throat tightened. I stumbled back a few paces, and Mystic Gorge caught me in his arms.

"Enough!" Ye Hua's father stepped in. He turned to me and said, "It was Demon Emperor Qing Cang who killed our son. Ye Hua offered up his primordial spirit to stop the Eastern Desert Bell from destroying all under the sky. He sacrificed himself to save the sky and earth, for which the Sky Emperor has given him a notable honor. Le Xu is too upset to think straight. You mustn't take what she's saying to heart. But you need to hand over our son's body now. The two of you had an engagement agreement, but you were never married, and it is unreasonable of you to be appropriating his corpse like this. Our son was named heir to the Sky Clan when he was born. According to the Sky Palace's inviolable regulations, he must be buried in the Thirty-Sixth Sky's Wuwang Sea. I implore you, Goddess, please do not stand in our way."

The day Ye Hua was taken back up to the Ninth Sky was overcast, and a breeze was blowing. I covered his face with kisses: all over his brows, eyes, cheeks, and nose. As I placed my lips upon his lips, I nursed the absurd notion that he might wake up, place his lips against my forehead, and say, "Qian Qian, it was all just a joke." It was nothing but a crazy delusion.

Ye Hua's parents placed his body inside an ice chest and carried him out of Qingqiu. They left me with nothing but his bloodstained black cloak.

Sometime before this, Zhe Yan had given me a peach tree, which I had planted at the foxhole entrance. I watered it every day and added fertilizer to the soil, and in no time it had sprouted branches. The day the tree had its first flower, I placed Ye Hua's black cloak inside a coffin to make a cenotaph, which I buried beneath the branches. I tried to imagine what the peach tree would look like with its branches all covered in blossoms.

"Don't forget you have a son, Your Highness," Mystic Gorge said. "Do you wish for me to go and fetch His Young Majesty and bring him back to Qingqiu?"

I waved a dismissive hand at him. Of course I had not forgotten I had a son. But at the moment, I did not even have the energy to care for myself. He would be much better off and well cared for in the Sky Palace.

I spent the following two weeks after Ye Hua's parents' visit sitting under the peach tree in a state of constant muddleheadedness, during which time I was often visited by hallucinations of Ye Hua. He was always wearing his black cloak, with his hair down and loosely fastened with a silk band. He would be leaning against my knees, reading a book, or sitting at a desk opposite me and painting. When it rained, Ye Hua would gather me up in his arms and shield me from it.

I might have been content; however, Zhe Yan, Fourth Brother, Mystic Gorge, and Bi Fang were not. On the evening of the sixteenth day I spent out there, Fourth Brother finally could bear it no longer, and he picked me up, carried me into the foxhole, and placed me in front of a water mirror so I could see myself. With barely suppressed rage, he said, "Look at what you've become! Ye Hua may be dead, but that doesn't mean you have to stop living."

Fourth Brother was right: I did not think I could carry on living. I was not sure if turning to dust flying and flames dying would definitely reunite me with Ye Hua; however, I had always thought that turning to dust flying and flames dying meant that there would be nothing left of you, all parts returned to the soil. If this were to happen to me, I would no longer remember Ye Hua, and I did not want that. At least now, every so often I got to enjoy seeing him standing in front of me and smiling.

The goddess reflected in the water mirror was pale and haggard. There was a thick white cloth around her eyes, with a few dried leaves stuck to it. But it was a different white cloth from the one I usually wore. My brain was turning very slowly. Oh, I remembered now, at the beginning of the month, Zhe Yan had grabbed me and placed my old eyes back in my head. He had made this white cloth and doused it in a special medicinal solution in order to protect them. It was a different cloth from the one Father had made for me.

Fourth Brother gave a sigh. "Wake up!" he said sternly. "You've been alive so long, surely you've seen enough life and death, separation and reunion. Can't you just accept your situation and move on?"

It was not that I was unable to accept my situation, more that I did not know how. If I had known how to, I would certainly have done it. When I got drunk and smashed up the soul-binding lamp that time, it had released my memories of what had happened three hundred years ago. For some reason, at that time, I had been unable to remember anything good about Ye Hua.

Since he had left, I could not think of a single misdeed: all that flashed through my mind were his good points. In the past I had castigated Li Jing from up on my high horse about how he always wanted what he did not have and never cherished things when he had them. But was I not just the same?

The moon was round in the sky and bright were the stars. It was late and there was no one about. There was nothing for me to do except sleep. I had never expected that I might dream of Ye Hua, but that night I did. He was sitting behind a desk, reading through a set of documents. He placed them to the side, took a sip of tea, and gave a slight frown. He placed the teacup down, lifted his head, and gave me a wide smile. "Qian Qian, come over here and tell me about the play you read yesterday," he said.

I was completely absorbed in this dream and did not want to wake up. Old Fate really had done me a favor this time. When I hallucinated Ye Hua sitting with me under the peach tree, he was unable to speak, but in this dream he was just like in real life. Not only could we take walks together and play chess, he could also talk to me.

From then on I started to dream about him every night. I started to adore sleeping. I had a shift in mindset, which made me feel a lot more comfortable. There is a story in the mortal world called Zhuangzi's butterfly dream. It is a classic tale about a mortal called Zhuangzi, who one night dreams that he is a butterfly and flutters around filled with joy. But then all of a sudden, he wakes up and finds that he is in fact a mortal called Zhuangzi and not a butterfly after all. He does not know if he is Zhuangzi who has just woken up from a dream about being a butterfly or a butterfly currently having a dream about being Zhuangzi.

In the past, I viewed my waking life as the reality and my dreams as illusions. But the reality of my life depressed me now. Was it not better to alter my perspective, therefore, to view my dreams with Ye Hua as the reality and my daytime life as the illusion?

Zhe Yan and Fourth Brother saw the color gradually return to my cheeks. The only problem now was that I was asleep so much. But they were clearly relieved and stopped keeping such a close eye on me.

No news came from the Ninth Sky about who would be the next heir to the Sky Throne. I had heard that Su Jin's immortal status had been revoked forever due to her negligence while watching over the Eastern Desert Bell.

Her dereliction of duty made her indirectly responsible for Ye Hua's battle with Qing Cang and led to him having to sacrifice his primordial spirit and his spirit flying. The Sky Emperor was devastated to lose his oldest grandson and also extremely angry, and as soon as he heard the part Su Jin had played in this, he banished her from the Ninth Sky and sent her into six reincarnation cycles, during which she would experience a hundred love calamities.

• • •

Changing my attitude toward life made me feel a lot better. Now I could still believe that Ye Hua was alive.

I no longer wished to see the cenotaph I had made for him, because it reminded me that he only existed in my imagination, while in reality Ye Hua was dead, dead and gone. I started to develop a phobia about going near the cenotaph, but I could not bring myself to ask Mystic Gorge to dig it up. Instead we made another entrance to the foxhole, and I used that.

When he had time, Fourth Brother would come around and pick me up and take me for trips to the mortal world. It was his way of taking my mind off things, while giving himself a nice day out too. While we were roaming the mountains, he would say, "Look at that mountain standing so tall it touches the clouds. If you stand at the top and look down, you'll see how insignificant everything in the world is. Doesn't thinking about that make your mind feel like it's expanding? Doesn't it make you feel as if your experience of sadness might be nothing but a cloud floating in the sky, which you might just wave your hand at and waft away?"

While in the water, he would say, "Look at the water rushing down from that waterfall and tumbling to join the river. It flows out day and night and never turns back. Don't you look at that waterfall and think it's just like life? You have no way to turn back, so you have to just keep looking straight ahead?"

When we visited market towns, he would say, "Look at all the mortals running around like ants. They are only on this earth for six or seven decades, and during that time, they are bound by the destinies Si Ming has set for them. The farmers spend most of their lives toiling hard in the field, the academics spend most of their time not achieving what they set out to, most of the good women raised end up marrying rascals.

But they go contentedly about their business all the same. How can you look at these mortals and think you are so much better than them?"

At first I listened to him, but he started to become fanatical about speaking like this, and his long-windedness started to annoy me. After that, I started to go to the mortal world on my own.

And that was where I was on the third of September: three years after Ye Hua departed. I was listening to a play when I spotted a young immortal called Zhi Yue who came from the immortal Fanghu Mountain. When you went to a play in the mortal world, you followed the local custom of throwing a handful of coins onto the stage during the applause at the end if you thought the actors had performed well to boost their morale and thank them for their hard work.

It must have been Zhi Yue's first time to come to a play in the mortal world, as she looked on enviously as everyone started tossing their money down from the carved mahogany railings, obviously wishing she had some to throw too. She could tell that I was an immortal in one glance and skipped over to introduce herself and ask if I could lend her some money to throw over, as she felt mean not giving any. I was slightly puzzled as to why a little immortal who obviously had magic skills would not be able to do a simple thing like conjure up a couple of coins, but I lent her a couple of night pearls anyway.

At the start we were more like acquaintances, but every time I went to the mortal world to see a play, I would bump into her, and over time we became friends. Zhi Yue was a lively girl, but she never pestered me by asking details about where I was from, who my family was, how old I was, and so on, which was fairly unusual. And it was wonderful going to plays with someone else and being able to talk about them afterward.

She and I must have gone to see more than ten plays over the course of two months.

Tonight's play was *The Peony Pavilion*, which was about a couple overcoming difficulties so that they could be together. It was the fifth of October, which, in the lunar calendar, was a good day for a marriage, but a bad day to have an argument or go to war. It was three years to the day that Ye Hua had departed. I took a sip of wine and looked to the stage, where an actress in a blue dress was dancing and making her sleeves shimmy.

"You are as beautiful as a flower and young as flowing water, but why are you sitting alone in your boudoir so overcome with sadness?" one of the actors was singing. At that moment Zhi Yue arrived. She walked in late without a hint of embarrassment and sat down next to me.

Halfway through the play, she turned to me and covered her mouth to whisper, "Do you remember me telling you about my talented cousin who died some time ago?"

I nodded.

Apart from talking about the plays we saw, Zhi Yue would often mention this older male cousin of hers. He had been a brilliant, wise warrior and an exceptionally talented young man, but had sadly died in battle when he was still very young, leaving behind parents so grief stricken they could barely carry on living and a feeble little son who spent his days sobbing. The poor things. The poor, poor things. Every time she sighed and said, "Poor things," she looked so full of sadness at their sorry fate. I found it hard to summon any great sympathy for her cousin's household. Perhaps I really had learned to accept the reality of death.

Zhi Yue reached for the teapot and poured herself a cup of cold tea to wet her throat. She looked around, covered her mouth again, and moved closer to me, saying, "Did I not tell you that my cousin has been dead for three years? The He Clan thought that all that was left of him was his corpse and that his primordial spirit had turned to dust flying and flames dying long ago. They made a black crystal ice coffin and lowered him into the sea. I was there, I saw it. Last night the waters of that sea, which had been calm for tens of thousands of years, suddenly started to swirl. The water splashed up, forming waves ten feet high, and the black crystal ice coffin floated to the surface. Immortal energy was curling around all four sides of the ice coffin apparently, and that was why the water was so choppy and these high waves were rising up.

"Don't you think it's strange that my cousin's primordial spirit turned to dust flying and flames dying and yet he still has such a powerful source of immortal energy protecting him? None of the He Clan knew what to think. Members of the younger generation were sent outside while the clan elders sent a message to our clan's revered god to ask what was happening. My parents think there is a chance that my cousin didn't die after all. Oh, if that's true, then poor little Ali will no longer have to spend his days sobbing and wailing."

Suddenly I was surrounded by a heavy silence. The cup in my hand crashed to the floor, and I heard my own hollow voice saying, "Is it the Wuwang Sea you are talking about? Your cousin . . . your cousin . . . he's not the Sky Emperor's oldest grandson, heir to the Sky Throne, Ye Hua?"

Zhi Yue looked at me, gaping, and then stammered, "H-h-how do you know?"

I rushed out of the teahouse and stumbled onto the street before I remembered I would need a cloud to get to the Ninth Sky. I summoned a cloud and stumbled onto it. I looked down to see a crowd of mortals kneeling on the ground beneath me and realized I had jumped astride my lucky cloud without making myself invisible in front of everyone in this busy marketplace.

I got off the cloud and stepped into the air. I was high above the ground. Looking down, I saw a vast expanse of fields. My mind went empty, and I could not for the life of me remember the way to the Southern Sky Gate. The more anxious and impatient I got, the emptier my mind became. I got on the cloud again and floated back and forth a number of times, not sure what I should do.

My foot slipped and I nearly fell off the cloud, but luckily I was a caught by a firm pair of hands. I heard Mo Yuan's voice from behind me. "How can you be so careless, nearly falling off your cloud like that?"

I turned around and grabbed hold of his hands. "Where's Ye Hua?" I asked in a panic. "Master, tell me where Ye Hua is!"

He frowned. "First wipe your eyes," he said. "I was just coming to tell you the news."

Mo Yuan explained how Father of the Universe had used half his godly power to make an immortal embryo so that Ye Hua could be reborn. After he had been reborn, this godly power continued to remain within him, hidden inside his primordial spirit. Mo Yuan had not appreciated that when Ye Hua slayed the four ferocious beasts from Yingzhou, he had received the other half of Father of the Universe's godly power, without which he would certainly have died.

Ye Hua must have used all of Father of the Universe's godly power to fight against the power of the Eastern Desert Bell and stop it from destroying everything under the sky. His primordial spirit was badly damaged in the fight between these two powers, and he fell into a deep sleep. Everyone had assumed his soul had flown and that he had turned to dust flying and flames dying. Ye Hua must have also assumed this.

He should have needed at least a few decades of deep sleep, but the black crystal ice coffin had some beneficial power, and despite being used as a burial ground by the Sky Clan, Wuwang Sea was actually a sacred site and had special properties to help assist recovery. Ye Hua was lucky, and he woke up after only three years.

I did not hear most of what Mo Yuan said. The only thing I properly heard was "Little Seventeenth, Ye Hua has returned! He is currently making his way to Qingqiu to see you. You must hurry back."

I had never dared to imagine that Ye Hua might actually still be alive. I had prayed for this a million times, but in my heart of hearts, I had always known that it was nothing but an absurd dream. Three years ago Ye Hua had turned to dust flying and flames dying. Buried under my peach tree was the cloak he wore as he died. Before he died, he had told me to forget him and urged me to live a happy life.

But. But Mo Yuan said that Ye Hua had woken up. That he was not dead. He had been alive all along.

I got onto a cloud and soared all the way back to Qingqiu, but I kept losing concentration and tumbled off four times along the way.

When I got past the mouth of the valley, I dropped down from my cloud and stumbled along the ground the rest of the way to the foxhole. Some little immortals I passed on the way called out to me in greeting, but I did not see them. My hands and feet started to shake. I was terrified that Ye Hua would not be there, that Mo Yuan had said what he had said just to trick me.

As soon as the foxhole was in sight, I slowed my pace. It had been a while since I had used the main entrance, and I had not noticed how big the peach tree I had planted there three years ago had become. It was the first time in three years that I was able to see clearly the bluish green of the mountains, the verdant lushness of the trees, and the emerald blue of the lake: the myriad colors of Qingqiu.

The sunlight filtered down through the clouds and shone onto the blossom-covered peach tree between the bluish-green mountain and the emerald-blue water of the lake, creating a gorgeous pink haze.

Underneath this haze stood a young man in a black cloak. He was leaning over, stroking the tombstone in front of him with his slender fingers.

It was like a scene from my dream.

Holding my breath, I took two steps forward, afraid that any sudden movement might cause the scene in front of me to just disappear.

As he turned his head, a breeze blew over the tree, causing the branches of petals to undulate, looking like a series of pinkish-red waves. He gave a slight smile. He was the same as before, with his fine face and his jet-black hair. Petals floated down from the pink sea above our heads, and between the sky and earth, there was no other color, no other sound.

He reached out a hand, and in a quiet voice he said, "Qian Qian, come over here."

ABOUT THE AUTHOR

Tang Qi is a writer of fantasy and romance novels. Her works include *Life Is a Flower That Blooms Twice* and *The Nine Realms: Hua Xuyin*.

ABOUT THE TRANSLATOR

Photo © 2015 Paul Ryan

Poppy Toland is a freelance literary translator who studied Chinese at Leeds University. While living in Beijing, she worked as an editor for *Time Out Beijing* and as a field research supervisor for the BBC's *Wild China* television series. Poppy is now based primarily in London. She wishes to thank Nala Changjing Liu for her help with the translation.